KING

Chloë Fowler

Hatchling
Press

For the women who built me, broke me,
and made me whole again.

PART ONE
Under the Spotlight

CHLOË FOWLER

Chapter One
Spotlight

The show ends as it began. Turned away from the audience, and her final line delivered into silence.

'Uh-huh. Thank you. Thank you very much.'

This is the moment Jess craves, the one when nothing happens. When the spotlight shuts off. Black. She loses her footing, but no one can see this deep in the dark. This is a moment to gather. A split second of mourning, disbelief that it is over so soon. Eyes closed, her head hangs, right hand on cocked right hip. Silence.

Then, the applause. She can hear the scuffles of an audience standing for an ovation, but she won't let herself open her eyes to see. Not yet.

She's performed her show, *The Wonder of You*, so many times, but each new audience creates tiny shifts in temperature and mood. Alone, she would punch the air. On stage, she just lets it wash over her. Opened again, her eyes adjust until she can make out the features of faces that have been pale smudges beyond the footlights. The smile she composes to greet them is gracious, feigning surprise, as if she's forgotten that they are even there, as if this had been a performance for herself alone. She presses cupped hands against her heart, then holds them back out. Her smile is one of thanks, a mutual gifting of pleasure.

Backstage in the cramped dressing room a few minutes later, sweating, thirsty.

'Fuck's sake.'

Jess backs up against the wall to steady herself and carefully pulls the satin fabric over her calves. She doesn't want the hassle of having any ripped seams mended, and the Edinburgh diet of beer and fast food is already messing with her waistline. A spritz of Febreze under the arms of her jacket because she can only afford to get it dry-cleaned every few weeks. She winds the thick bandages from around her chest, stretching her arms behind her to ease the ache in her breasts. She pulls a small leather pouch out of the pocket of her black Levi's, fingers inside to replace her wedding band with two heavy, bejewelled pinkie rings. The pouch, with the letters TCB pressed out in gold, was a gift from her father Martin, and is more precious than her wallet or phone.

Wincing, she peels off one sideburn and then the other, pats away the sting. A few cucumber wipes remove the heavy foundation, and she dusts powder across her forehead to smooth out the shine. Her hands stroke her quiff upwards, palming down flyaways. Although no longer in costume, her cheekbones, dark hair, and the curve of her lips retain the spirit of Elvis. Even if she could shuck his soul off more quickly, she wouldn't, because it would be a waste of the energy he has helped her create. The longer she inhabits his essence, the more power she has.

In a few minutes she'll head out, inviting the looks and the appreciative smiles of the audience who've stuck around for a glimpse, but first she grabs her phone. Her father sends messages as random thoughts occur. Today, he's attached a photo of another review he's clipped from *The Guardian*. The fact that her show, performed four-hundred miles from where he lives, is being covered by broadsheets never fails to dazzle him.

Copy in the post! That's my girl. Elvis is in the building! Chat this weekend? TCB until then. Dad x

This acronym is code they use between them, as Elvis did with his Memphis Mafia. Taking Care of Business. Jess has suggested, as she does every year, that her dad comes up to see the show but gets the same answer: that he doesn't want to cramp her style. For this reticence to make the trip, she blames her mother. Much as she blames her mother for withholding encouragement that Jess and her father have more time together, just the two of them. Her mother doesn't like any displacement from her creature comforts, crowds, or having to confront her daughter's lifestyle in all its queer glory.

As the month has worn on, her wife Sarah's regular messages have turned into sporadic, uncaptioned photos of their three-year-old daughter. Even the occasional 'come home soon' seems laden, not exactly a sign that she's missed, but at least a sign that she's needed. It's Thursday, Claudie's day for Little Kickers, so there are shots of her in the tiny kit, a blurry leg kicking a ball towards an invisible goal. More than once, Jess has wondered whether these are innocent pictures, captured impulsively, or whether they mete out code: 'I'm such a good parent, I've got this, but get back soon to take over.'

Jess *has* been missing proper check-ins with her daughter. Claudie's schedule is precise, and out of sync with Jess's away from home Edinburgh hours. By now, Claudie will be exhausted and cranky after the afternoon activity and unused to having her same mother administer dinner, bath, and soon bed. Sarah will be tired, too, still adjusting to juggling Claudie and work. She wonders if her wife is experiencing the same see-sawing of emotion she does when she parents full time – when the lows (refusing to eat her dinner, not allowing her hair to be combed after a bath) threaten to plunge her into despair and the highs (the throwing of arms around her neck, a mispronounced word) tug her belly with love.

After a few weeks away, Jess has tucked guilt at her absence inside and has settled into the pleasure of her routines being governed solely by her own needs. The joy of taking a shower for as long as she likes, things being in the same place that she left them, not having to meal plan, or eat at all.

The Wonder of You goes up at four each afternoon. By the time she's done a stint at the bar, performed guest slots at late-night queer cabaret venues, and seen other shows, there isn't a mutually convenient time to call home. Jess sleeps late in the mornings, waking too late to call before Claudie goes off to the childminder. Her Edinburgh life is nocturnal, a throwback to a time when all-nighters weren't simply vigils at the bedside of her sleep-resistant daughter. When she does catch them, after a perfunctory chat ('How's work?', 'Fine. How's the show?', 'Going alright, I think.') Sarah will stick the camera on and hand the phone over to Claudie, requiring that Jess talks for long enough for Sarah to put on a wash or go to the loo. But Claudie is too young to know how to hold the handset properly, and more often than not, Jess ends up chatting with the ceiling, coaxing her back from the other side of the room, calling her name into the void. Occasionally she catches Sarah in a chattier mood. They'll prattle back and forth, undiscussed tension forgotten. This pleasure is a reminder of when all they had to talk about was themselves, not bills, whether the cleaner cleaned enough, plans for the weekend. Before their friends deserted London for Brighton or Bristol.

Jess zips her suit into its custom-made bag and hides it on the rail behind a bunch of other costumes, so it won't get damaged. Standing close to the full-length mirror propped against the wall, she stares at her reflection. Not bad, she thinks. A final check that her turn-ups are level, looks at herself again, twists this way and that.

When she opens the door, the muffled noise of the show that follows hers seeps into the corridor. Renewed adrenaline courses through her as the memory of applause rings in her ears. In an August of daily shows, the post-performance high lasts a month. On a rare low-confidence day, all she needs to do is remember the coveted five-star review she got from *The Scotsman* or look at her spot on the listings chalkboard which now says 'sold out'. Her interactions with the cast of other shows have subtly changed too. At the start of the month, they were all in it together, but as one or another show started dominating the 'one to watch' listings, a pecking order emerged. She's no longer treated like one of them but as someone to defer to.

Jess strides down the back stairs and into the bar. Hips tilt forwards, shoulders back, his laconic swagger still inhabits her bones. Possessed. The bartender, Ray, has already pulled her pint, prepped, ready for when Jess turns to greet her audience.

'Still hearing good things,' Ray nods at some people who stare and nudge their friends in recognition that the star is in the bar. 'Your fans are in. As per.'

Jess has made a point of befriending this tall, heavy-set girl who has confessed that she's only recently come out and is still finding her feet on the scene. A slight blush spreads across the young woman's cheeks as they chat.

'Pays to keep the punters happy,' Jess smiles and nods her thanks as she slides a note across the sticky wooden bar top, including enough for a generous tip. Taking her first sip, she takes stock in the mirror behind the optics.

Her show draws a mixed crowd, but she can spot the women who've come to see her because of who *she* is, not because she's Elvis, the King of Rock and Roll. With so much queer content on offer, the more discerning hunt out the stuff that's light on angst, or more than queeny camp. These are the classy gays, in their 'casual not casual' clothes, shorn hair, good shoes and expensive tattoos. The ones that dig her schtick, who understand that she's not merely an impersonator, that she is telling a story. Who appreciate that she has soul as well as rhythm.

The Wonder of You doesn't require prior knowledge of Elvis but rewards it. The obvious lines (the uh-huh's) draw laughter from everyone, but the less familiar ones ('ambition is a dream with a V8 engine') are only spotted by aficionados.

Four true fans, Japanese girls in matching calf-high white socks and tartan skirts, have come to see her three times now. They were initially inconspicuous because they were late to the queue and forced to separate. The second time – first in line. When the stage manager told Jess they were there the third time, she'd performed several songs in their general direction. In the few minutes before the auditorium cleared at the end, she'd thanked them in person for coming. They'd nodded their heads, shaken her hand, and looked so dazzled, hands over their mouths as they giggled, that Jess felt like Elvis during his Las Vegas residencies.

Sometimes she'll be ambushed by older straight couples. They'll proffer anecdotes about when they first heard his music or where they were when he died. Earnest in their adoration, excited to be in the presence of an artist, husbands pump her hand up and down, but their wives hang back, struck by sudden shyness they don't know the cause of. Jess knows why she has this effect on straight women and recognises the quickening of their breath and coy smiles for what they are.

She embodies Elvis as his younger self. The smooth skin, the shiny hair, the smiling eyes. Hips and lips. The innocent, grafting, kind man – the son, GI, performer, friend, husband, father. The Memphis King of their imagination. These women are caught between lusting for Elvis the man, and the fascination that Jess is a woman. Not androgynous, but proudly masculine. This confident, post-performance stance that makes her entrancing, even arousing, is why she does not want him to slip from her grip too fast.

Jess has perfected nonchalance as she greets her lesbian fans. Unlike the straight ones, they appreciate her transgressions and how she's politicised the more familiar Elvis narrative. Butch women nod briefly, identifying her as one of their own. Femme women flirt. Stopping to chat, folding into their banter, Jess is herself, but amplified. Happy to accept a second and third drink, sometimes more. Storing compliments to bask in later but batting them away in the moment.

Jess spies a familiar face in the crowd. Lol and her friends came to see her show earlier in the week. They ended up dancing in a gay bar until the early morning. Tonight, she's here again but alone. Lol is flirtatious, even as she stands up to give Jess a hug. A brunette, not generally Jess's type, her glossy curls bob on her shoulder when she laughs. Jess's post-show voice is still deeper than her real life one. She speaks more slowly, allowing her audience of one to savour each word. They pat each other's thighs and arms, elbows jostling on the table. When one of them leans forward, the other does too.

'Can I tell you something?' Lol asks.

'Shoot.' Jess says.

'Sounds weird, but I'm a bit starstruck. I kinda feel like I'm actually having a drink with Elvis. Like with Elvis *and* you. Both at the same time.'

'He'd be on the softer stuff than I am.' Jess waggles her pint glass. 'He'd probably have asked for a Pepsi. Cheap date. Hope neither of us disappoints.' Jess smiles, knowing she's anything but disappointing.

'No way,' Lol says, reaching up and gently stroking Jess's quiff. 'He was cool. But you're amazing.'

'Uh, thanks. Not sure what I've done to qualify, but I'll take it. Did you tell me you worked in finance?'

'That sounds flasher than it is. You'll think I'm really boring if I tell you more.'

'I can tell you're not boring. Go on!' Jess goads.

'I'm just an accountant. I know, judge me now.'

'A job's a job,' Jess laughs, but she is disappointed despite herself that Lol doesn't do something more interesting. 'We've all got to pay the bills.'

Jess feels Lol's knee slide between her own. There is no apology. Lol does not draw away but catches Jess's eye and holds her gaze. For Jess, these flirtations are acceptable parts of her post-show persona – the space between her authentic self and the fiction she creates on stage. Acting on any of these harmless, fleeting interactions is a line that Jess will never cross. Lol suggests a nightcap at the club across the road, and for a moment, Jess is tempted. But when they stumble outside, Jess steers Lol towards the line of waiting taxis. Lol is shorter than Jess and stretches a little to kiss goodbye, her lips resting on Jess's cheek longer than they need to. When Jess pulls away, the disappointment is clear in Lol's eyes.

Safely solo, a taxi bears her through the Edinburgh streets back to her digs. Each of the routes to her temporary home are familiar now. The steep incline up from the Grassmarket, the long road bisecting the meadows, the up-lit Castle receding behind her. Sweeping past hoardings, a chaotic decoupage of posters. It's past-midnight, too chilly for late-night gathers on the Bruntsfield links, and street sweepers clear the road of the festival detritus – takeaway containers and empty cans – that will appear again tomorrow.

Climbing the stairs to her apartment, Jess is weary but buzzing. Nearly twenty years ago, she first came to Edinburgh and shared a tiny flat with five other girls – three to a room and only enough space in the hallway and kitchen for their luggage, costumes, boxes of flyers. Clumps of hair in the shower, the bathroom bin overflowing as one by one they got their periods. Jess, not usually prone to nostalgia, finds herself hankering for when she still had true artistic ambition. When she and her classmates were still protected by the safety of drama school. When the idea of taking a role purely for cash was anathema and the darker the work, the more appealing the poverty and lack of fame that came with it. Now, Sarah insists on paying so Jess can live on her own. 'After all,' she'd cajoled as they scrolled through Airbnb, 'profit isn't the point.'

'Just curious,' Jess had asked her. 'What *is* the point? For you, I mean?'

'Art, Darling. Art. And it makes you happy. Which makes me happy.'

After transferring large sums of money to secure the apartment and pay her producer and PR agency, Jess wondered if Sarah's generosity was an investment or a write-off. She will never bring this up because she knows the response – that it's not an issue because Jess is the stay-at-home parent who gave up full-time performing when Claudie came along. Jess has never been entirely sure if renouncing her dream was her choice, or another of the clever negotiations that makes her well-paid wife so good at her job. If she tries hard enough, sometimes Jess can even forget the truth – that her wife funds these excursions into art and that she is here on gift, not graft.

Letting herself into her empty apartment, Jess feels a momentary ache at the silence. Back home in London, however late she gets home, she'll tiptoe into her daughter's room and press her nose against Claudie's hair, inhaling the heavy scent of toddler sleep. She'll undress quietly on the landing, creep into bed, and lie beside her sleeping wife, who if she wakes at all will just turn further away, resisting any possibility of being touched.

Reaching into her pocket to remove the pouch of heavy rings, she pulls out the piece of paper with her number on it that Lol had pushed at her when they parted. Jess leaves it on the kitchen table. She will throw it away tomorrow.

Chapter Two
The Interview

It's only as Jess walks down the corridor, towards the suite in the fancy Apex hotel, that she remembers she didn't check a photo attached to one of Tiff's *LEXI* articles. As soon as she's knocked, the door opens quickly, and despite having nothing to go on, Tiff does not look the way Jess expects. Petite and toned, the physique of an athlete rather than a gym bunny. Hockey? Netball? She has blonde curly hair, carefully manicured eyebrows, nude lipstick slicked across her lips. She's wearing a black leather skirt (short enough to stop above her knees), and her toned, well-shaved legs are tanned. Like her bright white, freshly unboxed Converse, Tiff has clearly set out to make a good first impression. It's worked.

'Jess?' Tiff holds out her hand.

'Tiff?' Jess takes it and they shake. It feels an oddly formal gesture between two women, but having never met or even spoken before, a hug would feel too intimate.

'So good to finally meet you,' Tiff says. 'An Edinburgh trip is a perk of the job.'

'Pleased to oblige ma'am,' Jess says, surprising herself by doing a quick salute and clicking her heels. Unsure where this gesture has come from, she laughs.

'On my god, that's uncanny.' Tiff laughs back, gesturing that Jess should come fully into the room. 'The hype doesn't lie. Mind blown.'

'Let's hope I don't go downhill from here,' Jess says.

'No chance,' replies Tiff, 'I can already tell this is going to be ace. Coffee? Take a seat, we'll get cracking.'

Tiff's hamstrings tighten as she bends into the minibar and then hands Jess a small bottle of sparkling water. A waft of citrussy perfume. The warmth of a blush threatens to spill up from Jess's chest to her cheeks, and she fusses with the pour to deflect attention. More used to dealing with blushes from others, her fluster is unexpected.

'You're going to go easy on me, right?' Jess asks.

'We'll see. People have a habit of opening up. But if I dig too far, let me know.'

Blue eyes framed by black-rimmed specs and pen poised over the creamy page of a new Moleskin notebook, Tiff leans forward in her scarlet velvet chair.

'So why Elvis?'

'You tell me?' Jess meets Tiff's gaze head-on.

'Magnetic, sex symbol, an icon?'

'You got it.'

'His appeal never goes away, right? But how did it start for you?'

Jess sits back on the matching plush sofa and basks in the luxury; normally, interviews are in noisy coffee shops or the venue bar. Tilting forward, legs apart, elbows resting on her thighs, she's trying to strike the right balance between alert and relaxed. Jess readies the explanation that she sees herself as an artist. A Drag King. She morphs, not mimics.

'My dad,' she starts, 'he's the ultimate fan. He's been a massive support. The real deal, he gets all the credit.'

Encouraged by a nod from Tiff, she explains that it all began when she was eight and fought her teachers to let her play Joseph rather than Mary. The pleasure she felt inhabiting the male character, the thrill of that first burst of applause. The pride her father showed, his warm hand resting on her head as they chatted with other parents in the assembly hall after the show.

Tiff's right, she has a talent for getting people to reveal themselves and Jess finds herself opening up, losing the inhibitions that usually cause her to paint a glossier version of the truth. Jess was no prodigy. At fifteen, she'd stopped wanting to be noticed by anyone, at all, ever. Sweat leaked from her, staining the rust-coloured, Aertex shirts she was forced to wear at school. Back then, she'd envied everyone else's bodies, even those of the girls who were bullied or shamed. Given a choice, she would have swapped her sweaty body for their greasy, lumpen ones in an instant.

When she turned seventeen, the sweat quite literally evaporated. She moved closer to people again, practiced walking like the girls at school she wanted to befriend, learned their expressions, discovered what made them laugh. She learned how to assimilate. To mimic. Those years brought attention which she now wanted back, with interest. An introvert at heart, a performer by design.

Now, amongst non-performers, she is careful with her phrasing and intonation because she doesn't want to come across as a luvvie or narcissist (both things that her wife can't abide). It's when she is performing, as Elvis, that she feels most alive, most powerful. She inherits the adulation that was all his, but with an extra whack that she's earned herself.

'Wow.' Tiff sits back in her chair, twists her wrist to release the ache from notetaking. 'That's amazing. Do you think Elvis would have identified with all that?'

'He wasn't as confident as we think he was. His parents were a huge support, so were his aunt, his grandmother. Then his mum died way too early. Such a tragedy, I'm not sure he ever got over it.'

'There's a lot of heartbreak in his story. I think we forget that. And that's even before we talk about Priscilla. His one true love?'

'We'll never know, will we? It certainly didn't end the way they expected. Life's messy.'

'Love certainly is,' Tiff laughs. 'You mentioned your dad earlier. Are both your parents as supportive of you as Elvis's were of him?'

Jess hesitates. She generally avoids talking about her perfectly normal, middle-class upbringing or her strained relationship with her mother at all, even to Sarah. There is nothing specific to hide, but little she's proud enough to share. But Tiff's open-faced curiosity, and the unexpected connection she feels, encourages her to carry on.

'For sure, Dad's always encouraged me. Mum's a bit more complicated. I think she doesn't quite get it. Me, or Elvis. Maybe she feels a bit left out.'

Her father had practically forced her to audition for drama school, desperate that his daughter pursue her dreams – hinting at regrets that he didn't do the same. Mountview had been a revelation. She'd written and performed her own angry monologues, realised she was gay and thrown herself into the London scene. She'd drunk too much cheap red wine, smoked weed, hinted at an adolescence of vague traumas to make herself sound more interesting. When her father had pressed her to talk about her drama school adventures, she'd presented edited versions that made her sound more successful than she was.

Her mother had stepped back, claiming she wasn't clever enough to understand any of it, and when Jess came out, had stayed a polite distance. A committed relationship with Sarah, then their marriage, had been received with tentative warmth, at best. This tepid space has only grown cooler since Claudie was born. She has never discussed it with her father, but she's sensed he's aware because his enthusiasm has redoubled, as if he's offering support and love for them both.

'Not sure this is the direction your article should take,' Jess says, suddenly anxious that despite choosing to share, she may have said too much. 'Can we keep that bit off the record? Maybe focus on the show?'

'One hundred percent.' Tiff smiles. 'The show I can't wait to see. Especially now.'

Jess hasn't shared everything, though. That being Elvis, and amongst fans, is beyond intoxicating. That being a wife and a mother between shows is a distraction from the craving, but not quite enough. These permitted excursions into performing are a reminder of the life she once fought so hard for and has now, mostly, given up. She can't always remember now if that was her choice, Sarah's, or just the inevitable sacrifice that one parent sometimes makes when a child comes along.

As if she's heard Jess's thoughts, Tiff asks, 'You're married?'

Jess touches the thin matte silver band on her left hand. 'Six years. Sarah.'

'And you've got a daughter?'

'Claudie. She's amazing. I'm very lucky.'

'How's motherhood?'

'Claudie's three going on thirteen. She has her moments. But don't we all!'

'Go on, show me.'

Jess scrolls through her app looking for the right photo and can't help smiling as images of her daughter's blonde head, her grinning face, her tiny frame whizz past. When Tiff leans over to look, Jess self-consciously skips over photos that feature her wife. Jess knows what Tiff will be itching to ask, that she will have been trying to spot a resemblance in the pictures but will be avoiding asking what might be an insensitive question.

'Sarah is Claudie's birth mother. When we were trying to get pregnant, we already knew that she'd go back to work quickly, and I'd do most of the day-to-day. I'm the lucky one who gets to spend so much time with Claudie. She's starting nursery in September; things will likely change a bit.'

'And now? A full month away? Must be tough to be gone for so long.'

'I see her on camera, but it's not the same. Missing her like crazy.'

'Claudie, or your wife?'

'Both. Obviously.'

'The reviews you've been getting are great. She must be proud.'

Jess wants to steer the conversation away from Sarah, and what she may or may not think of her show, or her acting at all.

'And you?' she asks. 'Who's waiting for you at home? You must travel a fair bit too.'

'Only Collette,' Tiff pauses for effect. 'The cat.' As Tiff plucks imaginary fur from her top, Jess's eyes are drawn to her chest, the faint outline of Tiff's lacey bra under her white shirt. 'Though she's about as much trouble as the ex.'

'Sorry to hear that,' Jess says and then adds, 'I mean about Colette. Not the ex. Sorry, I'm prying now.'

'I'm over it. The ex, not the cat.' This banter feels natural. 'What does your wife do?' Tiff asks.

'Marketing. She's the MD of her Agency. It's a corporate job, pretty different to this world.'

'The breadwinner then? Lucky you!' Stung, Jess tries not to let it show as Tiff carries on. 'When I told the girls I was interviewing Elvis, they were all jealous. Now I've met you, I feel I'm even luckier.' Jess wonders if she can detect a slight blush on her cheeks but Tiff stands up too quickly for her to be sure.

'We'd better crack on. Ready for your close-up?'

'Born ready.'

Tiff signals that Jess should head into the adjoining bedroom where she sits on the edge of the bed, and two women come in and start unpacking their plastic cases. She smells face powder as their fingers flutter across her cheeks. They gossip above her; she is not expected to join in. There is coffee on the breath of one of them as she applies mascara to Jess's lashes. Her cool fingertips press gently on her eyelids to keep them shut.

Jess hasn't heard from Sarah yet today, and the distance between them feels fresh again. Not only the miles but the differences between what they're experiencing. Jess craves these forays into her culture and her art, but she wishes Sarah could be there more often to see her in it. She wants to be admired by her, the way she respects her wife when she hears her negotiate deals on the phone, subtly chastise her team, or joke with a client. If here, Sarah would be putting everyone at ease, making them laugh. Jess is outgoing on her own terms but knows that she dims around her confident, witty wife.

Hair and make-up complete, she takes a selfie.

Gussied up!

Totally forgot. Soz. Having fun?

It's weird. Got to get my game face on.

You'll be amazing. Sexy you. My King.

Jess treasures these moments of fondness between them, usually subsumed by the effort of co-parenting. When the banter between them feels intimate, less like a to-do list. She goes back into the small lounge area, quickly transformed into a makeshift studio with reflective screens and lights.

'You look fab.' Tiff beckons her over.

'Scrub up well?' Jess wipes her palms, suddenly damp, on her jeans.

'Seriously. You'll be great.'

The photographer comes over and shakes Jess's hand.

'Mattie. Good to meet you. Relax.'

'Do you want me to be me?' Jess asks. 'Or more like him?'

'A bit of both. We'll try out a few different poses until we get the right one.'

Mattie's androgynous all-black look suits her. She wears gold wire-framed glasses, hair shaved short against her scalp, one small gold stud in her left ear lobe. When Mattie comes over to position her in front of the screen, Jess sees tribal tattoos on her dark skin. Her cologne is spicy, with a hint of tobacco and leather. Jess enjoys having her shoulders twisted this way and that, the feel of Mattie's hands.

Mattie asks Tiff to bring over a black metal chair, and Jess straddles it, her arms resting lightly on the back. The lights flash. As instructed, she moves into different poses and curls her lip on cue. It took her a long time to master, but now she can do it on command and knows its effect. Quicker than she expects or wants it to be, the shoot is over.

'All done.' Mattie says as her assistants start dismantling the equipment. 'Fancy a look? To be honest, they'll only need a tiny bit of touching up; your skin is amazing. See what you think.'

Tiff steps forward quickly from where she's been standing in the doorway of the adjoining bedroom. 'Ooh,' she says, 'can I have a sneak peek?'

In order to see the screen, Tiff has to stand close to Jess and their shoulders touch as Mattie rewinds through the shots. There's one of Jess pouting at the camera, playful, her eyes smiling. In another, she's side on, a thoughtful gaze through the window, and one, perhaps Jess's favourite, where she's looking straight at the camera, beckoning, sexy.

'Mattie,' Tiff says, 'these are incredible.'

'Not bad, huh?' Mattie replies.

Jess isn't sure what to say, not wanting to come across as big-headed, but astonished that she's been captured so well. The photos don't just make her look (and feel) sexy and powerful but have also managed to capture the part of Jess that is most like him.

'I've never really got the whole Elvis thing, to be honest,' admits Mattie. 'But I think you've converted me.'

Tiff hangs back after the crew have finished packing up and have left the room.

'I wasn't sure until I'd met you, but I'm going to pitch to make you the cover. Your story is brilliant, but the photos nail it.'

'Wow.' Jess's hand automatically reaches up to touch her quiff. 'I wasn't expecting that.'

'Can't make any promises,' Tiff laughs, 'but I can be pretty persuasive.'

'I bet,' Jess says, as Tiff's cheeks redden. She can already imagine buying extra copies. Sending one to her dad, perhaps getting it framed.

'I reckon your wife's going to love them too,' Tiff laughs.

Jess smiles back, but she is already wary of Sarah's reaction. They've scoffed at the magazine in the past; the butch wedding suit ads and full-page advertorials for lesbian-friendly holiday resorts. Sarah has often said *LEXI* made her feel embarrassed to be a lesbian and that if this was a club, she wouldn't want to join it.

'Well, thanks for letting me know. About the cover. I'm chuffed, really.'

'See you in a few hours then? We've got tickets for later.'

After the formality of their initial handshake, Jess senses that their connection calls for a different response. Perhaps sensing her indecision, Tiff leans in for a hug.

'I'll make it a good one. Just for you,' Jess adds for clarity.

'Maybe we can grab a drink after. Raise a glass and all that...'

'Definitely,' Jess replies. 'It's my turn to ask you some questions,' she laughs. 'I've talked too much already, and I don't know a thing about you.'

'I'll hold you to that,' Tiff smiles.

Jess, left alone, looks back at the room, now empty of women, and her heart still races.

Chapter Three
The Anniversary

The interview has coincidentally fallen on a poignant day in the Elvis fan calendar: August 16th, the anniversary of his death in 1977. Jess has planned a special moment for the performance. It's a date she and her dad mark with each other too, at least in some small way. The anniversary has felt even more loaded since Claudie was born. Jess thinks about the global outpouring of grief for the King and has often wondered how his then nine-year-old daughter, Lisa Marie, coped with his loss. A little girl, cherished, then abandoned.

The Royal Mile is as chaotic as usual, and Jess resists the urge to overtake the slow-moving crowds. There is a palpable difference between the clumps of sensibly-dressed tourists and the hipper crew at her venue. She pauses to watch performers drumming up ticket sales, takes flyers when she's offered them, remembering the agony of the hours pushing her own into people's hands. They try to make eye contact as each flyer is handed out, as if that moment of connection will guarantee a sale. Then they see them dropped on the ground a few feet further up the road, trodden on, footprints stamped on their faces. The disappointment, the waste, the desolation of unsold tickets, and any hope of a small profit diminished.

She pauses in the theatre bar where a group of her fellow performers cluster around today's edition of *The Scotsman*, cups of tea and empty crisp packets littering the table. They give her mock salutes when she walks up.

'Nice one, Jess. Another stonker,' says David, waving a copy of the paper at her. 'I'm really bloody jealous.'

'Yeah, you can't even pay for reviews that good,' says Alicia. 'Trust me, I've tried.'

David and Alicia are two-thirds of the cast of Sarah Kane's *Blasted*. A difficult play to stage in the first place, their run has been decimated by walkouts and crap write-ups ('a tortuous hour', 'wish I'd been blasted to the next venue'). Although Jess has seen their show and agrees with the reviews, she's told them that it's powerful, and commends them for being so brave with such murky work. Spending time with other performers is another gift of Edinburgh. When she's here, she never has to apologise for wanting to act, losing herself on stage and being buoyed by audience energy. Feelings that feel hollow, even pretentious, amongst her non-industry friends and even her wife.

'Cheers, guys,' Jess says. 'It's the King, not me, that deserves the credit.'

She gives them an Elvis-style wink and carries on through the bar and up the stairs to the dressing room. Rather than going straight in, she carries on up a few more flights and stops by a window at the end of a landing where there will be no interruptions and good reception.

Her father answers the phone.

'Hey,' Jess says gently.

'Hey, pumpkin. I was hovering, driving your mum crazy. Knew you'd call. Big day.'

'Big day. We'll be making a special toast to him during the show,' Jess says. 'Go on,' she smiles. 'Tell me where you were when you heard. I know you want to.'

Her father chuckles. 'Your mum and I were still courting, not even married yet. She'd finally convinced me to go and see that James Bond film, *The Spy Who Loved Me*. She had a thing for Roger Moore. I wasn't so fussed, something a bit smug about him.'

'And there was only room in your heart for one man,' Jess jokes.

'Now, now. Anyway, the projectionist turned the lights on right at the start of the credits, and he said, 'Elvis is dead'. Just like that. And the whole audience sat there in silence, wanting to ask questions, only there was nothing more he could tell us. Everyone started crying, your mum, me too. It wasn't like today, love, no internet. Well, your mum could see how cut up I was, so we went straight back to my bedsit and played records until morning. As soon as it was light, I went out and got the papers, and there it all was. The answers. I cried again, right there, in the street. Like a baby.'

'Don't cry, Daddy,' Jess says, and they both laugh lightly at the in-joke. 'I know how much he meant to you.'

'But thanks to you, my clever girl, I've got him back in my life again. I'm so proud of you, you know that. I'm the lucky one. I got to watch my little girl grow up to be an amazing woman. He never did.'

'I'll do him proud tonight. You too.'

'Do it for him,' her father says.

'For *both* of you. Look, I better go and get ready. I'll call at the weekend. In the meantime, I'm...'

She pauses for a moment so that he can join in.

'Taking care of business.'

The line goes quiet, but Jess stays for a moment longer. She remembers being waltzed around the living room when her father fished through his stash of vinyl each Saturday night. The rest of the family would groan and hang back, but Jess would jump onto the carpet, copy his moves, mouth the words. Her dad would pepper conversations with facts about his idol and ask her to quiz him. There were no answers he didn't know. They'd pour over photos in yellowing magazines he'd saved from back then, and he'd talk about the trip to Memphis they'll take one day. 'Beale Street,' he'd say longingly. 'Breakfast at the Arcade, and we'll stay in the Heartbreak Hotel.'

'There's not actually a Heartbreak Hotel, Dad,' Jess had protested once.

'Oh yes there is. It's as real as Graceland. He never actually went there, but still...'

When Jess had stopped seeking out auditions because Sarah and then Claudie came along, her father had made no secret of his disappointment. Then, it was him that led her to discover her own Elvis – the one she carries not only in her heart but in her bones. The start of it all.

When he'd turned seventy a few years ago, her parents had gone all out and booked the best suite at the local hotel in Milton Keynes, invited everyone they could think of. Instead of her brother, it was Jess he'd asked to make a speech. Rarely excited about performing in front of friends, especially her parent's friends, she'd decided she owed him and that she must do it.

After putting a newly born Claudie to bed, Sarah had helped her stick strips of sequins on an old white suit they found in a charity shop. They choreographed Jess's moves by studying endless videos on YouTube. Jess had assumed that it would be her first and last performance, but she'd put the hours in all the same. On the night, they endured dinner but skipped dessert and snuck back up to their bedroom to change. Sarah helped push Jess's fringe up so she could spray it into the best quiff she could. They laughed as they stuck on that first pair of clumsy sideburns. Costume on, Sarah perched on the edge of the bed and looked up at her.

'You actually look really fucking hot,' Sarah said and pulled Jess down towards her. 'My King.'

'Oi, watch the quiff. This thing's precious.'

Before they opened the door to leave, Sarah had surprised her by grabbing her again. Rarely the instigator of any intimacy, especially after she'd had Claudie.

'Hey, King,' she whispered into Jess's ear, putting her hand down to Jess's crotch. 'Do I get my own show later?'

'Uh-huh,' Jess whispered back. 'Let's do this.'

Sarah's nickname for Jess, King, had stuck; but only to a point. Used by her wife when she's in the mood. The mood that's so infrequent now it's practically extinct. Sarah's job, Claudie, Jess's lack of desire to wear anything more alluring than jeans and t-shirts at home – these are not precursors to romance. 'We should have more date nights,' they've said to each other, more than once. For Jess though, the effort of organising a sitter, co-ordinating Sarah's diary and booking a restaurant is more than she can be bothered to do. Their treat, these days, is not sex, but an evening on the sofa with a TV crime drama and a takeaway.

That first night as Elvis, Jess had asked the hotel staff to dim the lights. She'd only prepped to do one song, 'I Just Can't Help Believin'. But once finished, everyone stood up, shouting and clapping, louder than any audience she'd experienced for a long time. From her place on the makeshift stage, and having sung about misty mornings and hands in hands, she'd seen her dad wipe tears away. With nothing else prepared, she performed the same song again. She crooned to him that the girl is going to stay. After the encore, she stood at the front of the room and bowed. Still in character, she walked up to her dad. Her mother, sitting next to him, smiled tightly.

'Happy Birthday, Daddy,' she'd said.

He stood up and pulled her into his arms. Pride, love, surprise, acceptance. It was everything. And the start of something. Her hair is now permanently cut to help her sculpt the quiff. The lip curl, shoulder flicks, and hip twitches have become her own. She no longer acts, she just becomes.

Jess shakes herself from her reverie and heads back downstairs to get into costume and hover backstage until it's time. The changeover between shows is always flurried, even if everything is running to time. The performers before her swoop past, laden with props, nodding a good luck. Alone now, Jess hears her pre-show playlist and the audience's low hum. Bouncing up and down on her toes, swinging her arms in circles behind her, she ensures her muscles are limber for the opening sequence. Alone, peeking out from the wings, she sees the house is nearly full, while a few stragglers side-step gingerly down the steep steps to get to their seats.

The auditorium lights lower on cue, and the audience falls obediently silent. They expect her to enter in full cape and rhinestones, but she toys with them by simply wearing black, tight jockey shorts and a white vest, her breasts bound so her silhouette is as androgynous as possible. She walks slowly across the gritty boards to the teasing horns and drumbeats of the *2001 Space Odyssey* soundtrack which Elvis himself borrowed from Strauss's 'Also Sprach Zarathustra'. The drums beat faster, and she can almost hear the audience gasping in anticipation. They cannot envisage how a woman in underwear will be able to transform into the King. They wonder if they've been mis-sold a ticket.

Jess takes a few steps forward as the stage goes black. She turns away from them and takes a deep breath through her nose, summoning all her power to complete the first movements of the show. They require precision and explosive energy, not strobe but staccato. The rush of blood to her head is so full it pounds, but it's not a headache. It's love and lust and passion and fear and freedom.

Blackout.

Backlight beams full on.

Nobody could say exactly how, but she has started to change. Her shoulders are squarer, her hips fuller. Her head high, she is already mesmerising,

Two seconds later, the lights plummet back to black.

Then on again.

Her right leg points out, her knee twisted inwards, weight shifted onto her toes. Left arm taut behind her, index finger pointing. Transformation intensified.

Blackout.

When the lights come on again, the track crescendos. She's on the tips of both toes. Her knees twisted sideways; arms flung up behind her. A moment of motion, the iconic pose is timed to hit the split second of illumination, so they can all believe that maybe, just maybe, he has been born again.

The next thirty seconds are a chance for them all to catch their breath. The music switches from classical to the fast bars of 'See See Rider': drumbeats, guitars playing underneath, a refrain that continues until the mood has temporarily settled. Elvis used this time to pace from side to side, flicking his cape behind him, connecting with his band and audience, revelling in the frenzy that even just being in the building created. He'd bow his head in mock humility, tap his foot on peddles at the front of the stage. Let them have what they're there for – a long look. For Jess, still capeless so early in this show, this is a chance to pump herself up, to take the deep quick breaths she needs before she starts using her voice.

It's the audience's first proper look at her too. Some will feel awkward, even confused. They won't know why they feel embarrassed to stare at the semi-naked woman on the stage in front of them, why their heart rate has quickened, why their palms have gone moist.

Over the next forty minutes, Jess will tell the story of the women that Elvis loved. His young bride Priscilla, of course, but also the women that history doesn't remember as clearly. His messy loves. She'll give Dixie, his first girlfriend, her rightful place as the girl who loved Elvis before he was the man he became. She'll allow Anita the heartbreak of losing Elvis to Priscilla; Ann-Margret the chance to be more than simply one of his affairs. For Ginger, his fiancée at the time of his death, Jess will reserve yet more loss.

Enlisting her dad's encyclopaedic knowledge of Elvis's discography, Jess has been careful to include enough of the big numbers. Elvis's early hits are framed in the comparative innocence of his first loves. 'Heartbreak Hotel' suggests that Elvis's initial attraction to teenage girls was his way of staying grounded, having been thrust prematurely into the adult world of fame. 'Surrender' becomes a chance to examine more overtly sexual motifs, and the choreography becomes more suggestive. During a slower track, 'Are You Lonesome Tonight', Jess takes the opportunity to slip on the satin trousers that she hung up earlier. The material slides up her legs as tenderly as a kiss.

Jess and her dad tussled over which songs to close the show with. But before that, she needed a final fast-paced number, during which she puts on the jacket, though still incomplete without the final piece of her costume – the cape. Her father wanted something well-known, a crowd-pleaser, but Jess fought for 'Let Yourself Go', a track from *Speedway* an Elvis movie she loved. To her, it's the sexiest song in the canon, but it's also about power, the singer instructing the object of his affections to let go and take it slowly. The beat is fast. He's urging her, he's teaching her about love, making love. There's something about the rhythm, the dubious message, that fires Jess up. She moves fast across the stage, tugging on her jacket until she's fully dressed, dazzling. Ready to be crowned the true King.

After that comes 'Separate Ways', the penultimate number. It's not one that a less committed fan will know, which makes it even more impactful as the lyrics take hold in the context of her show. It starts innocently enough. She kicks the microphone cable to one side, turns as if to whisper to an invisible band behind her. As Elvis did, she smiles directly at the audience, making eye contact with people that she can see in the front row, seducing them.

She tucks her fingers under the rim of the waistband that covers her midriff, smoothes out the satin. Finally, it is time to clasp the cape around her neck. Only now, at the show's climax will she be fully dressed, turned away from the audience, arms outstretched.

As she sings about the change that's happening in their lives, she's aware that most will be unfamiliar with the lyrics. They won't know what's coming. She slows herself down, strolls towards and from the audience, hangs her head, holds it up again. She sings about love slipping away, two people who are becoming like strangers. The audience is holding their breath. Total silence unless someone quietly gasps, the shushing of a tissue, unable to stop their tears. Her final line, devastating, lingered upon. Nothing is left. She lets the vocal die out, part hums, part sings, and sobs the final few bars. Because this is a story of heartbreak.

To Jess, the power of *The Wonder of You* lies in the queering of the love stories it depicts. It asks the audience to question the nature of Elvis's love and desire of women. Because it's performed by a woman who loves women; but dressed as a man who stole hearts, filled them, and broke them. Her Elvis is tender and kind but also powerful and dominant. His treatment of women was controversial, but through her Drag King lens, it explores whether love between women completes, softens, or just complicates the narrative. The audience leave the auditorium confused and enthused. They wonder whether Elvis is to be adored or whether history should further explore his motives. Straight women find themselves irresistibly drawn to Jess and question whether it's Elvis they want, or her. Gay women applaud Jess's acknowledgement that lesbian love is a kind, rousing gift.

Without having to spell it out, it's clear to the audience that this is not a singalong show, and if anyone does start humming or mouthing the words too audibly, they are shushed by others. Tonight though, this sad anniversary, Jess has decided to allow them a chance to sing.

The title song of the show is her final track each night. Tonight, she has asked that the house lights are put on and while the first bars kick in, the ushers file down the steps and hand out plastic cups of prosecco to the audience. Beckoning them to stand, Jess temporarily abandons the character.

'Hey folks,' she says, as herself. 'I'd like to invite you to sing with me, to him. I'm sure most of you know the words.'

Sweeping her eyes across the rows, she looks out for Tiff, who is quickly wiping a tissue under her eye but now smiling and laughing. A slight nod of her head to show she's been spotted.

The song starts; how no-one understands him but the lover. Although they begin quietly, the audience quickly increases in volume. They sway, clap hands against their plastic cups. Some even take on the higher pitch of the backing singers. She sees Tiff nudging her colleagues, their arms across each other's shoulders, getting into it.

When they get to the part where a touch of the hand makes him a King, Jess smiles and takes a quick bow with the applause. During the instrumental, she walks back and forth across the stage and holds her hand out so that people in the front row can touch her. At the final line, the title of her show *The Wonder of You*, Jess takes a few steps back to the middle of the stage, holds her arms out, and the bright blue lining of her cape is dazzling. At the final drumbeat, she turns away from the audience. They can see the full glory of that infamous eagle, picked out in gemstones, across the white satin. She takes a bow.

The high after tonight's performance feels particularly potent. If her dad had been in the audience, Jess knows he'd have bellowed along with everyone else. Her mum, she suspects, would have dutifully stood up but refused to sing, keeping her hands clasped on her handbag in front of her so she could beat a speedy getaway.

Jess is in such a rush to get through her post-show routine and get out to see her fans, Tiff amongst them, that she almost forgets to check her phone. She wonders if Sarah will have remembered that tonight was the anniversary performance and might have sent her a special message or a jokey reminder that Jess should go to bed early because she's arriving tomorrow. But nothing.

Phone tucked away, Jess heads out to the bar. In her haste, she's removed less of the eye make-up and kept her quiff at full height and still feels as though Elvis's spirit is inside her. Walking tall, hips thrust forward, she feels amazing.

Tiff has paired her leather skirt with a gauzy black top, her Converse replaced by wedges that emphasise her taut calf muscles.

'Wasn't sure what you'd like. Took a punt.' Tiff hands Jess one of two glasses on the bar next to her. 'G&T. A double.'

Jess hates gin. Or at least, tonic. 'Perfect.'

'I knew you were going to be good, but I didn't know how good. You were brilliant. Better than brilliant. Seriously though, and I'm not just saying it, you got me. Here.' Tiff presses a fist up against her heart.

'I'm so glad.' Jess affects mock humility. 'It would have been embarrassing if you'd thought it was crap.'

'Oh my god, no. It's genius. You're a genius.'

Jess spies a table over in the corner and gestures to Tiff that they should go and sit down, away from the crowd. Normally she'd resent not having the chance to chat to her fans, but tonight she's happy with this one on her own.

'Did the others enjoy it?' she asks. 'Where are they, by the way?'

'They loved it. Mattie said it made her think about Elvis in a whole new light, think she actually really likes him now. But...' Tiff's eyes flick down to the table, and she smiles in mock-apology. 'I told them a little white lie to be honest. I said you had tickets for a show straight after but only one spare for l'il old me.'

'Well, I'm honoured.' Jess feels a flutter deep in her belly. She's received plenty of compliments before, but this one really means something.

Tiff leans forward suddenly and takes Jess's hand. 'Your rings! Close up, they're even more amazing.'

Jess pulls her hand back quickly and fumbles in her jeans pocket for the pouch. 'Oops, forgot to take them off. Got dressed in a hurry.'

'Shame,' Tiff laughs, 'I thought they were kinda hot. Don't think they'd suit me though,' she waggles her short, neon pink nails at Jess.

'No, maybe not. Not that yours aren't great though.'

'In my head, I'd thought that Priscilla was his one true love, that their divorce was a mistake, and that if he'd lived, they might even get back together. Not like I knew much, but maybe that's what I wished for. But your show has made me think. Is there such a thing as one true love? Or maybe that's just my cynical singleton voice speaking.'

'Don't be so hard on yourself. It's out there for you, I'm sure. And who says there's such a thing as *one* true love, anyway?'

Their eyes meet for a second, but Jess immediately looks away. When she speaks again, her tone sounds unnaturally jaunty, even to her. 'Hey, you promised me that I could ask *you* some questions since the interview was all about me. So, I'll start with an easy one. It's too hectic in here, and I know a late-night bar that's never too heaving. Fancy it?'

'I'm all yours,' Tiff says.

Chapter Four
The Visit

Jess spends the morning deep cleaning the apartment in preparation for Sarah's arrival. It's been in the calendar since she arrived but now it's here, she feels frazzled and unprepared. Plus, her eyes are puffy from the 2am finish after a later night of drinking than she planned with Tiff. She moves the framed picture of her two girls on a country walk, from the coffee table to beside the bed, buys flowers, bacon and eggs, checks the date on the milk. Changes the sheets. Sarah should already be en route to the station when a message arrives at lunchtime.

Slight change of plan. Running late. Really sorry. Won't make a massive difference.

??

Work thing. Got a new train booked. Arriving at 8. Can't wait. xx

Jess flings her phone down on the bed and sits down hard, wishing she felt she was her wife's priority, for this weekend at least. Sarah will have dispensed with any obligation to stick to the plan ('clients come first') and will have got her PA (the one she actually pays) to book her a new First-Class ticket. As usual, any inconvenience Jess faces is the collateral damage of Sarah's job, her income, and the privileges it affords them both.

She messages back, offering to collect her from Waverley, but Sarah replies that it's probably going to be too late, she'd rather jump in a cab. An hour later, Jess messages again, hoping to come off as chirpier than she feels.

How's it going, my lover?

SLOWLY. This train is being powered by donkeys.

Relax. No rush.

Run out of wine.

At last, Sarah says she's in a cab.

Forgot how scruffy Edinburgh was. Students and tourists. Yuk.

Finally, a taxi pulls up, and a familiar blonde head appears. Jess runs down the stairs, two at a time. Because they wait until the front door is shut behind them to kiss it feels awkward and a beat too late.

Jess hurries them up the stairs so the timed light doesn't go off before reaching the top.

'Here's home.' Jess lets Sarah into the flat ahead of her.

'It's good to be here. Finally.'

'Come here, you.' Jess moves over to give her a proper hug, but after only a few seconds, Sarah pulls away.

'Too many free crisps and sandwiches.' Sarah rubs her belly. 'Seriously bloated.'

'So, what do you fancy doing?'

'Oh, I don't know. Only just got here. What do *you* fancy doing?'

'I'm here all the time, so it's not really up to me. I've booked some stuff for tomorrow, though. Fancy a quick drink in the pub? Are you hungry? Or I've got some wine in?'

'Would you mind if we did that?' Sarah says with a hint of apology. 'Maybe a quiet one tonight, a good sleep, and a big one tomorrow? Sorry. Is that really boring of me?'

Even in her first hour, Sarah has taken control, and Jess feels her sway diminish. Sarah smooths Jess's hair back off her forehead, kisses her briefly on the lips. 'I've missed you,' she says.

'Missed you too.' Jess opens a bottle of red wine. The sofa is only a two-seater, a little too small for them both to sit comfortably. The first time they're face to face in weeks, so much to catch up on. Jess has nothing to say.

'How it's going, though?' Sarah starts. 'Are you the hot ticket in town? Surrounded by adoring fans in the bar afterwards? I'm here to claim my wife back. For 48 hours anyway.'

'It's all good,' Jess replies. 'Full-on, but fine. Had the interview with *LEXI* yesterday. Think it went okay. How's my baby girl?'

'Bollocks, sorry, I forgot to ask. I can't wait to read it though,' Sarah says, but doesn't press for further details and Jess, although primed to tell her more, stays quiet. 'Claudie's missing you,' Sarah says. 'I don't think she has as much fun with me. Little madam. I'm being a bit strict, she says. *Mama wouldn't make me brush my teeth twice a day.*'

'I so would,' Jess laughs. 'It's my job to take her to the bloody dentist!'

Sarah leans forward to pour herself another glass of wine and then sits back again. She arranges cushions around her, creating a pillowy barricade between them.

'How's work?' Jess asks.

'A nightmare, to be honest. A re-org in EMEA. It's not the fact of doing it that's the issue, it's the extra work. And the pitch was a nightmare. If they don't want to work with us, that's fine. I wish they'd just say so.'

'I'm sorry, sounds pretty tough.'

'This is your weekend, remember? No more work chat. What time is it anyway?' Sarah picks up her phone to check. Now it's in her hand, she starts automatically checking her messages. Deleting some, writing short responses to others.

'Sorry, sorry,' she says as she types and pats Jess's knee. Her manicured fingers dart across the screen. 'Got to sort something out.'

'Of course.' Jess goes into the bedroom and lights a scented candle, knowing they'll be going to bed soon, sensing they both need today to be over. Already, Sarah has filled the space. Her perfume has altered the smell. The small rooms had felt spacious enough with the high ceilings, but seen through Sarah's eyes, everything feels dingy and cramped.

Jess's phone pings as she's draping the cheap woollen throws back into position and rearranging the cushions.

Hey, you!

It's from Tiff.

Had a great time last night. Not often you get to party with the King!

Then another.

Heading back to London tomorrow afternoon. Fancy brunch before? Read a great review of a place near where I think you're staying? I can come to you.

Sarah calls out from the bathroom, 'I'm all done in here.'

Worried that she'll seem rude if she doesn't reply, Jess types quickly.

Can't. Sarah's here. Enjoy your last day.

Forgot that. Hope you have fun.

Sarah has fully unpacked, even for two days: laid out her eye-creams, moisturisers and foundation, stuffed her brushes in the small mug Jess put there specially.

'Cosy.' Sarah is lying in bed already, duvet pulled up to her chin.

Jess climbs in, the mattress sags; both bodies slowly drawn together, like quicksand. They reach out and hold hands under the duvet. It is big enough for one, but for two, like the sofa, it feels small.

'It's good to have you here.' Jess squeezes Sarah's hand. 'I've missed you. Love you.'

Sarah rolls up onto her elbow and looks into Jess's eyes. 'Love you too.' She kisses Jess on the lips then rolls back down.

Jess reaches up to turns the light off.

'Sleep well, darling,' Jess says into the dark.

'Night, King.'

Jess smiles to hear her nickname, a signifier that her wife is happy and that all is good, despite the awkwardness of her arrival. The weekend suddenly feels full of possibilities. She lies in the dark, listening to the sound of her wife's breath. When Sarah transitions to sleep, a slight snore catches in her throat. Two days of laughing, hanging out, making plans. And tomorrow afternoon, Sarah will be in the audience of her show, and that, she thinks, will make it even better.

In this temporary home away from home, if it's raining, the buildings opposite turn black, but they are pale grey and gleaming this morning. Sleep has diluted any stickiness of the night before. When Jess gets back into bed after making them both tea (already slipping back quickly into her wifely routines), Sarah sits up, leans forward for a mouth-closed morning kiss, smiles, and stretches. She asks what they're doing that day and in the same sentence suggests that they head out to brunch. This is a 'quorder' – an order disguised as a question – a mode of communication that is favoured by Sarah.

The next hour or so is spent sitting side by side with their backs against the headboard, communicating with other people. Sarah Facetimes her mother so they can speak to Claudie.

'You two look well-rested,' Judith says. 'Your gorgeous daughter has been good as gold, as always. We're just glad you've managed to get away,' Judith says. 'Let me go and find her.'

As Judith walks with her phone, the view transitions from Italian marble tiles to the Persian rug and stops above where Claudie is playing. The lens swings up, and there she is – moving things in and out of a dollhouse. With her wife in the same room but her daughter so far away, Jess gasps and presses her hand over her mouth. Every inch of this tiny body is as familiar to her as Jess's own – the nobbles of her knees, her little fingers. She knows how long before her nails need cutting, how to separate her hair into miniature bunches, and avoid combing over the raised birthmark above her left ear. Although it is biologically impossible, there are still times when she catches herself thinking that she can see herself in her daughter.

'Hey, ragamuffin, what are you up to?' Jess calls into the phone. 'Wave at your mummies.' Judith urges Claudie to look up. Claudie stands, her ankles peeping out above the legs of her pyjamas that she's already outgrowing. 'Are Nanna J and Grandpa spoiling you rotten? Did they maybe give you a chocolate croissant for breakfast?'

'Oops. Sprung.' Judith's arm reaches around the camera lens to wipe the smear away with a crumpled tissue.

Jess and Sarah take it in turns to try and engage Claudie in conversation but with so many distractions on offer, eventually they tell Judith they'll check in later. After goading Claudie to press the red button, they fall silent.

'They're so good with her, aren't they?' Jess puts a hand on Sarah's thigh. 'We're lucky, you know.'

'They love it.' Sarah asks, her tone tentative, 'Have you called your parents recently?'

'No. I will. Maybe later.'

'Go on, do it now. I'll chip in,' Sarah promises.

For all that her dad has embraced WhatsApp, Jess's parents don't entirely understand why a phone needs a camera. Instead, she dials their landline, and it keeps ringing; she wonders if they've already headed out for their Saturday chores. If the phone is picked up, it will be by her mum, who will answer cautiously, despite seeing it's her daughter on the caller-ID panel.

'The Ellis residence,' she says, sounding a little breathless.

'It's Jess, Mum. You alright? Sounds like you've run a marathon.'

'Sorting out some stuff for your dad. You know what he's like. Gets these ideas in his head. It's so hot down here. And now he wants to empty the shed. Today of all days.'

'He should have waited until I get home. Or at least give my lazy brother a call. Why can't he come and help?'

'Don't be glib, Jess. It's not nice. They're away, remember? Frinton.'

'Oh yes, glamorous Frinton. The summer holidays dreams are made of.'

Her mother sniffs. 'I can see your father coming up now. Hold on, I'll get him.'

As Jess hears her mother calling out, she pictures her dad lumbering, a little stooped in recent years but gathering speed when he knows it's Jess on the line. Her mother tutting a little when he comes in without wiping his shoes.

'Jessie! How are you, pumpkin? It's bloody hot down here. What it's like up there?'

'Hot. For Scotland. How are you doing, Dad?'

'I'm fine, love. Nothing to write home about.' He changes the subject. 'How's my star? How did the big Anniversary show go? Did they love the singalong?'

'It was brilliant, actually. They really got into it. And now Sarah's here.'

'Hi Martin.' Sarah, overhearing their conversation, calls out from where she's unpacking on the other side of the room. 'Seeing the show this afternoon, I'll report back.'

'Thanks, Pet,' Martin calls out to his daughter-in-law. 'And where's my beautiful granddaughter then? Home alone?'

'She's with Judith and David, Dad. You know that.'

'We could have had here too, you know. We might not be as sprightly as we were, but I reckon we could cope for a weekend. Anyway, love, I better go, you heard your mother, but you carry on being brilliant. Take care, love. Sing your little heart out. Take care of business.'

'Always, Dad, always.' With a click, he's gone.

It's noon by the time they've showered and dressed. Sarah in boyfriend jeans, a Breton top, white Birkenstocks (new ones each summer) and her hair tied her up in the casual ponytail that Jess watches her perfect for fifteen minutes.

'New top?' Jess asks.

'Maybe,' her wife smiles across the room at her. 'You don't think I look like I'm trying to be twenty again?'

'You look great. Twenty or um, twenty-plus.'

'Oi!'

'Thirty-nine soon, and then you know what that means!'

'Don't rub it in, and you're only a few years behind me, you know.'

Sarah swipes at her, grinning. Jess notices that Sarah has had a mani-pedi in preparation for the weekend. Having spent so long apart from her wife, Jess feels a little giddy with pleasure, remembering what she loves about her wife, her isms and quirks.

'You look pretty good yourself, King,' says Sarah as they walk down the stone stairs. She laughs as they simultaneously reach for their sunglasses. 'Wifey twins.'

Sarah's Chanel's are oversized, a last-minute purchase at Heathrow before a business trip. They set off down the wide pavements, and then Jess pauses to switch them around.

'Ant and Dec,' she says as she takes Sarah's shoulders and moves her to their established sides of the pavement. Sarah laughs and takes Jess's hand, a gesture of rare spontaneous intimacy. Jess often watches Sarah shower Claudie with kisses, pulling up her t-shirt to blow raspberries on her soft belly and wonders how long it's been since Sarah has touched her with the same looseness. She misses it, but not enough to make it an issue.

They find a table at a Bruntsfield cafe, outside and in the sun.

'Glorious,' Sarah says as she looks over the menu. 'Do you think they have cortados up here?'

'What, in Scotland?' Jess laughs. 'Apparently, they even have cars. And Wi-Fi.'

After breakfast, they wander across the Meadows. The city glistens ahead of them, but even so, the mood has shifted slightly after their morning's flirty banter. Shading her eyes with her hand, Jess looks up at Arthur's Seat framed against the bright blue skies.

'How is Jonty? Linny and the kids?' After Sarah's brother and sister-in-law, Jess works through a list of other people: friends, colleagues, and a client going through a bitchy patch. Jokes about all the holiday spam on their Instagram feeds. Sarah gestures that they should pause on a wooden bench. A young couple walks past, clutching each other as they walk, stopping to kiss every few steps. Sarah breaks the silence.

'We're good, aren't we?'

Jess feels her body tense and hopes that Sarah doesn't notice. 'Wow. That's out of nowhere.'

Sarah continues. 'I guess I'm just conscious that with my work and your show and Claudie and everything, we don't ever really check in with stuff like that. Sorry if it came out like a big thing, it's not. Honestly. I'm not trying to start anything major here.'

Sensing that this is a statement, a start of something but not quite a conversation, Jess knows the only answer she's expected to give. Her mind briefly turns to the question about true love that Tiff asked her, the one that, after many years of marriage and a child, is not one she even thinks about anymore. She pushes the moment down again.

'Of course, we're OK. Better than OK, I reckon,' Jess says. 'I mean, life is going to change soon anyway, right? Claudie's about to start nursery... which makes it feel like the last three years never happened.'

'She'll be great. It's all down to you. I know you work hard to make sure she has loads of playdates and clubs and stuff. I do appreciate it. I feel bad that it's stuff I don't do.'

'Hey, don't apologise.' Jess play swipes Sarah. 'That was the deal, remember? It's cool.'

They lapse back into silence as a family walk past, the woman pushing the stroller, a sleeping baby swaddled inside.

'Do you ever get a bit bored?' Sarah asks.

'Blimey, twenty questions!'

'It was only that you said it, made me wonder. You know you can talk to me about it if you want.'

'Hey, let me get this month done. I'm happy. It's all good. Back to real life soon.'

Even as she says it, Jess resents how quickly she's reverted to accepting that her real life is so different from the one she's living in Edinburgh. A way of living that she hasn't challenged and hasn't, until now, even thought to. 'Something on *your* mind?' Jess presses.

'No. It's all good.'

The man, his wife trailing behind with the buggy, urges his older daughter into running races, faking a loss each time. Jess remembers when Claudie was young enough to fall for it too. Jess feels Sarah take a deep breath. Her wife may be trying to keep her voice light, but it comes off as loaded and the minute Sarah starts speaking, Jess feels her chest tighten.

'We got a letter though. From the clinic.'

Jess knows what her wife is referring to, but still asks, hoping her breath doesn't sound as constricted as it feels. 'The clinic?'

'You know, Harley Street. They've sent a letter about the donor.'

'Oh right,' Jess says, her voice noncommittal. 'That's come round fast.'

'I guess,' Sarah says. 'It's been nearly four years now. It's routine.'

'What does it say?'

'Nothing really. Just a reminder of what was in the original contract, remember? That if we want Claudie's sibling to have the same donor, we've got time for that. But not *that* much time. I should have sent a shot of it, but honestly, it was just a first letter. I'm sure they'll send more, and you'll be back by then. We don't have to chat about it now.'

Sarah scuffs the earth underneath the bench. Pushes a cigarette butt around with the toe of her sandals, straightens the shoulder of her top. Jess wants to make eye-contact but her wife is gazing in the direction of the town and when Sarah speaks again it's to change the subject, a sign that the conversation, for now at least, is over.

'What time do we need to be there?'

'We should get there by 3 o'clock latest. Want to make sure you get a good seat! Curtain up at 4.'

Jess is looking forward to walking into the venue with her wife, squiring her around, introducing her to other companies and new friends.

As they cross the Meadows' calm expanse, Jess points out the coffee shops that serve the best cake and the venues her friends perform in. Jokes that they can climb up to the castle tomorrow – she has said this before, knowing they never will.

'My King of Scotland. It suits you.' Sarah puts her arm through Jess's. 'Hope we can drag you back to boring old London after all this.' As they walk into town, memories of the great shows so far, the appreciative audiences, the interview, Tiff, the thrill of tonight's performance a few hours away, Jess's life in London has never felt so far away.

CHLOË FOWLER

Chapter Five
Sexy Little Rabbits

Sarah already has their drinks lined up when Jess emerges after her show. It went well, and she knows it. Not quite her best performance, unable to completely lose herself knowing her wife was in the audience, but still worthy of the lengthy ovation she received. Sarah stands next to a younger couple who turn towards Jess as she approaches, slow clapping in unison.

'You were brilliant,' Sarah says. Jess, poised for a proper kiss, is disappointed when Sarah's lips simply brush her cheek. 'I knew you would be. I don't know how, but it's got even better since I last saw it.' Sarah turns to the people standing next to her. 'Surprise! You remember James? From work? And this is his wife, Cassie.'

Out of context, it takes Jess a moment to place him, and she hopes the face she composes to greet them is pleasure and not the sting of annoyance she feels. James, she remembers now, is one of Sarah's latest protégés, her partner in crime on a pitch that involved many late nights of preparation, phone calls and messages. He's not dressed for a weekend at the festival, a city in which layers and comfortable shoes trump more fashionable choices. His faun chinos and blue check shirt make him look more corporate than she suspects he really is, and as he leans forward to shake her hand, she sees a vintage watch and tattoos snaking from his forearm to his elbow.

'Of course, good to see you again, James. And meet you, Cassie. Thanks so much for coming. Sarah didn't say you'd be here. Sorry, it took me a moment.'

It is only Saturday afternoon, but Cassie is dressed for an evening out. Slim-hipped, wearing a baby pink silky shirt over a balcony bra, she makes no attempt to hide the outline of her nipples. A Monica Vinader pendant nestles between her breasts. Even her hair looks expensive.

Cassie's cheeks flush when Jess kisses her on the cheek. Jess tries to catch Sarah's eye to collude in the private joke they make about how often straight women blush around Jess. But Sarah is talking to James and does not notice.

'Seriously,' giggles Cassie. 'I had no idea you were so talented. Sarah said you were good, but I didn't know you'd be *that* good.'

'Agreed,' says James, drawing back to them. 'And listen, I'm not talking shop, honest, but you should do our Christmas party. Be the emcee or something. Don't you think she'd be amazing, Sar?'

'We'll see,' says Sarah. 'It's not such a bad idea.'

'There's no such thing as a bad idea.' Sarah and James say in unison and laugh.

Sarah stands close to Jess, and now the introductions are over, takes her hand, kisses her on the lips, happy to stake her claim, in company at least. They drink fast and signal for another round, and then another. James and Sarah take turns to pay, but later, Jess notices they haven't tipped, and catches Ray's eye and slides her a surreptitious fiver across the bar.

Sarah is becoming giddy with the freedom from home and sharing in the limelight that shines around Jess. Though Jess is the performer, when they are together, it is usually Sarah who dominates. Sarah is better versed in taking charge within group situations, prepped with small talk, and knowing what questions to ask to bring out the chatter in people. It's why she's so good at her job. Jess is only more extroverted when she's not accompanied by her wife, when they are not trying to compete subconsciously (and sometimes consciously). When she is in costume. When she has Elvis by her side.

'We hope you don't mind. We've booked a table for dinner,' Cassie says. 'It's supposed to be good. James says we were lucky to get a reservation.'

'Of course, I don't mind,' Jess replies, glancing at Sarah. 'I've booked some tickets for things, but a few no-shows won't matter.'

'Oh King,' says Sarah. 'I should have said. You don't mind, do you?'

It's the same subtle manipulation she feels when she collects Claudie after nursery and is begged for a playdate, the look on her daughter's face, imploring, and excited. She can never say no to her gorgeous daughter, nor, it seems, to her powerful wife.

'Don't mind at all. A nice change from pie, chips, and cheap beer.'

'Then let's get this party started.' James puts his hand in the small of Cassie's back as he shepherds her to the door.

'And there was I thinking I had already got the party started,' Jess says as she drains the dregs of her pint, takes Sarah's hand and follows the younger couple out of the bar.

'I hope this is alright,' Sarah leans into Jess. 'I only found out they were here this weekend, and I wanted to show you off. My talented, sexy wife.' This is a rare compliment that Jess is happy to take, despite knowing that 'surprise' isn't quite the truth. If anything, Sarah will have encouraged her protégé to choose this weekend to visit the city.

James summons a cab, and darts around it to allow the women in first, choosing the front seat for himself. Sandwiched between the warmth of Cassie on one side and Sarah on the other, Jess bridles. She usually performs the chivalrous gesture, especially when traces of her post-show Elvis remain, and she resents being treated like one of the girls.

Her ownership of Edinburgh ebbs away as James tells the taxi where to go – the posh restaurant at the top of Harvey Nichols, looking down on, but not part of, the festival throng. Until now, she's had no need of the fancier shops of New Town, where the buildings are a sandier stone in contrast with the austere grey of Old Town.

Again, James makes a show of standing back and ushering the three women ahead of him with a showy bow each time they approach the base of the next escalator up to the restaurant. Cassie quips about borrowing his credit card. Sarah jokes that it might be time for some gift-for-selfing. Jess says nothing. She wants to resent this man and this rare evening alone with her wife that's been taken from her. Still, something is endearing about his puppyish, if misplaced enthusiasm, and there is pleasure in seeing her wife relax amongst others. It will also be the nicest meal she's eaten in a while.

Sarah and James order martinis before dinner, very dry with an olive (they say this with a faux Scottish accent). When Cassie tips her head back to drink champagne, her slender throat constricts. Jess swills her amber Old-Fashioned around the ice cubes and tries not to wince at the strength.

James and Cassie are still tanned from two weeks in Greece.

'Have you been?' Cassie asks. 'Honestly, it's so beautiful. The food's amazing.'

'Oh…' Sarah slumps back in her chair. 'I'd kill for a proper summer holiday. Something to heat up my bones. Just, you know, with Claudie and…' She waves her arm at the twinkling lights of the city beneath them as if being here is the Festival's fault, instead of Jess's.

Edinburgh, Cassie and James tell them, is their mini-break chaser after Greece and their honeymoon not long before that. Jess imagines them fucking against whitewashed walls, the bright blue sea beyond, a white curtain billowing in the breeze.

James proposes a toast. 'To being in the presence of greatness,' he says, tilting his glass towards her. 'May this King never leave the building.'

'To Jess. And the King,' the others chime in.

'Seriously, though, you should be on the big stage,' Cassie says to Jess.

Jess thinks she is on the big stage already but says thanks.

James and Sarah get side-tracked talking about work, heads pressed close together. Jess has forgotten the power that emanates from Sarah when she slips into professional mode, how quickly she slides between being the boss and the confidante. Dandling naivety, never conceding too much of her real self. Jess wonders how often she's been handled the same way.

Cassie puts her hand on Jess's arm. 'James thinks Sarah is brilliant. He loves working with her. He won't shut up about her, actually!'

'She has that effect on people,' Jess laughs. 'I guess it's why she's so good at her job. Congratulations on getting hitched, by the way. Recently, right?'

'Six months ago. It was amazing.'

'Do you feel any different?'

'Oh, you mean now that we're married? I don't know, good question. But yes, actually, I suppose it does feel a bit different. I sometimes hear him talk about his wife, and it takes me a second to remember that he means me.' Cassie has a similar charm to her husband, aware of how much attention to take and how much to give. 'But we're not at all interesting. I want to hear about you. How did you and Sarah meet?'

Jess and Sarah are deft at telling their story in public, rolling their eyes on cue, and switching in and out of each other's lines as if it is the first time they've told it. But Sarah and James are still in full flow on the other side of the table, and Jess doesn't want to interrupt.

'Oh, it took a while,' she explains. 'We first met at a party. I didn't remember it, to be honest. We met again at another party a few years later. She promises me she wasn't stalking, just an accident. Anyway, this time she reeled me in, and didn't let me go. I'm her bit of butch from the 'burbs. She's the North London Jewish Princess.'

'It sounded romantic until you said that!' Cassie says. 'And now you're married, and you've got a daughter. I remember James told me that.'

'Claudie. Just turned three.'

'I bet she's so cute. I mean, Sarah's gorgeous, so she must be.' Cassie's eyes widen. 'Oh gosh, I didn't mean, sorry, that was really insensitive.'

'I'm sure she'd take it as a compliment. But yeah, she's adorable. But it means we're pretty boring now, really.'

'You're not boring,' Cassie insists. 'You're a power couple.'

Jess notices that Sarah is already getting sloshy, something that happens at a work do but less often with friends, rarely when it's just the two of them. At least, not anymore.

When they're called, they follow the waiter into the restaurant, and she hears Sarah and James arguing about who will pay. The wine flows.

When they finish eating, James calls an Uber. Jess has been going to the sorts of clubs that aren't appropriate for this slick couple and her polished wife, so yet again, she concedes to a suggestion James has up his sleeve. Sarah holds Jess's hand in the taxi. There's a short queue outside when they arrive. James and Cassie pause to snog.

'Young love,' Sarah says. 'This is fun, right? I know it's not exactly what you had planned, but that's what Edinburgh is all about – being spontaneous, right?' Sarah whispers into Jess's face, her words slurred.

Once they're inside, James asks Cassie to dance, but she shakes her head and says she wants to finish her drink first. He holds his hand out to Sarah instead, and they wind their way to the dancefloor. Through the crowds, Jess sees them spinning around. James occasionally catching Sarah's waist to steer her away from other dancers.

'What's it like knowing that everyone in the audience is there to see you?' Cassie nudges Jess. She turns her attention back to this pretty woman with her eyes wide open.

'Oh, it's pretty good,' Jess says.

'But don't you get nervous? I'd be terrified that I'd forget my lines or trip over or something.'

'You get used to it,' Jess says. 'Something takes over.'

'I could tell that.' Cassie reaches out. 'Like you were under his spell or something.' Her eyes glisten in the dim lighting. 'I'd love to have a dance now, actually,' she says. 'Shall we?'

She stands up and reaches her hand out to Jess, then leads them over to where James and Sarah are dancing. Instead of spinning her around, Cassie takes hold of Jess's hips and pulls her in close. Her grip is surprisingly strong. Jess catches her floral perfume and the tiniest whiff of sweat. Cassie's skin is so damp from the heat of the room that her shirt is starting to cling. Jess puts her hands on Cassie's hips in return, feels her thin waist swivel.

'If I close my eyes and think of you on stage, it's like dancing with Elvis,' Cassie says.

The two couples occupy a small space on the dance floor. They pair off and split up, sometimes dance as a foursome. James divides his attention between the three women as if he has an equal claim to each. His style changes with each new dance partner. With Jess, he plays the joker; they laugh as they egg each other on through the twist, the fishing rod, the car boot. He dances closer to Cassie, hands roam her back, snake down to her buttocks, pulling her in for a kiss.

Mirroring them, Jess pulls Sarah close, cups her face in her hands, kisses her lips, then puts her hands in the back pockets of Sarah's jeans. Her wife wraps her arms around her neck in response. Even though Jess knows this intimacy is fuelled by alcohol, it's a welcome reminder of how well they fit together, when they remember to.

James calls the server over, orders more champagne, raises his glass for a toast.

'To love.'

'To new friends.'

Sarah and Cassie go off to dance. This time, it's Jess and James who are left alone.

'I think Cassie's got a bit of a crush on you,' he jokes. 'I get it. You guys are amazing,' he says. 'Sarah's literally the best boss I've ever had.'

'The best wife I've ever had too.' Jess laughs.

Something about his earnestness appeals to her; his desire to please and to show off, but with an underlying self-consciousness.

'Lesbians are great,' he slurs at her. 'You've got it all sorted. You can have everything you want, and you don't have to have dicks like us hanging about. Smart.' He drains the last of his glass, she sees his

Adam's apple bobbing. Sarah and Cassie loom into view.

'I've got to sleep, King,' Sarah says, knocking into the table. 'Take me home?'

They stumble outside and call taxis. James and Cassie cling to each other, whispering and kissing.

'We'll do this again, yeah?' says James. 'Got to hang out in London. We want to be your friends.'

Sarah is giggly in the cab, forgetting their rule to keep affection to a minimum if they're not totally sure they're safe, and keeps snuggling up to Jess. She tries to snog her, but Jess pushes her gently away with a smile.

'We're nearly home,' she says. 'Wait until we're back.'

'And then,' Sarah growls at her, 'what are you going to do with me?'

'Shh.' Jess holds a finger to Sarah's lips.

Sarah goes straight into the bedroom when they get into the apartment, sits on the end of the bed trying to tug off her shoes, clumsy with drink. Jess puts a pint of water on each of their bedside tables, lights the scented candle, and turns the light off. She pulls Sarah's top over her head and pulls her forward a little so she can unclasp her bra, pushes her back against the mattress, and peels off her jeans and knickers. In recent years, Sarah would signal that she wasn't up for anything else by rolling away and reaching for her pyjamas. Tonight, she stays still. Open.

'They're great, aren't they?' Jess hears Sarah's voice in the dark. 'James and Cassie. Like sexy little rabbits. I bet they're up to something right now too.'

Jess kneels between Sarah's legs, noticing how recently waxed Sarah is. 'Tell me what you think they're doing,' she says. 'Go on, tell me.'

CHLOË FOWLER

Chapter Six
Always On My Mind

Having expected to feel revived after the visit from Sarah, with the brief conversations they did have and the longer one they didn't, Jess feels oddly sluggish. Brilliant though it was to see her wife, Sarah's presence has pricked the bubble of her Edinburgh existence and Jess is finding it harder to plug back in. Yet she still has two weeks of her run to go; there is time for her to re-discover it.

Whenever she'd pushed her father to name his favourite Elvis songs, 'The Wonder of You' came top, but the lyrical apology of 'Always on My Mind' came second. It's the midpoint of her show. The audience hears her singing about a man never taking the time and wishing he'd said and done different things, but as the words come out, she is thinking about her wife. Wishing they had more time together when it was the two of them, and then hating herself for even imagining less time with Claudie. Jess walks the vintage mic stand slowly from centre-stage to downstage left. Dropping her arms down by her sides, tilting her head, taking in the energy of the pause inside herself. The heat from the rig burns the back of her neck. Her eyes close against the glare of the bulbs, but she is careful not to scrunch. She knows how long she can stand in this position, directly above the footlights, before she becomes disorientated when she opens them again.

Pitch-perfect, she captures the swoops and dives of his vocals, the subtle twitches in his face, the way his hands clasp the microphone. Once the first few slow bars of the piano kick in, eyes still closed, she feels an electric current rip through the audience. This is it; they are thinking, this is the one. Only her mouth moves as she tells the story of someone who wishes they'd treated the other person better. Slowly tilting her head up, she raises her right hand, not quite a full gesture, simply a steadying. She opens her eyes, stares straight at the audience, confronting them with the apology. She wraps her hands around the microphone, sways slightly to the rest of the verse, rocking back on her heels, further away from the mic, as her volume increases.

There is a photo of her at this moment, taken by her producer during the tech run. It's one that she returns to when her confidence falters, and she needs to remind herself how good she is at being Elvis. The stark black of the stage contrasts with the dazzle of her pale skin and white underwear. Her hair dark against her cheek, quiff perfect. The muscles she's worked hard to sculpt across her shoulders and calves, throwing shadows on the rest of her body. She could be a man, a woman, a boy, or a girl. But at this moment, she is unmistakably him. The audience is free to stare, and she knows that they do. It is during this moment of raw vulnerability that she feels most powerful. But this afternoon, for no reason that she can think of, she feels afraid.

Spots have appeared on her chin. She covers them with concealer and hopes they're invisible to the audience. Her poor Festival diet has caught up with her, pushing at the seams of her costume, her waistline, the tops of her arms. She is aware of the irony that Elvis, too, had to adjust his costumes to encompass his swelling girth. The stage lights are unforgiving, and she can't afford for her body to fill out too much more, already having to suck in her tummy during the first twenty minutes of her show. She promises herself that she'll lap the Meadows before most people are up. The only earth on the running shoes she brought with her is from Clissold Park, back home.

She tells herself to buck up, get moving, get out there, make the most of it. Continuing to chalk up great reviews, it's only a few days until the Fringe Firsts are announced – though she knows their decisions will have been made by now, her fate sealed. She no longer worries about the box office. Her show is sold-out, and a queue for returns snakes around the building each afternoon. Talking to David and Alicia over dinner, both still plugging away at *Blasted*, she finds that they too have reached the halfway slump. They reassure her that this is normal, remind her that she's lucky – they will make a loss or, at best, break even.

'And what's next for you?' David asks. 'Soho, November.' Jess says. 'You guys?'

'Back to auditions,' Alicia sighs. 'When my agent starts returning my calls. You're so lucky that you don't have to worry about all that.'

Again, there it is, the sting. The implication that she is merely playing at performing, while her real job is at home with her daughter and wife. Claudie, who she is longing to hug, smell and tickle. But also, in the gaps between missing her, the guilt that she's revelled in their time apart. After Soho, she thinks again, after Claudie starts nursery, then I have to plan. Talk to Sarah. Commit to *something*.

The three of them toy idly with heading to The Pleasance to see if there's anything decent on but the enthusiasm isn't there and they part ways. As usual, her apartment is silent and empty, chilly in the cooler evening air of the last week of August. She sends a quick text before bed.

Hey love, missing you. Was great having you here. Can't wait to see my girls again.

She waits to see if Sarah's online, hoping she'll see her typing. Maybe even have a pre-sleep chat. But there is no response.

She sends a new message, not to Sarah, but to Tiff.

Hey, get home safe. Got everything you need for the big write up?

Hey back. Home. Missing the bright lights.

Jess types a reply, then deletes it. As she's considering whether to write a different one, another pops up from Tiff.

It was amazing to hang out. I'll send you the copy when I've written it up. Night!

Can't wait. Make me sound great.

Impossible not to. xx

Jess notes the two xx's and smiles. Anticipating the article, the photos. Handing her money over in the newsagent, waiting to see if she's recognised by the cashier. At least one copy for her and Sarah each, and one for her dad.

Jess wakes up, groggy, dry-mouthed, and on instinct, picks up her phone to check the time. Normally left on ring in case Sarah has an emergency overnight with Claudie, she had forgotten to take it off silent before she went to bed. Her wife's name is on the screen; she's calling. A bubble of anxiety forms in her chest whenever Sarah calls. She can't help imagining a litany of catastrophes that might have befallen her daughter or wife. She knows it's probably nothing, just Claudie awake early and wanting to talk. A kind response to her messages the night before.

'You okay?' She picks up, her voice still a morning croak.

'Oh, Jess.' Sarah says. 'I'm so sorry.'

'For what?' Jess asks. 'What's wrong?'

'I've woken you up. You haven't seen your messages. I'm so sorry.'

Sarah keeps repeating it, and yet still Jess doesn't know what she's sorry for.

'Your Dad, Jess. Your poor Dad. Oh, Jess. I'm so sorry.'

'I don't understand.'

'He had a heart attack, Jess. Late last night, early this morning, I don't know the details. I'm sorry. Your mum has been trying to call. She eventually rang me because she couldn't get hold of you. I thought you might still be asleep. I'm so sorry.'

Jess's stomach lurches, her skin clammy, her hands shake.

'Oh, God. Shit.' Jess says. 'Let me call Mum. I'll call you back.'

'Of course. And Jess, I really am so sorry. I love you.'

'I'll call you back,' Jess says again and rings off.

Her phone buzzes with a warning that she's nearly out of battery, unplugged since last night. The charger cable isn't quite long enough, so she has to half-crouch and half-stand as she calls her mother. There they are, the slew of notifications that she's slept through – the missed calls, the new messages stacking on top of each other.

'Mum? It's me, it's Jess. Oh, Mum.'

'Jess.' Her mum's whisper is so slight that Jess wonders if she's been given something to keep her calm. 'Love. He's gone. I don't know what happened. I don't know what to do. Maybe it's my fault, I don't know. I wasn't there for him.' The whisper has turned to sobbing, the sound of panic.

'Slow down, Mum. You need to breathe, just breathe. I'm not going anywhere. Can you tell me what happened?'

Through tears, Jess's mum tells her that her dad had felt fluey earlier in the week but had assumed it was a summer cold, nothing to worry about. Certainly, nothing so amiss that a hardy seventy-three-year-old would think of bothering the GP.

'I spoke to him loads this week,' Jess interrupts. 'He never said anything.'

'Of course, he didn't, Jess. He never wants you to worry about a thing. He loved you so much, Jessie.'

She'd made him take it easy, her mum insists. Cancelled a few plans, made sure they ate a bit earlier at night, and laid off the stodge. His spirit had been fine even while his body seemed tired, his movements slower. There had been nothing to suggest there was a ticking bomb in his chest. Last night he'd gone to bed early, complaining he was exhausted. Her mum, earplugs in so she didn't hear him snore, had spent the night fast asleep next to him. Unaware until 3am, when she was woken up, sheets bunched around him, writhing, that he was dying.

'Oh, Mum, I don't believe it. I'm so sorry. I'll come home right now. Let me pack, I'll get a train, I'll be there really soon. I'm so sorry.'

'Thank you, Jessie. I'm so sorry too. It's the shock of it. I don't know what to do.'

Jess sits, stuck, on the edge of the bed. Staring at the bar of battery life as it creeps up. Clenching her fists and then unclenching them again, a gulp of stale water, swallowing two Ibuprofen, though she's not in any pain. Picks up the phone and finds herself scrolling through Instagram, on reflex. Realising what she's doing, she slams the phone down again, ashamed, angry.

Her phone screen flickers.

Did you get through?

Yes.

You okay?

I don't think so.

It's horrible. I wish I was there with you.

Yes. Can't speak. Need to pack.

Knowing she should be getting up, calling a taxi, Jess lies down again. Images and conversations with her dad flip past like black and white negatives, spooling, spooling, spooling.

Messages pile up in her feed. Her mum, her brother, his wife, Sarah, Sarah's mum. She can't face them. Finally, she calls her producer and tells her that her remaining shows will have to be cancelled. She understands the cost implications, a reduction of profit, maybe even a loss of reputation. But this is her father, her inspiration, her idol. She knows she should not be thinking about this now and apologises. It is the shock talking, she explains. She is in overdrive.

She moves tentatively around the flat as if something is broken. Scooping up her belongings, putting things back where they belong so the owner won't complain. Everything in the fridge and cupboard gets tipped into the bin. The reviews that her dad has sent her are pinned to a corkboard, his scrawled annotations in green pen. It feels weird to take them home, but she doesn't want to throw away either. She fingernails each tack, folds the clippings, and sticks the small wedge of paper in her back pocket. For the first time since she's heard the news, tears fall down her face. Forcing herself to chew a piece of dry toast, she gags.

She showers, dresses, and calls a cab to take her to Waverley. The driver is cheerful, used to ferrying performers and their gear to and from the station. He gets out to help her with her luggage.

'All done, are you?' he asks in his thick Scottish accent. 'Heading home?'

'Yes,' she replies quietly.

'I hope you've had a good wee run of it up here. Some of us complain, but it's only a good thing for the city. We miss you when you're gone.'

The station is chaotic. A new train disgorges fresh tourists every few minutes, all charging up the platform with their wheely bags trailing behind them. Jess feels invisible as she walks against them, pushing against the eager crowd, without even the will to apologise when her case runs over someone's foot. Once on the train, she finds a free seat and puts on her headphones.

In a few hours, she should be heading to the venue, unzipping her costume from its bag, warming up her vocal cords, drinking her Red Bull, going through her pre-show routine. Instead, she is on a train home. Home. The graffiti-covered concrete sidings slip away, slowly, and then faster. Shrinking back in her seat, headphones in, she wedges her shoulder between the cushion and the window and wills herself not to cry. Not here, not yet, not with the last glimpses of the city she loves receding behind her.

Wanting to block out the sounds of the cheerful holidaymakers leaving Edinburgh, she presses play. It's 'Always on my Mind.' The dread she felt during the show last night suddenly makes sense, and she can't bear the fact that the last message she sent was not to her dad but to Tiff. A woman she's only just met, means nothing to her and is not part of her life or family. Not even really a friend, but a journalist she is trying to impress and whose attention is flattering, fuelling her ego. The sound of Elvis's voice, normally one that warms her, is unbearable. She rips the headphones from her ears and stares out of the window, tears running down her face. Her Dad and Elvis. Both gone.

Part Two
The Show Goes On

CHLOË FOWLER

Chapter Seven
Don't Cry Daddy

The heat on her neck is not from stage lights. The muscles in her legs are not limber, not poised for explosion. They are shaking. There are no rhinestones, no white satin. There are no gasps, there will be no applause. Only silence. The faces she sees are not shrouded by the darkness of an auditorium; they are the pale, tear-swollen ones of her friends and family. There is a coffin.

When her mother first asked her to sing, Jess wanted to say no. She didn't think she'd manage it, worried that her voice would come out as a choke or a whisper. She'd talked it over with Sarah, whose voice has become permanently kind and gentle, and they'd decided that it was the only thing that she could do. The choice of song, in the end, was easy.

'Just Pretend' was one of his favourites, and he'd always said he preferred it in the higher key that Jess sings in. Not a greatest hit, but a gut punch. Now that she's standing, alone, only having summoned the courage to practice once, she's never felt more afraid of the eyes watching her.

Pretend, the song asks, that I'm holding you. Jess sees her mother's shoulders, which have remained taut until now, crumple. Then, how he'll fly to you. Jess's voice carries across the congregation, up to the stained-glass windows, out towards the heavy oak doors at the back of the crematorium. Still, she manages to breathe. By your side is where I belong; tears start to race down her cheeks, and she steadies herself because she does not want to falter. She clenches her fists so hard, the heavy rings bite into her flesh. Wearing them is the only concession to costume that would be appropriate on this day, the leather pouch safely in her pocket. Despite the fact that she can hear his tone reflected in her voice and that she's looking at her father's coffin, both men have never seemed so far away.

A few months later, standing in the dumping ground that is the spare room, Jess shivers, arms prickling with goosebumps. It's early October, too soon for her to feel that keeping the radiators on all day is acceptable.

By 11am, the warmth of the early morning heating has leaked out through the old sash windows, and the Victorian house feels chilly and damp. Beyond the garden wall is Abney Park Cemetery, where Jess can see autumn leaves float down amongst the graves. This is not the manicured resting place that her father lies in, but a tumbledown jumble of history and decay. With her daughter at nursery and her wife at work, the house is too quiet.

Grief creeps up on her in surprising ways, but this she knows is normal (because people keep telling her). But while it is alright, reassuring even, when her eyes fill with tears at a sudden memory of her father, the other source of her grief feels more indulgent. It's a private grief, not one she can talk about. Not even to Sarah, especially not to Sarah. Her wife has been kind since her dad's death, creeping around as if sudden movement will startle, her voice low, gentle. Tender pats and hugs, gentle, not passionate. But the loss of him, Elvis, the other man in her life, also punches at Jess. She feels as abandoned by him as she does by her father.

Jess has come into this room to force herself to face her costume. Her Soho show, the one she'd assumed would be her triumphant return to the London stage after Edinburgh, is just over a month away. She can't hide from it any longer. Her producer has pinned a note to the bag. 'So sorry,' it reads, 'for your loss.' Unzipping and then plunging her hands into the stiff canvas bag, the fabric feels stiff and scratchy. Prising it off the hanger, Jess traces the gemstones and white satin, noticing faint grey patches that weren't there before. Mildew masked by the lingering smells of Febreze and sweat. `Away from the dressing room, the heat from the rig, the applause, it looks garish, cheap, unloved. It too has suffered a loss.

Although she has sung for him at his funeral, Jess feels there's another resting place she has to find for her grief. Martin had never made it to Memphis, though he'd talked of it often. Every few years, he and Beverley got out to Spain and took even more sporadic river cruises. But Jess's mum was suspicious of America ('all those guns'), and a twelve-hour flight was not on her bucket list. Since her father's death, Jess's dreams have been full of Memphis, or what she thinks is Memphis, neon lights and music pouring out of the open doors of every bar on Beale Street. Is this the time, she thinks, to make the pilgrimage? This isn't something she can talk to Sarah about. Their holidays have been sporadic since Claudie's birth, and although she often says she wishes they could get away, Sarah uses financial or work excuses to stop any planning in its tracks. As she doesn't earn any money herself, a long-haul trip is not something Jess feels she can even suggest.

Sarah has been the model of a supportive wife, and Jess knows she should feel grateful for the time and space she's been given to grieve. Sarah tiptoes around, has taken on some of Jess's jobs at home, asks Jess repeatedly how she's doing, tentatively, as if she might break. Instead of these kindnesses bringing them together, she feels a distance between them that she can't describe and doesn't want to analyse too deeply in case it ushers thoughts that are bigger than she can name. It is a temporary fog, like the first flush of grief; it will surely lift.

Alone in the house, her costume unpeeled from its shroud, Jess still isn't ready, but knows that new life needs to be breathed back into her body if she's to perform to his standards, convincingly transform. Stripped of her clothes, her skin is pallid in the dull light, blue veins snake across her limbs. There is a dusting of dark hairs on her legs; she has not shaved in a while. Twisting right and then left, she pinches her waist to see how much the skin pulls away. Her eyes mine her torso for the outline of muscles that will need toning to be stage-ready in six weeks. Her hair has grown out, the longer sides nag at her until she tucks them behind her ears. That too will need addressing, and she makes a mental note to call her hairdresser, who understands that she prefers a male cut to a female one.

She slides one careful foot in the left leg of the trousers first, then the right, stifles the memory that the last time she did this was in her dressing room, the muffled hum of other shows pushing through the walls. The jacket next. She'd asked her tailor to sew weights into the seams and, crouching down to measure her inner thigh, mouth muffled by pins, he'd suggested that so many gems and sequins would restrict her movement, and she'd explained that no, the heavier the better so she can feel truly rooted on the stage.

Her Elvis skin on, pressure gathers behind her eyeballs, and she collapses into the emotions that have been building. Here it comes, this smack of grief, the sting of hot tears down her checks. Crying for her father, the messages she no longer gets, his constant reassuring, kind presence. Her father's messages have slipped so far down her WhatsApp list that she has to scroll to find them now. The connection they shared, the one that helped her create the man she embodies. The mundanity they stand for, the love.

Headphones on, Jess scrolls through her playlist, knowing that she'll have to accept the music she once loved back into her life; she stands, feet apart, in front of the full-length mirror.

Grinding her toes into the thick carpet, her weight spread evenly amongst the soles and balls of her feet, she turns up the volume. There is a restraint to the vocals, chosen especially for this moment. There is no crescendo, no howl, roar, or stomp, just a gentle buzzing in her throat that tells her that she is making a sound. She is singing again.

In the final verse of 'Don't Cry Daddy', she presses her palms and fingers against the cold mirror. Tensing a little, but not too much to force the door on its hinges, she brings her left foot forward to steady herself as the orchestra fades away.

A few minutes later Jess leaves the room and notices handprints smeared on the mirror. Instinct tells her to grab the Windolene from the bathroom and wipe them away. But she doesn't.

Later that day, Claudie is finally coaxed into the bath. Jess looks forward to this ritual more than her daughter does. The little girl sits sideways in the tub, tiny knees crossed, smacking bubbles with her palms until they burst. The slip mat underneath her, the mesh pouch for tiny buckets, beakers, and floating animals suctioned to the tiled wall, just within reach. Dressed, Claudie sometimes looks older than she is, adopting poses and using phrases that sound strange and hilarious. In the bath, she looks tiny again, so defenceless and soft that Jess wants to wrap her up safe, never let her go. Jess kneels, rinsing out the sponge when she hears her phone ping on the landing, pushes off the rim and instructs Claudie to wash her own bits and bobs for a second, long enough for her to grab her phone but not let her daughter of her sight.

'Naughty Mummy is on her way, but she's not here yet,' Jess tells Claudie when she crouches back down, grabbing the plastic jug so she can pour water over her head before the shampoo. 'Extra story time for you and me. Aren't we lucky?'

Careful not to chivvy, Jess lets Claudie choose two books and budges her up against the wall, her eyelids already sinking. Tancred the bear is clutched to her chest, and she's nearly asleep when they hear the key in the lock. Sarah talks as she chucks down her keys by the front door, a thoughtless thwack. Still in her post-work bubble, Sarah is laughing into the phone, happy and relaxed. Claudie sits up straight, eyes wide open. Jess is annoyed – all the work calming her daughter down, undone by the anticipation of seeing her other mother, perhaps eking out her stories for longer.

Footsteps on the stairs, a head pokes around the door, then a body. Sarah's tailored, burnt umber suit looks fresh and uncrumpled, even after a day at the office. Despite the interruption, seeing her poised and attractive wife, Jess's heart beats a little faster. Sarah undoes her high-waisted belt and peels her jacket off, untucks her silk shirt, kicks her heels off by the door. Jess, in tracksuit pants and a hoodie, her hair un-quiffed, is suddenly aware how scruffy she feels next to her meticulously groomed wife.

'My two best girls,' she kisses the top of their heads. 'You look cosy.'

'I'm getting two stories tonight,' Claudie says.

'Oh, lucky you! I won't interrupt. Night, night, darling, sleep well.' She bends down to kiss Claudie again. 'Love you, Snugaroo.' She walks slowly out of the room but turns back, hand on the door. 'Sorry I'm late. I wanted to say goodnight. I'll leave you to it.'

Sometimes Sarah stays in the room while Jess is reading. She'll lie on the rug and lift her legs in the air, one after the other, peeling off her socks, transitioning from professional to parent. She'll laugh at the lines that are supposed to be funny, chant along with the rhymes. Tonight, she bends to hook her shoes with the fingers of one hand and half shuts the door behind her as she leaves the room.

Jess finishes the story and urges Claudie up for a final pre-sleep wee. Claudie grumbles and then concedes, she knows it's a ritual she cannot skip. Leaning down for a kiss, Jess whispers, 'Night, night Claudie-Bear. Love you.' Walking down the landing, past their own bedroom, Jess hears Sarah chuckling on the phone, and does not disturb her.

Thursday evenings are Jess and Sarah's first chance to catch up after a long week. All they usually eat is pimped-up versions of Claudie's nursery suppers. Sarah's family cooks for pleasure, but Jess has inherited a lack of culinary imagination from her mother. Friday night is usually spent with Sarah's family, where they're guaranteed a great meal. Thursdays come with the lure of the approaching weekend, wine, and a Deliveroo.

As she's waiting for Sarah to come downstairs, Jess sifts through the pile of 'admin' that Sarah always leaves pointedly next to the family calendar. The letter from the clinic is face-up, impossible to ignore. Jess does not know why the letter, which is simply a reminder that they have a choice ahead of them, has created space for the start of a conversation that she'd prefer not to have. She wants to ignore it, but the fact that it's been left here, so overtly, means Sarah wants it to be noticed. This is not going away and it won't be long before her grief, and the distraction it creates, is no longer an excuse.

It is already 8:15, so late that Jess is tempted to root in the freezer instead of waiting for a delivery.

Back downstairs, Sarah asks, 'Have you ordered yet?'

'Of course not,' Jess snaps. 'You know I don't order until I know what you want. I've been busy too.'

'That's not what I meant. I'll eat anything,'

'Oven pizza?' Jess is conciliatory. 'I could bung one in?'

'How about Thai?' Sarah says, opening the app on her phone. 'I'll choose my bits, and then you add yours. I'm sure it won't take too long.'

'Great.' Jess decides it's not worth protesting that it will take ages to come.

'In here?' Sarah walks into the living room and drops down on the sofa. They sit in silence, side by side. Whatever it is that's still between them, Jess does not want to feel she's the one to blame for pulling away first, so she puts her hand on Sarah's calf. Sarah reclines against the arm of the sofa, swoops her hand through her hair.

'Long day?' Jess asks.

'The usual.' There is no elaboration.

'I tried the costume on again today. Finally.'

'Oh.' Sarah pauses, and Jess sees her take a deep breath. 'You okay?'

'I guess so. I had to do it sometime and I'm glad I did. But it didn't feel totally right yet, if I'm honest.'

'I get that.' Sarah pauses. 'Listen, I hope it's not too soon, but I have been wondering.'

An unnamed flicker of anxiety pulses through Jess, which she deflects with an attempt at humour.

'Wondering? That's sounds dangerous.'

'Hey, hear me out first,' Sarah smiles gently.

'Shoot.'

'I guess I wondered what you were thinking about doing after, you know, after your next show? I know it's all booked and you're committed. But I mean after that.'

'What do you mean?' Jess hopes that her quick intake of breath isn't audible and removes her hand from Sarah's leg.

'I suppose I just wondered, the way you've been recently, a few things you've said. Death makes people think, doesn't it? About change.'

'Change?'

'Honestly, I don't know. Like maybe this is an opportunity for change. For both of us. Like maybe performing a few times a year isn't for you anymore. Or that you were over it. And that maybe we, as a family, could change things.'

'Over it? You mean acting? The one thing I've ever really loved doing and been good at.' Jess resents that her voice has become higher pitched than she wants.

'Acting is not the only thing you're good at. That's ridiculous. You're an amazing mum, just for starters.'

Jess chooses to ignore this disingenuous compliment, especially in this moment.

'And when you say, change, what do you mean? What do you want to change? Or is it that you want *me* to change?' Jess's voice stays taut, unwilling to concede that she's had similar thoughts.

'I don't really know what I mean. It's just a conversation, right? Maybe I shouldn't have brought it up. It's not as though I've got a solution. I was just thinking.'

'I didn't even know we had a problem. Or rather, that *I* was the problem.'

'Can we just forget it?' Sarah twitches in her seat. 'I do think we need to talk about the future, but clearly now is not the time. I don't mean just *your* future either, I meant all of ours. You, me, Claudie.'

Sarah stands up and crosses to the window as if looking out for the imminent food delivery. 'Babe,' she remonstrates. 'Please don't be angry. I'm just trying to communicate. I feel like we haven't done that much lately.'

'Gotcha,' Jess says, still not looking at her.

When the doorbell finally rings, it is after nine, and it's clear that neither of them is hungry. Jess is embarrassed by the number of plastic tubs that sit between them, the sheer waste of plastic and food. They eat mechanically, any pleasure gone.

Chapter Eight
The Weekend

Sarah's parents live in a large semi-detached house near, but not quite in, Hampstead. Compared to Jess's own parent's home, it's not far off a mansion, but Judith and David Allen joke that they can only afford to live in the less-desirable end of the village.

Sarah sprawls on the sofa. David presents Claudie's drink with a flourish – dropping in a glacé cherry and a tiny pink umbrella. Claudie takes the drink but stays glued to Sarah's side. Although she's a regular visitor, it takes her a little while to relax and gain the confidence to explore on her own. Jess, too, is a little slow to settle, though she's never been given any cause to think she isn't welcome. She loves Sarah's parents, her brother and sister-in-law, and the ease with which they navigate the world. Sarah and her brother were brought up to exude confidence to own their own space, buoyed further by expensive schooling.

'How's your poor mum?' Judith asks.

'She's alright, just about.'

'It's awful for her. Poor thing. Such a shock. I guess you're having to spend a lot more time there now, picking up the pieces?'

'I try to get there as often as I can,' replies Jess, knowing that she's not there as often she could be, that spending time with her mum alone is painful for the wrong reasons.

Unlike her own mother, her mother-in-law expresses curiosity about what Jess is up to. 'And what about you? Any plans now Edinburgh is over?'

Jess looks sharply over at Sarah and wonders what she's sharing with her mum. 'A short run in Soho in a few weeks. Then we'll see.'

'Well, your hands are pretty full with this little one, aren't they?' Judith nods in Claudie's direction. 'And this big one too!' waving her hand at Sarah.

'Oi,' Sarah says. 'Enough of the big, thank you.'

The doorbell rings, and Hannah and Oscar charge in a few seconds later. Unlike Claudie, her cousins don't wait to be told what to do or where to go. Jonty, Sarah's brother, holds the door, and his wife Linny slides past him, Ezra encased in a papoose on her front. As usual, Linny looks elegant and immaculate in her skinny jeans, Veja trainers, and a navy cashmere sweater.

Jonty thrusts flowers at Judith, and although the gesture appears throwaway, the bouquet looks like it might have cost fifty pounds.

'Sorry we're late, Mum.' He kisses her cheek and holds a bottle of wine out to his father. 'Rioja. Board meeting. Nightmare.'

'Go on in and get a drink.' Judith pats his shoulder. 'It's the weekend. You're here now. Relax.'

Sarah jumps up, suffused with energy that she lacked before. She hugs her brother and sister-in-law and lunges for Ezra, unpeeling him from the papoose.

'Oh,' she peers into his face and kisses his cheeks. 'He's delicious, Lin. You make such good babies.'

'He has his moments,' Linny laughs. 'Should've seen him an hour ago. We were at the door, and he literally took one look at Jonty and lost his lunch. Right down my top.'

'I'd have done the same,' says Sarah, miming a puke at her brother.

Judith ushers them into the dining room. 'You know your places,' she sweeps her hands out in front of her.

They take their seats at the heavy pine table, set with candlesticks, silver salt and pepper mills, napkins wrapped in ornate rings. It's a formal setting for an informal family, but Jess knows it's all part of the Friday night tradition that Judith likes to uphold. Sarah offers to keep Ezra so Linny can eat her dinner with both hands. She sniffs his head, turns him backward and forwards, puts him over her shoulder, folds his tiny hands in her own.

'You'll make him sick!' Jess jokes and puts her hand on Sarah's knee.

'I have done this before,' Sarah says a little sharply. Jess takes her hand away.

Judith ferries in dishes of tortilla, patatas bravas, sweetcorn quarters, chicken wings, mushrooms with herby butter, bowls of bread. She goes back out to the kitchen and comes back with more.

'I'm such a bad Jew,' she trills as she places down dishes of prawns in garlic sauce and small glistening chorizo sausages.

It wasn't until she met Sarah that Jess learnt the difference between the Orthodox Jews, like the ones she queued along with at the bus stops on Stamford Hill, and the wealthy, cultured Jews who make up the Allens' North London set. Even now, she does not fully understand which bits of Jewishness her in-laws choose to keep (Friday night dinners, Passover, debate) and which bits they've dispensed with (keeping kosher, attending synagogue).

The Allens are shouters; conversations start and finish in the same breath.

'Any plans for your birthday yet, Sarah?'

'Knife and fork, Oscar, please.'

'Bloody Tories!'

'Sorry, sugar, when IS half-term?'

Sarah is different amongst her family than at home, at work, or with her friends. She's a touch petulant but also funnier, wise-cracking with her brother and teasing her parents. Jess was shocked when they first met by how free they all felt to discuss topics that would never have been covered in her own home: politics, TV shows, scandals, money, theatre, art.

Aside from politics, Jess has opinions, but she doesn't feel she con-tributes equally or as articulately as the Allens. It always feels somehow like work, or a test, which she fails. Sometimes she starts to speak, but by then, it is too late because the conversation has swerved in another direction.

Sarah is sharing an anecdote about a meeting at work, one that Jess has not heard before. A pang of disappointment. She used to know everything that was going on in Sarah's world. Another realisation that this is how they used to be, but the blur of life with Claudie, Jess's time away, the death of her father, her preoccupation in general, have created gaps in her knowledge and more distance than feels natural. Surrounded by her in-laws, she feels a wave of love for her wife. Grateful to have been so folded into this family. She puts her hand back on Sarah's knee to show this appreciation and strokes it gently. But there is no recognition from her wife.

Staying long after dessert is not expected; the energy drops as quickly as it grew. The dishes are cleared, children are rounded up, and there is a recapping of future plans as if they need to reassure themselves that they'll be doing this again, soon. Only in mid-October and with Hanukkah a way off, the topic of Christmas (another non-Jewish celebration the Allens happily embrace) rears its head.

'You might not know what your plans are this year?' Judith gently asks, 'You may need to spend the day with your mum?'

'We don't know yet,' Jess says. 'I'll find out. But thank you for thinking of it.'

'We can top and tail, come over that evening, or even Boxing Day. We'll figure it out,' Sarah says. At the door, she reluctantly hands Ezra back to Linny. 'Fancy a swap? Now I've got him, I don't want to let him go.'

'Sleepless nights and nappies?' Linny laughs. 'You're joking, right?'

Driving home, Claudie is dozy in her car seat, and Sarah is quiet.

'You alright, love?' Jess asks.

'All good,' Sarah gazes out of the window. 'Just tired. Ready for the weekend. Ezra's gorgeous, isn't he? So nice to see them all playing together.'

'I do love your family, you know,' Jess says. 'I don't ever take it for granted.'

'I know. They love you too. We're very lucky, aren't we, Clauds?'

Sarah turns back in her seat and smiles at their daughter, fast asleep.

'Our little girl.' She puts a hand on Jess's knee. 'Growing up too fast.'

But the gesture is too late. Jess wanted to feel Sarah's hand on her own over dinner, surrounded by the family, in the middle of the laughter and the chatter. Here, in the dark of the car, it does not feel enough.

The following day is Saturday. Jess scoops up the post and spots a stiff-backed envelope nestled amongst the mail.

'Let's go and pack your bag,' Sarah urges Claudie up the stairs. 'We're leaving soon.'

Saving the large one for last, Jess sifts the junk letters into the recycling. She spots the sender's logo and address, and her heart beats fast, glad she is on her own to open it. She carefully slides her fingers under the gummed-down strip, keen not to rip the contents. A Post-it note is stuck to *LEXI*'s cover.

We're really proud of this one. Hope you like it. Drink to celebrate? T xx.

Although she was emailed the image to approve, Jess is still taken aback seeing it printed on the glossy cover paper. Her face – his face – winking at the lens. Her skin and the quiff that rises above her forehead are flawless, the red lipstick she would never have chosen for herself. No stranger to her own reflection, she allows herself to believe that she is, captured at that moment, stunning.

She remembers feeling Mattie's hands positioning her on the chair. The connection with Tiff, all the pleasure of Edinburgh is back inside her, for a second. Even Elvis makes a reappearance, for a moment. Hearing Sarah and Claudie coming back downstairs, she tucks the Post-it in her pocket and leaves the magazine on the island while she gets their lunch out of the fridge.

'Wow.' Sarah comes into the kitchen and picks it up. 'King, you look bloody amazing.'

'It's not bad, right?'

'Seriously, it's brilliant.' Sarah comes over for a kiss, pressing her quickly against the fridge. 'I'll read it properly later. But wow. Claudie!' She calls out. 'Lunch! We've got to get a move on.'

Jess is disappointed that Sarah hasn't made more of a fuss but doesn't say so. Although they've complained about the magazine's preoccupation with gender and sexual politics and the naff ads, it's a publication that matters to her. As a teenager, newly aware of what it might be that made her feel so different from her boy-obsessed classmates, Jess had ventured to further flung newsagents to buy her copy. She'd read it covertly, stashed it in piles of stuff her mum wouldn't find. Reading LEXI had been the first time Jess remembers knowing that it was going to be fine, that she was not the only person who wanted to look like her, love women like her. Sarah has been open about the fact that she's never felt the same need to ally herself with a tribe, that she's comfortable and confident enough without one. How lucky for you, Jess has thought to herself, to have never suffered the same taunts and rejections. She'd been hoping Sarah might even scoop it up and take it to show their friends; to take it herself would appear big-headed. But Sarah doesn't, and it's left there on the island. Marooned.

They set off shortly after they've eaten. The boot is loaded with wellies, coats, and overnight bags, and at the last minute, when Claudie realises they are going to the seaside, in go the buckets and spades. Their house is off Stoke Newington High Street, and Jess loves driving through the city on weekends to get out of town. They're quickly through Dalston, sweep past the Saturday calm of Liverpool Street, get through the slow lights at Bank, and she jokes that London Bridge is falling down behind them as they cruise towards the A23.

'So good to be leaving London. It can sometimes feel like too much.' Sarah sniffs the air as they hit the motorway, as if she can already smell the sea breeze.

Of their Stokey friendship group, Caz and Bex were first to get civil partnered and then convert to marriage. The first to get pregnant. Jude and Lisa quickly followed Caz and Bex down to Brighton, lured by the larger and more affordable houses, the seaside, the scene.

As they near Brighton, Sarah leans back to shake Claudie's leg to wake her. Jess doles out gummy sweets to speed up the process, and they sing a few rounds of 'Who Can See the Sea'. As soon as they pull up to Caz and Bex's house, the door opens.

'Mate.' Jude pulls Jess into a hug. 'Your dad, I'm so sorry.'

Still getting used to handling commiserations from others, Jess deflects attention by gesturing towards the kids haring off down the road towards the beach.

'We better move it.' Bex says over her shoulder as she runs down towards them.

Joined by Jude and Lisa, who live nearby and who'd already arrived, the six women and their children traipse down to the seafront. Jess walks next to Lisa, bringing up the rear with the buggy. Her curly hair is stuffed under a beanie hat, and the style of her clothes is different from when she lived in London. There is more wool, more pattern, more elastic. Jess notices that she isn't wearing any makeup.

'I know I look a mess but trust me,' Lisa says. 'But if you had two toddlers, you'd be grateful just to get dressed. I'm so sorry to hear about your dad. It must still feel really raw.'

'It's shit, it was a shock, but you know, you got to keep on. But how are you doing?' Jess asks.

'Honestly? Exhausted. I love Maya to bits. She's amazing, totally chilled. Only a year apart, but Scarlet is definitely the boss. You watch. She'll have all of them doing what she tells them in half an hour. Hard work, though.'

'I bet.'

'You think it can't be that bad, but sometimes, I just want to shut the door and leave it all behind. Sorry. No more whinging, I promised Jude.'

'What do you mean?'

'Don't tell her I told you, but she's on a mission to get you guys moving down here. We need you. We miss you!'

'No way, mate.' Jess laughs. 'Sarah wouldn't live anywhere that wasn't within a five-mile radius of Selfridges.'

They manage forty-five minutes on the rocky beach before it starts to rain. Back in the house, Caz sticks on a DVD and dumps biscuits and juice boxes down for the kids.

When Caz and Bex lived in Stoke Newington, theirs was the flat Jess most envied. Bex had a collection of vintage vinyl mounted into frames and had sniffed out original pieces of fifties furniture and crockery before any of the rest of them had taste or money. The frames are hung on the wall here, and the vintage leather chair is in the corner but covered in coats, soft toys and cushions. The walls are painted in weird, too-bright colours, and the carpet doesn't meet the wall in one corner.

'Don't judge!' Bex laughs. 'We're gonna get it all done. Trust me. There's no point while the kids wreck everything in their path.'

'I love it,' Jess said. 'It's cosy, that's what family homes are for.'

'Bugger,' Caz says. 'I forgot to get garlic for tonight. Any chance one of you lot could pop out?'

'Sure thing.' Jess pats her pocket to check for her wallet. She feels something crinkle and pulls out the Post-it from Tiff, and she quickly sticks it in amongst her credit cards. 'Jude, come with?'

Setting off down the road, Jess suddenly feels tongue-tied, though this woman is technically her best friend.

'I'm really sorry, mate.' Jude stops suddenly and puts a hand on Jess's arm. 'I've been a terrible friend. I should have called and asked more about your dad. Lisa kept nagging me, but I didn't know what to say. You know it doesn't mean I don't care, right?'

'Don't worry about it.' They hug and then slap each other on the back.

'You good, though?' Jude looks closely into Jess's eyes.

'Getting there.' Jess stuffs her hands into her pockets and kicks gently at a lamppost, ridding them of invisible mud. 'Think we're both finding it tough at the moment. It'll pass.'

'Just keep talking,' Jude urges. 'You and Sarah are good. But I'm really gutted for you mate, I always liked your dad.'

'He liked you too. Remember after you first met him after uni and I'd just come out, and he assumed you were my girlfriend. He gave us his blessing.'

'Bless him. He never got that every woman you introduced to him wasn't *actually* in love with you.'

'Well you say that…' Jess laughs.

Jess resists the urge to check her phone as she waits outside for Jude to pop into the corner shop. There's no reason for there to be another message from Tiff after this morning's flurry, but she can't help hoping. She hasn't told her friends about the interview yet either. She's planning to weave it in somewhere later, subtly enough that it won't look like she's showing off. She's even wondered if Sarah had quietly stashed it in her bag before they left and will bring it out later, with a bottle of bubbles, so they can celebrate in style.

Jessa and Jude walk back the house slowly, but neither starts up a conversation. The only questions Jess thinks to ask feel trite, it'd be just chat, not meaningful conversation. She knows that this is part of life, of growing up, of spending more time with friends and family on their doorstep than the ones that go way back and live further away. It used to only take her and Jude a few minutes to resume banter and the retelling of ancient anecdotes, but today the energy between them feels lacking. She wonders if Jude can feel it too but just before they go back into the house, Jude says, 'Mate, you should call me more often. We should hang out. Not with the kids and the wives, just us.'

'Deffo.' Jess squares her shoulders. 'You're on. I'm on at the Soho in a few weeks, maybe come and stay? Have a night out.'

'Deal. Send me the dates.'

Back inside the house, bottles of wine and beer are opened, and the mood gradually loosens. She sees Sarah's eyes track around the room, taking in the chaos of a family home, so unlike the tidy space and life she's cultivated for herself and that Jess works hard to maintain. In the past she'd have spotted judgement in Sarah's eyes, but tonight she's smiling, even wistful.

'Can't believe the size of the garden,' Sarah says to Bex.

'I know. Can't believe the size of the gardening Caz doesn't do,'

Bex teases. 'We call it the mudroom. If the twins are playing up, we stick them in wellies and coats and shove them out there until they're quiet.'

Caz urges everyone to sit down so she has room to finish cooking dinner. They cram awkwardly around the small kitchen table while Bex wipes up smears and crumbs from the kids' tea. Jess is hemmed in at the far end of the bench seat, back pressed against the wall, opposite a high chair rather than one of her friends. The conversation splits apart as the six adults talk over and under each other: house renovations, politics, schools. More wine is opened and quickly drunk.

'There's a meat one here.' Caz points to a cast iron dish of lasagne in the middle of the table. 'And a vegan one for the rest of you. Garlic bread. Salad. Just help yourselves. You know the drill.'

Conversation stops as they pass serving dishes around. Bex offers to make Jess's plate up for her because of the awkwardness of where she's sitting and it makes her feel childish, pandered to.

'So how was Edinburgh?' Bex asks, as she passes Jess a slice of garlic bread. 'I know you didn't get to finish the run, but how was it before that?'

'Pretty good, thanks,' Jess says.

'She's being modest,' Sarah chimes in. 'It was brilliant. And she's only the cover of this month's *LEXI*!'

Jess looks up from her plate, surprised and glad that Sarah has found a moment to celebrate her. She waits for Sarah to say more, perhaps wave the copy around, brandish some champagne. But instead of raising a toast when she holds up her glass, Sarah just takes a swig. The honour is left to Jude who tilts her beer bottle at Jess in lieu of a toast.

'No way,' Jude says, 'that's great, mate. Nice one. Cheers.'

'You've all got to buy a copy now.' Jess grins at them all.

'That'll mean at least four copies sold then!' Sarah says.

'Ouch,' Jude says. 'It's not that bad.'

'Shit, sorry love, that's not what I meant.' Sarah blows a kiss at Jess, but the damage is done. Jess laughs along but fiddles about opening a new wine bottle, so nobody sees as her eyes fill with sudden tears. The moment darts away as quickly as it came, and Jess pushes the rest of her lasagne under some salad leaves to hide her hurt.

The frenzied jollity of the earlier part of the evening is never quite matched after that. As soon as they've eaten from tubs of half-eaten ice cream, Jude and Lisa claim they have to get home because of playdates tomorrow, and nobody tries to stop them. Jess's offer to help clear up is refused and Sarah is already in the small double bed in the spare room when she gets in.

Sarah puts her hand on Jess's back.

'You know I didn't mean it about the article, right? What I said was horrible and stupid. It came out wrong. I'm sorry. Too much wine, I honestly think it's great. I didn't have time to read it properly, but I'm looking forward to it. I'm proud of you.'

'It's fine,' Jess replies, but doesn't turn around.

'I think you look amazing in the photos. Can you buy some extra copies? Maybe even get hold of the prints so we can blow them up or something?'

'What, for the downstairs loo?'

'I'm just saying, they're really nice.'

Jess knows that Sarah is being kind, that she feels awful about her remark, knows she can't entirely undo the damage that the truth has caused. 'I know, love, thank you,' she says, not wanting to end the night on a row.

'My head's gonna hurt tomorrow,' Sarah groans. 'Remind me not to drink so much wine again.'

Jess lies down, wishing she was in their own house where she could go downstairs, listen quietly to some music, think.

'Let's not rush off tomorrow,' Sarah's voice comes out in the dark. 'Claudie loves it here. And it's nice, isn't it, being amongst friends.'

'Yup,' Jess says. 'It's all good.'

Sarah is silent for a few moments more, then her voice seeps into the dark.

'Maybe it wouldn't be too bad to live down here after all. I could commute.' She pauses. 'Sorry, sorry, I seem to be coming up with a lot of stupid suggestions recently.'

'Go to sleep, love. Remember the hangover.' Jess hopes Sarah can hear the smile in her voice.

Jess can hear Caz and Bex downstairs in the kitchen, unloading and reloading the dishwasher. Amongst her friends, tucked up with her wife and daughter, Jess knows she should be happier than she feels.

Chapter Nine
Birthday Girl

'That was nice.' Jess lets her leg linger over Sarah's naked torso and props herself up on her elbow. 'Happy Birthday. Again.'

'Happy Birthday to me.'

Jess pushes dense feather duvet off and leans across to the bedside table to hand Sarah her half-drunk glass of champagne.

'Thanks for arranging all this.' Sarah gestures at the hotel room. It is one of Sarah's favourite places, mentioned whenever she longs to get away. Jess booked the room months ago, aware that leaving it too late would disappoint her wife. After a tricky few months, she knows she needs to make it up to her. The cost per night, let alone the spa treatments and dinner, is well beyond her budget. Her limited personal resources are becoming an increasing frustration, and although Jess knows that Sarah is comfortable being the breadwinner, the lack of her own autonomy is starting to grate. She has her own credit card, but since Edinburgh she's aware of the mounting total and can no longer afford to pay anything but the interest off each month.

'I wanted to do something lovely for you. You've been amazing over the last few months, everything with mum and dad. I know it's what we expect to do for each other, but I really appreciate it.'

'Of course,' Sarah touches Jess's cheek. 'It's truly shit that he's gone. There's nothing more helpful to say. I'm also sorry that I've been a bit of a grump recently too.'

'Hadn't even noticed.' Jess lies. 'Honestly. How about some more presents?'

Sarah props herself against the studded headboard, tugs the duvet up over her chest, and rifles through a gift bag. She selects one gift at a time, shaking each gently, sniffing the paper to see if they betray a whiff of what might be inside. The bag was handed over when they dropped Claudie off with David and Judith.

'Mum,' Sarah had protested. 'I'm too old for presents.'

'Just a few little tokens,' Judith had said, though Jess knows that the contents will have amounted to several hundred pounds.

The Allens approach gifting as they do all things – noisy, lavish, but done with love. Discarded paper is chucked carelessly, even gleefully, on the floor as the gifts pile up: The White Company, SpaceNK, a candle from Diptique. Jess has learnt to keep up. Her own gift to Sarah was a necklace unwrapped earlier and cost Jess nearly £300. More than she could afford to spend but upsold from a cheaper one by the shop assistant at Dinny Hall in Islington.

'Lovely, lovely, lovely,' Sarah says. 'I feel very spoilt.' Then, after a moment's silence, 'What time is dinner? I'm starving.'

'Must be all that exertion,' Jess smiles. The luxury hotel, the clean, smooth sheets, the promise of a whole night alone had stirred them both into rare lust, and the sex they've had was fast, hard, and passionate. Of the two of them, it's always been Jess's role to take charge of their lovemaking. Although she sometimes feels it lets Sarah off the hook from working as hard, there is more pleasure in knowing that her fingers, and tongue still have the power they do. The sex this afternoon has loosened them both, and the way they smile at each other is a reminder of how they used to be together. And how much more often.

'Just going to jump in the shower.' Sarah hops out of bed and walks naked to the bathroom, swooping down to pick up discarded clothes on her way. Jess notices her wife's Caesarean scar stretching under her belly like a smile, her firm buttocks, the stippling of cellulite at the backs of her thighs. She appreciates how good Sarah looks, not just for her age, but because she looks after herself. Sarah would have reached automatically for her robe at home, even for the short walk between rooms. Her lack of inhibition in this luxe cocoon is a further reward for Jess's generosity. Sarah's hair has ballooned around her head, puffed up by the oil from a massage earlier. Jess feels another butterfly of lust in her belly.

'Might join you in there,' she calls out.

'Give me a minute first.'

Jess cups her hands around the back of her head, waits to hear the loo flush. Then she joins Sarah in the vast rain shower, turns her around, and soaps her back using oversized dollops of the expensive, spa-branded product in bottles lined up in a turquoise tiled recess in the wall. She gently tilts Sarah's head back and shampoos her hair, massaging her scalp, watching the water pour off, the final remnants of suds slipping down the plughole.

'You're sexy, you know that,' Jess whispers, pressing her breasts against Sarah's back.

'Not so bad yourself, King.' Sarah turns around to kiss Jess. 'Now, you get out and get dressed. I won't be long.'

'We're in no rush.' Jess ekes out the moments of intimacy before they will have to leave the bubble of their room.

The pre-dinner martinis they'll drink will make them giddy and expansive, but the bottle or more of wine they'll have when they eat is likely to tamp down their energy, usher in more introspection and honesty.

Chivalrous role continuing, Jess takes Sarah's hand and squires her across the cobbled courtyard from the annex and through the heavy oak doors of the main building. Released from the need for taxis or the time pressure of getting home for the sitter, the way they walk, even the way they touch each other, is sexual. Jess senses they're noticed in the bar and does not resent the attention, pleased with the impression they make. She's in a crisp white shirt, black trousers, shiny brogues, and a black cravat, hair quiffed high. Tonight, she embodies the perfect marriage of Elvis and her true self, the purposeful stride, a smile playing on the edge of her lips. In her high heels and low-cut dress, Sarah could have chosen from a pre-planned selection of jewellery but has selected the Dinny Hall necklace. Jess is grateful, putting her hand in the small of Sarah's back as they weave behind the maître d' as he leads them to their table.

They play at guessing each other's choices when they're handed the thick, creamy, freshly-printed menus. Not long after, the amuse-bouche arrives – a tiny earthenware mug of truffled wild mushroom soup, a perfect miniature crouton nestling on the plate.

'To the birthday girl,' Jess toasts her wife.

'To the star, good luck for next week.'

'I'd forgotten about that for a minute,' Jess says. 'Think I'm a bit nervous. Not sure why.'

'You'll be great. First-night jitters, probably. You'll never forget that your show in Edinburgh, well, you know, ended the way it did. This is your chance to reclaim the stage. Can I ask you something? It's an observation, really.' Sarah carries on when Jess nods. 'You normally talk a lot more about a show when it's coming up. Is something up?'

'Wow, you've gone deep.' Jess's smile falters.

'That'll be the wine talking. Nothing too heavy. Just chat.'

'I guess it's just all a bit complicated.'

'Tell me.'

'I'll try. But please, this isn't a 'fix it' conversation. It's *just* a chat, right? I'm trying to be honest about what's going on and I'm not sure it's making much sense, even to me.' Jess takes a swig of her wine. 'I knew how much my dad meant to me. But I don't think I realised how much he was connected to how I feel about Elvis.'

'Carry on.' Sarah's gaze is too intense. Jess looks at her hand as it traces an invisible mark on the tablecloth.

'With the way the run in Edinburgh ended, the article, the show coming up – I feel like there's something I'm missing. Like losing my dad means I've lost a part of Elvis too. Like maybe I won't be able to do either of them justice anymore. I'm worried. That's all. I want the show to be a success. Maybe more than ever. But sometimes I wonder if it's all enough.' Jess looks up and holds Sarah's gaze. 'Sorry, that was a lot. Just feelings. And too many martinis.'

'Oh Jess, I'm so sorry. I've been a really bad wife, honestly. I've been thinking more about how you feel losing your dad, but not thinking hard enough about the other stuff.' Sarah takes a sip of her wine. 'It's confusing, I guess. It's such an amazing show. You've worked on it for so long. I know it means a lot to you.'

'It's not the show. It's something more than that. You've got your job. You're amazing at it. I don't have that, or I do, but only as Elvis. I think I'm losing sight of who I am.'

'You have Claudie. You nail it all the time. You're patient, you make her laugh, you know how to chill her out. Stuff I'm way less good at.'

'And I love it, I really do. She's incredible, you're incredible, we're great. Maybe I'm nervous. It'll be fine, I'm sure it will.'

The waiter interrupts. He takes ages to explain every item of their starters, and by the time he goes, the mood has shifted. Sarah's concern has turned to sadness.

'I'm really sorry, J. I wish I could fix things for you. I do. I'll try harder.'

'I don't want to be fixed. But it's good to talk. Listen, we've drunk a bit. Let's drop it. This is a weekend away, remember? Your birthday.' Jess reaches her hand out across the table, takes Sarah's, rubs her thumbs across her wife's knuckles. 'You are my everything. You both are.'

Sarah pulls her hands away and starts fingering the necklace Jess gave her earlier.

'You're my everything too. And I really love this, by the way.'

'Do you really?' Jess asks.

'I love it. It's perfect. And I love you. We're a good team, right?'

'The best.'

'And Claudie's doing brilliantly.'

'She's her own little person, cracking on with life.'

A waiter swoops over before she can pour and tops up both their glasses, the bottle empties and he asks whether they'd like to order another.

'Shall we?' Sarah gestures.

'Go on then. Why not?'

'We don't have to drink all of it.'

By the time the main course arrives, Jess feels the heavy pull of exhaustion that comes from rich food, more alcohol than she's used to drinking, the weight of the conversation. The chef has won awards, is famous for foraging and fermenting. She pushes her venison loin around the plate, cuts tiny slivers, takes tentative bites. Her throat feels sticky from the butter and cream in the parsnip puree. She wishes she'd had the sea bass, something she didn't have to chew or slice.

She exhales, sets her knife and fork down, and looks to her wife, hoping they will share a smile and acknowledge to each other that they are being beaten by the rich food.

'What about you though?' Jess asks. 'How are you feeling about stuff at the moment? It can't all be about me and my existential crisis.' She wafts her hand over her face, a thespian swoop. An attempt at humour that doesn't quite land as Sarah's face turns serious.

'OK,' Sarah says. 'So, my birthday seems like the best and the worst time to bring this up, but after what you've just said, maybe it *is* the right time.' She takes a deep breath and carries on. 'I'm thirty-eight, well, thirty-nine now. I'm healthy. We've got a great life. Claudie is amazing. And you know we got that letter right, from the clinic? About the donor sperm and how long we've still got access to it? I've been thinking about it a lot and, to be honest, feeling pretty broody, and I wondered, how would you feel about, you know, having another baby?'

Jess reaches for her glass and bats the waiter away, a little too brusquely, when he rushes over to refill it when she's done.

'I guess I thought maybe you'd been thinking about it too,' Sarah continues. 'I left the letter out. I think it might be really nice for Claudie to have a little brother or sister. Maybe also with what you're thinking about, you know, the future, a new baby could be part of it?'

Jess knows that unless she says yes, whatever she says next will disappoint her wife. The clues she's ignored click like *Guess Who?* tiles in her mind – the frequent mention of siblings, the pleasure of seeing all their friends and their offspring in Brighton, the desire to cuddle her nephew, Ezra. The desire not to let him go.

Her silence is clearly making Sarah anxious, and her voice is sharp. 'It can't be that much of a shock. We always talked about two.'

'I'm so sorry, Sar. I've been preoccupied with dad, the show, Claudie.' Jess hopes that Sarah interprets her reaction as surprise, being caught totally off-guard, not a response more worrying than that. 'I really am sorry. It's not a no, honestly. It's a big decision, you know. I need to think about what it means, you know, for all of us. For me.'

'I didn't think you had a plan,' Sarah says, her voice quiet with disappointment.

'I don't know, maybe I have. Maybe I haven't. Honestly, can I think for a little bit? It's a lot to take in. Especially after all the wine.' Again, Jess's attempts at jollity fall flat.

'Sure, of course. We can keep talking. Another time.'

The waiter tries to top up their glasses again, but there is more left in the bottle than Jess has the stomach to drink.

'I'm bushed,' Sarah says. The adrenalin that propelled her to finally say what she wanted has left her deflated. The makeup around her eyes has smudged to grey circles. 'It's been a really lovely day. Maybe I didn't pick my moment too well. Classic me. How about we head to bed? Talk more tomorrow?'

The duvet has been turned down while they were at dinner, crumpled towels have been replaced, a sapphire blue glass bottle of water sits on their bedside tables. The lights have been dimmed, but all the warmth of intimacy between them has gone.

'Shall I go first?' Sarah asks, already peeling off her dress, but this time around the corner, no longer willing to be on show.

'Sure,' Jess sits on the armchair and lets Sarah go into the bathroom, where she will remove her makeup as meticulously as she put it on a few hours ago. Jess wiggles and pats both her pockets.

'Damn,' she calls out, 'must have left my phone on the table.'

'It'll still be there tomorrow,' Sarah calls back, her voice muffled by her toothbrush. 'We're not going anywhere.'

'I think I'd feel safer having it. In case there's an issue with Claudie.'

Sarah comes to the bathroom door, a smear of toothpaste on the side of her mouth.

'I'm sorry if I landed that on you,' she says, wiping it with a towel. 'I've had an amazing day. Thank you.'

Jess walks over and kisses Sarah's forehead.

'The conversation isn't over, I promise, we'll keep talking. Maybe not tonight, but we will. I'll be back in a minute. Don't wait for me.'

Sarah climbs into the bed and pulls the duvet up. 'Don't be too long. And Jess? Love you. Thanks for an amazing day. Really.'

'My pleasure.' Jess does a mock bow as she leaves the room. 'Back soon.'

The air outside is chilly, the lights in the hotel are dim. The remaining restaurant staff glide around, some setting places for breakfast, others sweeping the floor.

'We didn't want to disturb you. Here you go.' Her phone is handed over. 'Have a good night.'

'You too,' Jess says.

Back outside, she sits down on the bench by the ivy-clad hotel frontage and stares out into the blackness of the driveway and the fields beyond. Hears the faint whisper of traffic on the motorway. Checks her phone and sees an unread message. It's from Tiff.

Boring Saturday night here in London. Not as fun as next week will be. See you at the Soho! xx

Can't wait. She types quickly, as though even replying is a betrayal. *See u next week.*

Jess types two x's at the end of the message and then deletes them. Wonders if Tiff will notice. Wonders what it means that she's edited herself in this way, if it means anything at all.

She's tired, but the fresh air has turned her brain from muggy to churning with thoughts. If it wasn't so cold, she'd stay out here longer, allow more time for Sarah to fall asleep. Thoughts and decisions hover at the edges of her brain. Jess wishes the conversation hadn't happened, not here. Earlier, she'd imagined them ending the night a different way. Her wife, naked in bed, wanting her. Crouching over her body, stroking, kneading, running her short fingernails across her wife's thighs and back. All to herself, the way she used to be.

She doesn't know whether she's been offered a choice, or whether Sarah is presenting another baby as a quorder, that order posed as a question. She's confused. Has she been handed power over their future, or has hers just been taken away?

Chapter Ten
The Soho

Climbing on through the back door of the 73, Jess grips the mustard yellow stair rail as the bus jerks off quicker than she expects. It's only Wednesday and not rush hour yet, so she can select her preferred section of the upper deck – halfway down and by the window. Out of superstition, more so now than ever, Jess never listens to Elvis before a performance, but the choice of other music to go with her journey is critical. She spends too long scrolling through her playlists, seeking the right track to match her mood. Unsure what to pick and unwilling to make a wrong choice, she keeps the headphones in her ears to muffle the sounds of people and traffic.

The bus drifts through the many lights on Essex Road. Jess watches people congregating on the benches at Angel station, others leaning against the wall. Waiting. The local shops have replaced pumpkins with Christmas decorations and sparkling lights. Sarah has started compiling gift lists and scheduling nights out with friends between her client dinners. Jess is yet to feel festive.

Her preparation before a show usually buoys her excitement further. She adds weights to her runs and enjoys seeing her arms, back and shoulders regain definition. She'll hum Elvis around the house, start dancing while she's cooking, if not for practice, but at least to make Claudie giggle. But it's taken her longer than normal to get prepared for Soho. Without her father to act as coach ('you've got it, Jessie, you've really got it') and the sense that Sarah is no longer quite as supportive as she was, she's lost confidence. She's watched videos on YouTube, listened to Elvis on loop, and it's only now the run has finally started that she feels more ready.

Forty-five minutes later, the bus is nearly at Oxford Street. Over her earlier indecision, Jess lines up her Swagger playlist. As soon as the first electronic beats of 'Break My Stride' kick out, her head starts bobbing, her hips twitch, and her steps quicken. Nothing will stop or slow her down now. Not yet in her costume, the pedestrians don't know who she's about to become, but the energy she emanates is enough for her to gain some appreciative looks from women she passes.

Paulie has been a fixture at the Soho for so long that no one can remember when he wasn't guarding the desk at the stage door. His salt and pepper hair is in a tight ponytail that emphasises his cheekbones, a silver ring on each finger, bracelets jangling. He usually treats performers, and stage management with disdain, but his soft spot for Elvis means Jess gets the full beam of his campy warmth.

'Oh darling,' he tells her, 'I had so many posters of him on my wall you could barely see the paint. Mother used to think I liked the records, but it was a different type of groove I was after.' Paulie's phlegmy chuckle ends in a cough. 'Get on with you now. You've got a show to put on. Knock 'em dead, sweetheart.'

'A friend might pop in,' Jess says. 'Tiff. I've told her to sign in here first.'

'A friend of yours is a friend of mine, darling!'

'See you later, Paulie.' Jess waves and walks upstairs to her dressing room.

Jess shares the space with a young comic called Lexi, flush with the success of her debut run at Edinburgh. It's not the generous, well-lit space that punters might imagine dressing rooms to be, but it is more than the make-shift cupboard she shared in Edinburgh and it is theirs for the week. She is alone as she puts the final touches on her thick foundation when she hears footsteps stop and pause outside.

'Knock, knock.' Tiff sticks her head around the dressing room door. 'I hope it's not bad luck to visit the star before a show?'

'Too late now!'

'Damn, knew I'd be overdressed.' Tiff laughs and points to Jess's costume of black jockey shorts and a white singlet.

'Nah, you look fab.' Jess fusses around the room, clearing stuff off surfaces so that Tiff has a place to sit. Tiff does look great. She's wearing knee-high black boots, sheer tights, and a short jumpsuit that plunges down her neckline. Femme, but not girly.

'Sit,' Jess gestures to a chair she unearths from underneath her coat.

'How do you feel before a show?' Tiff asks. 'I'm not making you nervous, am I?'

Being in the theatre, spending time with an in-awe Lexi, now seeing Tiff, any flickering nerves have disappeared. Jess smiles.

'I don't do nervous.' As she speaks, Jess realises that she's genuinely not, and for the first time in a while.

Lexi comes back in after a smoke, says hello, and shakes hands with Tiff.

The tinny blare of the Tannoy calls time for Jess's show; she hears the distant sound of bells in the foyer and bar.

Tiff stands up quickly.

'I better go get my seat. Break a leg, or whatever you're supposed to say.' As she goes, Jess smells the familiar waft of her citrussy perfume.

'She seems lovely,' Lexi says.

'Chuffed she could make it.'

'I can see now why your daughter is so cute.' Lexi gestures to a framed photo of Claudie that she keeps on her dressing table.

'Oh, Tiff's not my wife,' Jess laughs. 'She's a friend, a journalist.'

'Oh god, sorry.' Lexi blushes. 'I saw you guys together and assumed. That's so embarrassing.'

'Don't worry about it.' Jess turns away to grab her costume before winding her way through the corridors to backstage. She's still smiling as she calls out a final good luck to Lexi and heads off to her own stage.

Jess knows it is taking her slightly longer than usual to morph from her own self to becoming Elvis. The costume is the same, the rings, the lightning bold stud in her left ear; but the transition feels clunkier than it has in the past. She feels her father's presence on her shoulder, a grief that reassures as well as saddens. There is something else too, the weight of a question she doesn't know how to ask of herself, or answer.

But as soon as she's on stage, there it is. She nails the jumps, kicks and swivels that she has worried will be hard to execute after the long hiatus off-stage. Her voice soars and swoops, she croons. A stomping ovation.

Lexi's show has gone well too. They high five and dress fast, both eager to get out and meet their friends and fans.

'Feels good, huh,' Jess says, tugging on her jeans, fastening her belt, tucking her shirt in and then out again.

'It really does,' Lexi replies. 'Edinburgh was amazing, but this is next level.' She turns to Jess at the door before heading out. 'Hey, Jess,' she says, 'thanks for being so supportive this week. I was bricking it, but you've made it really easy. So, thank you.'

'No sweat,' Jess says. 'It's a funny old business. Listen to the people who love you and ignore the ones who don't, and you'll do fine.'

Initially disappointed that she was sharing a dressing room, Jess will miss it, and Lexi. The young comic's enthusiasm and willingness to accept advice has reminded Jess that her experience is hard won and valuable, at least to someone. Once Lexi's gone, Jess takes a moment to check she hasn't left anything behind. No message from Sarah. The 'good luck' and 'hope it went well' notes that she used to get before and after every show haven't come this time. Sarah did get Claudie to scrawl a good luck card before her first night, and has made sure Jess's favourite late-night snacks are ready for when she gets home. It's the specific questions about her show – when it goes up or when it's over, how big the audience is, how appreciative their applause – that are being withheld.

The prospect of an evening where she will be the object of appraising glances from her fans in the bar and in the company of Tiff is tantalising. As usual, Jess's final ritual before heading out is to remove the heavy pinkie rings and replace them with her wedding band. She leaves one on; the heavy metal is gold-plated, black lightning bolts run up either side, and TCB is picked out in tiny diamantes. It's a ring that doesn't let her forget that she's carrying him with her; she often finds herself stroking the underside with the thumb. Leather jacket over a white shirt, hair quiffed high, kohl pencilled under her eyes, an extra button on her shirt undone, she looks good, and she knows it. She smiles his slow smile, the one that's never from her eyes. The glide and slink of her hips.

Jess described Tiff as a friend to Lexi, but as technically they've only spent one afternoon and evening together, messaged a bit, she isn't sure how she'll know when, or if, they've passed the gap between acquaintance and friend. It feels odd and exciting, like the first few dates of a new relationship. A warm glow, a faint fizz, somewhere between adulthood and adolescence. For obvious reasons, she hasn't told Sarah about Tiff. It's an omission, not a lie. She has done nothing wrong, she has not broken any rules, but something in her feels the thrill of the illicit.

Downstairs, Tiff is waiting, standing by the theatre door, a glossy faux fur coat slung over her arm.

'Didn't know if you wanted to stay here and hang out with your fans.' Tiff swoops her hand at the crowded bar. 'Or we could head straight to Ruby's?'

'Ruby's?'

'My member's club. It's great, and I need to justify the extortionate membership! They make a mean martini.'

Jess, hoping to have a drink or two in the theatre bar, wants people to come up and congratulate her and for Tiff to bask in the accolades showered on her new friend.

'I'll do you a deal,' she says. 'One drink here, then Ruby's.'

'Done,' Tiff says.

Jess shepherds Tiff to the bar, a protective hand on her waist to steer her through the crowd and stop her bumping into other people.

'Such a gent,' Tiff says when they get to the bar.

'Uh-huh,' Jess says.

As predicted, the bar is full of fans. Groups of women, more gay than straight, cluster together and nudge each other when they see she's arrived. She's exuding the magnetic androgynous confidence that makes her so powerful as Elvis, but post-show, powerful as herself too. Aware that Tiff has noticed other people looking, she basks further. Accepts a few handshakes and nods at others who nod at her. Most people won't interrupt, they can see she's with a friend, but it's obvious she's there to be seen.

Tiff has noticed too. 'You should start charging them,' she jokes. 'Quite the celebrity.'

'Better not let it go to my head.'

'Like the way it did to Elvis's?'

There it is again, Tiff's ability to drop in that she knows, and cares, about who Elvis really was.

'It's all about choices,' Jess says.

'Oh yeah? We've got a date with a cocktail or two, and I'm going to disappoint your fans by stealing you away. I think it's time Elvis left this building.'

'Steal away,' Jess says as she pushes the door open for Tiff to slide past. Jess takes Tiff's coat and holds it open so she can slide her arms in and tie the belt tight around her waist. Out on the cold pavement, Tiff shivers.

'Again,' Tiff laughs, 'such a gent. Southern charm!'

'Shall we?' Jess offers her arm, and they walk down further into Soho. She likes the feeling of having this pretty, petite woman on her arm, an echo of the Elvis she's just been, with a tiny Priscilla under his wing.

The door to Ruby's is tucked between two restaurants, so discreet you could walk past without spotting it. Tiff walks up the stone steps first, presses the buzzer, and a woman in a strappy red dress opens the door.

'Babe!' she cries out. 'Been ages!'

Jess, having relinquished control of the evening, follows Tiff into the long, thin bar. The panelled walls are painted a dark moss green, setting off the gold mirrored frames and neon artwork, double-wicked scented candles waft in corners. Tiff leads Jess to a pair of leather armchairs in a room where the lighting is set intentionally low, candles flicker. Jess catches a whiff of her own smoky fragrance, with it, a vision of home. She pictures her wife and daughter. Her daughter asleep, her wife watching TV, feet up on the sofa. She does not envy them or want to go home. There is nowhere she'd rather be than out, in Soho, with an attractive friend who is making every effort to impress and be present.

The bartender pours liquid into the silver shaker, shaves orange peel, and waves a lighter underneath the curled fronds. They've been silent for a few minutes, and Jess wonders if this is an awkward moment, a sign that thoughts of friendship are misjudged. But as soon as their drinks arrive, Tiff raises her glass. 'Cheers. To your stunning cover. And a bloody brilliant show. Another brilliant show, don't think I could get tired of it.'

'Hey, there's always a ticket for you. And cheers to you and *LEXI*. You made me sound and look great. Much cooler than I am.'

'A humble brag,' Tiff smiles, 'you know you deserve all the accolades. And more.'

They clink glasses and sit back against the studded leather chairs. A cashew lands on Tiff's chest when her manicured fingers scoop a few hickory-smoked nuts from a bowl. Without thinking about it, Jess leans forward and plucks it off.

'Oi,' Tiff laughs.

'Finders keepers,' Jess says and drops the cashew into her mouth.

Tiff settles back, comfortable in her surroundings and the company.

'So, tell me,' she asks, 'your last show, especially after what happened in Edinburgh. How are you doing? Really?'

Still buzzing from tonight's performance and in the presence of this charming, inquisitive woman, Jess feels free to talk. Editing any mention of Sarah, or the possibility of another baby, she focuses instead on her dad and Elvis, a conversation that she started, but never finished, with her wife.

'They both made me, I guess. I can't quite work out who I am without them. Sometimes when I'm in the show, I feel like I'm the better me. The me that borrows from Elvis. The confident, sexy, got-it-together me. It makes the other me, the grieving, snappy, disillusioned me, feel way less appealing. If that makes any sense at all.'

'I think I could tell that,' Tiff says. 'I mean that I've seen the show before, and you were great then, but tonight was different. Like you captured the bit of Elvis that was sad, ground down, but also the side of him that was so magnetic and amazing you could never imagine life without him. You were really, really good, Jess. Even more real now than before maybe.'

'Thanks. Honestly. It helps to hear it.'

'Have you talked to Sarah about it?' asks Tiff.

'Yeah. A bit. We've got stuff going on, though.'

'Well, you've got me in the meantime, or at least for tonight,' Tiff says. 'And I'm all ears. So, what is next?' Tiff tucks her feet underneath herself on the oversized armchair.

'What do you mean?'

'So, it sounds to me, tell me if I've got this wrong, that you're more in love with performing than ever, but that maybe the Elvis thing has got more complicated. Too sad, brilliant, of course, but different now that your dad has passed. So maybe the Universe is leading you to something else?'

'You are a good listener,' Jess says. 'If journalism doesn't work out, you should be a therapist. You might be right. I hadn't thought about it quite like that. I'm not quite ready to let him go. Either of them. But something has to change.'

'I guess it must be hard to juggle, though,' Tiff observes. 'You know, home and work. But I guess if you've got a dream, you have to follow it.'

'Uh-huh,' Jess channels Elvis for a moment. 'The juggle is real.'

'Ha-ha.' Tiff leans forward and swipes Jess's arms in mock despair. 'I hope your wife knows how lucky she is. She must be pretty amazing if you've stayed at home rather than getting famous on the stage. Maybe it's your turn now.' Jess doesn't mention that she's wondered the same.

'I see what you're doing here,' Jess sits back and waggles a finger. 'You're getting me to talk all the time and not letting me ask about you.'

Tiff pauses, runs a hand through her curly hair, and there it is, another waft of her perfume.

'Honestly, *LEXI*'s special. It matters. It helps people be seen.'

'You're right. And I agree.'

'We're not for everyone, not even for all lesbian, gay, bi, trans, and all the other women. But it matters to me. Like I say, I want people to be seen. Like I want *you* to be seen, you're special.'

'You're doing it again,' Jess laughs. 'What about what's next for you?'

'Good question. I totally love what I do. I thought I wanted to be a writer and then realised I hated being on my own for days on end. For me, it's about stories. Bringing them to life. TV is something I'm into, maybe film. It's a tough industry, but I've been working some contacts. There are so many amazing ideas out there. It's always about finding the truth. You know, about people.'

'You have a gift for that. Really. It's rare that I open up as much as I do with you.'

Jess offers the compliment and then, embarrassed, decides it would be a good idea to have a change of scene. Hearing the pulsing music from downstairs, she suggests they go and dance. When they squeeze past other women, a few make eye contact and smile. More of those flirty, approving looks. It's been so long since she's been out in town, been noticed, been appreciated, and she's full of energy and up for it. This is how life used to be. When she and Sarah would go to lesbian bars (when there were lesbian bars), she knew they looked great together. Other women would look at them and feel envious, knowing they didn't stand a chance. But that was back then when they went out at all.

They order another drink from the bar and wait for the track to end. It's too loud to talk normally, so when Tiff tilts her head up to shout in Jess's ear, her breath tickles. Jess looks down to mouth a response, their heads close together. The track changes, Jess pulls Tiff into the middle of the dance floor. Jess knows she's a good dancer and quickly discovers that Tiff is a great partner. Feet planted far enough apart that she has balance; her thighs, hips, arms, and neck all move together. It's not a slow track, but Tiff is dancing slowly enough that every movement is visible and sexy. Alcohol and the thrill of a great night out with an attractive woman loosen Jess's inhibitions, and she puts her hands on Tiff's hips to guide her moves. They match.

'Wow.' Tiff stands on her tiptoes and shouts into Jess's ear. 'I love this!'

'Love what?' Jess mouths back.

'Being here. Dancing with you. Guess you don't need his music to still be as cool as the King.'

Other couples on the dancefloor part a little to give them more room. Jess feels the beat of the music in time with her heart, and she feels, for a moment, as good as she does on stage. They head to the bar and Tiff signals to the bartender. They get handed a shot, neck it, and quickly ask for another.

'Really?' Jess raises her eyebrows at Tiff as the glass comes to her lips.

'It's not a school night. Relax. You know you want to.'

Jess knows she is drunk, much drunker than she's been in a long time. And it feels great.

Jess is shocked when she glimpses the time on someone else's phone. 3am. Way later than Sarah, even knowing Jess will be doing post-show socialising (and not knowing who with), will think is acceptable. Standing still for a moment, she sees Tiff stumble, unsteady on her heels. It's time to go. Jess bends down and yells into Tiff's ear.

'Tiff. It's time. I need to get home.'

'No!' Tiff tugs at her. 'We're having too much fun.'

'I reckon we've drunk enough. C'mon, let's get outta here.'

Jess reaches out, takes Tiff's hand, leads her towards the staircase, and doesn't let go until they're at the top. Tiff makes to turn back and go downstairs, but Jess puts her hand around her waist and turns her back again, keeping her hands there as she steers her towards the door. This gesture feels intimate away from the dancefloor, but Jess does not pull away.

The woman in the red dress is perched on a stool behind the desk when they get upstairs.

'Taxis?' she asks. 'It's cold out there.'

'Get a cab,' Jess urges Tiff, 'it'll get you home safe.' She turns to the door lady. 'Yes, please.'

'You ladies wait inside. Will let you know when it's here.'

Jess leads Tiff further down the hallway to an alcove where a telephone would once have been. Tiff leans back against the wall.

'Hey.' Tiff reaches up and gently strokes Jess's quiff. 'I had a great time tonight.'

'Me too.'

'Which one of you? You? Or Elvis?'

'Both.'

Tiff stands up a little bit straighter. 'I really like you, Jess.'

Jess smiles. 'I like you too. We both do.'

'Which one likes me more?'

Jess hears the lady at the door call that Tiff's taxi is outside.

'Unfair question,' Jess laughs.

Tiff pushes herself off the wall of the alcove and stumbles a little. Jess catches her.

'Hey.' She kisses Tiff on the cheek. 'That one's from me.' Tiff looks up at her. 'And this one's from him.'

Before she thinks about what she's doing, Jess kisses Tiff on the lips. Shocked, she pulls back. Then kisses her again; prolonged, smoother, hotter. Then it's over. She takes Tiff's hand and walks her out towards the waiting cab.

The cold outside is a smack.

Jess opens the back door and helps Tiff get in.

'I'm sorry,' she starts saying, but Tiff presses a finger on her lips.

'Shh,' she says. 'A lady never tells. I had a great night.'

'Text me when you get home,' Jess says, standing up and shutting the car door.

Alone on the pavement, Jess rocks on her heels. So, so drunk. It's so late. So cold. She weaves a little way down the pavement, away from the club.

'Fuck,' she says, crouching down as though she's been hit. 'Fuck.'

She pushes herself off the pavement, stands, and walks down towards the night bus stop on Oxford Street. Hugging herself against the cold. A deep breath in, her diaphragm steady, a deep breath out. It was nothing, she thinks. A brief moment. Nothing, but still something.

Chapter Eleven
The Emcee

Jess has been dreading tonight. James came good on the request he casually tossed out back in Edinburgh – that she emcees Sarah's office Christmas party. Wyatt & Webb has expanded under Sarah's committed stewardship, now sprawling enough to call for a venue takeover, a live band, an internal awards ceremony. Jess, having avoided this type of work, felt she had to say yes. Sarah, to her credit, has not put the pressure on, but Jess is wary of adding another 'no' to the growing pile of things she's resisting.

The Soho show has helped her regain some of the confidence she'd lost after Edinburgh. Great reviews: the programming team has already suggested that she come back early next year, perhaps for longer. They've asked if she's got a new show up her sleeve. The relief that she hasn't 'lost it' bubbles away in her brain and distracts her from what's happening at home, where the conversation remains mundane, even perfunctory. The mood is muted. Sarah asked polite questions about Soho but didn't come to see it.

Jess's late night / early morning during the run hasn't been mentioned either. Presumably Sarah assumed she was out with friends but didn't ask which ones. Jess has pushed the memory of kissing Tiff to the base of her brain, but when it bubbles up, she can't help resisting the fizz of warmth it creates. Any flirtations she's indulged in before have been a direct result of women seeing her show and contained within the bubble of performance, but she's never over-stepped the line like this before. She has no excuses to make, even to herself. But she cannot let it happen again.

Christmas is coming, more distractions. All of it points away from what they don't want to discuss or don't know how. Being nice enough that they can't accuse each other of being unkind, but without the warmth or intimacy that would prove nothing is wrong.

Her act tonight is totally different from her show. It's showmanship, not really acting. Jess normally dons her costume slowly over her hour on stage, the final stunning reveal reserved for the last few minutes. As the emcee, her wow must happen on entry. She binds her breasts and checks the wide bandage can't be seen under her crisp white shirt. Her stage show makeup is designed for a more distant audience – it's blocky and angular, the lights and the content requiring a more explicitly masculine look. Under these unforgiving fluorescent lights, knowing she will be close to her audience, she takes more time perfecting the contouring of her foundation and powder, blending with care.

The final spritz of hairspray is the punctuation mark of her transformation. Tonight she keeps her finger on the nozzle for a few seconds longer, because up-close she needs her quiff to be as rock-solid as her vocals and moves. Tonight is straight-up impersonation, not drag, not queer. Jess isn't sure how she feels about it. Perhaps it's a betrayal of the version of Elvis she wants to tell, perhaps it's the start of something new.

Leaving the dressing room, she can already hear the crowd down the heavily carpeted corridor, mainlining complimentary champagne and canapes, tanking up before dinner. Approaching the security-manned heavy doors are two men. They're wearing suits, but their ties are undone and dangle down their shirts like parallel stains. Unlike the way her fans usually look at her, they do not break out in smiles, do not nudge each other in recognition, and don't hang back and turn shy. They merely look her up and down, carry on talking, and sail past security and into the room.

The banqueting suite has been decked out with retro Americana props to celebrate the successful pitch of a small slice of Coca-Cola's marketing pie. Neon signs hang over the bar, a Hollywood sign studded with tiny white bulbs is next to the photo booth, equipped with a large trunk of Dolly Parton and Elvis wigs. There are themed cocktail stations – a Wild West saloon offers tequila or whisky, an art deco Manhattan bar offers vodka or gin. All of it laced, of course, with Coke.

A deep breath. Sauntering slowly, legs wider apart, hips first, Jess drifts amongst the guests to get to the front of the room. She hears some appreciative laughter, spots pointing and nudging as she gains their appreciation. Jess's smile gradually relaxes, but she makes sure her head retains his familiar tilt to the left, her shoulders pushed forwards, an intentional gait. Even without a paying audience, the silence and spotlights, it's not as hard to transform here as she thought it might be. Although she doesn't have her script or even the music, she's settling in. Taking people's hands when offered, cupping them within hers, nodding her head slightly. Warming to her, women crowd around, wanting to be close, while the men hang back.

'Thank you,' she says slowly to people who smile at her, milking the drawl. 'Pleasure's all mine, honey. Uh-huh.'

The volume increases, the lights dim, and a spotlight beams onto the stage, the cue for everyone to make their way to the front. Jess saunters up the stairs, stands centre stage, and waits for a hush to fall. This silence would be absolute during her show, and she would be totally in control. Tonight, the audience takes longer to fall quiet, and even then, there is loud chatter and laughter from the back of the room. Wyatt & Webb have sprung for a top-notch covers band. They've met briefly to run through their numbers so when she nods to the bass player, the clubby beat of the 'A Little Less Conversation' remix kicks in. There is nothing she can do, she cannot wait any longer, she realises the silence may never actually come. The audience cheers.

Her show is paced slower at the start and doesn't allow for this kind of rock-star opening. Jess twists, turns, jumps. Her hips thrust, and her legs twist. Swept in by the crowd's euphoria, she adds some showier flourishes to her routine. She hears them yelling words back at her, *bite, bark, fight, spark* and *satisfy me*. The song finishes, and the audience are already clamouring for more, not satisfied with just one song.

'Good evening, y'all.' Jess has to pause, pace the stage, take another bow; the audience is still clapping and calling for more. 'I sure appreciate the lovin'.' More whoops from the crowd. 'But right now, it's my pleasure to welcome your MD to the stage. To my mind, she's way too pretty to be anyone's boss but apparently, she's mighty smart, and I sense she might have some real fans out there. Ms. Sarah, where are you, darlin',' come on up!'

Sarah walks slowly up the stairs in her short, bright green dress and red heels, a pair of Louboutins that she bought a few years ago and only wears once or twice a year. They're kept in the box, and whenever Sarah tries them on, she takes them off at once, claiming she's too fat, that they constrict her feet, that a less showy pair will have to do.

Sarah's short speech is passionate, funny, rousing. Jess hasn't seen her wife speak in public for a while and she's impressed again by how self-assured and confident she is. Sarah finishes up and tells everyone to have a great night. She moves to walk off the stage. But Jess steps in and grabs her hand.

'Hold on there, little miss, we're not done yet.'

Although Jess has prepped this moment, she's unprepared for how unnatural it feels. How she's acting in more ways than just the ones she's being paid for. This is not something they have discussed. She knows Sarah will not appreciate the lack of control, the public display of affection. Sarah, caught off-guard, takes a step backward. Jess holds out her hand to steady her and nods to the band.

'Uh-huh, ladies and gentlemen. This here is one exceptional lady. You know that, the Chairman knows that.' She laughs in his direction. 'And because I'm her wife, I know that. This song is for you, Sarah. If you know the words, sing along y'all. And if you don't know the words, sing anyway.'

The slow beat of 'I Just Can't Help Believin' kicks in. It's the song they chose for their first wedding dance. A love song, intended to be soft, and kind. Jess takes the microphone from the stand and slowly dances around Sarah. Initially thrown, Sarah allows Jess to take hold of both her hands and pull her in and out of an embrace as the beat picks up. The audience cheers and whistles as the song continues. As the song ends, Jess puts her hand on the small of Sarah's back, bends her backward, and kisses her, before standing up and winking at the crowd. Before signalling to the band to play the first tracks that will guarantee a packed dance floor, Jess takes one more bow.

'Have a great night, y'all.'

Jess, or at least Elvis, has been invited to stay for the party so she moves down into the crowd of people who pat her on the back, ask her to dance, touch her. Keen to find out Sarah's reaction to her act, especially the reveal that they're married, Jess seeks out her wife, who has melted into the crowd. Jess spots the back of her green dress standing amongst a group of colleagues. Now that her moment on stage is over, she is flushed, relaxed and she hopes that the high spirits of the evening have created the same in her wife. A brief thaw in their chill.

She walks up behind her, and Sarah's team nudge and point to get her attention. Sarah turns around. But her smile is not the full beam Jess has hoped for. Annoyance, imperceptible to others, flickers at the corners of her mouth.

'Ma'am,' Jess says, still in character, 'I wondered if maybe you'd like to dance?' She holds out her hand. But the request has wrong-footed her wife again, and Jess can tell she doesn't want to.

'In these shoes?' Her laugh is tinged with an edge. Sarah leans forward to whisper in Jess's ear, but Jess can see that she's smiling in case anyone is looking.

'Can we not?' she says. 'I'm really not in the mood.'

Smarting but not wanting others to notice she's been rejected, Jess stands and holds a hand out to a colleague instead.

'May I?' she asks. The young woman giggles and allows herself to be swept away into the crowd, enjoying the envious glances of others. For the next hour or so, if they're in danger of getting too close, either Jess or Sarah drift quietly further away from each other.

Later, Jess finds Sarah and James at the bar, hoping her mood will have softened with the alcohol and the success of a great party. James suggests they each do a shot.

'Sure,' Sarah says, 'let's do it.' But then she shifts to talk to the person on the other side of her. James turns to Jess.

'You were amazing,' he starts. 'I knew you would be. Sarah says this isn't your usual kind of gig, but you nailed it.'

'More fun than I thought,' Jess replies. 'And I do what the boss says.'

'Me too! Cassie says hi, by the way. I think she has a bit of a crush on you.'

'Say hi back. Don't tell Sarah, but I've got a crush on her back. How's she doing?'

'Good. I mean great, in fact. Better than in the first trimester anyway, she got pretty bad morning sickness.' Jess's surprise must show on her face. 'Oh, maybe Sarah didn't tell you, we're expecting.'

'Oh wow. That's great news. Congratulations. When are you due?'

'April. We think it must have happened in Edinburgh, actually. Another shot? To celebrate? While I'm still allowed out at night?'

Jess can feel that Sarah has stiffened, her shoulders rigid. They neck another shot each, and Sarah makes her excuses yet again, 'Better go mingle.' Jess is left alone, reeling. Aware that any hopes of a cheerful debrief on the journey home are over.

By midnight, most of the agency is drifting off. After some searching, Jess finds her wife sitting at a table with a group of the younger ones, a large glass of white wine in front of her and a half-empty bottle standing nearby. She's smashed, and her colleagues are too, but none of them will leave while Sarah is still there holding court.

'Hey, you.' Jess puts a hand on her wife's shoulder. 'Think we better shoot.' Jess holds out her hand.

'See, now MY boss is telling ME what to do,' Sarah slurs. But Sarah dutifully follows Jess out of the ballroom, they collect their coats from the cloakroom, and Sarah slumps against the desk. Jess asks the door attendant to call them a taxi. Sarah presses herself up against the window in the cab, as far away from Jess as she can. Her fists are clenched white in her lap, and she stares out at the dark streets.

'If Carlsberg did Christmas parties…' says Jess, 'that was a great one. You pleased?'

'Better have been. Cost us a fortune. Looks like you enjoyed it though. That was quite an act you pulled up on the stage.' An edge creeps into Sarah's voice.

'I thought you'd be proud of me. I'm assuming that most people knew who I was?'

'Well, they do now. I just found it all a bit, I don't know, embarrassing.'

'If you're embarrassed by me, then why did you encourage me to do it? You know it's the sort of performing I hate. I did it for *you*.'

'It looked like you were having the time of your life.' Sarah mimics their voices. 'Your wife is so talented, your wife is so sexy, she's so cool.'

'They said the same to me of you. Though they didn't mention the sexy part, might have been overstepping it a bit.' Jess's attempt at humour fails.

'I'm their boss. They have to be nice.'

The edge in Sarah's voice has tipped over into aggression. There are things Jess knows to say to smooth things over, placatory titbits that would have done the job in the past. But she is angry too. Sick of feeling manipulated, asked to collude in decisions she isn't ready to make.

'Nice to see James again,' Jess tries.

Sarah snaps, 'They didn't even have to try, you know, it just happened.'

And here we go, Jess thinks. She wills herself to keep quiet and not be goaded, not say something she will regret. She has not drunk as much as Sarah, but still enough that if she's sufficiently riled, she won't let go. Sarah continues.

'It's so easy for them, right? BAM, one weekend away, and she's pregnant.'

'Love,' Jess tries. 'I get that you're annoyed. But can we talk about this another time, maybe wait until tomorrow?'

'Wait, Sarah! Wait, Sarah! What am I waiting for, exactly? Huh?'

'Please stop.'

'Wait for Claudie to go to nursery, wait for your show to be over. Wait for Cassie to have HER perfect baby. Wait for Jess to feel less sad, wait for Jess to have an idea about what to do with her life. Wait, wait, wait. Wait for WHAT?'

'Stop it. Sarah. Just stop it. This is a big fucking decision, you know. It's not like, 'Shall we get new doors on the patio?' It's a tiny bit bigger than that.'

'Is it, though?' Sarah asks. She looks so sad, tears rolling down her face; it both breaks and hardens Jess's heart. 'Is it really such a big decision, Jess? We're great parents, we have an amazing daughter. We can do this. I can do this. I want this so badly.'

'I know you do, Sarah,' Jess takes her hand. 'I want to want it as much as you. I just can't give you the answer you want, not yet. I have to be sure.'

Sarah pulls her hand back, her whispered fury a rasp away from full volume.

'I don't get it. I literally do not get it. I work fucking hard all year so that we have choices. This is a choice I really, really want to make. I thought maybe you were stubborn. Now I think you're just being a cunt.'

CHLOË FOWLER

Part Three
ElvisCon

CHLOË FOWLER

Chapter Twelve
The ETAs

Sarah used to perch on the end of their bed and play fetch when Jess packed for a trip; bringing in chargers from other rooms, Imodium ('just in case'), padded hangers for Jess's costume. In their early days together, if one took a trip, the other would tuck a love note in the suitcase to be discovered when the case was unpacked. Today Jess is getting ready alone, and she knows there will be no note.

Christmas was navigated gingerly – both bruised, careful not to cause more hurt. They'd channelled all their energy into Claudie, who'd become so dazzled by the falsetto brightness of their attention that she became whiny and sullen.

New Year's Eve in Brighton with their cluster of friends was a date they kept, but the proximity of happy families was too much for Sarah, whose behaviour deteriorated shortly after midnight. As the twelfth bong sounded, the three couples moved together for their private kisses, but Sarah and Jess only touched lips briefly and then retreated to opposite sides of the room.

Sarah's avoidance of Jess was palpable, and Jess sensed Sarah's distance was a tactic to stop herself from going on the offensive. But drunk, Sarah couldn't help herself, and when the attack came, once all the couples had retired to bed, Sarah had smashed the duvet down with her hands, all her frustration and anger erupting. Not prepared to retaliate because she did not blame her wife for being angry, Jess had crept downstairs and slept on the sofa, the narrow double bed in their friends' spare room too small to hold both their hurt. Jess accepts the punishment for her indecision, knowing that if her wife knew about her kiss with Tiff, she'd have even more cause to be furious. Not biting back is her penance for her betrayal. Sarah doesn't understand why she's unable to concede, and Jess doesn't know why either.

The deadline for deciding looms. Not an actual deadline, but an artificial and invisible one when Sarah will tip from irritation, to anger, to fury, to disbelief. Jess doesn't know what will happen if she says no. When she's with Claudie, or even just thinks about her, she feels a consuming, crushing love. In those moments, she can't imagine why she isn't saying yes to a second child, one that would likely be as amazing and precious as the first. But try as she might, she cannot picture siblings charging up the narrow stairs of their house, two sets of bicycles, two sets of tiny wellington boots. If she imagines anything at all, it's the stress of needing to find and then move into a bigger house, the crush of expenses, double the worry. When she watches frazzled mothers urging toddlers to get out of the way of babies' strollers, urging two children on and off buses, all she feels is pity, even horror. None of these are feelings unique to her; she knows this. Parents of one child always wonder what change will come with another.

But she has another fear, one she can't articulate. The one she doesn't think Sarah will understand. By creating space to parent and love another child, will she lose sight of what keeps her whole and makes her... *herself*?

Performing is in her soul, the time when she feels most herself, and she is not prepared to give it up. If anything, she wants it more than she ever did and her conversations with Tiff, the surprising unlocking of honesty, has made this clearer still. Jess knows she'd have to start at the bottom, fight for parts, suffer the rejections. Be away from home more, those late nights or early starts to get to set. She senses that performing is a lifestyle that's incompatible with parenting full-time, not least a new baby as well as Claudie. It's certainly, it would appear, incompatible with her marriage and the vision that Sarah has for their life.

Nearing what she senses is a crisis, Jess wonders whether this trip to ElvisCon is running away or a chance for them both to breathe. Perhaps this final foray into a world of Elvises will put paid to her ambitions. Either way will be an answer of sorts. It's certainly an opportunity to be apart.

Her dad had stumbled on ElvisCon through Google. When he'd first suggested she join the Elvis Tribute Act championship in Birmingham, she'd laughed and explained to him that she didn't see herself as an impersonator, and that to join their ranks would be demeaning. But in a fit of grief after he'd died, she signed up, wishing so much he was still alive to know. Maybe he would even have come with her. A Memphis taster? At the very least, a chance taken too late to make him proud.

When Jess had suggested that Sarah and Claudie join them for the last day, Sarah had demurred, saying this was something that Jess should work through on her own and that it would be a bit much for their daughter. Jess has wondered whether Sarah hoped this would be a final resting place for her private Elvis, a private Graceland. Her wish might yet be granted.

Despite the frost between them, Jess's imminent departure seems to have thawed Sarah a little.

'Give Mama a nice goodbye kiss and a big squeezy hug,' Jess hears her wife instructing Claudie in the other room. 'We won't see her for a few days.'

Jess kneels to say goodbye to her daughter and feels those little arms snake around her neck.

'Be good for Mummy.' She strokes Claudie's warm head. 'I'll be back in three sleeps.'

'We'll miss you,' Sarah had said, her chin resting on Jess's shoulder. 'I'm sorry. For everything.'

'It might be so awful that I'll come straight home. It's all a bit daft, to be honest.'

Sarah pulled far enough back that she could look into Jess's eyes. 'Love you.'

Jess waited until she was at the end of the short path at the front of the house before calling back, 'Love you.'

Now at Euston, Jess keeps an eye out for fellow ETAs (Elvis Tribute Acts), half-expecting to see fully clad Elvises queuing at Greggs or grabbing painkillers from Boots. But if they are here, like her, they are still in mufti, keeping their powder dry for the main event. It's on the train that she starts noticing Elvis fans. A group of women, hair puffed high by hairspray, cram their luggage into racks and squeeze in around a table. They open cans of pre-mixed cocktails, and she can hear them crooning from her end of the carriage.

When they pour off the train an hour or so later, a Hilton courtesy bus is lined up outside Birmingham International. A poorly handwritten sign inside the passenger side window says 'ElvisCon: Europe's largest ETA Championship.' Jess winces as she watches the driver fling her costume bag onto the back of the bus and then climbs on. The women from her carriage are already there. Nobody speaks to her, but they fold the driver into their banter, 'Go on, darling, bet you've had all the best ones in the back of this bus.'

The journey from the station to the Hilton Metropole is short. They pass the NEC and Resorts World, and with each mini roundabout, Jess feels further and further away from her comfort zone. There's a queue at check-in, and her costume bag is wedged over her arm like a weighty sling. She kicks her small suitcase ahead of her as they all shuffle forward as the desks open one by one.

'Charming,' says a woman with dyed pink hair and furry boots who stands behind her in the queue. She nods to Jess's luggage. 'He makes you carry the bags while you do all the heavy lifting. I'd have a word with him, I would. Go on, love, there's a space open over there.'

The first showcase isn't due to start for over an hour, so Jess has plenty of time to take her bags up to her room before coming back down to complete her registration for the competition. The faux-marble corridors echo with laughter. A man in a familiar white jumpsuit darts into a lift as she walks past – tall, perma-tanned, unsmiling.

'There goes Mr. I Love Myself,' laughs one of the women walking in front of her. Her heavy-set friends, each carrying bags emblazoned with sequined Elvis heads, join in. They're wearing matching sweatshirts emblazoned with the dates of last year's Championship.

One of the many doors leading off the dark brown carpet, her room is shabby and dark. Running her hands down the satin trousers and jacket to smooth out creases from the journey, she dares to hope it might bring her good luck.

Conscious of her lack of allies, no stage door hello, dressing room banter, or final checks with the tech team to act out her pre-show routines, she sends Sarah a message.

Arrived. All a bit nuts.

Sarah is typing a reply; she waits until it appears.

You the winner yet?

Steady on. Just arrived.

Sarah's next message appears while she's still typing hers.

Claudie says hi. Says she misses you.

Missing her back. And you. Gonna go downstairs and check out the competition.

Slay.

The warmth in the messages is cheering and briefly reminds her how strong they are, or at least how strong they can be, how different this experience would be if Sarah was there with her. She wonders again what it is that's stopping her give the answer that would melt all their tension. Looking in the mirror, Jess is glad she's decided not to make her quiff too pronounced for now. Unsure when the judging officially starts, something tells her it's too early to draw attention to herself.

Back downstairs, she follows signs that point towards the competition registration zone. An older woman sits behind a makeshift desk – the tablecloth is strewn with clipboards, lanyards and a shiny red cash tin. Shirley, her name badge says, is wearing heavy foundation; beneath her bronzed cheeks, her whiter, pouchy jowls look crepey. She barely glances at Jess and keeps up a conversation with another woman. Eventually, Jess leans forward and asks whether there was someone else she should notify that she's arrived. Perhaps she is in the wrong place?

'Oh, sorry, love,' Shirley says, with a thick Birmingham accent, 'I assumed you were waiting for someone. You know, to register him. He has to do it in person, I'm afraid.'

'Oh, I'm the performer,' Jess explains. 'I've registered already. I got an email telling me I needed to come and tell you I was officially here. J Ellis-Allen.'

Leaning over a little to scroll down the list of names on Shirley's clipboard, she points when she spots her name. 'There you go, that's me. Right here.'

'Oh.' Shirley's face freezes, and she snatches the clipboard away. 'I'm sorry. It said 'J,' you see.' She holds it back out, pointing. 'No full name. Can you wait here a little minute for me?'

'Surely, Shirley.' Jess's attempt at humour fails, and Shirley looks flustered as she locks the cash tin, pockets the key, leaves the table, and ducks into one of the rooms. Through the open doors, Jess sees clusters of Elvises. Limbering up, enlisting their wives to help them zip up their costumes, back-slapping and chatting. It won't be long, Jess thinks, until she's part of their gang. A King amongst Kings. After a minute or so, Shirley comes back out. A tall man with a thinning ponytail follows her out.

'This is the lady.' Shirley picks up the clipboard and holds it in front of Tony's face. 'See, it just says J Ellis-Allen.' She turns back to Jess, and her face is part apologetic, part irritated. 'This is Tony. He's the founder of ElvisCon,' she explains.

'Is there a problem?' Jess tries to keep any anxiety out of her voice, but her blood rises, and her breath quickens. 'You can see there, I did register. A month or so ago. I've paid up too. Got my room, used the discount. Ready to rock and roll.' Again, her attempt at humour is met with blank faces.

Tony is wearing faded black jeans, a leather belt with a prominent Elvis buckle, and a black button-up shirt. Dressed like a roadie, he has the swagger of a bull-rider; a roll of duct tape looped through his belt like a pistol. He leans forward, his fingers press down on the white cloth, the tips of his fingers glowing white.

'Tony.' He offers her his warm, clammy hand. She can feel his Elvis pinkie ring pressing into her palm.

'Just come over here for a tick, love.' He beckons her away from the queue. 'What it is, see, and this is a bit awkward for me to say as it goes, but the thing what it is, is that well, you're, um, well you see, Elvis was a fella, the tribute artists are all fellas if you get my drift. No offense, love, it is what it is.'

Jess feels eyes from the queue burning into her back.

'There's nowhere in the rules that says contestants can't be women,' she says.

'I'll have to review that. I suppose we never really thought we had to spell it out, thought it was obvious.'

'It is what I do,' she remonstrates. 'I'm a performer. I've paid to be here. It's not against the rules. I double-checked.'

'I'm not sure it will be quite as easy as that.' His smile is as greasy as his ponytail. 'We're a bit of a family, see. Most of the ETAs are top of their game, been coming for years. The judges are professionals, top class. And, of course, we'll need your backing tracks. If we don't have those, we can't let you use any old thing.'

'You've got them,' Jess says. 'Sent last week. So, I reckon I'm all set. Right?'

'I'll have to let the judges know. I can't guarantee they'll be happy about it, mind.'

'Thanks, Tony,' she says. 'It's truly a pleasure to be here.'

'Shirl, love.' He pauses for emphasis. 'Give Miss Ellis-Allen her wristband. If you have registered, you'll have been assigned a seat.' He nods to an easel by the door, and his eyes don't meet hers as he slopes off.

Jess doesn't know where to put her anger or embarrassment at being so publicly dismissed. Having spent most of her adult life being attuned to side-eye in more homophobic towns and cities where people might judge her for looking gay, it has been a long time since she's been judged because she is a woman. The interaction with Tony has straightened her spine; she's more determined than ever to prove her worth in the face of his attitude.

Jess stands in front of the makeshift seating plan and Jess makes a point of taking longer than she needs to spot her numbered chair. Weaving her way through a dozen tables to find hers, she does her best to look as though she knows where she's going. Once at her table, she takes stock. It's obvious who the other ETAs are, regardless of whether they're in costume yet or not. They swagger, with their small entourages clucking behind them, carrying bags, looking busy.

Jess usually feels at home amongst other performers: the push and pull of mutual praise, the mock self-deprecation, how to gloss over a duff review. But these guys are different. They're not luvvies, there's no air-kissing, no braying. They're not theatrical; their one outlet for costumes and microphones is in spaces like this. They're grafters. These events loom large in their calendars, on Facebook groups for months, stirring up the rivalry, making plans. Being Elvis for them is an act of respect and reverence, a heartfelt tribute. They are, she thinks, like her dad, and he would have loved to have been here. They are his people, and she's suddenly wondering what it will take to make them hers.

Around her, people catch up with old friends, discuss tactics, and lay down friendly predictions, marking their territories with recently purchased Elvis merchandise, pints, and large sharing-bags of crisps. But there is an undertone of something less warm pervading the air of jollity, and Jess is unsure what it is or why.

The lights dim, and the emcee tries to settle the audience, many still milling about finding their seats, in a chorus of 'Viva Las Vegas,' but the response is lacklustre. He introduces Tony, who says a few short words and reminds everyone that the first official heat is later that evening. More whoops as the first showcase act takes to the stage, but once the performance starts, Jess only detects muted enjoyment from the back of the heads of bobbing permed hair. She had expected more cheering. A few shoulders twitch, or a small group of women get up and dance and then sit down again as swiftly, chided by others.

As her feelings of unnamed discomfort grow, Jess is grateful that her heat isn't until the next day. Is she unsettled because she's here on her own and everyone else has an entourage? Because she's a woman in what appears to be a man's world? Whatever it is, it's not a lack of confidence in her skill; she knows she's good. It hasn't occurred to her that she would feel so othered here, in a space where her gender alone seems to cause consternation, never mind her sexuality. Suddenly, she realises that her assumptions – that she'll be amongst fans, compatriots, new friends – are entirely misplaced.

She feels an urge to message Sarah, to smooth her anxieties by finding humour in the ridiculousness of it all, the shabby hotel, the unwelcoming crowd. But fearful that her wife won't understand, instead will urge her to sack it off and come home or, worse, tell her she knew that would be what it was like. She takes a deep breath and messages Tiff instead. This is not something she's allowed herself to do since their night at Ruby's, but something about this environment so far from home (and Sarah), and being back in her Elvis element, creates a new sense of permission.

Hey you! You'll never guess where I am.

She waits, hoping that the grey ticks will turn blue, that she'll get a reply as quickly as she used to. They do.

Hey stranger! Thought you'd never get back in touch. How you doing?

Sorry about that. Awkward. Anyway, here I am.

There's a pause, and Jess wonders if Tiff will choose to pause the conversation or reply at all. But the blue ticks, and a reply quickly follow.

Go on then. You've got me curious now.

ElvisCon! Google it. It's mad tbh.

Crazy. I guess this is a chance for you to test a few theories? You doing okay?

Jess can't help feeling gratified that Tiff has remembered the depth of their conversation at Ruby's, despite what came at the end of it.

Thanks for remembering. Yeah. Lots to think about. How you doing?

Good. Also got career stuff on my mind. I'm excited.

Tell me more?

Maybe over a coffee or something? No funny business. Promise.

Jess is relieved that Tiff has been the first to acknowledge what happened between them and realises how much she's missed the fizz of new friendship.

You're on. Gotta go.

Nice to hear from you. Honest. And remember, you're the best King there is.

The sense that someone *is* invested and interested in her experience here, and is willing her on, gives Jess renewed purpose. Even if that person is not her wife.

After seeking respite from appraising eyes in her room, an hour or so later, Jess heads back downstairs, where she can instantly see the mood has shifted. Women have gussied up, changed from jeans and hoodies to high heels and tight dresses, applied layers of make-up. Their husbands are in button-up shirts, pressed slacks, slicked-back hair. Jess hasn't anticipated a dressier evening; it's yet another misstep of the uninitiated.

The mood in the performance space has turned from the quiet appreciation of earlier to an audible frenzy. Reunited friends cluster, empty glasses, and bottles create messy centrepieces. She is on a table with nine others, but they barely acknowledge her, too busy gossiping. Two of the older women ask her to move her chair over a little further away from the table so they can make space to sit together. Her instinct is to refuse, she was here first, but she thinks better of it and scoots over. If they bother to thank her, it's inaudible.

The compere bounces on stage, now in a shiny suit, hair quiffed, forehead glistening. He waves to the judges, sitting motionless around a central table; they smile, turn to acknowledge the crowd, then turn back to their scorecards. He explains that each ETA has pre-selected two songs that they'll perform back-to-back, the judges will score them, their cards collected straight after each heat. The scale of audience enthusiasm will make a difference. The more whooping and hollering they deliver, the better.

Jess has her first opportunity to size up the competition. With six Elvises per heat, the other five loiter in the darker recesses beside the tech desk. Some swig from water bottles; others bounce on their toes, wheel their arms behind them. Some chubby blokes have forced their bellies into white jumpsuits, accessorised with belts, the capes, jewel-encrusted rings wedged onto their fingers. Latter-day Elvises quickly break a shiny sweat, and Jess can see that each swivel and thrust is causing them pain, but for their five minutes, they'll ignore it. They'd be laughing stock in any other environment for trying something they can't quite carry off. But here amongst fans, any weakness is forgiven. They're performing with younger men whose voices are still good enough to carry the high notes and whose hips have more sway. These are average guys who would command gigs as wedding singers in tribute bands, a bit of Johnny Cash to make a little extra on the side.

The crowd seems to have their favourite ETAs pegged before they've performed, even walked on stage. Table by table, the audience stands up and cheers according to who is up next. Women nudge each other, smile, dance. If the judges are marking on enthusiasm alone, the winner will be one of the youngest performers: mid-twenties, slim-hipped, dark-haired. He winks, leers and holds his hand out to older women near the front of the stage, sweeping along the front row. He comes off as smug and insincere to Jess's mind, a baby-faced pretender to the King's throne. His chutzpah hides his failure to hit the high notes and he sails off the stage to foot stomping.

The final performer of the heat is announced.

'This young man placed second last year, and he could be the one to beat this time around. Put your hands together for Mark Vegas.'

This guy looks the part. Jess is instantly convinced, and she sits up a little straighter. His walk, the way he plucks the microphone from the stand, the Southern drawl of his introduction. He gets no more applause than the others as he walks on the stage, and there's no entourage pacing in support, but he at once sounds and looks like the real deal. A rival, finally. The track he's chosen is a classic. 'Hound Dog' has no instrumental to guide him. He grabs the microphone and let's rip. His hips thrust; his knees move in time to the music. He stands on the tips of his toes and twists from side to side. His face and eyes capture the true spirit of the man they're bringing back from the dead, even if for a few minutes.

It's his second track that shows the breadth of his range. 'Always on My Mind' is one of the songs in Jess's show that creates a moment of silent awe in her audience, occasionally tears. Mark's performance is no less mesmeric, and once again, Jess is transported. The shabby room, the cheap tablecloths, the whispers of the crowd melt away. The spirit of her father sits beside her. She imagines his hand briefly patting hers on the table, a shared glance. Her own eyes fill with tears for what she has lost. A true Elvis in the building.

When he's done, Jess wants to stand up and whoop. Still, the applause following his act is surprisingly lukewarm. His lack of entourage clearly affects his fanbase volume. Unlike the others, swooped up and into the green room by their wives, mothers, or girlfriends, he picks up the pint he's left on the compere's table and slips back into the dark auditorium.

The heat is over, the house lights go up, and the audience is reminded to head to the Jungle Room for the first night party, but Jess can't face it. Older audience members stand up, pausing to unbend creaky knees and regain their balance before pushing off and out. These older fans are like her father – amplified because they've followed their passion out of their armchairs and the LPs into this competition territory. Short of visiting Graceland, this is as close as they can get to the real thing. But the 'real thing' in this room, in a shabby chain hotel off the M42, feels about as remote as the moon. Still, they love Elvis like her dad loved Elvis, and she wants, suddenly more than anything, to be loved by them. This is no longer a silly jape, a fool's errand. This is a competition that she wants to win.

CHLOË FOWLER

Chapter Thirteen
Tony's Cronies

Tony's cronies have evidently spread the word. Even while queuing to be assigned a table at breakfast the following day, people nudge each other, pointing her out. Jess is given a table in the raised area, away from the bigger spaces reserved for larger groups. The upside is privacy; the downside is that she must walk further than she'd like to get to the buffet. The same crowd she saw last night in their finery clearly think breakfast is for comfort eating, and dressing. Faced with sweaty tureens of eggs, soupy beans, and fat-crusted bacon, a yoghurt is all she can handle.

She slept badly. Every time she drifted off, people called their good-nights out to each other, slamming doors down the corridor. The Jungle Room party she'd avoided had clearly been a late one, and the contest timetable has kicked in. The hotel bubble involves days spent shrouded in either the darkness of the performance hall or the fluorescent public spaces. The difference between daytime and night-time is irrelevant in this micro-climate of music and booze.

She notices Mark Vegas, the guy who'd had nailed his round yesterday, hunched over his phone, stabbing at the screen. As she passes his table on the way back to her room for her final preparations, she takes the opportunity to talk to him, the first ETA she's spoken to since she's been here.

'Sorry to disturb you. I thought your performance last night was amazing. Blew the competition out of the water, in my opinion anyway.'

'Cheers.' He puts his phone face down on the table. 'Hard to gauge with this lot.' He waves his hand around the breakfast room. 'I'm guessing you're the famous woman who's daring to be Elvis?' he laughs.

'I had no idea it would be such an issue, to be honest. But I'm not backing out now.'

'Don't let them put you off. It's the judges that matter. I call them the wolfpack. You're fresh meat.'

'The judges or the other ETAs?'

'Not the judges. Not even the ETAs. We're just here to get on with it. It's the fans, they're the ones to steer clear of. They don't like strangers, so watch your back. I'm Mark, by the way,' he holds out his hand. 'Mark Vegas.'

She holds hers out in return. 'Jess. And thanks for the advice. See you out there.'

He purses his lips and mime's a wolf's howl.

Hers is the last heat of the day. After that, only the semi-finalists continue through the competition. Of course, there is no female green room, so Jess contorts herself in the tight cubicle in the lady's loo. Trying to avoid letting her trousers drag on the floor, she hears a few women talking as they wash their hands.

'I reckon Jonny Pelvis has got it in the bag this year, Jules,' says one voice.

'Could be right. Top form, that lad. He's going to go far,' says the other.

'You know what's coming next, don't you, Jules?'

'Seriously. Tony's spitting, and I'm not surprised. She's got some nerve. Apparently, they're going to change the rules to stop it from happening again.'

Jess thinks about hanging fire and hiding until they've left, but the minutes are ticking down, she needs to be lined up with the other guys in her heat and this is her first opportunity to bite back. The cubicle door creaks as she pushes it open. Her suit clings to her curves, and under the LEDs of the toilet, the gemstones glitter. Her quiff is perfect; unlike most blokes she's seen so far, it's dark and full, she doesn't have to wear a wig. As soon as she's in costume, her confidence returns. The swagger, the charm, it's all back, and it feels good.

'Right, better go and give Tony what he's been waiting for,' she says over her shoulder as she walks towards the door, then holds it open, forcing them to walk out ahead of her. 'Enjoy the show, ladies.'

In the green room, the Elvises in her heat are putting the finishing touches to their outfits. Limbering up their voices and bodies, lunging and jumping up and down to get their circulation going. She's used to be being stared at now, but the silence as she walks up to them is unnerving.

'Gents,' she nods at them. She tracks her eyes across all five, forcing them one by one to acknowledge her. A few nod, stay silent, look at their feet. One of the older Elvises steps forward. His suit strains at the waist and thighs; moisture pushes past the heavy layer of the foundation he's wearing. He holds his hand out to her. 'We're not saying we agree with this, but we're all gentleman here, aren't we? We'll fight fair. And may the best man win.'

One by one, they file out. Jess lets them all go and looks at the green room behind her; a battlefield of irons, ironing boards, mirrors, discarded sideburns, plastic bags, hairspray canisters. This one's for you, Dad, she thinks to herself. And for you too, buddy. She looks to the ceiling.

From her vantage point, the crowd is getting antsy. Four hundred fans have been cooped up for twenty-four hours already, only walking as far as they have to for food, drinks, and sleep. Only the smokers will have been outside. Conference fever is not doing her any favours.

Her slot is at the midpoint of the heat. Each time a new performer turn is announced, the other guys slap them on the back and wish them luck. They are passable, not excellent. None are a patch on Mark, and none she thinks, are a patch on her. Two more 'Hound Dogs,' a 'Blue Suede Shoes,' a shouty 'Viva Las Vegas.'

Mark Vegas is sitting at a table near the front. When they make eye contact for a second, he tips his pint at her and purses his lips in a wolf's howl again, mouths good luck. When she readies herself to run onto the stage, there is only a smattering of applause, though she hears whispering, shushing, some laughter. Everything about this moment feels different to her usual performances. This is not drag, it's impersonation. She adjusts the microphone stand, tries not to focus on the spittle from other ETAs. Too afraid of hecklers to say anything yet, she gestures that she's ready. She's been told to nod to the tech desk when she's all set, that they'll press play on the backing track.

Nothing.

She clears her throat and says 'track please' to the back of the room. The audience stays immobile and has now fallen silent. Still no music.

'Track, please,' she says again. She sees someone running from the tech desk to speak to the stage manager. He frantically beckons her over. She leans down to hear him.

'There's a problem with the music.' He's a little breathless. 'We queued it up in the break, but something's happened, it won't play.'

'Fuck's sake,' she whispers. 'You're joking, right?'

'I'm not, love. Get off the stage again, we'll get another guy up, and then you can go at the end, after the break.'

'No way. I'm here now. I'm doing this. Track or no track.'

She walks back into the centre of the stage. There are rumblings of dissatisfaction, people wondering what she's about to do. She closes her eyes. The room grows quiet again.

'Get off the stage,' she hears someone yell out from the back of the room, anonymous in the dark. Even in this environment, the vitriol is unexpected. But she hears other voices too. 'Just let her sing, mate, let her get it over with.'

She shuts her eyes, wraps her hands around the microphone, and starts singing 'If I Can Dream.' Her muscle memory kicks in, the knowledge of who she has to become. This is not a track for dancing, not even swaying. Her body is suspended between breaths. With no instrumental to guide her, her timing is slightly off. But she knows she has the tone and the pace to get going and that her confidence will build along with the track's crescendo when she asks why her dream can't come true. The questions seep out with all the power she can muster.

The silence in the room is no longer threatening, but she doesn't sense the tide has changed in her favour yet. As the next verse continues, she pushes her breath from the depth of her belly and increases her volume so she can hit the final notes. The trumpets and the backing singers are in her head, the drumbeats are propelling her towards the bridge. These songs are as familiar to this audience as the alphabet; they don't need the music to know the power suspended between walking, talking, thinking, and dreaming. Life and death.

They are with her now, willing her to hit those notes, knowing that she will. But as soon as the song is over, the fine thread connecting her, and the audience is severed. She does not get the wild applause she expects or deserves. A slight ripple, not an ovation. She summons the last of her energy to power her through the second track, her final chance to impress. This is the one that will show them that she isn't his voice; she is also his mouth, hips, knees.

Unlike 'If I Can Dream,' 'Let Yourself Go' isn't one that she can perform without the beat behind her. She nods at the back of the room again and hopes desperately that the tech desk has sorted out the music, that it wasn't just sabotage all along. The audience takes a collective intake of breath, waiting to see what will happen. The beat starts. The rhythm of this track is sexy and provocative. It defies the audience not to tap their feet and let their shoulders twitch. The track starts with a few handclaps that set the pace, and they slowly kick up to a faster pace as she prowls across the stage. Despite her nerves and the unforgiving audience, the beat carries her through. She's determined to teach them what love is about. She will stop them being afraid, make them relax. The words urge them to enjoy. She won't let them fight her any longer.

Some of the younger women at the front of the crowd stand up and dance along with the music. Her body relaxes more into the movements that she's practised and practised. She knows precisely where to wink, when to let her mouth curl, how to let her hips tilt forwards and backward. During the bridge, confidence gained, she struts across the stage to pay attention to the other side of the room. Seduces, as only she knows how. Men in the audience just sit at their tables, arms crossed, refusing to engage. Women smile and sing along, push to the front of the stage, show their appreciation by getting closer. She risks a peek at the judge's table, but they stay impassive, some looking at their scoresheets instead of her. Not even tapping their pens.

Despite the temporary thaw, once the lights go up and she passes the compere on the stairs, the applause subsides. Deflated, she leaves the room. As she brushes against the other Elvises in her heat, a few pat her on the back, grudgingly approve. The green room is empty. She puts her hands down on a nearby table, presses her palms in until her wrists hurt, willing all her anger, grief, frustration, and shame to pass through the wood, the metal legs and the floor. A man's voice.

'You showed them,' Mark says. 'Seriously, you nailed it. Can't believe they fucked up your track too.'

'I'm not easily beaten. You were right, tough crowd. So much for Elvis having buddies. Don't suppose you fancy a drink, do you?' she asks. 'Not sure I'm ready to go back in there yet.'

'First one's on me. What'll you have?' Mark asks. 'I'll bring them over.'

Dressed not unlike her, he's in Levi's, a checked shirt and Timberlands. A good-looking guy, in and out of his Elvis suit.

'That was nuts,' she says when they sit down. 'Wasn't sure how it would go. Can't help wondering if they stuffed up my track on purpose. Maybe I'm paranoid.'

'Fuck 'em.' Mark holds out his pint to chink against hers.

'You here alone? Most of the other guys seem to have come mob-handed.'

'Yeah. It's complicated.'

'I hear you.' Jess takes a swig and looks him in the eye. 'Complicated is… well, complicated.'

The sound of the backing track and an off-key version of 'An American Trilogy' filters through from the nearby corridor.

'Not sure I'd attempt this one with that voice,' Jess says.

'Or the face,' Mark laughs. 'He's one of the regulars. They love him whatever he does.'

Jess feels her satin jumpsuit slipping on the fabric as they lapse into silence, leaning back on the velour banquette. She stares at the carpet. Hoovering sticky glitter and fake gems out of carpets and wiping hairspray off mirrors must beat picking up dog shit during Crufts. But still, it's not exactly the Ritz.

'Well, you're the first fucker here who hasn't treated me like a weirdo, so cheers for that,' Jess laughs.

'Each to their own,' he says and sweeps his hands back over his quiff, a gesture that's so like her own that she instinctively mirrors it. His hair is naturally full, certainly fuller than others, but is thinning a little at his temples, and he'll have to wear a wig if he carries on performing.

'What's funny?' he asks.

'Nothing really. Just smiling. This is the best chat I've had in a few days. It's nice.' The banter, the change of perspective, makes her feel comfortable and relaxed.

'You heading to the Jungle Room later?' Mark asks her.

The after-party, named after Elvis's famous basement at Graceland. She'd stuck her head around the door earlier – a little beyond the performance area, rigged out with a small stage, cabaret seating, and cheap tropical props. A space for the ETAs to let their hair down, metaphorically of course, and a live band that takes requests (Elvis only, of course).

Mark is at the bar when the last heat finishes and people start filing in, stocking up on drinks before the Jungle Room opens. Two couples in their fifties have squeezed themselves into the banquette behind hers. The women are arm in arm, sitting next to each other, drunk and singing. One of them glances behind her, right at Jess, and then turns back.

'It's not right, Sharon. Is it? It's not right.' She is whispering, but it's loud, clearly loud enough to be overheard. 'I mean, he'd turn in his grave. Wouldn't he Shar, don't you think?'

'She wasn't half bad, though, was she?'

'But it's not right. It's messed me up. He was a man; the performers are meant to be men. It's not right.'

'They'll change the rules. I heard someone say that Tony said they'll change the rules. It won't happen again. She can't ruin it for everyone else.'

Appalled and embarrassed, Jess wants to retaliate and have it out with them. Instead, aware that she needs to look busy, she gets out her phone, not checked all evening. A message from Sarah.

How's it all going?

Yes, she told Sarah it was laughable, silly, embarrassing. But that was yesterday. She hasn't conveyed her own change of heart, how much this competition matters to her now, how much she's determined to prove everyone wrong. She changes her mind and sends the shortest message she can get away with.

All good.

If Sarah wanted to know the answer, she'd still be online, but the ticks stay resolutely grey.

CHLOË FOWLER

Chapter Fourteen
The Jungle Room

The air in the Jungle Room is chilly. Absent of bodies until now, the air-conditioning has been pumping out cold air, and goosebumps quickly form on exposed arms. The band troops in. The drummer, belly resting on his thighs, taps the snare idly and the lanky bass player twangs a few strings. They'd look like a low-budget wedding band in any other context, but the crowd treats them like rock stars, though they're yet to play a note. Territories are claimed, chairs re-arranged to create cliques. Jess and Mark find a corner of an unoccupied table at the back.

An eighty-or-so-year-old woman shuffles in on her walker. Her hair is neatly curled and coiffed, gold bangles chime on her wrist, heavy rings on her fingers, and when she speaks, her voice has the gravelly purr of a long-time smoker.

'Anyone sitting here, pet?'

Surprised that anyone is choosing to talk to her, so used now to being ignored, Jess says, 'Please,' and stands to help her from walker to chair.

'You were really giving it some welly up there earlier. I was impressed, for what it's worth. My name's Jean, by the way.'

'Pleasure to meet you, Jean. Jess.' Jean's hand is warm, and her grip firmer than Jess expects from this elderly woman. 'I take it you're a regular here, then?'

'Oh yes, pet. Me and my hubby have been coming for ten years now. We love this weekend, so much better than the one in Wales, better quality hotel, better quality food. And the ETAs are world-class. We met at a record shop back in the day, both buying the same record. Elvis, of course.'

'Shall I get another chair for him?'

'Oh no, love, you're alright. He died; God rest his soul. February last year, after the last competition. Heart attack it was. Sudden like. But I said to myself, 'Jean,' I said, 'he wouldn't have wanted you to stop having fun.' So, I thought if I could get myself here, I would. So here I am.'

'I'm sorry for your loss,' Jess says, 'that's really sad. I lost my dad too, last year. He was the biggest Elvis fan I ever met. He would've loved it here.'

'I'm sorry to hear that too. We fans have to stick together, it helps us all feel better. People are ever so friendly they are, aren't they?'

'Hmmm.' Jess is non-committal. She can see ETAs dotted amongst the crowd, ready to accept the touches and requests for selfies from fawning fans. Nobody yet has approached her, though she sees them looking. Jean notices too.

'Don't you worry about a thing, darling. You're fine. Is that your hubby, then? Quite the pair!' Jean nods at Mark, chatting to another of the ETAs near the table.

'Oh gosh, no!' Jess laughs.

'But you are married, love, aren't you? A lovely girl like you. He's a lucky one.'

'She's a lucky one, actually. But she's not here this weekend. I'm flying solo.'

'Oh, right you are then,' Jean says, unphased. 'That's nice. My niece is a lesbian, as it goes. Stella. She's got an ever so nice, what do you call it to be politically current and all that – partner.'

Jean pats the top of Jess's hand, resting on the white tablecloth in front of her.

'You stay happy, darlin'. Treasure every day. That's what me and Derek did. My treasure, he called me.'

'I will, Jean, I will.' Moved by Jean's comment, Jess sends a silent message to Sarah. A thank you, an apology, an 'I love you.'

Tony's back on stage. Flushed with the success, the crowd in the palm of his hands.

'Ladies and gentlemen,' he crows, and the drummer taps his snare a few times. 'Welcome tooooo, the Jungle Room! Are you ready to dance?'

The crowd yells back at him.

'I said, are you ready to dance?'

The crowd yells louder.

'And are you ready to hear more from our amazing ETAs again?'

Everyone is standing now.

'Then let's get this party started!'

Tony clearly fancies himself as a bit of an Elvis, but it's clear that whatever his skills are, it's not singing. The band starts to play 'Viva Las Vegas,' and he showily tilts his microphone to the audience so they can shout along with the chorus. This is the eleventh time Jess has heard the track that day, and the mood is what she imagines Las Vegas to be like – a city full of crazed, sleep-deprived wannabes. It's not a song she'll want to hear again.

After Tony has done his turn, several of the ETAs take to the stage. Knowing they're no longer being judged, officially, and buoyed by booze, many are better than they had been in their heats. There is a pecking order of popularity, and an unofficial relay is established. Every so often, one of the less popular ETAs or even a member of the general crowd pushes up to have a go, but when that happens, the atmosphere shifts from full party to a chance for others to go to the loo or the bar.

A few braver people even come up to their table and, using the excuse of talking to Jean, nod at Jess and say a few quiet words of encouragement. Not praise, but not as overtly dismissive or judgemental as before. The pints she's drunk are chipping away at her own reserve, and the next time Mark beckons to her to dance with him at the back of the room, she stands up.

'You alright on your own for a bit Jean?' she checks.

'You go for it, darling. Don't waste your night on an old bird like me. Give 'em hell.'

Mark goads her. 'Go on, mate, give it another shot. Get up there. They can't say no this time.'

'I dunno,' she laughs, 'don't want to push my luck.'

'What've you got to lose? Chicken. I dare you.'

'I'll think about it.'

When the current song is nearly over, Jess makes her way over to the keyboard player taking the requests. Elvis is with her now; her hips start twitching, her shoulders square up, the moment of physical transformation she needs before her voice will emerge.

The band starts playing. She's chosen 'Surrender.' The beat is fast, but there are a few bars of guitar and percussion to give her time to get poised. The atmosphere feels different from how it had done a few hours ago in the main space; she finally senses the adoration and frenzy that she's felt on stages before. But she can also see Tony and some of the A-List ETAs at the back of the room, standing in a line, arms crossed, turning their heads occasionally to mutter.

Pacing, making eye contact with the women in the front row as she sings about her heart on fire and curious desire, the vibe is entirely within her. Possessed, exhilarated, and for a moment, the happiest she has felt for months. Even more so than Edinburgh, certainly more than Soho, when the shadow of recent loss still hung heavy in her. Now, Elvis is beside her, within her. She can see the other guys, the lesser mortals, not measuring up. They can only dream.

'Surrender' is less than two minutes long, and when it's over, the women on the stage in front of her call her to perform another straight away, yelling for an encore. A few of her competitors stand by the side of the stage, awaiting their turn, keen for their own applause. But this moment feels so powerful that she's not prepared to give it up just yet. She knows the perfect song, how well she can deliver it in his perfect voice.

At the front of the stage, holding up her hands against the swell of the noise, she motions for quiet. This feeling of stillness, the poise, is what she'd expected to feel earlier when it was her heat. The moment that was taken from her by the casual rejection of Tony's team. Some judges are in the audience now, too, no longer marking their cards but keeping score. Turning away from the audience, nodding to the bass player, she holds her right arm up and clicks her fingers in time to the beat. Tilting her head a little, tapping her foot, waiting for her cue.

The slow beat of 'Fever' kicks in, and still, she waits to turn and face them, undulating ever so slightly. They cannot see it, but a slight smile, his smile, curves her lips. Controlling her breath so they can hear each intake, there is power in the stillness of this song, the song she's watched videos of Elvis performing hundreds of times. She knows that the merest twitch of her hips is what the audience is here for. For once, they don't need the tricks, the showy moves. She is perfect, and she knows it. The act she came here to perform, the beginning and not, she hopes, the end.

Women at the front of the stage hold their hands out to her, and she swipes them lightly as she leaves the stage and joins Mark at the back of the room, accepts air kisses and back slaps as she goes.

'That's more like it,' she grins as he offers her another shot. She tosses it back. She swipes the drips off her lips with the back of her hand.

By now, another Elvis is on stage hammering out 'A Little Less Conversation' (another track she won't want to hear for a while). She feels a tap on her back, and two women in high heels are standing there, swaying a little and holding on to one another.

'We think you're amazing, we do.'

'Thanks so much, ladies, appreciate that.'

They start pulling at her hands and encouraging her to dance. She lets herself be drawn into the crowd, quickly surrounded. The women who press against her now, touch her back and hold her hands, are not like the women she attracts at home. But they are real; their desire for her is honest and visceral. They have forgotten themselves, and flush with their lust, she has forgotten who she is, her Jess-ness. She is him. Slugs of white wine spill from their glasses. Jess is properly drunk now, lost somewhere between Elvis and real life.

'Ladies,' she starts pulling away from the crush. 'I'll be back.'

The Jungle Room is over-heating now; hot, writhing bodies are no match for the air con. She can feel the sweat on her chest and the backs of her thighs as she swaggers towards the loo. Two heavy-set men stand outside when she comes out again a few minutes later, not talking, waiting.

'Alright, lads?'

Their matching Elvis bomber jackets make them look like they're in Grease costumes, but as they close in, she can smell the beer and fags on their breath, and there is nothing funny about them. Cold air creeps up her neck, and her stomach flutters.

Placating them, holding up her hands. 'Everything alright?'

The larger man of the two takes a step towards her. Her back is already against the wall, so she can't step back to avoid him.

'We're trying to figure you out, is all.'

He takes his time, his eyes sweeping up and down. When this quiet menace has happened in the past – in a misjudged bar, a bus-stop, walking down the street – Jess has been quick to fight back, rather than flee. But here, dressed in a white satin suit, lights refracting off the gemstones, without an obvious exit, she holds her hands up to either side of her head.

'Calm down, lads, we're all good. It's just a bit of fun, a friendly competition, right?'

'Not sure the other ETAs would say that,' the smaller man says. 'They take this pretty seriously as it goes. We all do. You know, out of respect.'

'That's it, Dave,' the larger one says. 'Respect.' He doesn't turn to walk away but takes a few steps back, keeping eye contact. Jess swallows.

His mate joins him, and they start walking away. Just a few steps later, the smaller one turns back. Jess is so shocked that when the spit lands on her, she doesn't even think to react. A few seconds later, she goes back into the bathroom, grabs wedges of paper tools from the dispenser, and scrubs at her lapel. More towels under the tap, more water, more vigorous wiping. The moisture makes the white satin turn grey and the towels turn to mush.

She hears footsteps and goes into a stall, puts the loo seat down, and locks the door behind her. She lets her body go completely stiff, squeezes her eyes shut tight but looks up at the ceiling, willing herself not to cry. Her fists are clenched in her lap. She's not sure if she's angry, humiliated, shocked – probably all three. She can't stay in here forever.

Jess recognises one of the judges coming out of the stalls, heading to the basin next to hers. She's one of only two women on the panel. Dressed all in black, with patent flat-heeled boots to complete the look. Her hair is permed and silvery grey, assisted by a bottle but made to look naturally cool. Their eyes catch in the mirror.

'Think I caught the tail end of that. Are you alright?' she asks.

'I've had worse,' Jess turns to face her.

'Listen, love,' Liz says, checking again that they're alone in the Ladies. 'They're not ready for new. And I don't mean this to be rude. But these competitions aren't for you. You're pretty good, even Finals standard. When we see these men up there, we know they're not him. We know some are good, some are great, some are pretty lousy.' A wry smile. 'But they're as close to him as we'll get. They're keeping him alive, doing us all proud. I wanted to tell you because, well, you'll have felt the people in there cheering you on, maybe even changing their minds a bit. But tomorrow, when the scores come out, you might be disappointed.'

Liz's bracelets jangle as she swipes on some lipstick, tugs down her long silk shirt, and adjusts her wrap. 'I probably shouldn't have said anything. Just don't stop performing. You're good. But you can't win.'

Mark is waiting outside for her, pacing, worried. 'You've been gone ages. Mate, you okay?'

'I'm fine, just fine. Maybe I realised that my Elvis has left the building.' She tries a smile but unwanted tears form. She sniffs and shakes her head, wishing them away.

'One for the road?' Mark asks, his voice slurry. 'Just one more, go on.'

'I don't think so, mate. That's it for me. But thanks.'

Back upstairs, Jess turns the shower on, peels off her costume, lets it crumple to the floor and then kicks it into the corner. She can't wear it again. All the good luck it once brought her is gone now. She'll have to buy another. More expensive, more gems, more golden. As the water melts her quiff and the water muddies from her foundation in the white plastic tray of this cheap shower, she wonders how she'll kill time before her train tomorrow. She knows she'll be avoiding the crowds downstairs. She has lost so much, and although she knows she can't get her dad back, she isn't ready to let Elvis go. Not yet. Her ElvisCon may be over, but there is still a dream alive, and it's worth fighting for.

CHLOË FOWLER

Chapter Fifteen
Slow Dance

Jess puts her phone down on the sticky tray table in front of her seat and settles back as the hoardings of Birmingham International Station recede. It vibrates, and she picks it up again.

Of course. I'm here. Come anytime. Will cheer you up. xx

The refreshment trolley looms into view. A spotty youth swivels his head left and right, asking whether anyone wants anything.

'A tea, a Coke, and a packet of Wheat Crunchies, please.' She hands over the cash and winces as the hot paper cup is handed over, along with a floppy plastic stirrer, milk and sugar. As the tea cools, she sips the Coke, waiting for the sugar to hit her system. The bacon-flavoured crisps are the best cure for a hangover she knows. She quickly finishes the small bag and wishes she'd asked for two.

At Euston, Jess trails her small suitcase behind her and heads straight down to the Tube, so anxious to reach her destination that she barely bothers to stop it wheeling over other people's feet. Heading south, nine stops on the Northern line, heading away from town, the carriage is empty. Street-level at Kennington, her phone guides her through the unfamiliar area. She keeps returning it to her pocket because she doesn't feel entirely safe. The bric-a-brac stores (or tat shops as Sarah would call them) are heaving, and she skirts crowds of people who've stopped to chat near the litter bins outside McDonald's.

Finally, she stands near the pin she dropped on the map. Having navigated through the maze of towers to find Acacia block, she reads the instructions for the keypad. 'Seventh floor,' a tinny voice calls out and then a buzz. She tugs and then shoulders the heavy metal door.

Tiff is standing by her front door. Smiling, the first friendly face after a morning of strangers.

'You made it, I'm so pleased. Come in.'

The flat smells of clean laundry, a space of pales and pinks, the occasional flash of neon. It's feminine but with enough edge not to be girly or counter to Jess's own taste, as is Tiff. Her boyfriend jeans sit low on her hips, held in place by a black leather belt studded with large silver rings. Under her pink cropped sweater is a thin, tight white t-shirt that shows off her abs. If she's wearing make-up, it's skilfully applied so she looks natural.

'It's small, but it's all mine. Journalist's salary.' Tiff shrugs her shoulders up with an apology.

'It's great. I love it. And thanks again for letting me come over.' Jess runs her hand through her hair, aware that it's not as carefully quiffed as it usually is and that there are dark rims around her eyes.

Tiff steps forward and interrupts her with a hug. There is no awkwardness, despite their kiss that drunken night all those months ago and not having seen each other since. In fact, Jess almost feels as though she's been here before. Right at home, shucking her shoes off at the door.

'Hey,' she asks, 'where's Colette?'

Tiff does a double-take.

'Wow, good memory. She'll be around here somewhere, she's a bit shy. Unlike her namesake. Give her time.' She heads into the galley kitchen and Jess rests against the wall, watching her rummage. 'Didn't know what you might fancy.'

This tiny space showcases Tiff's style – a matching Smeg toaster and kettle, Orla Kiely caddies lined up along the wall. Tiff dips down to the under-the-counter fridge and comes back up with two brown bottles of craft lager tucked between her fingers.

'Beer?'

The last thing Jess wants is alcohol.

'Do you know what I'd really love?' she says. 'A mint tea. Sorry if that's a bit lame.'

'Of course, it's not lame. Do you want fresh, or a bag?'

'Oh my god, you're literally amazing. Fresh. Please. And can I use your…'

'Loo? Of course. Right down the hall. Can't miss it. There are only two doors.'

Studying herself in the mirror, Jess takes a moment to remind herself why she's here. The bathroom is spotless. Bottles are arranged with all the labels facing out – Jo Malone Pomegranate Noir, Bumble & Bumble hair products. No bath toys or slip mats. A home for adults only.

Resting her hands on either side of the sink, she stares in the mirror, splashes her face, and uses the water to smooth her hair back a little. She's conscious that she's in London, not in Birmingham, where Sarah will expect her to be. She hasn't told her that she's come home early, hasn't been sure what to say. Jess tells herself that she'll stay at Tiff's for a few hours and then surprise her wife and daughter with an early arrival. She'll have decompressed, be ready to walk in, all smiles and hugs. This is simply a pitstop.

When she comes back out, Tiff sits on the sofa and pats a cushion. When Jess sits down next to her, it feels small, and their knees touch. She wonders if she should move it away but doesn't want to be rude. Before she decides, a lumbering, fluffy cat ambles over from where she was hiding.

'Oi,' Tiff laughs, sensing why Jess is smiling. 'We're not all petite you know. She's very sensitive.'

Colette jumps up and after a brief sniff, settles down on Jess's lap.

'I wasn't expecting that,' she says.

'She's not normally so forward.' Tiff leans forward and Colette tilts her head up for the kiss. Jess can smell Tiff's shampoo and it's a relief when she sits back. 'She must really like you. As does her mum.'

Tiff laughs her flirtatious comment off, dismissing it as quickly as it came and then changes her tone. 'Are you okay? Sounds like a rough few days. I'm really sorry. Want to hear all about it, whatever you're happy to share.'

Jess's instinct is to bat the question away like a kid when they first get home after school. But Tiff has welcomed her here, and despite herself, she's ready to talk, in fact, she needs to. Tiff is attentive, and Jess sits back more comfortably against the cushions. Tiff expresses shock, anger and laughs when it's appropriate, cajoles for more details. Tiff is perceptive too.

'But is it what you needed it to be?' she asks, and Jess pauses for breath before she answers, stares out of the window, strokes under Colette's chin. 'Maybe,' she says, 'maybe.'

She tries to verbalise her feelings; that she doesn't want their approval, not that group of small-minded, mostly untalented wannabes. That it's fired her up, even more, to explore Elvis in his own world, go to Memphis, and measure up alongside the true professionals.

'You should totally do that,' Tiff urges. 'You shouldn't let this stop you. Go. Just do it.'

'It's not that easy though, is it? Wife, kid.' Jess laughs then changes the subject and asks about Tiff's life, asks for stories, encourages gossip about the queer community. Tiff is a good storyteller, peppering her tales with observations that make them laugh. But it's not long before Tiff steers the conversation back to Jess.

'What's Sarah's take on all this?' she asks. Tiff will know that Jess hasn't shared her experience with Sarah yet, that in fact, she's in Tiff's flat in Kennington because she's not at home with her wife in Stokey. Or in Birmingham, where her wife still thinks she is. She wonders briefly what's behind Tiff's question and whether she's made a terrible mistake coming here.

'Communication isn't our strong point right now.'

'Oh.' Tiff's lips purse in sympathy. 'Wanna share? Safe space and all that?'

Jess's bones are tired. She's tired of constantly thinking and not talking, really to anyone, about what she is feeling.

'I might be ready for that beer now if it's still on offer.'

'You got it.' Tiff leaps up and comes back with a bottle, then tucks her feet under her thighs, props her head on her hand, and listens. She knows when to make an appreciative sound or one of surprise or empathy; she does not leap in with questions or try to compare Jess's experience with her own. She seems genuinely interested and invested in what Jess might have to say.

Jess does not tell all. She knows when to stop. She talks about work, her dad, Claudie. Doesn't bring up Sarah, the baby (or 'not baby'), her marriage, her sense of isolation. These are private anguishes and for her alone.

'It's not selfish to realise you want something different,' Tiff says. 'It's how you feel. It's good that you're honest about it.'

'Thanks for listening. Honestly, I'm sorry I've wanged on so long. You make it so easy.'

'I like hearing you talk,' Tiff's voice calls back from the kitchen where she's gone to make them both some food. 'To be honest, so many of my friends don't have much interesting to say, so it's great talking to someone with a bit going on.'

'Older, you mean?' Jess laughs.

'Maybe just wiser,' Tiff laughs back. 'Sounds as though you've got quite a lot to figure out.'

Jess knows this is when she should say no, that she should be heading home. Her mood has improved. She even feels happy. Hearing Tiff humming under her breath in the kitchen, the clink of plates and cutlery, she knows it's too late to leave right now.

Jess looks more closely around the room. The IKEA bookshelf full of novels that she's heard of but hasn't read, a fitness manual, travel guides. Matching photo frames show Tiff pressed against other women, tongues out, faces painted, rainbow flags in the background. The Pride shot that's the same as the one she used to take with Sarah, when the gang used to head into Soho once a year. There are holiday photos too, Tiff on the beach somewhere tropical, then somewhere that looks like Amsterdam. This woman is only a few years younger than Jess, but she feels a generation ago. The life she has is the one that Jess had too.

'Need a hand?' she calls out.

'You're alright,' comes back the reply. 'Though I'll sling you a bottle to open while I finish off. It's picky bits, really.' Tiff's arm snakes around the divider wall; Jess takes the bottle of white wine and opens it. Tiff comes back out with a tray of artfully arranged snacks. Olives, a bowl of hummus, vine leaves.

'Wow,' Jess says. 'Amazing.'

They drink the wine, topping up almost as soon as they're halfway down the glass. It's sloshing in her, mixing with dolma, and there's a faint sting of garlic in her cheeks.

'I can tell a lot about you from the things you have in here,' Jess nods at the room.

'Oh, like what?' Tiff laughs.

'You read. Like proper books, interesting ones. You've got lots of friends, you have adventures. I spotted a few books about TV production too, are you thinking about that?'

'You remembered.' Tiff looks down at her lap. 'Yeah, I've been developing a few pitches. I think I'm really going to go for it.'

'You should.' Jess taps Tiff on the knee. 'I think you'd be great. Smart, committed, and like I've said before, amazing at digging until you get the truth.'

Tiff bobs up and down while they eat and drink, lighting candles when it gets dark, putting on CDs and reverting to Spotify, darting from track to track. Her cheeks are flushed; she does not pull her t-shirt down when it rises, showing more slivers of midriff. When Dolly Parton's 'Jolene' comes on, Tiff whoops, claps, and jumps off her chair to dance on the geometric rug. Jess wouldn't have guessed Tiff's taste to be so old-school. Tiff kicks the coffee table out of the way, smooths out the rug so she won't trip, and sings, her curly head framed against the twinkling lights of London.

Jess's shoulders start moving along with the music, and when Tiff holds her hands out, she allows herself to be easily pulled off the chair, and they dance together. They twirl, shimmy backward and forward, move closer to hurl the chorus at each other, and hold hands. A track by the Dixie Chicks comes on, and again, Jess is surprised.

'Didn't peg you for a country fan!'

'You kidding me? I know it's not cool, but I love it. If you offered me a beach in Thailand or a bar in Nashville right now, Nashville all the way. You?'

Sarah has put paid to Jess's love of Country. 'Such a lesbo cliché,' she'd groaned when Jess had tried to play some early k.d. lang. The pace slows when 'Heart's Content' by Brandi Carlile comes on.

'Wow,' Jess says. 'Finally, another fan!'

'Oh my god, she was on in Islington a few years ago. Literally blew my mind.'

'I was there too.'

'Really. Great night, right?'

Jess had been there. The gig was so close to home that she reckoned she could tempt Sarah to come, hoped the live experience would convert her. The audience had been full of more gay women than she'd seen in years. Sarah drank beer, joked about the burps, was affectionate, and even chatted idly to other women at the bar. But the support acts started late, and Brandi started even later. It was nearly 10pm before she even got on stage. By that time, Sarah was drunk, and her elation had turned to exhaustion. She didn't know the songs, the noise was too much; it was an unseated gig, so her personal space was constantly invaded by clusters of other drunk women.

'You can stay,' she said to Jess, 'but I'm done.' They'd waded through the crowds, pushed outside, and sat on the 73 bus home in silence.

Tonight, the beat slows, and so does time. The wine and lack of sleep, the catharsis of honest conversation, Tiff's dense perfume and her flushed cheeks, her tight skin, the central heating. After two days of rejection amongst strangers, the sense of being understood and the intimacy with a sexy woman is exciting. As the track draws to a close, Jess's chin is resting on Tiff's shoulder. Tiff tilts her head back, and they kiss.

As their lips meet, Jess starts pulling away. They're still holding hands, but suddenly awkward, Jess pulls away.

'Sorry,' they say in unison.

'I can't, Tiff…'

'No need.' Tiff waves her hand. 'Put it down to the power of Brandi. Maybe no more dancing for us.' She lunges for her wine glass.

'Good call,' Jess says, and they sit back down on the sofa, listen to the music, and don't look at each other.

Jess breaks the silence. 'Just for the record, though, thank you again.'

'And just for the record, I suggested you come here because I like you. You're a friend. You seemed like you needed a shoulder.'

'I like you too.' Jess lightly touches her wedding ring. 'I appreciate you listening to me. But I can't like you, not like *that*.'

'And I'm not here to break up a marriage either. I think you're really talented, and I don't like seeing you even thinking about compromising. That's it. Like I said before, I want you to be seen.'

They drink more wine, laugh, the danger of the last few moments passes.

An hour later, it's past 10pm, she's drunk, and it's too late for Jess to go home. The idea of a cheap London hotel occurs to her, but heading back out into the cold, leaving the cocoon of this flat, does not appeal. There's a danger in staying that edges into Jess's mind, but it's not a feeling she wants to lose.

'Listen,' says Tiff, as if she's read Jess's mind. 'Stay here tonight. I'm a night owl; I'll clear up and chill. You go sleep. And don't worry, I'll kip on the sofa.'

'Oh my god, I'm like the worst person. I turn up for mint tea and a whinge, and I end up with dinner, dancing and a bed for the night. You're amazing.'

'We're not talking about the dancing, remember?'

'Well, thank you. I'll get out of your hair early tomorrow. Good job, I've already got my toothbrush,' Jess says as Tiff hands her a clean towel.

Jess pushes the door shut, puts on her pyjamas, the musk of two nights' sleep and the antiseptic hotel still clinging to them, and gets into bed. She thinks back to the brief kiss from earlier. She already feels guilty about the second kiss, even though it ended shortly before it began. Somehow though, she doesn't feel worse than the first time and wonders if she should. She's been absent from her wife for a few days, but the emotional absence has been longer. Are they even trying? Sarah hasn't messaged her today, she hasn't asked how she's getting on.

In the face of Tiff's intense interest, how her own wife is treating her feels like neglect. Just when Jess needs her the most. Dimly aware of the sound of plates and glasses being washed up, a room being re-arranged, the murmur of late-night telly, she lies there, half awake and half asleep. Hoping and dreading.

Without needing to look, Jess knows Tiff is in the room. They both knew that the promise to sleep on the sofa was to keep Jess there and would never be a reality. Tiff's spicy perfume wafts closer, and the mattress shifts as Tiff gets in. After a few minutes, the silence between them is so complete that they can't hear each other breathe. Jess reaches an arm behind her, feeling out. In response, Tiff shuffles closer, spoons around Jess's back and thighs. An arm snakes over her waist. Jess is warm, dopey with drink, stirred by the feeling of this woman's skin, her smell, breath on her neck. She has not felt desire for someone, not like this, for a long time. Silencing the inner voice that tells her to stop, stop, stop before it's too late, she rolls over.

Jess leans over Tiff, feels their breasts touch, kisses her. Instantly, their tongues are inside each other. She tastes Tiff's toothpaste and is momentarily worried about her own sour breath. There are hands on her breasts, squeezing her nipples. Jess kneels, pinning Tiff's legs to the bed underneath her, gesturing for her to sit up enough so she can pull off her tee-shirt. Confident in her own body, Tiff lies back down, arms crossed above her head, a shadowy invitation in the dark.

'Hey,' Tiff whispers. 'Hey, you.'

'Shh.' Sweeping her tongue over Tiff's earlobe and down her neck and shoulder blades. Further down to her nipples, taking each one by one into her mouth until they're hard, folds and puckers against her tongue. Snakes further down, hearing Tiff's breath quicken, allowing her hands to trace this woman's firm, muscled body. Jess moves back up, kisses Tiff's mouth again, lies flat against her right side.

'You're soaking.'

Her left-hand slips inside Tiff's shorts, warm and wet against her hand.

'Get in, just get in,' Tiff breathes, pushing her head against the pillow.

Not long after, Jess feels Tiff coming underneath her hand. Even in the heat of this moment, she feels proud that she knows exactly how to do this right the first time. Tiff tightens and loosens until clenching completely. Jess's own muscles stiffen only when she is sure that Tiff has come.

'Fucking hell,' Tiff whispers.

Smiling in the dark, Jess stretches up and kisses Tiff again. 'Okay?' she asks.

'Don't think you need an answer to that.' Tiff pulls Jess's head down, so it rests on her shoulder. 'Just another of your talents.'

CHLOË FOWLER

Chapter Sixteen
Home

Hours later, Jess is on her own doorstep. A deep breath. Keys in hand, pulse-racing, she assumes they'll still be in bed, Claudie snuggling up with pre-breakfast weekend screen-time while Sarah drinks tea and reads. She's messaged that she'll be home early – telling Sarah that she's cut short her trip and caught an early morning train back from Birmingham. All this, of course, is a lie. Her red-rimmed eyes, if quizzed, will be blamed on the final night in a tiny single bed with a terrible mattress and three days of poor-quality hotel air.

Along with the lack of welcome, she expects the atmosphere to be awkward, marked by a chilly whiff of irritation that she's interrupted Sarah's Sunday plans. Instead, kicking off her boots, she hears scuffling.

'Shh.' Sarah's voice, a loud stage whisper. 'We don't want Mama to know we're here, do we?'

Thrown, but as her instinct to play along kicks in, Jess dumps her bags down with a theatrical clunk.

'It's awfully quiet in here. They must still be asleep. Lazybones! I better go and wake them up.'

'Surprise!' Claudie rushes out of the kitchen in a tiny curly-haired rugby tackle, plunging headfirst into Jess's thighs. Her arms wrap so tightly around her legs that she has to shuffle her way into the kitchen. Bending down to pick up her daughter with an, 'Oof, when did you get so heavy?' Jess kisses her face and ruffles her curls.

The house is fragrant with coffee, orange juice and freshly baked cake. She's the only place she wants to be, and yet, along with her bags, she's carried shame in with her like a foul odour. She wonders if her wife can smell betrayal. But Sarah kisses Jess on the cheek, her kindness making Jess feel even worse.

'We wanted it to be a surprise.' She swipes her hand towards the kitchen island, a wonky cake sitting proudly on the surface.

'I made it,' Claudie yells. 'I made the cake.'

'All by yourself?'

'All by myself!'

'Star Baker for you. Wow. It's amazing!'

Jess dutifully stands over the chocolate construction, cooing, pointing at the tumbling piles of Smarties and the words she can pick out, lined in Haribo. 'Welcome Home, Mama.'

'Can we have some NOW?' Claudie jumps up and down. 'We don't have to wait, do we Mummy? You said it was for when Mama came home, and she's home now. Please!'

'Gosh.' Jess rubs her tummy. 'It's very, very early for cake.' She takes an exaggerated look at her watch. 'How about you let me grab a quick shower and then we'll have some cake, and you can tell me all about what you've been doing. Deal?'

Claudie's face crumples into a conciliatory pout. 'Deal.'

'Now that,' says Sarah, complicit in this game of compromise, 'is a cracking idea. Mummy and Claudie can have a little piece of toast now and then by the time we're done, Mama will be back down and a lot less stinky, and then we'll have cake.'

'Oi!' Jess raises each arm to sniff her pits, an exaggerated waft of her hands. 'But now you say that... I'm DIS-GUST-ING!' She is rewarded by a giggle. 'I'll be back down really soon.'

In the brightness of the warmth she feels from her family, Jess almost forgets, for a second, the awful thing that she's done. She turns to Sarah, an adult-to-adult voice.

'That alright?'

Smiling, Sarah comes over and kisses Jess on the cheek again, and it's almost more kindness than she can bear.

'Take your time. It's nice to have you back. Can't wait to hear all about it.'

'Ugh,' Jess shrugs. 'It wasn't the best. Hope I haven't got in the way of any plans you had today. I know I'm back early.'

'Nothing planned at all. We're glad to have you home. Now, go.'

'Just got to do something first.' Jess goes to the drawer under the sink and reaches for the roll of bin bags. Sarah follows her back into the hallway.

'Hold it open for me?'

Jess passes a bag over, and Sarah fingers it open. Jess digs into her luggage and pulls out her crumpled and stained costume, jammed in carelessly, angrily. The jacket has shimmered and glistened at audiences in Edinburgh and London, embodied a King, but the stint in Birmingham was its last appearance.

'Blimey.' Sarah's eyes widen. 'That bad?'

'Pretty much.'

'But it cost you a fortune. You love that suit.'

'It's done its time.' Jess shoves her elbows deep into the black bag, pushing down and down.

'Oh,' Sarah says. 'I won't make you tell me now, but I want to know.' Jess sees that her wife's face has already changed from warm to excited. Her mind is already charging ahead, full of possibilities. Already wondering if Jess has given up her Elvis, perhaps for good. 'You sure you don't want me to keep it safe just in case?'

'I won't. So, no. Chuck it.'

Sarah follows Jess to the bottom of the stairs as she heads up for the shower, hand stroking the banister as if swiping for dust.

'Maybe let Claudie watch a naughty Sunday morning movie and talk in a bit?'

Jess listens for the steel, a glint of accusation that she's sniffed out the truth. But it's not there, there is only warmth, and it's winding her so much that she wants to be sick.

'Sounds good. I'll be down soon.'

She'd gone through all the scenarios on the Tube, swirling them around until she was so muddled that she can't remember what she decided. The truth? A half-truth? Flashes of Tiff slip unbidden into her thoughts, not just the feel of her body but her warmth too, the quickening breath that comes with being truly wanted. These thoughts are not okay, not remotely okay, and she squashes them down again.

A few hours earlier, Tiff had fallen asleep quickly, and as soon as she heard her breath change, Jess slipped out of bed and gathered up her clothes. She spent the rest of the night sitting upright on the sofa because even allowing herself to lie down would have felt too kind to herself. Adding insult to treachery. Watching for dawn, willing the hours to pass and also not to pass because sunrise would mean she'd have to face a new day.

The remnants of the central heating had eventually leaked away. Close to the chilly window, her left shoulder grew stiff and sore. She hadn't managed to find her socks in the pitch black of Tiff's bedroom and punished herself by keeping her feet on the floor, not allowing herself the warmth of tucking them under a blanket. Exhaustion, combined with thrill, remorse, arousal, and shame, muddled together as the minutes crawled forwards. She'd felt herself grow delirious with anxiety, had wanted to shout out but couldn't.

'Well, that was a surprise,' Tiff had said when she left, leaning casually against the lintel of the living room door, one naked foot resting on the other, her oversized tee shirt slipping off her left shoulder. 'It's still early. I could make coffee?'

Jess, allowing herself one moment of eye contact, pushed her hair up from her forehead, even in this moment too vain to allow it to lay flat.

'I should go, and I shouldn't have let things go so far.'

'Text me later, let me know you're alright.'

Jess had kissed her, chastely, on the cheek, and left. Wondered whether Tiff's forgiving goodbye might mask tenacious pursual in time. Speeding down the reeking stairs, tugging open the heavy front door of the building, blinking in the morning sunlight, Jess had felt a flash of anger. Smashing her suitcase against the paving stones, taking no care as she hurled it up the concrete stairs to the pavement, she wanted to blame Tiff for what happened.

But this isn't fair. She knows she has blurred her own lines, made her own wrong decisions, and feels as guilty about the texts, the conversations, the making of plans as she does about spending the night, or at least some of it, in another woman's bed. There is fault here, but it is not Tiff's alone. There is also connection, and it's become harder to ignore.

Safe in her own house now, Jess dismantles as much evidence of her trip as she can. Her clothes go straight in the washing basket, suitcase tucked back in the spare room cupboard, sponge bag stowed under the basin. Hot water, scalding even, pours over her in the shower. She accepts the sting and takes time soaping between her legs, neck, breasts, and any part of her that Tiff may have touched; hates herself for the cliché she is, the guilty shower scene from countless movies and TV shows. Surely, Sarah will take this is as a sign of transgression. She will smell a rat.

Jess is aware that she has now joined the serried ranks of the unfaithful, the legions of people who must scrub away their infidelities, compartmentalise their communications, make excuses. She has worked so hard to rise above her normal, predictable upbringing but now, she is like all the other bored housewives who've strayed. A cliché.

The bedroom was a place of sanctuary, a space she could have mapped every inch of in her sleep. Now, she feels like a stranger within it, each memory tarnished. Sarah has changed the sheets to prepare for Jess's return and put fresh flowers above the Victorian fireplace. The dresser, discovered at a Cotswolds antique fair, sanded down and spruced up one weekend with Annie Sloan chalk paint. The bright ceramic knobs drilled into the wall for Sarah's jewellery, scavenged at a Saturday market in France before Claudie was born and when mini-breaks were still a thing.

Tips of wet hair drip onto Jess's shoulders. Patting the bedcovers for her phone, she realises she's left it downstairs. Damn. There are messages she wants to delete. Pulling on newly-washed jeans, combing hair back from her face and buttoning up her shirt, Jess knows, with absolute clarity, that she will not tell Sarah the truth, not now.

Seeing her daughter again, her beautiful, innocent, warm, funny daughter, has reminded her of everything she has. Love, a marriage, a home, a child. Jess is still not sure she wants another baby, but she doesn't want to lose the one she has. Horror and exhaustion press in on her until she knows the only way to stamp it out is to offer something, do something, that will make another person so happy it will eclipse the shame. Her reasons for demurring any further are no longer good enough. Not worthy of hacking away at the rift that has grown between them until it's threatening to pull them apart completely. She's held on to the power of this decision for long enough, it's grown too heavy, she doesn't want it anymore. It's in her gift to make her wife happy, and the only thing she can do now is make it all okay.

Back downstairs, Sarah has poured water into the cafetiere and pushes the plunger down, brown liquid and grounds threatening to spill over the glass rim.

'Watch it.' Jess attempts jocularity. 'Bit too keen there.'

'Now, now,' Sarah says. 'If you want some, be nice.' Smiling, she pours the coffee and pushes a mug over to her wife.

'Claudie?' Jess asks.

'*Frozen*. Again.'

'Let it go, let it go,' Jess croons.

'Ha ha.' Sarah sits down at the kitchen table. Her face is open, warm, sincere.

Jess joins her.

'You first.' Sarah says.

Jess takes a deep breath.

She smiles and looks Sarah straight in the eyes for the first time since she's got home. 'So, I've been thinking...'

Even before she can say the actual words, Sarah is grinning, standing up, clapping her hands. From the other side of the kitchen, Jess's phone pings. Once, twice, and then again, a succession of messages typed and sent quickly.

Standing, bouncing with excitement, Sarah pulls Jess into her arms.

Jess says the only thing she can.

'I'm sorry, Sar. I'm sorry it's taken me so long. Let's do this. Let's have a baby.'

Part Four
The Band Plays On

CHLOË FOWLER

Chapter Seventeen
Hyde Park

The London sun is not yet at summer strength, but it's warm enough to draw crowds. Skirting clumps of tourists who are sprawled on their jackets and dodging office workers with their M&S bags of lunch, Jess spots a vacant bench. She's purposefully given herself time to be soothed by nature, a final chance to get her head in gear.

She used to meet Sarah at this Hyde Park pond, not at this exact spot, but on the other side, closer to Sarah's old office in Mayfair. Jess would bring the picnic, selecting quiches and artisan salads to please her soon-to-be wife, avoiding onion or garlic before Sarah's afternoon meetings. Basking and nibbling, Sarah would talk about her work. Jess, hearing about a professional life so different from her own, would encourage, laugh, and placate. She'd loved that wicker basket – leather handle, pre-loaded with pastel tubs and elastic straps to keep the dinky salt and pepper shakers in place. It's now stowed deep in the loft.

There is a unique pleasure in an inner-city park, surrounded by nature and London landmarks looming in the distance. Jess watches ducks cruise the pond, dog-walkers tensing their arms against straining leashes. The hum of traffic in the background, the occasional flash of a red bus through the trees. How nice it is, Jess thinks, that there is so much green in the middle of this city. A park flanked by exclusive addresses, luxury hotels, and shops she'd need to dress up to go into. Sarah's stomping ground. In their early days, she'd been dazzled by the ease Sarah showed swooping into Harrods or Harvey Nicks – a loyal and regular customer. Sufficiently well-bred to nod her thanks to the doormen, not common enough to say an actual thank you.

As Jess had hoped, when she dropped Tiff's name casually into the conversation, Sarah's forehead creased as she tried to remember who she was. Jess had prompted her, 'You know, the journalist from *LEXI* that I did that interview with last year. We've kept in touch on and off. She says she's got an opportunity to talk to me about – would be daft not to hear more.' Sarah had nodded and said she hoped Jess had a good meeting. Jess had decided not to mention that it was less of a meeting and more lunch at the swanky restaurant in the park. It's a relief that Tiff means absolutely nothing to her wife; there is no cause for anxiety, and Jess is safe.

Though safe is not quite the right word. Every time Tiff's name pops up on her phone, her heart booms, and her stomach lurches. Jess tries not to think back to 'that night,' not because she's ashamed (though she is) but because the flush that comes with remembering the connection she has with her, the ease she can talk to her, her hair, her skin. Despite knowing that the safer course of action would be to delete her number and cut off all contact, they have exchanged messages now and again. Jess has not told her to stop. In fact, the initial booming and lurching of fear have been replaced by a thrill when she sees her name. She's ashamed by how flattered she is by the attention, lapping up compliments like a cat drawn back to its own sick. She wants to ask Tiff so many questions, wants to know everything about her but has to limit herself to the occasional question and be satisfied with that.

She knows, of course she knows, that everything about these exchanges is wrong and that if discovered, would need some explaining. There's nothing inherently illicit about their correspondence. Still, it's more intimate in tone than Sarah would expect between her wife and a journalist she met nearly a year ago and has merely 'kept in touch with'. Dedicating most of her time to her daughter, her wife, and planning for the insemination, this separate slice of thought is one she feels she can partition away from the rest. It's a rare treasure, something just for her. After each interaction, she instinctively locks her phone and turns off notifications, ignores the whiff of betrayal she feels.

Her phone pings. *On my way!*

Standing up, Jess shakes the cuffs of her jeans down her calves, pats her quiff to check it hasn't grown wispy in the light breeze and walks towards the cafe. There is a queue, and she's idly scrolling through Twitter when she feels a tap on her shoulder.

'Hey.' Tiff tilts upwards to kiss Jess's cheek. 'You got here first.'

'Wasn't sure how busy it would be.' Jess gestures towards the line ahead. 'I guess everyone had the same idea.'

'Should've met at Ruby's after all,' Tiff teases.

When Jess had finally agreed to meet, Tiff had suggested her Soho club again, where they'd be guaranteed a table on the rooftop terrace. Jess had offered the Serpentine Cafe instead, keen that they meet on equal territory. Queueing is awkward and not moving fast enough to cover anything other than meaningless, awkward small talk.

'So, how have you been?' Tiff asks. 'Busy?'

'You know, school runs, playdates. Same old.'

'So domestic!'

'Got any plans for the summer?' Jess asks.

'A weekend away with the girls in Mykonos. A week in New York. Nothing major. What about you guys?'

Thankfully, before Jess has to say they've only got a week booked in Cornwall, they're next to be seated. 'Inside or outside?' they're offered.

'Inside,' Jess says, but Tiff says, 'Outside, surely, in this weather?'

'Have a lovely lunch, ladies,' the host says as they're led to their table.

When the sun blazes out and glints against the glass walls, people bend into bags for their sunglasses. The bifold doors have been pushed back so that servers can get to tables without squeezing past each other. It's noisy, enough of the buzz that Jess had been hoping for but not so loud that they'll have to bellow. Their menu is titled 'Late Spring/Early Summer', with seasonal ingredients listed with wearying specificity.

'What are you having?' Jess asks, more out of habit than curiosity.

'Probably the salad,' Tiff says. Jess can't face the cliché of hearing herself ask which of the four salads listed she means. 'Or I quite fancy the gazpacho, but I fear for my dress.' Tiff looks at her lap, and despite herself, Jess's eyes track down too.

The last time she saw Tiff was in her flat. Just out of bed, she'd been wearing an oversized tee-shirt, her skin the pale cream of midwinter. Today, she's light caramel, as if she's already been on her quota of summer trips. Her dress reflects the trend – all puffed sleeves, tight bodice, cinched in waist.

'You look lovely,' Jess says. 'Summer suits you.'

'You're not so bad either,' Tiff says and corrects herself. 'Sorry, strictly business. No more compliments, I promise.'

When the server comes to take their order, they start with drinks. Jess asks for sparkling water, but Tiff says she'll have a spritzer. The sun is shining, and she's out for lunch with a friend; why not? The server turns back to Jess.

'Go on then, a Peroni.'

Conversation skirts and darts when their food arrives. Any intimate details about their personal lives are glossed over. Instead, they talk about what they're watching on TV, the weather. First drinks turn into another round. Jess asks about Tiff's work and hears that she's got something exciting to talk about but will wait until after lunch.

'Tease!' Jess laughs. 'But I'm really glad things are working out for you.'

'And you,' Tiff asks, turning a touch serious, 'how are you feeling about work?'

Yet again, Tiff has asked the right question at the right time. Since ElvisCon, Jess has found it harder and harder to get back into the zone. Usually, she'd have her venue in Edinburgh booked, a few one-off gigs set up here and there, but she hasn't sought them out, pretending (at least to Sarah and partly to herself) that this part of her life is over. Another punishment, the source of which is sitting, smiling, in front of her right now. She shares some of this with Tiff but omits to mention anything about Sarah or the possibility of a new baby.

'Wow, so you're thinking of hanging up the rhinestone jumpsuit for real this time? How are you feeling about that?'

'I don't know. I think I feel sad, but also as though he's letting myself go.'

'Maybe Elvis and your dad are telling you to move on,' Tiff says. 'But I bet neither of them want you to quit performing. But you don't need Elvis, you know that. You've got so much else going for you.'

'You don't know that,' Jess says.

'True. But it's a good guess.'

Jess does not know who she is without 'him', a part of her life for so long that she can't remember whether she has any other talents left. Losing Elvis would be another level of heartache. Without him, she is nothing but a mother, a wife, a daughter. And for all the love she feels for them, it does not feel like enough. There is a piece of her still missing, and she senses that she won't feel whole, or settled, until it is found.

Messaging is one thing, meeting is another. She can feel herself slipping into the easy familiarity of conversation with Tiff and fears how she'll pull back again. Suddenly keen to leave, she wonders why she thought it would be a good idea to come. Placing the menu face down on the table, she says she won't have a dessert and should head home. But Tiff pushes her into sharing a panna cotta. They're back on safer ground with sun and alcohol relaxing her bones by the time it arrives. Fifteen more minutes won't hurt.

Their spoons clash over the creamy dessert.

'Finders keepers,' Tiff laughs, a throwback to something Jess had once said to her. Nudging the final mouthful with her finger, she licks it, and smiles. 'I didn't get you here under false pretences,' she says. 'I wanted to run something by you. You can say no straight away, obviously, but hear me out.'

'Sounds ominous.'

'Don't panic,' she laughs. 'It's nothing bad. The opposite, really.'

Tiff takes a breath, a swig of her drink, eking out this moment. 'I think I mentioned my friend Jak to you before. They're the real deal, you know? They're one of those people you meet, and you know they're really going somewhere. The first non-binary director who's made it onto mainstream TV. Really impressive.'

Tiff explains that she got to know Jak after interviewing them for *LEXI*'s Top 100 Influential LGBTQ+ list, and then tells her the little she knows about the show.

'It's set in Shropshire. It's called *Hefted*, and it's basically a drama about two sisters, one gay and one straight, who run the local pub which burns down, and they have to figure out who did it. Think *A Star is Born* meets *Happy Valley*. So anyway, they've got a problem. The actor playing the gay sister, you can see where I'm going here, is also a country singer, and she's been diagnosed with vocal polyps, so she's had to pull out. I started joining some dots. Remembered how great you sang along with Brandi. Singer, gay, country music.' She smiles. 'Born to act and hot to boot. I thought of you.'

'Holy shit.' Jess sits back in her chair. 'I literally had no idea where you were going with this. Wow. Sorry.'

'I've told them all about you. They want to meet up. I think they're pretty serious. And honestly, it would help me out too. I really think I can get into producing and this could be a great way in for me.'

Tiff says she's already sent links to the snippets of Jess performing that she's found on YouTube, some so ancient that Jess had forgotten they were there.

'Stalking you, sorry!' Tiff laughs.

Despite her anxieties about her future, acting, especially in anything as high-profile and difficult to break into as TV, is something she's pushed to the back of her mind. She's assumed her only options would be to get an office job, maybe retrain as a teacher. Something she'd hate. Sarah has never encouraged her to audition or devise new work. Jess has never asked her opinion, worried that the answer would be hurtful.

Beaming at her from across the table, her voice loud with excitement, Tiff seems serious about this opportunity. It's too specific to have been made upon the pretext of getting Jess to have lunch. It feels real.

'Christ. I mean, wow, again. I need to think,' Jess says finally. 'It's not that I'm not grateful. I need to think. Is there a catch? There must be.'

'No catch. Not unless you've got something going on I don't know about. The shoot is in a few months, you said you didn't have any shows lined up. So why not give the audition a go at least?' Tiff shrugs. 'The first step would be a meeting. But having bigged you up so much, they're chomping at the bit. If it's a no-go, they're kinda back to the drawing board. Honestly, it could be exactly what you need. A change of direction, but still using your voice, your talent. A dream opportunity.'

The bill arrives, but before Jess can fish in her own pocket, Tiff is already digging her purse out of her bag. 'Let me,' she says, 'and if this show makes you rich and famous, you can return the favour.'

'Look,' Jess says, 'I'm serious. I'll think about it. And I really appreciate you thinking of me. Especially, you know, considering.'

'Considering what? That you ran out on me? Left me high and dry?' Tiff, leaning forward, puts her hand on Jess's arm, but she's smiling.

'I'm so sorry, Tiff, I really am.'

'Hey, I was only teasing. This isn't about us, I know that's not a thing. But actually, Jess, I really believe in you. Something in your show got me.' She puts a fist against her chest. 'I don't know why, but I figure that if I can help you, I will. You're too good to have your talent wasted.'

'I don't know what to say,' Jess replies. 'I guess you're like a guardian angel or something. I'll make it up to you one day. I'd love to hear some of your show ideas, you never know, maybe I can help you back.'

'I'd love that.'

When it's time to go, they meander across the grass towards Park Lane. When Tiff teeters on her wedged sandals, Jess steadies her. As soon as Tiff is upright again, Jess steps further away and steers them towards the safety of the tarmac path.

'Shame you can't stay for more of the sunshine,' Tiff gestures towards the groups of office workers who have skipped out of work early, lunches replaced with cans of pre-mixed cocktails.

They draw near the main road and hug briefly, kiss on the cheek, the arms of their sunglasses clashing.

'Call me, yeah?' Tiff asks.

Jess watches Tiff walk off. An afternoon with an attractive friend, warm from a few drinks, reassured that their night together has been (mostly) safely stowed away. Tiff is clearly on to better things, perhaps even a new girlfriend she hasn't mentioned; there's nothing to worry about. An opportunity in the offing, one that probably won't happen, but is worth pursuing.

Fuck it, she thinks.

'Oi, T!' she calls out. Tiff turns around, grinning. 'Tell them yes, tell them I'll audition. Let's do this. I'm excited.'

'You're on. You won't regret it. Just remember, if you get it, dinner's on you.'

As the bus ferries Jess home, she smiles so much it hurts.

CHLOË FOWLER

Chapter Eighteen
Landslide

Jess checks her phone, forgetting that there will be no good luck message from her wife. She knows she should have told Sarah about her audition straight away. Should have billed it as a vague opportunity that will probably come to nothing. But it seemed sensible to wait until she knew the outcome rather than start a conversation that might not be necessary after all. As far as Sarah is concerned, with no show in the offing and the costume ditched, if Jess is thinking about employment, it should be a steady one, with an income.

At the table in the artisan coffee shop around the corner from the meeting, Tiff fishes through a mustard yellow satchel for her lipstick. She repeats everything she knows again; her nerves seemingly match Jess's own. Her knowledge of the industry is impressive and Jess can tell that there is a stake in this for Tiff too. An opportunity to dazzle by proxy, a chance to prove her usefulness to a well-known director is to be cherished. Jess's heart pounds as she sips her scalding tea too quickly; she worries how soon she'll need the loo.

'Come on, let's get you there.'

Tiff, all in black, tugs the hem of her loose-fitting but flatteringly tailored silk jacket down. Jess, having taken Tiff's advice to look 'character adjacent', is in jeans and a short-sleeve shirt, the white of her singlet poking out above the two top buttons. Tiff leads the way, a short walk around the corner to the office.

'Thanks for coming with me.' Jess turns to Tiff as they approach the revolving doors. 'I really appreciate it. I know nothing is in the bag yet, but even being here feels good.'

'I'm glad. I don't know why I'm so excited for you. I just am. One last thing.' Tiff pauses to check her reflection in a shiny shop window, then turns back to Jess. 'Remember, you're amazing. Just be *you*. This is your chance to move beyond Elvis. You don't need him anymore. I'll be out here when you're done. Own it.'

Jess may not need Elvis within her anymore, but she makes a silent plea to the other man in her life. 'Be on my shoulder, Dad,' she thinks. 'I'm doing this for you.'

The introductions are swift. Jak's grip is firm. They have broad shoulders and spiky salt and pepper hair, eyes hovering between blue and grey. Jono, the casting agent, is the only man in the room, and he looks Jess up and down as he says hello. Then Paula, the writer of *Hefted*, scruffy and shapeless underneath baggy linen trousers and a linen shirt. Finally, the two producers. Jess immediately forgets which one is which.

This is a building designed to show off the people within it. Minimal furniture, a few discreet white gloss cabinets, a sleek trolley placed inside the door with bottles of expensive water and pale blue crystal glasses. The exterior window has a faint tint, so though the sunlight pours in from a soundproofed Soho beyond, nobody needs squint.

'Great that you could come so quickly, Jess.' Jono starts off. 'I think you know the situation. It's not her fault her voice has gone, but we really need this role to be played by someone who can really sing. The audience really has to believe in it. Jak, over to you.'

'Thanks, pal.' Jak leans forward and rests their right ankle on their left knee. 'Like Jono said, these things happen. For me, the voice matters, but it's the character too. We need someone who's been through some stuff, you know. Em has had a tough time. She's got grit as well as graft.'

'It's a great script,' Jess says. 'Hope I can do it justice.'

Jess was one of fifty women the last time she auditioned, over a decade ago, all lined up on chairs outside a bland rehearsal room in Acton. Called to the room one after another, handed a clipboard with a short chunk of text, told to read, and then ushered out as quickly as they filed in. Conscious of wanting to give off a relaxed vibe, to appear to be the natural choice, Jess sits back and settles her shoulders. Despite her nerves, being back in a space like this is thrilling, helping her feel sure that this is where she wants to be.

'So.' Jak leans forward again, holding Jess's gaze. 'Talk to me. Where do you see yourself in Em?'

'I don't know how much Tiff has told you about me. I'll assume not much. I read Em's character as someone who's lost something. Sure, she can sing. It's clearly the one thing she's sure of. But it's not enough. It hasn't stopped the pub from burning down, from having an enemy. Their livelihood's literally gone up in smoke. I lost my dad last year, so I have an inkling of what she's going through.'

'Sorry to hear that,' Jak interrupts.

'When he went, I lost more than just him. Same as Em. I know you've seen clips of *The Wonder of You*. I've been performing as a Queer Elvis for a few years now. It's been amazing. I love it. I've loved being him. But it's like him and my dad were the same, and now I feel like I've lost them both. I guess it's that loss that I felt when I read the script. It really touched me.'

'Thanks for sharing your truth with us,' Jak says. 'Grief's a bitch. And you're right, that's absolutely what we want to see with Em. There's light in the story too, but her character is one that really struggles. This is a story that needs to be told.'

'Just conscious of time,' Jono interrupts the conversation and turns to Jak. 'I've put a call into Michaela, she says she's downstairs.' He turns to Jess. 'We'll have you read together, and then it would be good to hear your voice, your singing voice, that is.'

'I'm ready.' Jess swallows.

'Nice one.' Jak checks their chunky, aviator-style watch. 'Let's do this.'

There's a jostle for position at the elevator as they try to cram into the same one and then realise, a little too late, that it will be an undignified squeeze.

'The execs are on their way.' Jono turns to Jak as the others fall back and allow them to take the first elevator with Jess.

'Divide and conquer,' Jak says. 'You do your job, and I'll do mine.'

Nobody speaks as the elevator continues down and down to the basement. Jono says he'll wait for the others, so Jak leads Jess through the maze of corridors. In contrast to the polished concrete of upstairs, the floors down here are carpeted; even the walls are clad in grey felt.

'Elvis, huh?' Jak says, setting a brisk pace. 'Used to listen to him with my dad. 'Blue Suede Shoes' and all that.'

'Left them at home today,' Jess says, gratified when Jak laughs.

'Known Tiff long?' Jak asks.

'Less than a year actually. We met in Edinburgh. She interviewed me. She's really smart, talented.'

'She's ambitious, that one. I'd love to find a way to work with her more. And I'll owe her one if this works out.'

So far, Jak hasn't asked Jess anything particularly personal, and Jess doesn't know if her wedding ring has been spotted. If Jak thinks she and Tiff are an item, they don't say.

After a few more turns left and right, Jak pushes in a code and opens the door to the studio. 'We'll get you set up, and then we'll be ready to go as soon as Michaela arrives.'

The studio is cold, and once the heavy doors are shut, sound proofed. A young guy, wearing the standard techie outfit of faded black jeans and a polo shirt, speaks into hanging microphones, and adjusts settings on cameras arranged at various angles. There's another sound guy through a glass panel at the back of the room, fiddling with levels on the mixing desk, and beyond him a bank of leather sofas and armchairs.

The door in the viewing room opens, and people from the meeting upstairs file in and are joined by an older woman in a scarlet pencil skirt and black heels, and a grey-haired man, muscles showing under his shirt. These are the network execs, redolent of money and power.

A faintly familiar, dark-haired woman bounces in. Rushing up to Jak, they kiss, and she gushes, 'Here I am, right on cue.'

Jess realises that Michaela is a well-known character actor from numerous TV dramas. Suddenly, this feels real, and so right.

As she digs the script out from her bag, Michaela switches from luvvie to professional. 'Where do you want me?'

'Reckon we'll dive straight in.' Jak hands Jess a thin section of the script. 'Jess, for your benefit, Michaela plays Siobhan, Em's sister. You'd be playing Em. They run a pub and times are tough. Think rural community and all the dramas that come with that, two women against the world. In this season, Siobhan has to tell Em that they're at risking of closing down and Em has to respond. I want to see desperation, but not panic. Anxiety, but also resilience. Just feel it out, let's see where we get to.'

Jess moves to the other chair and perches, hands on her knees. Jak walks to the back of the room, their boots noiseless on the carpeted floor. 'Just start when you're ready.'

Michaela turns. 'Break a leg,' she says quietly. 'You set the pace. I'll follow.'

A deep breath. Jess starts reading, feeling her way into the character through the first few lines of dialogue, remembering to flick her eyes up to Michaela every few words or so. Years of Claudie's bedtime stories have prepared her for skipping ahead a few words in her mind.

The dialogue flows, her tone quickly pushing forward with emotion, pulling back when she senses Michaela's turn. It's working; she's in the zone.

'This is great. Really great. Just try that line again.' Jak positions Jess's shoulders at an angle. 'Look to the left when you speak. I know we're not blocking the scene yet, but it might help to get the feel of it.'

Michaela's reading voice shifts from the slightly breathless, girly lilt that's her authentic voice (if it is) and switches into a deeper Midlands burr.

Jak paces and asks them to jump from one section of the script to the other, moving so fast that Jess stops worrying whether she's doing it right and follows the suggestions. Even without fully knowing the storyline, Jess already feels she's inhabiting the character, knowing instinctively what to bring and when.

'Great,' Jak says, nodding to the viewing room. 'Let's move on. Michaela, that's it for now. But stick around if you want.'

Jess automatically does the same as Michaela stands up, putting the script down on the chair behind her.

'Nice, you did great. I really felt that,' Michaela says.

'Thanks,' Jess replies. 'You made it feel natural.'

Jess isn't sure what happens next, so she stands, hands in her pockets, looking more composed than she feels.

'Reckon, we need you to do the easy bit now, well, easy for you anyway,' Jak asks. 'Ready to sing? Do you want any backing? I'm guessing you'll want some Elvis?'

They laugh.

This is the moment that Jess has been thinking about since the audition moved from thought to reality. She hasn't sung anything other than Elvis, in public, for years. Elvis is, or was, her shadow, her energy. Jess has felt disloyal prepping alternative tracks, as though she's turning her back on the men (she includes her father in this) who have given her everything. Betrayal is dogging her on all fronts. Jess blinks. She cannot go down this rabbit hole of personal agony, not here.

All she says is, 'Actually, I've prepped something else, if that's okay.'

Jess sees people moving about, chatting, drinking coffee, checking their phones in the viewing room. She feels like a voyeur but knows she is the one being scrutinised. Jak nods and leaves the room, and a few seconds later, Jess sees them join the others. Attempting to read their body language, Jess sees them shaking hands with the execs, pressing the Nespresso for a coffee.

Alone now in the airless, silent space, Jess grounds herself in the mountain pose, anchored, hands down by her sides. She takes a moment to imagine herself on a stage, lights warming her face, an audience beyond. She is not wearing a rhinestone jumpsuit and does not need to twist, bounce, wink, or curl her lip. Her final song on that awful stage in The Jungle Room at ElvisCon was her goodbye, and this is a hello. A rebirth.

She used to sing 'Landslide' by Fleetwood Mac to Claudie as a baby. The lyrics, burnt into her brain but unsung for years, carry her away, swaying, diving. She takes her love and destroys it. She climbs mountains and hills. At the point at which the track's tone shifts up a note, Jess looks up, gazing beyond the window into the room behind. There is no movement, but she wouldn't notice it even if there was. She tilts her head up a little, hums the bridge, and taps her thigh gently.

As she lets Elvis go, she opens the door to Em, her future. Whether this is freedom or a betrayal, hearing her voice swoop clear of the King allows Jess a moment of release. Tears course down her cheeks as she sings out sadness, apology, her confusion. There are thoughts of so many people muddling in her brain and it's impossible to truly separate what she feels about whom: Sarah, Claudie, Tiff, her mum, her dad, Elvis? Despite sensing she is on the cusp of something magical, she feels only loss.

Only when she's finished does she trust herself to look up at the viewing room properly, a silent movie. The Channel Four execs are smiling, Jak and Jono are high-fiving, and everyone is clapping. This is not the same applause that she's used to – not the stomping and whistling that crashes into her when she's on stage. But the euphoria feels the same, and she has to stop herself from taking a bow. Sarah's face swims through her mind, and then as quickly, it's gone. So many moments they've shared, but this is one she's experiencing on her own. Except she's not, because waiting for her outside is Tiff, the woman who has made all this happen and who she feels drawn to in ways that she can't ignore. And increasingly, isn't sure she wants to.

Jak comes up to the glass and beckons Jess to join them in the viewing studio. She is introduced to the execs, both offer vague compliments, but Jess knows that it is not their job to praise too heavily until contracts are offered and signed.

Eventually, she's ushered back up the long corridors. Jono says they'll be in touch.

'Assume you know the shoot is pretty soon?' he asks. 'September, straight after the summer break. No reason you won't be available, right?'

Jess wheels through the months in her mind, silently panicking about the timing. But it's fine. Sarah's insemination date, the final dose of hormones, the Ultrasound, assuming everything is on track, isn't until late October.

'Nope,' she says, 'nothing to worry about.' Nobody has asked her about her personal life, what commitments she might have. Her talent is the only thing that matters to them, and right now, exploring it is the only thing that matters to her too.

Back in reception, Jak holds out their hand.

'We'll call.' Jess is held in that gaze again. 'Soon.'

Alone, Jess grins. Fighting the urge to share her exhilaration with a whoop, she pushes through the revolving door with force, at last a chance to push out some energy.

Tiff, waiting by the door, rushes up.

'So?' she asks, grinning.

'Pretty good, I think. Actually, it was amazing.' Her shoulders relax, and she exhales.

'I'm literally buzzing for you. This could be it, Jess, this could be it. You must be stoked. So, what happens next?'

'I don't actually know,' Jess admits. 'I guess I wait.'

'Ugh, the waiting game. I reckon they've got to decide pretty fast.'

'I still can't believe that you did this for me. Ever since Edinburgh, you've, I dunno, changed everything.'

'Thank me later,' Tiff laughs, 'when you actually get the part.'

Jess instinctively checks her watch but doesn't register the time.

'How about I start now. Drink?' she says.

They walk around the corner and Jess stops suddenly when she feels her phone buzz. She pulls out her phone to read the message. She doesn't think about her wife or her daughter but about the group of people who need her. It's not Elvis they want. It's her. A rush of hot white adrenalin courses through her, and all the feelings of anxiety, grief, and disappointment evaporate.

'Tiff,' she says, putting her hands on Tiff's shoulders. 'Oh, my fucking god. It's from Jak. They say there's the legal stuff to sort out, but I've got the part.'

'Just like that?' Tiff laughs.

'Just like that. It's all thanks to you, Tiff. You did this. *You* did this.'

Jess can't name the feelings she has, but they're the opposite of the confused, anxious, and grief-stricken ones she felt while singing in the audition. Amongst it all, there is euphoria, the need to bounce, jump or run, just to move. She takes Tiff's hand and pulls her down the street.

'C'mon,' she tugs, 'let's celebrate.'

A few steps down the pavement she stops again, and Tiff looks up at her. In that moment, all Jess wants is to kiss her. She does.

Chapter Nineteen
The Music Box

Sarah doesn't have to tell Jess that she has a headache, because it's permanent. If it subsides briefly, instead it's the hot flushes, the joint pain. All symptoms of the hormones she's taken to boost her fertility chances when the time for the IUI comes. Sarah's first insemination and pregnancy with Claudie was a honeymoon in comparison, but she was younger then. Now, in her late thirties, everything seems so much harder. When Sarah got pregnant the first time, relatively easy after two attempts, Jess had spent hours with her ear pressed to her wife's belly, pretending to hear a tiny voice asking for food that would satisfy a craving. They'd laughed at Sarah's gassiness, the frequent trips to the loo, even the weight gain.

Despite having fought for this second baby for so long, Sarah is constantly moody now that the process has begun. Her hormones spread over the house like a virus from which neither Jess nor Claudie are immune. It doesn't matter if Jess has done the chores that are 'suggested' to her, if Sarah's had a productive day at work or if Claudie has been good as gold. Jess hasn't mentioned *Hefted*, putting off the one reason that would give her wife a genuine reason for fury. But with the shoot in just a few weeks, she is running out of time.

'I'm not an invalid,' Sarah complains as Jess opens the passenger door, to set off for a long-planned weekend in Brighton.

'I didn't think you were,' Jess bites back. 'I was just being helpful.'

Sarah's parents are waiting by their front door when they pull up. Claudie pauses only briefly to wave before rushing inside as if she's relieved to escape the tension between her mothers.

Back in the car, no longer needing to play happy families for Claudie's sake, they only speak occasionally, exchanging testy opinions on which route they should take, whether they stop for petrol now or on the way home, if it's too hot or cold.

This is how it is at home too. Within their four walls, they split apart: orbit without touching. When Jess offers comfort, small gestures to show that she's noticed, she cares, Sarah flinches. Her wife has made no secret of how repulsed she is by her own body – the blotchiness, the moisture, the hot flushes that creep up on her and push beads of sweat onto her forehead. Jess can't win. If she asks, trying to be kind, if Sarah is hot and if there's anything she can do, Sarah is irritated. But if she appears not to notice, Sarah will flap her clothes around her body and huff, almost daring Jess to comment.

Sarah eventually breaks the frosty silence after twenty miles have passed. 'You seem preoccupied. Are you OK?'

This happens too, a moment when Sarah realises how vile she is being, when she tries to make amends with a question, a kind remark. A brief respite from the sulk. Jess senses an opportunity that she must take. The unlikelihood of even getting the part had made not telling Sarah about the audition an easy decision. Then everything had happened so fast, pushed to sign contracts, another whirlwind.

Jess had been on the cusp of telling her several times, but as she'd been about to spill, the phone had rung, a client had emailed, or it was just the wrong time. Then she'd put it off because Sarah was off for a scan, or her blood pressure had gone up, and each time Jess had felt a better time was around the corner. With the decision so well and truly made and the excitement building up inside her, she is terrified that sharing the news will usher in a phalanx of recriminations and not, she is sure, unfettered congratulation. But she must do it. Now.

'So, what's up?' Sarah presses.

But as she's about to speak, Sarah puts her hands up to her forehead, massages her temples and groans. The moment of softness has disappeared as quickly as it arrived.

'Oh, nothing really,' Jess says. 'Just tired.'

'Aren't we all,' Sarah snaps.

'Would you rather not go?' Jess asks. 'Honestly, I won't mind,' though she will. 'Maybe you'd rather have a night in at home?'

'Another one? No thanks. I'm sure I'll perk up when I see them all. And we're on the way now. Silly to turn back.' Jess does not vocalise her irritation that Sarah will perk up when they're with their friends, that they'll get the best of her when Jess gets the worst.

The traffic is bad, so they decide to head straight to the restaurant. They've passed on the offer of a spare room and booked a room in a boutique hotel on the seafront. 'We can mooch around The Laines on Sunday,' Jess had said, wondering whether Sarah would feel up for it.

The last time they'd spent a romantic night together was so long ago. When Sarah had told Jess she wanted another baby. When Jess was given power over their future that she did not want to have. So much has changed since then. There is nothing in Jess that wants to make love, but intimacy would be a start.

They haven't seen the Brighton crowd in several months, and released from the tension in the car, Jess downs a half-pint too fast and then orders another.

'Playing catch up,' she says to Jude with a wink. Sarah settles down at the other end of the table, a bottle of sparkling water prominently in front of her, instantly looking more cheerful than she has the rest of the day. Or week.

The curry house is all floral wallpaper, dark wooden tables, and cheap paper napkins. Jess wonders if Sarah would prefer to be somewhere posher, somewhere she can socialise in more style. But watching Sarah relax amongst her friends, rare pinkness in her cheeks, the smile back in her eyes, Jess misses her, sad that she can relax around friends but not around Jess herself. She is laughing, telling stories, and showing photos of Claudie on her phone. Not for the first time, Jess sees that this decision to have another baby is Sarah's to celebrate alone when she's happy. Only when she is miserable, anxious, or feeling unwell does she fold Jess into the hurt, and all of it feels like blame rather than love.

Jude proposes a toast, and although Jess had suggested that it's too soon to share their 'news, not news' with the gang, she realises she's done exactly that. Sarah's excitement amongst friends is palpable and Jess sees how important their approval is. 'Steady on,' Sarah laughs, 'there's nothing to actually celebrate yet!'

'Big news,' says Jude. 'You're a bit quiet though, you okay?'

'Of course.' Jess scoops bright yellow daal onto naan and puts it in her mouth quickly so it doesn't drip. 'Sarah's doing really well.' She lowers her voice. 'But sometimes it's hard to know how to be supportive in a way that doesn't make her want to kill me. And I guess it means other decisions are all on hold. I'm trying not to be selfish.'

'I hear you.' Jude signals to the waiter for more beers. 'Lisa was a nightmare. But as soon as the baby's here, it's different. Be patient.' She changes the subject. 'Got any shows lined up? Haven't seen much on your socials recently.'

Jess longs to tell her friend the news, see her eyes open, and hear the praise and congratulations. But for now, she says, 'Nope, nothing booked. Focusing on the girls.'

It's a Saturday night, and Brighton's restaurants are packed. It's noisy, and hot. Everyone is shovelling food in anticipation of their late night. Dishes of curry, rotis and other sides get passed around. Caz gets out a long strip of tickets, pulls them apart at the perforated seams, tells everyone to take one and pass the stack along. There's a friendly squabble over the bill, a debate about whether everyone paid Caz back for the tickets and who in each couple will hand over a card. For a moment, Jess feels they could be in their twenties again, pulsating already with the energy of a night in a club, not getting home until dawn.

Jess is giddy with beer, salty, spicy food, and friendship. Noticing that Sarah has gone off to the loo, Jess is tempted to send Tiff a message, maybe even a selfie, to show her that she has nights out too, that she's not old and settled as she must seem. She wonders what Tiff's doing with her Saturday night and notices how much she hopes it isn't being with another woman. She gets her phone out but then puts it away without sending one. Pathetic, she thinks.

It's a short walk down towards the Music Box. They pass groups of women heading in the same direction, other gay women who've made the pilgrimage to see one of their own.

Sarah trails behind, and Jess slows down to walk beside her. Sarah fusses about whether the car will be safe parked up by the restaurant all evening, whether she should call the hotel and tell them that they won't be checking in until after the gig.

'Honestly, it's fine,' Jess reassures. 'Try to relax. It's lovely to be out with you. We should do it more often.'

Sarah reaches out for her hand. 'I'm sorry for being a grump. Mood swings. It is nice to be out. You're right.'

'Jude was telling me how amazing she thinks you look. And you do look good.'

'Ugh, I feel so fat. My head's really bad again. That curry's given me heartburn.' Sarah's mood shifts again. 'Why don't I go to the hotel, and you come later?'

'It won't be the same without you,' Jess cajoles. 'How about you give it an hour or so, and if you really hate it, I'll take you then. Just an hour? For old times' sake? For Brandi?'

'Fine,' says Sarah, speeding up as though getting there sooner will make the time pass more quickly. 'I'm sorry, you know I'm not great with live music.'

It's been a long time since Jess has been at a gig, let alone a standing-only one. She's forgotten what it feels like to be carried along with a pulsing crowd. During the day, the mint-green latticed windows of the venue reflect the pebble beach and the sea beyond, but at night, it's pitch black, as if they're perched at the end of the world.

Straight through and into the cavernous, sea-level space, deceptively hidden under the street above. The temperature shifts up by several degrees. Sarah instinctively moves over to a massive fan at the back and stands with her arms crossed. It pushes warm, dense air into the space. Jess's shoulders creep up to create a protective zone, so she's not knocked in the queue for the bar. The first wave of refrigerated beers has sold out. The plastic bottle that she's handed, lid already removed, is warm and smells faintly of sick. Jude passes her a shot of sambuca, which she tosses back and washes down with more beer.

The six of them cluster in the spot at the back of the room that Sarah has claimed as their territory. Ten or fifteen years ago, they'd all have been down at the front, ready to dance and cheer with the crowd. They are not the only older people there, though they're outnumbered by trendier, sexier women. Appalled that her group will be classed as no different from the short-haired, thick-middle women in their Western-style button-up embroidered shirts standing still against the crowd swarming around them, Jess tries to separate herself a little from her friends. Time was they'd have spent the evening bumping into old friends and making new ones, creating collective memories. Tonight, she is with people she loves, but they remind her that she's someone she no longer entirely wants to be.

When Brandi is about to come on, the pre-gig country music turns into deep, throbbing bass. Jess turns to the stage and sees rows and rows of heads silhouetted against the lights piercing out from the front of the stage, spotlights swooping across them, shining columns of rapt faces. She knows this feeling. Brandi smiles and strums the guitar slung around her neck only when the crowd has fallen silent.

She starts with a slower song, one that everyone will know, 'Turpentine'. It's a song about loss and waste, about the hurt people can cause each other. She pauses after the first verse to usher in the applause and whooping she knows the crowd wants to give her, despite the mood of the song. The twins who form the rest of the band use this as their cue to file in and take their places. Jess and Jude nudge each other with recognition, mouth the words, swaying in a communal appreciation of a beautiful woman with a beautiful voice. A lesbian country singer, a trailblazer.

The following songs are faster in tempo. The audience gets more confident and dances as the electric guitars kick in. Lisa leaves briefly and comes back with more shots. Jess necks hers back, and when Caz refuses one, drinks hers too. The singer turns to the audience, and smiles as voices call out from the audience, 'We love you, Brandi' and 'Marry me, Brandi.' Jess turns to Sarah, sees that she is smiling, and takes her hand briefly, a moment of intimacy before her wife pulls it back again.

'Sorry lovely ladies of Brighton.' More catcalls and whistles. 'But I'm already taken. I will, though, play you one of my favourites. Reckon you might know it.'

Winking at the audience, Brandi takes a step or two back from the microphone, knowing that 'The Story' will be one of the songs they've come to hear, bounces on her toes, and then moves forward again.

The song builds from its gentler, folksy pace to a rocky, even angry scream. Aware that they'll have their moment to go crazy in a few verses' time, the audience sways quietly at first and then prepares to howl along with the singer. Jess usually loves this song, and in the past, she and Sarah have sung it to each other. It's about the things that happen to make a person whole. The good, the bad, the sad. But tonight, it feels too raw, and the distance she feels from her wife stops her from even looking at Sarah. It also reminds her of being in front of a microphone, connecting with an audience, and it's too much. She takes the chance to slip off to the loo, ducking through the crowd.

A voice stops her. 'Jess! Oh my god, you ARE here!'

Disorientated, it takes a moment for Jess to register the woman standing in front of her. Dressed for a big night out in Brighton – tight leather trousers, a skinny tee with the sleeves ripped off to emphasise her muscles, hair cut a little shorter, bright red lipstick a slash across her lips. Tiff.

Chapter Twenty
Our Song

Of course, Tiff is here. Jess knows that she's a fan of Brandi. They'd danced to her album all those months ago, during 'that' night. It hasn't registered, tucked in a flurry of messages earlier in the week, that when she said she'd be in Brighton, she meant this weekend, let alone here. In the same building as her wife. Now, hand in hand, cushioned by the crowd, Jess has only nanoseconds to turn her head so that when Tiff leans up for a kiss, her lips brush her cheek and not her lips.

'You're here,' Jess mouths at her.

'Of course, I said I was going to be in Brighton. She's amazing, right?' Tiff points to the stage. 'Total rockstar. Hey, come meet the girls. I've told them all about you.'

Jess's instinct is to run, because Tiff is in the same venue as her wife, but she's also excited, as if thinking about her had made her real, and doesn't want to walk off just yet. One by one, Tiff plucks women out of the crowd around them, cuter, more stylish, vivid, and younger than Jess's own crew. With an eye out in case one of her friends spies them, Jess is awkward, standing still in a sea of moving bodies, anxious that her body language could betray her.

'You having a good night?' Tiff nudges her in the ribs, then fans her face with her hands. 'Who are you here with?'

'Friends.' Jess is awkward. 'And Sarah too, obviously.'

'Sorry, bit pissed already.' Tiff ignores her answer, but sways along with the music.

'Me too,' Jess says, hips moving in time with Tiff's, gradually losing her inhibitions, trusting the crowds to hide her.

Tiff leans up to shout in Jess's ear. Her breath tickles. There is tequila on her breath.

'The shoot's really soon, right?'

'Still can't believe it, to be honest.'

'I'll bet. It's a long time to be away.'

Despite her anxiety, Jess reassures herself that there is no reason why Tiff and her wife should meet. They're on separate sides of the heaving venue. She'll spend a few polite moments here with Tiff, then slip away again and suggest to Sarah that if she wants to leave, she's ready too.

The song changes to one with an upbeat tempo, arranged for dancing. Jess and Tiff mouth the words to each other and move rhythmically together. This is the gig experience Jess has wanted. An artist she loves, a venue filled with collective energy, dancing with a woman she finds attractive, who she knows finds her attractive too.

Sensing that she's been gone too long, Jess leans down and shouts into Tiff's ear, 'I've gotta go. I'll find you later.'

'One more?' Tiff urges.

'Later, maybe.'

But Jess isn't ready to join her friends yet. The thump of the bass is in her feet, knees, shoulders. Head over the sink in the loo, she splashes some water on her face, then uses her damp hands to sweep her hair off her sticky forehead. All she can see in the mirror is the bright red tell-tale mark on her jawbone from Tiff's kiss. The tissue she uses to try and rub it off disintegrates too quickly in her fingers. She uses the scratchier hand towels, which leave a sore red patch on her cheek, and yet the outline of the lipstick remains.

By the time she comes out, Brandi is taking a break. Live music is replaced by country, and the lights have been turned up. The crush of people has moved from the front of the stage to the bar.

'Thought you'd done a runner,' Jude jokes when Jess joins them again.

'Bumped into a friend,' Jess says. 'Lost track. You know how it goes.'

'Lucky for some.' Lisa points her beer bottle at Jess's cheek. 'Someone's taken a shine!'

'Oh, that,' Jess jokes, rubbing her cheek with an exaggerated sigh. 'Occupational hazard. What can I say? The ladies love me. Where's Sarah?' she asks.

'Gone out the front for a minute, needed some fresh air. She'll be back.'

Jess relaxes. There's no chance that Sarah will have seen her and Tiff dancing. She and Jude reminisce about gigs they've been to, festivals, a road trip they all took through Spain.

'This your friend?' Caz gestures.

As Jess wheels around, she hears a familiar voice and panics again, checking that her wife hasn't returned without her noticing. Not yet. Jess tries to think of a way to get Tiff away without seeming rude. But

Tiff is standing next to Lisa, and she can't extract her without it being unfriendly. Tiff strokes the sleeve of Lisa's outfit.

'I love your dress,' she coos. Lisa, flattered, says something in return, and they laugh.

'You didn't say you were here with so many cool people? Naughty J.' Tiff laughs. Jude returns with a tray of drinks and offers one to Tiff because there's one spare.

'Cheers,' she says. 'So nice to put some faces to names. Jess has told me loads about you.'

The lights flicker, and instead of melting back into the crowd as Jess desperately wants her to, Tiff stays, drinks, grabs Bex's hands, and encourages her to dance. Bex, drunk and more than happy to whirl about with a sexy younger woman, is happily led away. Jess quickly loses sight of them as they get absorbed into the crowd.

Brandi walks back on stage to huge cheers, and the band starts off with a rocky version of one of her classics. Sarah's back and she looks exhausted. There are dark circles under her eyes, and her make-up has smudged. Jess senses her opportunity.

'Sar,' she says. 'You look done in. I'm happy to go. Honestly. Shall we head off?'

'I feel a bit better, actually.' Sarah surprises her with a smile. 'Just needed a bit of fresh air. Me and all the other decrepit lezzers sat on the wall and looked at the kids having all the fun. I'm fine.' Sarah leans over. 'Thanks for making me come.' She kisses Jess on the lips. 'It's actually really nice to be out.'

The tempo of the music shifts down a gear again as Brandi plays 'Late Morning Lullaby'. It's a love song to a new day and one they used to play on road trips, singing along as the wind from open windows whipped at their hair.

'Hey,' Sarah says. 'She's playing our song. See, I don't forget everything. You do forgive me for being so grumpy, don't you? I'm roasting, just gonna go and stand near that fan.'

'You sure you don't want to slip off?' Jess presses again. 'I could run you a bath in the hotel. I'm pretty beat too.'

'Nah, let's stay. Don't know when we'll get the chance again.' Sarah kisses Jess, and she walks over to the whirring fan. Jess tries to follow her, but Lisa grabs her arm.

'Wow,' she laughs, pointing at Tiff and Bex, who are no longer lost in the crowd but are walking back to them. 'Where did you find her? She's fun.'

Jess hears Tiff say, 'Wait, are you Sarah?'

She watches as Tiff approaches her wife and her heart races, terrified of what might be about to happen. Seeing these two women together is not something she has ever imagined. Unaware of any reason to wonder who Tiff is and what relationship she has to Jess, Sarah simply smiles back. Tiff must have paid her a compliment because Sarah's response back is warm.

A group of women pushes in front of her, a conga line of bright pink outfits, holding each other's waists tightly as they weave through the crowd. It is impossible to break through and Jess is forced to wait for them to pass. One of them is wearing a cheap tiara made of tiny bright pink vibrators, and a sash, the rest in matching tee shirts. They're drunk, verging on aggressive. As one of them knocks into Jess, she spills her drink down her top.

'Oi,' Jess says, but the woman mutters something and staggers off after her friends.

By the time she looks back, Tiff is no longer there. Sarah's face has slackened. With a sickening lurch, Jess walks towards her.

'We need to leave,' Sarah spits out.

For a second, Jess is relieved. She's escaped, and her wife has taken her up on the offer of an early exit and bubble bath.

'I want to leave now,' Sarah says again. 'You tell the others. I'm off.' Straight-backed, she pushes through the crowd and out into the lobby.

Jude is there beside Jess. 'She okay?'

'Not really, think it's all got a bit much. We're going to head back to the hotel. Message you in the morning, arrange brunch?'

'Not too early, mate.' Jude pulls her into a hug. 'No kids, lie in. Hope she's alright. Give her our love.'

Sarah strides ahead. The long flight of stone steps leads up from sea level to the street. Determined, expelling angry bursts of breath to get her to the top. Sober, to Jess's panicked drunkenness.

Jess, disorientated by the booze, the salty air, the conversation they're about to have, trips slightly on the steps.

'Fuck.' She knows Sarah won't turn around to check. 'Will you fucking slow down?'

But Sarah doesn't slow down, not once during the five-minute walk up the hill towards the car. Demanding the car keys and scowling as Jess pats all her pockets to find them, she gets in, slams the door, and starts the engine. Jess, panting, gets in beside her. Expecting Sarah to turn the car around and drive back down the hill towards their hotel, Jess is surprised when she pulls sharply out, a car honking behind them, and goes straight on.

'It's not this way,' Jess protests.

'There's no way we're spending the night in some fucking shitty hotel. We're going home.'

Winded, Jess sits back against the window and pulls herself tight and tiny against the glass. Fighting a voice inside her that wants to explain, to defend herself against whatever accusation is coming her way, Jess keeps quiet. A dangerous cocktail of anger and apology sloshes inside her. Instead, she waits for Sarah to start speaking, and even in the dark, she can see how her knuckles have whitened around the steering wheel. She desperately wishes she had water to wet her dry, anxious mouth.

Concentrating hard as they drive through Brighton, passing the clumps of lads outside kebab shops, dishevelled hens shouting at taxi drivers, Sarah stays silent. She still doesn't speak as they hit the long stretch of London Road, past Preston Park, towards the Downs. The streetlights peter out, and it's harder to see Sarah's facial expression, the taut set of her lips. Jess waits.

Sarah doesn't speak, in fact, until the A23 turns into the M23 and they're hurtling towards the M25.

'So how about,' Sarah stares straight ahead, spitting out her words. 'How about you tell me what the fuck is going on?'

Jess tries not to let her panic show. Without knowing precisely what Tiff has told Sarah, the magnitude, or multitude, of her lies and half-truths come crushing in. She opens the window for a second, hoping that the cold night air will blow away her fears and doubts. Her silence has saved her for now. Sarah starts talking first.

'A month.' Sarah spits. 'A TV show. A month. You know we've got appointments right? And then the insemination is literally just around the corner. Work is a nightmare; Claudie is starting school. These next few months really matter and anything that makes me even more stressed is just likely to make the whole thing less possible. I mean, really? Is now *really* the time?'

'I'm sorry,' is all Jess offers. 'I am.'

She calibrates what she wants to say carefully now. It's clear that the source of Sarah's anger is the shoot and that it's unlikely Tiff will have said anything about 'the other' betrayal. She feels relief and guilt because of how much secrecy she's allowed to creep into her life. There's an anger that grows in her too. The jubilation she shared with Tiff when she got the part, the acknowledgement that this was a break that her talent deserved – such a contrast to her wife's fury.

'I honestly, honestly didn't think it was going to happen. I keep expecting them to cancel, to tell me they've found someone better. Like an actual actor. But they haven't, and I think I've been pretending it would all go away.'

'But it hasn't gone away. But it appears that *you* will be going away. How humiliating that I'm your wife and I find out that news in front of all our friends from some woman who doesn't know shit about our lives. Tash or whatever her fucking name is.'

Sarah has tears running down her cheeks, and Jess reaches into the glove box and pulls out a packet of tissues.

'Something's really changed with you, Jess. Did you know that? I don't know what it is. It's like you've put up walls between us, and it's not enough whatever I do. I know I've been difficult, but I haven't been actually *lying* about everything. I'm supposed to be trying to have our baby, I thought that was *literally* the only thing that we were prioritising right now. That and me not losing my job so we can afford to have the baby in the first place. I thought we both wanted to do this, but honestly, I don't know if you're with me or not. I'm really confused.'

'Oh Sar, I'm so sorry. I'm not making an excuse, but you haven't been the easiest person to talk to lately either.'

Her wife's tone shifts. No longer spitting anger but slumped with sadness, confusion, loss. Without taking her eyes from the road, she reaches her hand out and gropes for Jess's, who takes it.

'Jess, you know how much I need you, right? I get that I can get really wrapped up in work, and my family, obviously. I don't know why I thought this would be all sweetness and roses, but it hasn't been, and I'm sorry. Please tell me that you understand that. But you've got to be honest with me. What I've just learnt is a massive fucking deal.'

Jess, taken aback by her wife's acknowledgement of the impact of her moods, feels so ashamed that she wishes her car door would open and send her crashing out onto the motorway.

'I'm sorry too.' She squeezes Sarah's hand and reaches for a tissue of her own. 'I think the momentum of it caught me off-guard. Suddenly, there was this situation unfolding, and they were all being so positive and excited. Jak, the director, you'll meet them sometime, is amazing and charismatic, and I want this, Sarah, I really want this.'

Sarah's hand pulls away and returns to the steering wheel, and Jess tells herself that it's not rejection, but an instinct to drive with both hands.

'And I have thought about what it means.' Jess steadies her voice to make sure she doesn't sound wheedling. 'It's only a month. They've guaranteed that. They've promised they'll have a car on standby if I need to rush back to London. And it's money too, like proper money. A chance for me to actually contribute more than just the washing up. You could even come visit! Bring Claudie. I promise Sarah, we'll make it work. I love our life, our girl. I do, I really do.'

Sarah is silent for a few minutes. Jess wonders if Sarah has noticed in return that she said she loved their life, but not her wife.

'Maybe,' she says quietly, 'we've needed to have this conversation for a while. Just promise me that this is all there is, J. I need you. We need you.'

Back in the Music Box, she'd feared that Sarah had guessed the truth about her and Tiff, or worse, that Tiff had told her. The knot of panic is already unravelling because *that* secret, the worst secret, is still undisclosed. This is her reset. She vows to stay faithful, be kind, be present. She will embrace the shoot, be professional, strive to let nobody down. Tiff must only exist in her past.

Although she doesn't feel forgiven enough to touch Sarah, to reach for her hand or her thigh to provide that reassurance, she knows her future is at home. With her family. If it was the spirit of Elvis, his magnetism, and his ability to love more than one woman that had allowed her to transgress so completely, he is gone now. She has run out of excuses.

'No more secrets,' she says.

'You promise?' Although Jess is looking straight ahead, she can sense Sarah glance away from the road and directly at her.

'No more secrets.'

Chapter Twenty-one
The Mothership

It begins in John Lewis. Ever since their aborted and revelatory weekend in Brighton they've been circling, attempting small gifts of kindness, but unable to fully find each other again. An uneasy détente. Sarah's been trying to get home earlier so she can share story time with Claudie, and Jess has redoubled her empathy with Sarah's headaches, flushes and achy joints. And today, Jess has suggested that they make the trip into town, hit up John Lewis and then take Claudie to Hamleys for a treat. She's had a project in mind for a while and thinks that retail will help liven Sarah's mood.

The upside of Stokey is the village vibes. Technically not far from Central London, but with the famous N16 postcode that assumes a distinct identity all of its own. When they moved here it was edgier and more diverse, once proclaimed the lesbian capital of London. The residents are more mixed now, and they are just like all the other couples with young kids living in tasteful Victorian conversions and with firm views on chain stores on Upper Street. The downside of Stokey is that public transport is limited, so it's reliant on the 73 bus and on a Saturday morning, they've forgotten how long it takes to get to Oxford Street.

They take turns trying to get Claudie to sit down instead of standing on a cushioned seat to get a better view. Sarah winces as Claudie touches every surface she can get hold of.

'She'd lick that window given half a chance,' Jess jokes.

'Shh, if she hears you, she'll try.' Sarah smiles back, a moment of levity that reassures them both.

As they near Oxford Street, Jess digs a fruit snack from her pocket, wipes Claudie's hands with a Wet Wipe and catches the gummy roll twice before it drops.

'Such a good mama,' Sarah says, resting her hand on Jess's arm for a moment.

'I'd have been smarter to have bought us some chocolate too,' Jess says, and bumps fondly against Sarah. 'I'm glad you're up for this.'

'You're totally right, it's time.' She touches her tummy. 'A more fun project than this one is proving to be.'

'Don't say that,' says Jess. 'I know the meds are making you feel pretty ropey, but once you're in it properly, and well, fingers crossed, actually pregnant, it'll be a whole different ballgame. But I do realise it's a lot for you. And I all I can do is sit back and watch.'

'You do a lot more than that.' Sarah takes Jess's hand. 'Remember with Clauds, you barely slept, just in case I needed something in the night. And you coped with all the gross bits. Better than I did.'

Jess laughs and blows a raspberry on Claudie's cheek. 'You won't remember this, but your Mummy was a right old windbag when you were in her tummy. A right trumpet trousers.'

'Oh God, don't remind me. I can only apologise in advance if it happens again.'

'It's not just me you have to apologise to. There are people in the next street who wake up when you let off.'

'Stop it!' Sarah laughs.

It's the first moment time they've properly laughed together, for months now. Jess squeezes Sarah's hand and Sarah squeezes hers back, remembering how easy it is to be close to the woman she's been with for so many years.

As if she's read Jess's mind, Sarah says, 'we need do to this more often'.

'John Lewis?' Jess jokes.

'That too, but really, just hang out. *Do* something together. As a family. We just get so caught up in the day to day that we forget that we can just get on a bus, go somewhere. I mean, we never even really go away. We said we would go on a proper summer holiday, but we've let another slip by. A week in Cornwall doesn't quite cut it.'

'Hey,' Jess says quietly. 'You've had a lot going on. We both have. And Claudie doesn't care, she's just happy if we are.'

'So, let's be happy,' Sarah says. 'I am if you are.'

'Always.'

They sit in companiable silence for another ten minutes and then Sarah starts getting visibly twitchy. She looks at her watch.

'Christ, we've been on this bus for hours now. London on the weekend is horrible. I always forget.'

'Nearly there,' Jess says. 'Relax.'

When it's time to get off the bus, Jess guides Claudie carefully down the stairs. Her hot sticky paw fits perfectly in hers. Watching Sarah glide into one of her favourite department stores – 'the mothership' she calls it – Jess feels more content than she has in months.

'Anything you need before we head up?' Jess asks as they walk through the Beauty Hall.

'Don't think so,' Sarah says, simultaneously swerving to spritz perfume on her wrists and neck. Jess tries to make a mental note to remember the precise name so she can put it on a future gifting list. 'Let's just head up before one of us loses the will.'

They're here to upgrade Claudie, finally, from her cot to a bed. It's a job they should have done a few months ago but the chill between them stopped them from properly engaging. Jess suggested they do a clean sweep at IKEA, but Sarah pursed her lips and suggested that her nerves couldn't take it.

'I know it would be cheaper, but IKEA doesn't exactly bring out the best of me. I work hard so my girls can have the best.'

Jess, constantly attuned to barbs, had ignored the comment, and decided not to bite back. Because Sarah is right, it *will* be her credit card that bears the brunt. Like so many decisions that crop up, if they face a crossroads, it will be Sarah that wins. This hasn't been discussed and is not something Jess has ever wanted to bring up, assuming it's just one of the unspoken deals that comes with long-term commitment and being the lower earner (by some margin). She has sometimes wondered though, what it would be like if she earned enough money to no longer defer, or whether another reason to secede control to Sarah would take money's place.

The minute they get off the escalator on the fourth floor, Claudie says she needs the loo.

'Standard,' Sarah says.

'I know, right, right on cue. You go take a seat, I'll take her.'

Jess, with the hurried gait of a parent who doesn't know how long she'll have before there's an accident, takes Claudie's hand and they weave their way across the floor. Jess's face is obviously showing the anxiety she feels, and she's waved through the queue by people kind enough to realise the peril of the situation. Once in the cubicle, Claudie is compliant, then insists on double-soaping her hands and demands to be lifted up so she can dip her tiny arms into the dryer. These are the mundane moments of parenting that she would never normally think of as precious, but after the gloom of the last few months it's a useful reminder of what she loves about her life.

She leads Claudie out of the toilet and then crouches down suddenly, face to face with her little girl.

'I love you so much, Claudie-bear,' she says, tears pricking her eyes. 'You know that, don't you?' The depth of her emotion clearly takes her little girl by surprise because Claudie reaches her hands out and cups Jess's face.

'Love you Mama,' she says.

They weave their way back to the spot they left Sarah and spy her sitting on a display sofa, phone in hand, her back to them. Jess goads Claudie into creeping up and shouting 'boo' so they tip-toe up behind her. Jess catches a glimpse of Sarah's phone screen and sees what looks like an estate agent profile. A small white house, a wide lawn in front of it, blue skies. Claudie, unable to hold the game any longer speeds up and jumps at her. Sarah gives her a snuggle and stands up.

'Thinking of moving?' Jess asks, with a surprised smile.

'Oh.' Sarah seems flustered as she locks the screen and shoves her phone back in her bag. 'That. Just a link that Bex sent.'

Jess's face obviously betrays itself. 'Doesn't look like London.'

'Hove, actually. Don't panic, J. Seriously. We were just messaging a bit and she's got a bit over-keen, and she keeps sending me links and I was just curious, so I clicked on a few.'

'Right,' Jess says. 'I mean that's kind of a big deal.'

'Honestly, it's nothing. Just a passing thought based on a silly conversation. Don't worry about it.' Sarah stands up and kisses Jess briefly on the lips and then deflects further by taking Claudie's hand and ushering her towards the small wooden beds. She's in full mum-mode, chitter-chattering, asking her daughter if she likes this or that, what she likes the most, all questions that she's incapable of answering. Caught up in her mother's enthusiasm, she giggles and happily throws herself onto the colourful duvets, pillows, and teddy bears.

Jess trails behind, still reeling from what Sarah has said and not yet ready to join in the fun. She knows her wife well enough to gauge that this isn't just a passing thought and nor was it just a silly conversation with Bex. She remembers the encouraging comments their friends made a few months ago when they went to stay, and then last weekend at the curry house, before everything went so badly wrong. If Sarah has it in her mind, even vaguely, that she wants to sell up, move to Hove, start again, then it is not unlikely to happen.

This is her wife's mode of operation. In her world, problems can be solved by spending money, changing a situation, and taking control. Whatever might be going on under the surface can be fixed by change. There will be discussion, of course, but Sarah is a skilled negotiator and will have stored up the benefits and have neat deflections from any concerns Jess might have.

Jess has set out to enjoy today, to reconnect with her wife and spend time together as a family. But now her mind is racing, and she can't focus on the scene in front of her. Sarah, seeming unconcerned, continues rushing Claudie around beds, play acts lying down and snuggling up together.

'A big girl's bed,' she coos. 'Isn't that exciting?' She calls over to Jess who is hovering, unsure where she fits. 'Jess, come and get in. Let's see if we can *all* fit.' Propping herself up on her elbows, she beckons. 'Come on J, I want you to be part of this decision.'

'Which one?' Jess can't help asking.

'Christ.' Sarah's façade drops momentarily. 'I told you that was nothing. I clicked on one stupid link. Let's drop it. We're here to have a good day out.'

Jess, still unsettled but determined not to spoil the mood, walks around the tiny bed, and tries to lie down next to her wife, her daughter filling the gap between them. But the child's bed isn't big enough for three, so she ends up on her side, the high sides digging into her. 'Not quite big enough for three,' she deflects with a laugh. 'The little one says roll over, so I'll just wait over here.'

She heads over to a selection of neon signs designed for children's bedrooms. She gazes directly at them, enjoying the temporary blindness. She looks back over at the two of them, cosy, content and now play-acting sleep, Sarah pretending to snore. She wishes she knew what was happening in her wife's mind. Once, she would have known, she'd have been able to second guess her thoughts and been able to pre-empt them, now she feels as though she's on the outside looking in.

Jess has bought salmon fillets for dinner, one of Sarah's favourites. Her wife has been trying to eat fewer carbs in the last few months, to get her body in the best shape possible before the insemination. This dinner was supposed to be romantic; she was going to light candles and use the grown-up placemats instead of the ones they use for Claudie's tea. Maybe even open some wine, something they normally don't do if it's just the two of them. While Sarah puts Claudie to bed, Jess cooks. This is normally something relaxing and then companiable once Sarah comes back downstairs, perching on a barstool watching Jess complete the final stages.

It's obvious though, that there are conversations to be had. Jess tells herself to stay calm, remember that her decision to take on the role in *Hefted*, and be away for a month, is one of the reasons they're in this state of mistrust. She cautions herself to listen and remain open-minded. It's not that moving to Sussex is a flat no, it's that she needs to be sure that any move would mend, not break them apart further. She hears Sarah come downstairs and tells herself, again, to keep schtum, be kind, listen.

'I think she's off,' Sarah says. 'Full of how many teddies she'll be able to fit into her new bed.'

'That's sweet. I'm glad you found one you liked.'

'That we liked,' Sarah says, 'It was a team decision.'

'Wine?' Jess asks, not wanting to antagonise any further. 'There's a Picpoul in the fridge.'

'Lovely.' Sarah starts getting out the best glasses. 'Thanks so much for cooking, it smells amazing.'

'Just thought we could do with a fancier dinner than shepherd's pie tonight. As it's Saturday.'

'And the last one we're going to have in a while,' Sarah says.

Jess wonders if this is snide but decides it's just the truth. She's leaving for the shoot and this time next weekend, she'll be there. About to start what could be the best adventure of her life, or the most ill-advised decision she's ever made.

Sarah passes her a glass of wine and holds up her own. 'Cheers. To your shoot. I hope it's incredible.'

'Thank you,' Jess holds up her glass and they chink. 'I know the timing is crap, but I really appreciate your support. I'm really excited. It matters to me that you're on board.'

'Look, I was shocked. It was the last thing I expected in a million years. I was humiliated too, it's not the kind of news you expect to hear from a total stranger, and in front of all your best mates. I just didn't know how to process it. And I'll admit, I'm kind of scared about it too.'

'Scared?'

'It's a lot. I didn't realise you had ambitions to ramp up your acting career again. And I guess I wasn't expecting it to be now, just as we're hopefully about to get pregnant.'

'I had mentioned it a few times though,' Jess remonstrates. 'I didn't know it was going to be TV, that I'd get this kind of part, but I had talked a bit about how I was feeling about losing Elvis, needing to find something else.'

'You're right,' acknowledges Sarah. 'I guess maybe I just wasn't listening. I think maybe you and I are both a bit guilty of not observing each other enough recently. I think maybe we've got a bit, I don't know, lazy?'

The salmon is ready and Jess gestures to Sarah that she should go and sit down while she brings over the food. The plates look scruffier than she imagined, she'd wanted to plate it up like a chef, but in her distraction she's broken the fillets, and the vegetable medley just looks plonked down, wilting and less glossy than she'd hoped.

'This looks delicious,' says Sarah. They eat in silence for a few minutes. Jess wonders if she should have put music on but it's too late to jump up now. 'I think I owe you a bit more explanation about earlier.'

'Earlier?' Jess plays dumb.

'What you saw on my phone, the house. Hove. I know I said it was just a passing thought, but it's maybe a bit more than that.'

Here it comes, Jess thinks. This is exactly what she has been expecting, the moment when Sarah reveals a plan that she positions as half-baked but is in fact, well on the way to being fully prepped.

'I think a change might really be a good thing for us. Hear me out. If we move soon then we can get Claudie's name down for good schools, not move her when she's already settled later on. Smaller classes, new people. Be near nature, the beach, all our friends.'

'And your job?' Jess asks, knowing that Sarah will have an answer ready.

'If I get pregnant then I reckon it's a good chance to re-shape my role. My workload isn't really working for both of us at the moment. I can maybe go down to four days a week, work from home more often, and there are great trains up to London from there.'

'Right.' Jess wills herself to stay calm. 'And what do you see me doing down there?'

'I guess based on our chats, I'd wondered if you might be thinking about looking for a job. Something different. Not full time or anything, and not even something that needs to pay a whole lot, but something that you enjoy doing.'

'I enjoy performing,' Jess says, allowing herself a moment of honesty.

'I know, and look, when I started thinking about this, I honestly didn't know that it was something that you wanted to pursue. You'd talked about feeling lost after your dad died, and I sense that your show has kind of run its course. Maybe I got that totally wrong.'

'I guess you didn't think I'd get a part in a major TV show.'

'No. I guess I didn't think you'd go to an audition without telling me.'

Here it comes, Jess realises. The moment when their conversation turns from amiable to direct, with disappointment and frustration laid bare.

'We've been through this. I've apologised and apologised again. I'm sorry. I'm sorry for not telling you sooner, I'm sorry that we're in a place where I felt I couldn't be honest with you. But we are where we are, and I'm not sure that uprooting everything in London and moving sixty miles is going to fix that.'

'I don't know what will fix it either.' Sarah puts her knife and fork down. 'I want to be excited for you, for us. But I'm just so angry, and so confused.'

'You and me both.'

'Jess?' Sarah asks. 'Does anything I've said make any sense?'

Unable to reply straight away, Jess gets up and starts clearing their plates away, loading the dishwasher, putting the pans in the sink.

'Maybe. It's a lot to take in. I'm leaving in a few days and then we're apart for a month. I guess that'll give us both time to think.'

There's a shout from upstairs, Claudie has woken up and is crying.

'I'll go up and check she's okay. I'll be down again soon, then let's keep talking.'

As she walks out of the room, Sarah pats Jess's back. Jess knows this is meant to be fond, but it's not a kiss, a hug, or even a chance to look into Jess's eyes. Jess starts the washing up and ten minutes later, Sarah has not reappeared. She can't hear any sounds from upstairs and she knows she's not coming back down.

Jess puts the mats away in the drawer and wipes the table. The last thing she does is put the candlesticks away. She never got around to lighting them.

CHLOË FOWLER

Part Five
All Hail the New King

CHLOË FOWLER

Chapter Twenty-two
Take Five

This is the moment she's been waiting for. Five days of trying but failing to ignore the cameras, the boom mics, the lights, the looping cables, the dollies, the people, all these people – each one doing their jobs better than, so far, she has managed to do hers. Before each take is a nanosecond of silence, pregnant with hope that this will be the one that makes the cut. That they can finally move on.

The scene they're shooting is one of the pivotal moments at the end of episode one of *Hefted*. Jess's character, Em, is a hard-working bartender known to the locals for her dazzling turns at their weekly live music nights. The paid performer is stuck in traffic and desperate that the show goes on, her sister (the pub's owner) has asked Em to give it a go, be brave, and urges her to find her courage. There have already been multiple takes of the moment Em washes her shaky hands behind the bar, wipes them on her jeans, and walks up to the mic. Her fingers have stiffened from the freezing water of the sluice sink, her thighs burn from the portable dryer that a set-dresser uses to re-dry her jeans after each take.

It's taken hours. The extras have become less giddy with excitement; there are fewer laughs as one, then another, loses concentration and drinks the pint of dyed water in front of them. They've learned to preserve their energy for the brief seconds they are paid to be present, aware of the cost of expending it on the in-betweens. Jess senses that Jak, normally so patient, is becoming restless and anxious about the full call sheet and the inevitable cost of falling behind.

Jess clenches and unclenches her fists, urging blood into the fingers that have gone numb from gripping the microphone. Rooted to the X duct-taped on the floor, she wiggles her toes. Her unfamiliar boots have rubbed a blister on her ankle. Jess doesn't want to complain or be marked out as 'that sort' of actor. Unwilling to draw attention to herself, she keeps all these movements to a minimum, wanting to appear more poised than she feels.

'Ready on set.'

Jess places her hands around the stand. The clapperboard snaps in her peripheral vision. She imagines herself as she used to be, standing in the wings before a show, knowing that she'd smash it. At the memory of having Elvis beside her, her mouth opens, her diaphragm expands, and even if her brain doesn't know what it's supposed to do, her body does. It is a glorious feeling, this swooping and diving of each line, the pit stops of the chorus that she heads towards and relaxes into. Just as quickly as they're memorised, lyrics are released from her brain once each shot is done.

On the floor in front of her, the extras are doing what they've been told – tapping their feet, smiling, and clapping noiselessly – only they're not acting anymore, they're feeling it too. It does not matter that the vocals from this take will be overlaid with the studio track she'll record later. Her authentic voice, the one in the moment, is the one that counts now.

Jess summons the panic and fear she's been directed to feel – that car ride, the tears, and the silence of that awful drive home to take herself there. One tear and then another tracks down her cheeks, and her knuckles tighten around the metal mic stand. The melancholy lilt she's practiced with her vocal coach, the slow drawl and husk of Country, the tamping down of any lingering Elvis tics.

And here it is. The suspended moment as her last note dies away. The extras are supposed to crash in with whoops and stomping, a pantomime of pleasure. But they are silent. There is nothing here but a voice, a person, a story, and they've all been transported. Finally, she is as possessed by Em as she's been by Elvis. The awakening of one character, the death of another, and her own re-birth.

'Take five,' the assistant director calls out. The set swarms back to life; people dart backward and forward. All except Jess, who stands on stage a moment or longer. For her, everything has changed. She's truly here, finally, where she belongs.

Her fellow castmates grumble about the early calls and the hours spent in the hair and make-up van, but Jess loves it. She's figured out what the girls (and only boy) drink. Each morning, she turns up with a cluster of oat milk lattes, and an extra hot Americano wedged in a cardboard holder, a sack of mini pastries dangling from her free hand. For this, she gets to sit nearest the small oil heater they stole from the green room portacabin, because the more seasoned cast members complained that the teams' fingers were cold against their skin.

'What's on today, then?' Sissy asks, securing a bib around Jess's neck.

'Ep Three. I'm meant to be having a bust-up with Siobhan.'

Sissy flicks through the ring binder to see today's make up design. 'Yup, that's it. Got to make sure your skin's not too cheery then.'

She wipes Jess's face with small cotton-wool pads, then tones, moisturises, primes, and starts with the foundation.

'This feels better than a facial,' Jess jokes.

'You won't be saying that in week three,' Sissy replies, gesturing towards the bank of products in front of her. 'This stuff really fucks up your pH. We'll be having to cover up spots by then.'

'I'll enjoy it while it lasts.'

The chit-chat here is different from other moments in the shoot. The length of time they spend together breeds intimacy, and this team becomes the unofficial team of agony aunts and relationship counsellors.

'Any new pics of your little one?' Sissy asks. She's only twenty-five, but she seems more attuned to adult life than some of her colleagues.

'Always!' Jess reaches into her back pocket, pulls out her phone and scrolls through. 'Always' isn't quite true. Sarah's pictures are sporadic, and Jess consoles herself by flicking through older albums before she sleeps each night. If the pictures have Sarah in too, she notices that she swipes through quickly. The woman in those photos isn't the same person who Jess remembers.

'She is very, very cute,' Sissy says. 'A right little heartbreaker. You must miss her a lot. Has she ever seen you on stage?'

'No, not yet, she's too young.'

Sissy spots a photo of Jess's dad. 'That your dad?' she asks. 'He's a handsome chap. There's a whiff of Elvis about him too.'

'Yeah, that's him,' Jess says. 'He died. Last year. But he'd definitely have taken that as a massive compliment.'

'I'm so sorry,' Sissy says. 'I didn't know.'

Jess has had imaginary conversations with her dad while she's on set too. She's told him about the intricacies of filming, filled him in with harmless set gossip. She knows he'd be proud of her, would egg her on to smash it each day. If he knew about it, he'd hate the distance that's grown between her and Sarah. His marriage to her mother was something he'd been so proud of. Every minor complaint swiftly followed with an admission that he couldn't live without her. And his absence from Jess's life feels as raw now as it did a year ago.

The day's filming finishes at 7pm, and a small cluster of cast and crew gather, waiting for the minibus that will take them back to the quaint village they're all staying in. The shoot is in a less picturesque location, more suitable for the gritty ambiance required of the script, so most of them are staying five miles away. It is her driver's day off, so Jess queues along with the others. But word of her performance that afternoon has got out, and the rest fall back, ushering her to get in first, choose where she wants to sit. Ignoring the flicker of embarrassment (and flattery) that she's being treated differently, she climbs on and sits next to the driver.

The journey to Granditon takes fifteen minutes; each twist in the road now feels familiar. The farmhouse on the left is so dilapidated that it shouldn't be fit to house the family that lives there. The industrial estate and the fleet of branded white vans parked up in the lot, the Starbucks on the big roundabout that Jess longs to visit for a full-strength cortado, but hasn't yet. The final stretch – fields, hedgerows, the prettier grey stone houses marking the entry to the village.

Like Edinburgh, time has suspended since she's been on set. Her days are governed by strict call sheets and being ferried back and forth between the location and her hotel. She's often unsure what day of the week it is, or what correlation there is between her day on set or Sarah and Claudie's routine at home. It gets dark earlier, but the glare of the lights around the location often makes her feel like it's still daylight, long after Claudie will have gone to bed, and it's too late to call. It's a reminder of her month in Edinburgh, the actual and emotional sense of missing something. Before everything changed.

Near the village, when reception improves, a message pings in her phone. It's from Tiff. They haven't spoken much since the Brandi gig. Jess can't shake the intense discomfort at seeing her wife and Tiff in the same place, let alone witnessing their brief, terrible conversation. She's tried to keep her distance but not be unfriendly, especially since the opportunity to be here, on set, is down to Tiff.

How's it going?

Going well, I think. Don't think they've realised how much I'm bricking it yet.

You'd know if it wasn't going well. I bet you're smashing it.

?? But it's amazing. And I love it. How are you doing?

Is it giving you what you needed?

The message arrives but she can see Tiff is still typing. As they pass the estate just outside the village, Jess waits to see what she's going to say next.

I'm good. Got a meeting with a production company tomorrow. They seem interested.

So pleased for you. Could be your big break?

Second big break. Tiff adds a smiley face. *You were my first.*

Conscious that they'll be at the hotel soon, Jess signs off.

Gotta go. Good luck tomorrow. Let me know!

And before she thinks about it, she closes with two x's.

There is enough time to pop into the shop before it closes. Jess has already decided that tonight she will have a bath and snack on chocolate and crisps in her cosy room in the guesthouse. She wants to process and savour the moment of triumph she experienced earlier; the moment she finally became the character she's been trying to inhabit.

For a short while after that conversation in the car on the way back from Brighton, the chill between her and Sarah had thawed. Sarah had asked tentative questions about the shoot. They'd said they loved each other, that it wouldn't be long. But now, a week into being away, Sarah's mood has soured, and the reality of her preoccupation with the insemination and Claudie's needs have dwarfed her ability to still pretend that this is all okay and that Jess is forgiven. There are no *I love you*'s in the occasional messages they exchange.

Wishing she could slip under the bubbles, watch some mindless TV, and then sleep, Jess calls home first. Sarah does not pick up on the first try, but Jess holds on, not wanting to have rung off so quickly that she could be accused of giving up. She is relieved that there is no answer, then ashamed for feeling it. She runs a bath, pours in the salts, and swirls her arm around. As she's about to submerge, her phone rings, and although she contemplates not answering, she decides that it will be better to talk now than have to call back again. Water drips on the bathmat as she wipes her hands. Because it is too cold to sit, dripping, on the bed, she quickly gets back into the bath before pressing to answer.

'Hey. How's it going?'

'Hey.' Sarah replies in a tone that tells Jess all she needs to know about her mood.

'You alright?'

'Yeah.'

'How's my girl?' She hopes that being able to talk about Claudie will draw her wife out of more than one-word sentences.

'Tired, cranky. Think she's got another cold coming.'

'Caught something from nursery, I guess. That place is a petri dish.'

'She only just got over the last one. Where are you anyway?'

Jess has been careful to position the phone so that Sarah can't see where she is, but the wet tips of her hair have given her away.

'Back from the set, it's been a long day. Having a bath.'

'Nice for some,' Sarah says.

'Hey, did the flowers arrive?' Jess asks.

'They did. Thank you.' There is a tinge of warmth in Sarah's voice. Since she's been here, Jess has sent brownies, flowers, and a few books for Claudie. Anything she can do to make her absence less stark.

'Any plans for the weekend?' Jess asks, aware that any mention of the shoot causes sharpness to creep into her wife's voice.

'Dinner at Mum and Dad's tomorrow. Then down to Brighton Saturday. We'll stay over. I did tell them that Claudie might still be poorly, but they said all their kids are sick too, so one more won't hurt.'

'Brighton, huh?' Jess attempts light humour. 'You're not going to buy a house, are you?'

'That's not funny,' Sarah says. 'You made your feelings on that pretty clear.'

'I haven't ruled it out, I know I was a bit harsh. It's a big deal, something I want to make sure we've really thought about. And talked about.'

'I've heard you. We're just going to visit the gang. I need to get out of London, and I could do with some extra pairs of hands for a few days.' Sarah's tone puts a stop to any further conversation.

'Give my love to everyone.' Jess tries to end the call on a better footing and adds a hopeful, 'I miss you.'

'She needs to go to bed, or she'll be a nightmare tomorrow.'

Her wife hangs up. Jess feels a flash of anger which quickly turns to disappointment and sadness. Every conversation they have seems to start or end with disconnection. I have a right to be here, Jess tells herself again. It's my turn, and it will be short-lived. Pushing her feet against the ceramic tub, Jess lets herself sink under the fragrant water.

CHLOË FOWLER

Chapter Twenty-three
New Friday Night Rituals

Jess studies Michaela surreptitiously, on and off-camera. Her co-star plays Siobhan, the lead. She's a well-known TV actor and has won awards, famous enough that her showbiz wedding featured in *Hello!* magazine. For all that, she's lovely. Although Jak is the director and confidently guides them through each scene, it's often Michaela who slips Jess a suggestion for how to move her hands or her face. They work together well.

Day by day, the connection with the camera, the thing she first feared she'd be unable to master, has become natural. Now, she can easily transcend the chaos of the set and its moving parts and exist, at the moment, for the lens. This ability to connect purely with the viewer and the story makes her powerful. She used to believe that the noise of the stage, the applause, the costume and the scale of a show made her come alive. That it was Elvis that got her through. Now she's realised that there is even more power (and pleasure) in the microscopic movements of her own face, body and heart.

Today's scene takes place as the two sisters have to watch their pub, their livelihood, burn down. Later, the audience will learn that it's arson, but the perpetrator won't be revealed until the final episode. For now, Jess's character has to stand beside Siobhan, her sister, in front of the green screen that will eventually become the raging fire. Every tiny twitch of their horrified shoulders will be captured by the cameras that are filming them from behind; even their backs have to act.

She and Michaela have kept themselves apart from the rest of the cast and crew all day, firming up their bond, preparing for the onslaught of their emotion.

'Have you ever lost something this big?' Michaela asks as they stand in their soot-stained clothes, ash expertly streaked on their faces by the make-up crew.

Jess thinks about the things she's already lost and the things that she feels are in the process of slipping away.

'I have.'

'I feel that in you.' Michaela reaches out and takes Jess's hand before the camera starts rolling. 'It's not really acting at all, is it?'

It's the cast and crew's first Friday night, and a new ritual is being established. There are three more weeks of gruelling days and nights, but there is an end-of-term feeling as they pile into the King's Arms. Everyone is trying a little too hard to show how much fun they're having – braying and shrieking as if they're old friends when the relationships are barely established.

The oak tables are permanently sticky where the varnish has given way to the wood underneath. Nobody has smoked here for years, but a stale tobacco scent lingers. In contrast to the dark pub corners, the polished brass pumps gleam, and the LEDs behind the optics shine through flavoured gins like a boozy kaleidoscope. The villagers, probably more plentiful than would generally venture out on a Friday night, are not bashful about their intrigue. Not to mention thrilled about the additional funds being made from renting out rooms, entire B&Bs, and regular spending in the village shops. They've ordered in items that aren't usually stocked – crates of avocados and oat milk. From the make-up girls to the leads, all are treated like celebrities. Jess has spotted them staring at Jak more than once. Not hostile, merely curious, unused to seeing such an androgynous person in their midst.

Whenever Jess has been recognised in the past, it's been because an audience has paid to see her perform – when they meet her, they're hoping to meet Elvis. The Edinburgh Festival was awash with people who either were famous or looked it; she was one of the crowd. But here, she feels different, marked out. She is walking a little taller, making eye contact more directly. Having spent her first week being nice, perhaps too nice, to everyone, she's now more discerning. She's been around Jak long enough to pick up ways to extricate herself politely from over-keen extras.

The shoot pecking order is plain by how the cast and crew have distributed themselves throughout the pub. Hair, make-up and costume are the most obviously transplanted from London and have dressed up for the evening, choosing to sit on the larger tables in front of the bar. Happy to be in full view, sharing bottles of cheap white wine, laughing loudly enough to be noticed. The runners huddle together in a corner, stretching out their pints because they're not being paid enough to get drunk. The tech crew still has rolls of duct tape attached to their belts and pencils behind their ears.

The rest of the cast is a mix of introverts and showier, anecdote-laden luvvies. Jess finds herself drawn to the introverts, surprising herself by wanting distance from the mannered delivery of her colleagues. High on the adrenalin of a show, among her people, she would join in more assertively, perhaps even lead the fray.

'Fancy a top-up?' The man who plays her gay best friend in the show, though much camper in real life than he is on screen, lunges over to grab a bottle of white wine from the ice bucket, now mostly water. Dripping, he hovers it over people's glasses.

'Ooh, watch it, Paul, you're making me all wet,' says Michaela.

'Not for the first time, darling.' Paul gives an exaggerated wink.

Her turn to buy a round, and Jess, suffused with largesse, dips into her wallet for a card.

'Want to set a limit, love?' the bartender asks, and Jess shakes her head. 'Happy to be generous.'

'Up to you, this lot looks thirsty!'

She feels a presence at her side, and it's Sissy, her favourite make-up artist. She's young, looks fresh out of college, all pep and confidence. There has been no mention of a girlfriend, no dropping of a tell-tale pronoun, but nonetheless, Jess has felt the girl's interest in her as more than passing.

'Heard your scene was amazing today,' Sissy says. 'Drink?'

'Think I should do the honours,' Jess smiles. 'Thanks for being so kind to me this week. You've made me look great.'

'Oh,' Sissy laughs, 'it was easy.'

'You here for the whole month?' Jess asks.

'Unless I mess it up.'

'I'm sure you won't,' Jess says. 'Not from what I've seen.'

Sissy giggles and rests her hand on Jess's arm. 'I'll do my best, don't want to let a certain someone down.'

It's been a while since a straight woman has flirted with her and even longer since the flirtation was based on her own personality, not residual Elvis. Jess is aware of how fast rumours spread and has caught wind of a few inappropriate temporary couplings. Although she hasn't been tempted herself, especially after everything that happened with Tiff, she can see how the suspension of reality has created a bubble – what wouldn't be fine at home is acceptable here.

Jak is positioned at a table by the door, happy to see and be seen this Friday night of the first week. They are surrounded by a gaggle of extras, all keen to impress in case they're upgraded to a few lines with their name in the credits. Jak is generous – taking their time to talk to each one to make them feel at ease. Having circulated around the other tables enough already and tired of the actor banter, Jess heads over.

'Ladies,' Jak says to the group of acolytes and stands up. 'Excuse me a moment.'

They walk towards the bar together.

'Friday nights on location,' Jak laughs. 'Something else, right?'

'Thought I'd come and say hi. Stage a rescue.'

'You read my mind,' Jak smiles. 'Actually, I fancy some fresh air. You up for a wander?'

Jess assumes that Jak will lead them out to the tables in front of the ivy-clad pub, but they loop around the back, down to the towpath at the end of the sloping garden. It's so dimly lit that Jess squints until her eyes adjust to the dark. Jak is striding on ahead, so sure of their footing. Fifteen meters down the path, past a small cluster of narrowboats that Jess hasn't noticed before, is a bench. Jak sits down, pats their pockets, and pulls out a vintage tobacco tin. They remove a long, thin joint, light the Zippo with a practiced flick, and draw the first toke down. A slow, audible exhale. Jess, still standing, kicks her heels gently on the dirt, smells the herbal smoke as it wafts towards her, and takes a step back.

Jak holds the joint out to Jess, who shakes her head. She hasn't smoked weed for years and isn't sure how her body would react. At best, it will relax her; at worst, she'll start giggling, not something she wants to do in front of her boss.

'So, how do you think it's going?' Jak asks.

Jess wonders if this is a trick question.

'Pretty well, I think, though I don't have much to compare it to.'

'You're doing fine. Some actors take years to get used to the camera. You're taking to it really well. We're really pleased. You'd know if we weren't.'

'That's a relief. I'm loving it, don't want to let you down. Especially after the first few days.'

'We all take a while to find our stride. You enjoying it, though?'

'Are you kidding? It's amazing. It's kinda crazy. I thought I loved the rush of being in a solo show – this is a whole other level. The collaboration, the way it all slots together, it's amazing.'

'Just keep at it. Don't be impatient. Head down, focus, it'll happen.'

Jess is flattered and pleased that her attempts to fully commit have been noticed. Jak takes another slow toke and then exhales.

'Jono's shared the early rushes with the Channel 4 execs, and they're pleased. They're going to throw extra money at the PR, start drumming up interest, get the word out.'

'I had no idea,' Jess says. 'Honestly, I've been taking it one step at a time.'

'You carry on. Don't change a thing. It's all good. Don't be surprised if there's more press interest than you might be used to.'

'I don't want to let you all down. To be honest, I wish it wasn't going so fast.'

'So, tell me, how is your wife coping? Can't imagine it was too easy for her to let you go.'

'She's pretty tough, but I think it's hard going. Claudie's hyper sometimes. But Sarah's supportive. We agreed that this was my time to do something for myself before everything. I don't think she's aware that this might not just be a one-time thing though.'

'I really hope it isn't. You've got a gift, you should use it. Bet you're missing your little girl, though.'

Jess's eyes tear up at the mention of Claudie, and when she replies, her voice is quiet. 'Yeah, I forget what it's like to be apart from her for so long. I think I'll be okay, but then I'm reminded how much I miss her.'

And she does miss Claudie. The weight of swinging her up onto her shoulders, thighs pressed around her neck. Listening to her play imaginary games with her dollies. Even being woken up by her in the middle of the night when she's had a bad dream.

'Well, look.' Jak drops the butt of their joint and grinds it into the dirt. 'This is such a good time for you, focus on the now. Your guardian angel was really looking out.'

Jess's confusion shows on her face, so Jak clarifies.

'She'll be here in a few days.'

'Who?'

'Tiff.'

Jess's heart starts racing at the mention of her name. Since her audition, she hasn't heard it spoken aloud by anyone else and now she's been mentioned, she feels real again.

'She's doing an on-set feature for *LEXI*. She's a great writer, and we owe her, given that she brought you to us in the first place. I'm getting chilly.' Jak pulls their leather jacket closer around their shoulders. 'Fancy one for the road?'

Jess wonders why Tiff hasn't mentioned her visit and decides she's meant it to be a surprise, and a strictly professional one. Tiff is sensitive enough to know that Jess will get anxious if she thinks there's more to it than that.

It is late; the pub will have called last orders, Jess's card is still behind the bar, and it's not the kind of village for lock-ins. But Jak fishes in their pockets and brings out a key attached to a large wooden fob. They walk back along the towpath, stop at the second boat, and lifts one leg over the side.

'Wow,' Jess grins, 'you serious?'

'Sure.' She hears Jak's voice call out from inside, then the clink of glasses and knocking of ice cubes out of a tray. 'As if being on a shoot wasn't shaky enough, fancied not sleeping on solid ground either. It's quiet, space to think.'

Jess climbs over the painted metal of the narrowboat's side and feels the boat rock. Two chairs are placed on the small aft deck, a little table, and some plant pots with wilting herbs. Inside, Jak is holding a match to kindling in the wood-fired heater. The flame catches quickly. Jak blows on it and then closes the glass door.

'This is amazing,' Jess says. 'Love it.'

The amber liquid catches the light when she's passed a heavy crystal glass. She doesn't usually drink bourbon, but right now, it's perfect: a small sip, the cool liquid turning to heat in her throat. Jak joins her, sits back in the chair and stretches their legs out. The wood crackles.

'I've never had the chance to ask much about you,' Jess says. 'I love your work. I'd love to know how you got where you are.'

'My cultivated air of mystery you mean,' Jak smiles.

'A bit like a therapist, never giving anything away.'

'Something like that.'

'Well, for what it's worth, and let me fangirl for a moment, I know you said I was doing a good job, but I reckon that's all down to you. I think you have a habit of helping people discover what they're capable of. Tiff is the same.'

Again, the opportunity to talk about Tiff with someone else, even if not she's not talking about anything personal, feels good.

'I'll take that,' Jak says. 'This is a pretty amazing job. It's about connection, really. Me, you, the camera, the audience. A series of dots. Emotions are the lines that connect them.'

'Love that,' Jess says, putting her glass down on the table beside her. 'And thanks for the drink and the chat. I'll let you get to sleep.'

'See you tomorrow,' Jak says, shadows from the fire catching their features.

Jess pulls open the narrow door, and cold air hits her face.

'And Jess,' Jak says.

'Yes?'

'It's none of my business. But a few things I've learnt in this game. Don't get distracted. Don't let the voices get in, and don't believe the hype. Just do you.'

Jess strolls across the grass back to the hotel. A whiff of woodsmoke follows her. She hopes it will linger on her clothes until they're washed. Jak has told her to be herself, but surely, she has to figure out who that is first?

CHLOË FOWLER

Chapter Twenty-four
The Arrivals

Tiff does not arrive alone. Early that afternoon, she is deposited along with three other journalists at the entrance to the set. Their shiny metallic suitcases and trendy clothes are interruptions from the outside world. Their comings and goings are reminders that reality is hovering nearby, that it won't be long before they're all shunted back into reality.

Slinging their press passes around their necks, the visitors are whisked off on a tour. Jess is mid-scene, so she can't do much more than a casual wave as they pause briefly to watch the action. Tiff is too far away for Jess to gauge her emotions, but even at that distance, seeing Tiff sets off a beat in Jess's heart that's both exciting and unwelcome, and she throws herself into the scene to distract herself.

Jak sends Jess off a few hours later to find Tiff and the other journos. They're in the Portacabin set aside for 'relaxing'. Bland and uncomfortable, there are clusters of stain-resistant foam couches, coffee tables strewn with paper cups and empty biscuit wrappers. More than one plea has been issued by Facilities for everyone to clean up after themselves, but like in the sixth form, no one bothers. When Jess approaches, Tiff blushes and pushes herself off one of the primary-coloured armchairs. Jess studiously makes eye-contact with the others before turning to Tiff in case she can't hide how she feels about seeing her again after so long.

'At last,' Jess says, her tone welcoming and warm, as she intends. 'Hunted all over.'

Regaining her own composure, Tiff kisses Jess on the cheek, then turns to the others. 'I know we're not 'officially' meeting you until tomorrow but let me introduce you. This is Dom from *The Times*, Laura from *The Guardian*, Andi from the *Radio Times*.'

Jess leans over and shakes their hands. 'Jess,' she says, 'I play Em. Welcome to *Hefted*.'

Laura, a woman in a bright yellow sweater and leather trousers, says, 'I haven't been to a set as buzzing as this one for yonks. I mean, the noise about this show is epic. You must be made up.'

'It's great,' Jess says. 'Got to live up to the hype now!' This bravado is new to her. Used to accepting compliments after her show, performed solo, she doesn't know quite how to take compliments that aren't for her alone.

'We've been told there's a bus coming to take us to the hotel,' says Tiff. 'We were beginning to think we'd been forgotten.'

'Doubt they'd do that. Imagine the headlines. I'll show you where to wait.'

As they walk to the pick-up zone, they pass the crew members readying the set for tomorrow's shoot; a few of them exchange a quick word with Jess, a quip, a joke. Jess feels even more at home in this new territory in the presence of the journalists, the on-set interlopers. She's been recognised in venues before, but she's shared the space, even the city, with so many other performers that she's felt anonymous. When she's dressed as Elvis, sure, she's seen (well, he is), but as herself, rarely. It's intoxicating, and she craves more of this fame now she's got it.

Stirred by a rush of adrenaline, swept up in a desire to impress, she nudges Tiff in the ribs.

'Fancy ditching this lot and coming with me? My ride's up there,' nodding towards the BMW parked a little way ahead.

'Fancy!' Tiff laughs. 'Look at you, the star.'

'I'll take the perks where I can get them.'

'Don't worry, I'll bring her back safe,' Jess says to the three other journalists as she squires Tiff over to her car, opens the door, and ushers Tiff to get in.

'Good day?' Jess asks her driver as he pulls away from the curb.

'Always a good day,' he says. 'Home?'

'Home.' She settles back against the leather seat, adjusts the volume of her voice, and turns to Tiff. 'Hey. It's good to see you. Quite the surprise.'

'Not a bad one, I hope? Should I have told you I was coming?'

'You're here doing a job. So am I, right? Nothing to see here.'

'Sure.' Tiff smiles and briefly pats Jess's leg. It's not a gesture that should mean anything beyond friendship, but even the lightest touch makes Jess shudder. 'Nothing to see here.'

Knowing she'll be out for the rest of the evening, Jess calls home.

'Just thought I'd check in.'

'Claudie's in bed.'

'I know, but I am allowed to call my wife, aren't I? It's hard to talk anyway when Claudie's running around. How are you?' Jess forces herself to smile, hoping her wife can hear it in her voice.

'To be honest, not the best.'

Jess knows she should be full of sympathy, not come up with solutions but listen and empathise. But her conversations with Sarah are fleeting and like this one now, angry and pained.

'I'm really sorry, Sar. I wish I could do something to help.'

'We are where we are.' There is silence on the other end of the phone. 'Listen, I meant to say, Claudie and I won't be here next weekend when you come home.'

Jess fights the disappointment in her voice. 'Why?'

'It's half term? Maybe your schedule has meant you don't remember that kind of mundane stuff. Jonty and Linny have rented a chalet in Center Parcs, and they've asked us to join them. Didn't see any point in saying no. Claudie can hang out with her cousins. She's had a pretty fun-free month. And I could do with other people helping distract her.'

'Oh right,' Jess says. 'Maybe I could join you? Could get the car to drive me straight there?'

'Honestly, why don't we just meet you back home? The chalet is tiny, apparently. We'll be fine. We'll see you when we get back.'

After nearly a month away, and feeling unable to complain because she'll just be told, again, that it is Jess's choice and her fault, she says quietly, 'I get it. I'll make sure it's lovely when you get home. And let me know if there's space after all.'

'Got to go,' says Sarah. 'Work call.'

Tiff sits at a table with Jak and the other journalists when Jess arrives at the King's Arms. Jak jumps up, gets Jess a chair, and puts it down next to Tiff with a smile. If Jak has any sense of the history between Jess and Tiff, they don't show it. Jess wonders whether she should find an excuse to move to the other side of the table, to a seat where she can't accidentally brush her leg against Tiff's or touch arms.

'I was telling this lot about how we're expecting big things for you,' they say. 'Bigging you up before the junket tomorrow.'

'Can I get you a drink?' asks Dom, the journalist from *The Times*, as he stands up.

'That would be great. Bourbon on the rocks. Cheers.'

'The hard stuff so early.' Tiff raises an eyebrow. 'Playing catch up?'

'Something like that.'

Dom brings over her drink, and Jess relaxes as she sits with them all and gradually releases any anxiety about saying the wrong thing. They laugh at her jokes, urge her to spill some beans. Relaxing too much, her thigh briefly brushes against Tiff's. A sudden jolt of electricity, a blush, a surprise physical reaction that she hasn't expected to have. Nobody can see this moment, but she can feel Tiff glancing at her. She suspects that Tiff is also unsure what her reaction would be. And the truth is, it's great to be sitting next to her, someone familiar after a month of being amongst strangers. Tiff is attentive, funny, and confident owning her space, and Jess remembers what it is about her that she likes so much.

As the group talks, they start and end each other's sentences, bantering, making each other and the rest of the table laugh.

'Well, I've got this one to thank for getting me this part in the first place.' Jess spots an opportunity to give Tiff a public thanks, not least in front of colleagues from other, wider-read publications.

'No way!' Dom asks. 'How so? You're a dark horse, Tiff.'

'I told you about Jess's show, right? Elvis? I had lunch with Jak, and they told me about what was going on, you know, and Jess came into my mind. Just a matchmaker, really.'

'Seriously.' Jess puts her hand on Tiff's shoulder. 'You changed my life. I owe you one.'

'Wish I'd seen your show,' Andi pipes up. 'Love a bit of Elvis.' She bounces in her chair the same way hundreds of people have done at Jess before, 'Blue, blue, blue suede shoes.'

Humouring her, Jess laughs.

'Just imagine,' Tiff says. 'I might be one of the last people to ever see that show.'

'What do you mean?'

'Well, if you're going be a big TV star, maybe Elvis will really have left the building.'

For laughs, and because she's feeling confident, funny, and wants to impress these journos, she turns to Tiff, takes a second to assemble her face, and says 'uh-huh' like Elvis. Tiff, delighted, turns to the others. 'See, told you, genius!'

The conversation continues to come together and split apart. Jess sits back to enjoy the sensation of being amongst clever, witty people.

Jak turns to Tiff and asks her a question. 'How's Bea? She seemed cool. Remind me how you two met?'

Jess, sitting between them, tries not to seem as though she's listening, hard.

Tiff's response is flustered, and she spills some of her drink in an effort to distract Jak from asking anything else. 'It's early days, just seeing how it goes.'

'Well, say hi from me. But avoid the urge to merge too quickly!'

Ignoring the quip, Tiff says, 'She'd say hello back. Think she was a bit starstruck.'

'It happens,' Jak laughs.

'My turn for a round I reckon.' Tiff works her way around the table. She nods at Jess.

'I'm alright actually. Think I need a bit of fresh air.'

Jess goes outside and round the pub where there's a bench against the ivy-clad wall. Sitting, hands pressed on her knees, back straight, she takes a deep breath. Trying to process how she's feeling. Tiff hasn't mentioned that she's been dating, and hearing about Bea, however quickly Tiff dismissed it as anything serious, she feels a plummet of jealousy in her belly. There's no reason at all why Tiff *shouldn't* be dating. But when Jess told her that they both have to squash the connection they share, it hasn't quite occurred to her that for Tiff, moving on might involve moving forwards, to someone else.

Footsteps. It's Tiff. Jess is glad that the darkness gives her a chance to gather a facial expression more nonchalant than she feels.

'Can I sit?' Tiff gestures to the bench and when Jess nods, she sits down. 'Wasn't sure you'd be coming back in. I guess you heard Jak ask me about Bea. I'm sorry, I was going to tell you. We just haven't had a moment. And honestly, there's nothing really to tell.'

'You don't have to explain,' Jess says. 'It wouldn't be fair to expect that. You don't owe me anything. I'm sorry if I made it awkward for you. I'm not exactly in a position to feel jealous. But if it's any consolation, I am.'

The silence between them grows. The sound of the pub reaches out in waves, people laughing, the beat of music.

'You're shivering.' Jess says.

'It's fine,' Tiff replies. 'I don't want to go in. Not yet.'

'I don't want you to go in either.'

'But I can't stay out here for long. They'll talk.'

Before she can stop herself, Jess reaches out and takes one of Tiff's hands. It's freezing and she can feel the bones of her slim fingers, her silver rings. Although it's now so dark that she can't see much beyond Tiff's profile, she can tell that she's looking at her.

'I've missed you,' Tiff says. And she moves just an inch closer on the bench. 'This,' she holds up their clasped hands. 'And this.' She shuffles a little closer on the bench. So close that their thighs and bodies are touching.

'Tiff,' Jess sighs. 'I can't. It's not fair.'

'No, it's not fair.'

Tiff tips her head towards Jess and then they're kissing. Jess has imagined this moment a thousand times and also told herself it mustn't happen. But now it is and it's all she wants.

'Hello you.' Jess kisses her, so intensely that their chins bump. Jess strokes the side of Tiff's soft face, so close now that there is just enough light for her to see into her eyes.

'Should we be…' Tiff says.

'Shh,' Jess whispers as she kisses Tiff's lips, the side of her mouth, her cheek and then the underside of her jaw. She swoops her tongue gently towards Tiff's earlobe and when she takes into her mouth, she feels Tiff press against her, a slight moan in her throat. Their tongues are soft against each other. Hard, then soft again. This is a kiss between lovers. Women who trust each other, want each other. All Jess wants is to move her hands down and touch Tiff's breasts, her waist, to pull her closer and closer. To take her hand and walk her down the dark road towards her lodgings, to laugh as she misremembers the key code twice, then take her upstairs. Take off her clothes, drink her in.

But she doesn't do any of this. Instead, her hands still cupped around Tiff's face, Jess says, 'I'm so sorry, Tiff, I just can't.'

They stop kissing and sit back, pressed against the bench, side by side. Wishing this moment didn't have to end.

Eventually, Tiff says, 'It's really cold. I better go in. If we keep doing this, we might not be able to stop. Are you coming?'

'I can't, Tiff, I don't think I can face them right now. Say goodnight for me?'

Tiff stands up, still holding Jess's hand.

'And Jess, I wish it wasn't like this. But I get it, I do. You've got a life to get back to. A wife. Your daughter. I get it.' She doesn't sound angry, just disappointed. It's enough for Jess to know that this is a kind goodbye, an exit, but not quite closure.

As Jess walks back to her lodgings, alone, she senses that something within her has changed. Again. Her first kiss with Tiff was a mistake, the night they spent together was a terrible and beautiful betrayal. The kiss they've just shared was something else. Something she can't define but that's made her feel sad, excited, and scared.

CHLOË FOWLER

Chapter Twenty-five
The Junket

The room she's been occupying for the last few weeks no longer feels like hers. She's started packing her bags, removing her keepsakes from the slim oak desk, and chucking away nearly empty bottles of water and product. No need to carry them all the way home. It's been a few days since she's called home, longer than usual, but she's messaged to say that their hours are unsociable to get it wrapped in time. Today's press junket is in an hour's time, but her car will be here in twenty minutes. Time enough that she should call, but not so much that if (or rather when) it isn't answered, she'll be gone by the time she gets a call back.

But the video call is accepted more quickly than she expects and when the face looms at her, it's her mother-in-law, not her wife. Despite herself, Jess feels relief.

'Jess,' Judith says. 'Good to see you. I've tried asking Sarah, but she doesn't share any of the juicy stuff. How are you doing?'

'It's hard work, to be honest. I mean, it's great. I'm definitely earning my pay.'

'Well, David and I think it's brilliant. We were saying to Sarah that it's such good timing, this job. Good to get it out of your system, I think. Home in just a few days. You'll need to be all hands-on deck when you get home. Your girls need you.'

Out of her system? Jess thinks. What does Judith believe this is, a field trip?

'Sorry, Judith.' Her voice sharper than she intends. 'Is Claudie around? I've only got a few minutes before I've got to go.'

'Sorry, Jess. Of course. I'll go dig her out.'

The video pauses as Judith walks through the house, calling out for her granddaughter.

And there she is.

'Mama,' Claudie stares at the camera, her face serious. 'Guess what?'

'What?'

'Something bad happened.'

'Oh no!' Jess plays along. 'Did the sky come tumbling down? Did you lose rabbit? Was there no more ice cream left in the whole wide world?'

'No, it wasn't that, silly Mama. I ran down the stairs too fast, and then I tripped, and I fell, and I scraped my knee, and there was blood everywhere.'

'Oh sweetheart, I'm so sorry. Is it still hurty?'

'It's better now. Look.' Claudie's face disappears from the screen, but she's too young to realise that it won't follow her. 'Look, Mama, I have a whole bandage.'

'Well, I'm sure you were a big brave girl. Did Mummy kiss it better?'

'Yes. But she cried too. Just as much as me. Maybe even more. I think she's very sad.'

'Oh, poor Mummy. Well, you must look after her too, darling.'

Jess feels tears coming.

'Look at me Claudie-bear,' she says. 'I'll be home. Really soon. To look after you both.'

And with that, her daughter puts down her the phone and runs off. She hears laughter from another room, recognises that of her wife, a laugh she hasn't heard in a long time and it's a reminder of the things that she loves about this woman. The one she's known for so many years, every inch of her, but who she's in danger of forgetting. A cliché that Jess hates, the gradual growing apart of two women who can companion nicely, but no longer want to touch.

Jess is left staring at the side of the sofa, the pictures of French landscapes on the wall above. She leaves it a few seconds, and then knowing that her daughter has got distracted and won't be coming back, she presses the red button, and the call is over. Jess, awash with guilt, weeps. Longing for the woman she loves, but who she knows she is no longer in love with.

An hour later, Jess is on set, coming face to face with Tiff any minute and despite having the time to think overnight, and this morning, she still doesn't know how to feel. The junket is held in one of the larger hangers. It's been tidied up, lights strategically placed, the tripping hazards of wires and dollies stowed away. The fact that they won't be filming in here again makes her and the rest of the cast a little melancholy. As much as this phase of production creates buzz for the network and audience, it's an ending for the cast and crew.

Jess is not ready to say goodbye, and she's dreading it. Being on set has awakened something in her and she doesn't want it to end. She doesn't need drag anymore, or even Elvis, she needs more. *This* is what she went to drama school for, what her father longed for on her behalf. What she'd planned to be her future until Sarah, then Claudie, came along. Not an occasional tryst with the stage, but a calling. None of this is what she can share at the junket; it's still too private and raw. A hope, but not an answer.

The leads are all positioned on director's chairs, their character names picked out in white stencils. There's a logo and press photo banner behind them, a small table with water jugs and glasses. The journalists will rotate between them for their strictly allotted twenty minutes. It's the first of these junkets that Jess has done, but not the last.

Aware that she wants to position herself carefully amongst the journalists, especially the ones from the most influential publications, Jess avoids looking directly at Tiff, not daring to make eye contact. She is terrified that what she'll see reflected back at her will take her back to where she was last night, resisting the urge not to step beyond a line she's already crossed too many times. All she wants is to communicate a private joke, special attention, but she knows she can't. Tiff eventually picks up on Jess's vibe, sits up straighter in her chair, and slips into professional interviewing mode.

Afterwards, Tiff hangs around in the room once the other journalists have moved next door for afternoon tea.

'Hey,' Tiff says quietly.

'Hey,' Jess replies. She's terrified that she's going to be asked to say more than she wants to, but equally terrified that all they'll do is say goodbye.

'Jess?' She's coy, and suddenly appears younger than she is. 'Do we need to talk?'

'Yes. But also no. If I'm honest, I'm really confused.' Jess wants to be kind, to make it alright, but the only words that come to her are clichés. 'There's a lot happening in my life right now. I'm struggling to process it all. All I know is that I really like you, even more than that.'

'I think it's mutual. And I'm sorry if I'm part of not making it easy. It isn't my intention. But I can't help the way I feel.'

'I'm trying so hard, Tiff, to do the right thing.'

'For who?'

It's a good question, another opportunity to be reminded how observant Tiff is, how much she seems to understand about Jess's life. Perhaps, she feels, more than Jess understands her own.

'Honestly, sometimes I don't even know,' Jess replies. 'I'm sorry that you've been dragged into this.'

'Hey, I'm an adult. I make my own choices.'

'I wish I had the same freedom.'

'Sorry for being so frank, but that's bullshit, Jess,' Tiff says, moving towards her. 'It may feel like these are the biggest decisions in the world but that's how it feels right now. Think about how you want to feel in six months, a year, I don't know, even in five years' time. What do *you* want? What do you think will make you really happy?'

The silence between them grows and Jess can't take it any longer. What she wants is to take Tiff in her arms, to hold her, to just talk. But she knows how unfair this is, to both her and Tiff, and even worse, to Sarah and Claudie.

'I can't do this,' Jess says. 'I'm so sorry.'

Tiff gathers up her bag and coat and busies herself to leave.

'Why do I feel like I'm being dumped when we weren't even a thing? I came here with zero expectations. But each time we see each other we end up the same way and it always feels so right. We can't seem to help it. But I need to stop getting in the way of your life. And you need to stop stopping me from getting on with mine.'

Jess, defeated, looks at the floor.

'I'm sorry, Tiff, really. I'm so grateful to you, and you deserve better.' More clichés to hate herself for.

Tiff turns to leave.

'I hope you figure it out, Jess. Elvis didn't and look where he ended up. I'm here for you as a friend, even if I can't mean more to you than that. I can't help you figure it out, but you have to find a way. You can't carry on like this. I certainly can't.'

The door does not slam, it just closes with a quiet click. Jess is left in the empty room, depleted of the energy Tiff brings into any space she inhabits. She knows that time is running out and she has to decide before it's too late. But the only thing she's sure of right now is that she can't do that here. She needs to be in a place where she can think, confront her past, commune with her idols, lay herself bare. The only place in the world where she might be able to figure out what her future holds. Memphis.

CHLOË FOWLER

Part Six
A Tupelo Boy

CHLOË FOWLER

Chapter Twenty-six
There are Lies and There are Lies

Jess has lied to herself and others recently, so her decision to delay going home and escape to Memphis feels like just another untruth on the list. Having been away for a month, and with her feelings about Tiff being stirred once more, she isn't ready to face her wife. Knowing that Sarah is off to Center Parcs with her family for the weekend, and having been told there is no room for her anyway, she decides to risk this final lie. She tries to call Sarah; to tell her in person seems the fair thing to do. But there is no answer so she messages instead.

Tried to call. Need to talk to you. Bit of an issue, they need a few of us to stay for a few extra days to redo some scenes. Know you're going away anyway. Hope that's okay?

Jess puts her phone down to finish packing and by the time she picks it up there's no missed call, but just a reply. It's terse, but not as unfriendly as she expects.

Sure, I guess these things happen. Probably more annoying for you tbh. We're not back until Tuesday anyway. Home by then?

She hopes the warmth in her reply will be noted too.

I really am sorry. Hopefully by then. Fingers crossed. Really missing you both and sad not to be coming home. xx

The blandness of their exchange, and the dutiful xx's that come back from Sarah without any accompanying message, feel meaningless. The carefulness between them is too polite, with so much unsaid. As she packs the photo of Claudie and Sarah that she brought with her, Jess gasps, winded, and considers cancelling the flight and booking a hire car so she can drive down to Center Parcs, to surprise them, to find a way to reconnect. But even as she does this, Jess knows this is not what she really wants. The next few days, in Memphis, may not be enough; but they might be a start. She convinces herself that they're not reckless. They're a reckoning.

The irony does not escape her that the last time she was at Birmingham International was when she headed from ElvisCon, unaware that it was the beginning of an end. Used to the glossier spoils of Heathrow and being able to take advantage of Sarah's BA Gold membership, Birmingham airport holds limited excitements. Although she knows there's no chance she'll be spotted by anyone she knows, she still feels furtive. Hunger gnaws at her, but she refuses to seek solace in food. There will come a time when she allows herself some pleasure, but it's not yet.

The first leg of the journey is a short hop to Paris. She turns down the offer of purchasing anything to drink because she can't face having to push past other passengers to get to the loo. She fights the urge to sleep but wakes up with a start each time she feels her head lolling, then jolting painfully up. The pleasure in what she has gained, the grief of what she has lost, the fear of what she might have to let go. All dart around in her brain like mosquitoes, thoughts she can never fully push away.

There are five hours to kill in Charles de Gaulle before her transfer to Atlanta. Even then, her trip won't be over, only ending in one final leg from Atlanta to Memphis. As an itinerary on paper, this journey seemed manageable, but numbed by the fluorescent strips and artificial air of the terminal buildings, it feels never-ending.

Jess wanders from one bank of leather and metal chairs to another, switching every hour to keep herself awake, looking enviously at the backpackers butting themselves up against spare walls and resting their heads on their bags to sleep. She buys a disposable toothbrush and toothpaste and tries to scrub away the synthetic onion that has coated her tongue from the cheap salad she bought in the first hour, and regretted for the following five. Milky water splashes down her black sweater. She looks as much of a mess as she feels.

Finally, her connection to Atlanta is called. Despite having money in her account, set aside for this very trip, she'd balked at the astronomical prices of Business Class, feeling that travelling in luxury would add insult to injury. At any other time, Sarah might have urged her to take the financial hit on a posher seat, tell her she'd earned it. But in the past, Sarah might have come too. A trip that would have brought them together, instead of what Jess is feeling now, that the decision to make the trip might be the final push that splits them apart.

Having booked so last-minute and in a panic, she couldn't even choose an aisle or window, so Jess is sandwiched in a row of five and contorts to tug each new thing she needs out of her hand-luggage. More than once, the chino and checked-shirt-wearing man next to her offers to put it up in the overhead locker, but she refuses. With so much of her life spiralling out of control, feeling her bag digging into her shins is the closest thing to a grounding she can get.

Her time in the air makes real life feel as far away as the ocean below. While she's clear on her reason for choosing Memphis, a pilgrimage, she knows she's also running away in a desperate bid to give herself space to make some decisions. She senses that it's within her to make the most destructive choice, but if she doesn't choose soon, it may be too late. Leaving her marriage was never something she thought she'd ever do, but the gap between her and Sarah seems to have grown and she doesn't know how to close it again, if that's even something Sarah wants.

She's been so consumed with her guilt and her own part in the undoing of their relationship that she hasn't given enough thought to whether it's her that's 'to blame', or whether Sarah might also be seeing a bigger picture. A future where they co-parent Claudie with love and care, but separately. Sarah is strong and Jess has always felt she is the stronger of the two of them; she has a safer foundation and a close family to help her move forward alone. Jess even senses that Sarah might still choose to have a second child, to adjust her professional commitments to get what she wants. Is there, she wonders, space for both of them to strive for what they need *now*, even if that's a momentous and heart-breaking choice?

Hefted has given her a glimpse of a different life – one that feels delicious and freeing. Jess entertains the possibility that she's being unfair on her wife, who has only encouraged (and funded) her forays as Elvis. But 'foray' is the rub: she's been allowed field trips, but once over, she's been expected to return home, her dreams satiated.

All she can envision now is a future where Sarah works harder to afford the life she wants, and thinks Jess wants, and in return, she will expect Jess to manage the house and the children. There is no gender difference to blame this inequality on, or complain about. It's the life they have, the way it's always been. Jess knows she's been complicit in this sacrificing of her goals but doesn't feel capable of imagining a compromise. Her answer has simply been to run away.

Thoughts of Tiff knock in her brain too, confusing her, causing her heart to beat in ways that she knows isn't okay. Tiff's skin, her hair, breath. Underneath her, or opposite her, listening. These are feelings she hasn't had for Sarah in a long while. If Jess has any choices now, they are impossible ones. A landslide that she can't even contemplate.

Her final flight is another short one. The air is suffused with tourist glee, the crew plays up to the passengers, crack jokes about Elvis, B.B. King, and BBQ. *Lonely Planet* guidebooks are tucked into bags, people circle the things they'd like to do on arrival. One more leg, Jess keeps repeating to herself. One more leg. Then she'll be in the city with all the answers. The home of the King.

Jess wanders further from her hotel than she intends, instinct telling her not to stop until she finds a bar full of locals rather than out-of-towners like her. The hats, the inflated cars, the portion sizes and the jaunty greetings muddle together with the blues, jazz, country and rock that seeps out from every open window and doorway. All of it bright and overwhelming – a cacophony that presses through her jetlag, as throbbing and persistent as the lie she's told to get here. It's all something she would once have shared with Sarah or more recently with Tiff, a WhatsApp with a cover photo, a cute remark. Now, her phone stays in her pocket, silent with disappointment. These are moments she experiences alone.

On the surface, the bars she passes all look the same – gaudy neon signs, wooden stages, mounted TVs permanently tuned to basketball. But this one, The Thirsty Moose, is out of the main drag; there are people sitting alone rather than groups of tourists, and Jess feels she can be suitably anonymous. She takes a seat at the bar, stares at her beer and avoids making eye-contact with anyone.

After a while, she's interrupted by voice at her side. 'Howdy, ma'am. I'm guessing you're not from around here?'

Jess swivels around and looks at the man perched on the stool to her left. His unnaturally jet-black hair looks brittle, artificially crisped by chemicals and heat. His dark denim jeans are pressed with sharp creases that align with the pleats in his Hawaiian shirt, a swirl of hibiscus flowers and tropical birds. His black cowboy boots look like they've never trodden in dirt. The first time she noticed people traipsing up and down Beale Street in boots like his she'd assumed it was little more than fancy dress worn by tourists – but now she senses that locals wear them too.

Jess smiles. 'You guessed right. London. The UK.' Contrasting with the drawl and throaty vocal fry of the accents around her, she hates the voice that emerges from her mouth – to her ears it's prim and terribly, awfully British.

'I figured as much. Welcome to Memphis.' Memfuzz, the 'phis' melting away into nothing, not the 'fiss' she uses.

'Don.' He holds out his hand. 'Pleasure.'

'Jess,' she says, holding out hers in return.

This is the first time she's spoken more than a few words to anyone in twenty-four hours.

Three craft beers later, Jess has learnt a lot about Don. Her preconceptions about Americans are confounded by his openness and charm. Bar staff top up his small dish of courtesy pretzels without being asked, people smile at him as they take their seats along the bar, though he insists he doesn't know them. She settles back, enough energy in her to listen but not enough to talk.

Don looks the sixty-eight he says he is – his three daughters scattered from Iowa to California and a fair few 'grand-kiddies who give him the runabout.' He's only a few years younger than her dad would have been, but seems so much lighter, more comfortable in himself than her father ever was. He is as strange and un-British as any man she has ever met. He shares stories of his life without asking anything for anything other than her attention in return. Jess would usually bridle at this arrogance, but with so many emotions, facts and questions swirling in her brain, she's happy for the lack of reciprocal attention.

He's travelled, he tells her, from East to West and North to South, mostly solo, sometimes paired with unnamed companions. His pock-marked skin is dark from decades of zigzagging from one hot state to another. He tells her he's been a roadie, a session musician, a portrait artist, a labourer, a chef. Broad shoulders, with muscles visibly flexing under his sleeves, his voice is soft and high-pitched, with the merest whiff of a lisp. Sometimes he giggles, a sound that sounds strange coming from an older man. The emotions of the last few days come at her like waves, and right now, she is so grateful to him for talking to her that she wants to cry. But then he pauses.

'Here's me, jabbering away, and I haven't asked you anything about yourself. You must be thinking I'm a typical American loudmouth.'

Worrying that her face may have been showing less attentiveness than she was feeling, Jess laughs.

'Honestly, there's nothing really to tell. Your life is much more interesting than mine. I want to hear more. Please.'

'Married, I'm guessing,' he says, not quite a question, 'but here alone?'

He pauses, nods to her wedding ring, looks up at her again. She takes a moment to weigh up which pronoun to use for Sarah. Aware that not everyone shares her politics or life choices, she doesn't want to anger, confuse, or worse, give him any reason to stop talking to her. Jess generally assumes that her appearance, even if it is a softening of the harder butch she once was, gives answers so she doesn't have to. But every so often, the need to consciously out herself all over again takes her by surprise.

'Sherlock!' she laughs, and wonders if he'll get the reference, but then lets it die away. 'It's complicated. Taking some time out. Time to think.'

'We all need a bit of me-time,' Don says. 'I guess your wife must understand that if she's let you come here alone.'

Jess's face must be betraying her surprise that he's understood her sexuality so correctly, despite her having said so little.

'When you're as old as I am and got so much under our belt, we learn to spot each other in the crowd.' He taps his finger to the side of his nose. 'Intuition from a kindred soul, if that's not being too forward. I came to my own truth later in life. Spent a lot of time searching for love in all the wrong places. But then again, I might not have had my kids, my grand kiddies.' Tapping his fist to his heart, he adds, 'I may not see them a whole lot, but they're right here.'

'You're gay?'

'You young people and your labels.' Don giggles again. 'I'm just me, honey, just me.'

Their conversation is interrupted by the announcement that the next artist will be performing soon. She comes on to muted applause, enough to reassure her that she's been noticed, not enough that she's celebrated, not yet. In her early twenties, she's wearing a short black dress, black tights and a pair of bright red cowboy boots that match her lipstick and a red streak in her hair. She perches on a high stool nestled amongst the speakers and lights, adjusts the microphone, checks the cable snaking out from her guitar, lengthens the strap around her neck, turns around to say something to the band behind her.

'She's not bad as it goes,' Don explains. 'Here the last few weeks. Probably not for much longer. I'm guessing you sing?'

Jess is surprised again.

'I do. I mean, I did. I dunno.'

'Elvis?'

'Yeah, a bit of him too.' Jess plays down her performing, again anxious that he might be like the men at ElvisCon, horrified that a female would dare to sing the King.

'I reckon you'd be pretty good,' Don says. 'I can't speak for your voice, but you look a bit like him.'

'Thanks. I've heard that.'

The singer's voice is husky and soothing. The mellow rhythm of the song lulls them, and they both sit and watch for a while. Jet-lagged, a little drunk, suddenly melancholy, Jess feels heavy and exhausted. She swirls the last few mouthfuls of her beer around in the glass, tips the last warm slug down her throat.

'I hope you don't think I'm rude,' she pushes off her seat. 'It's been such a pleasure meeting you.' Here it is again, the impossible British-ness of her voice. 'Must be the jetlag, I'm knackered.'

'Knackered.' Don chuckles as he repeats the word back to her, aping her accent. 'I like that. I might be way off beam here, but since my instinct was right the first time, this might interest you too.' He too stands up and fishes in the back pocket of his jeans.

He hands her a flyer, folded and unfolded so many times that the ink has worn out in the creases. Another one, Jess thinks, to add to the pile on the desk in her room. In the 24 hours since she arrived, she's flicked through them a few times but has felt overwhelmed with the choice of bus and walking tours, the discounted bundles for Sun and Stax Studios, the Gibson Guitar Factory, the Civil Rights Museum. All landmarks, all places she should visit, and would do if she was with

Sarah, or maybe even her dad. Places she knows she won't go to now, not alone. Apart from Graceland.

She unfolds it in front of him. It's badly typeset but the headline reads 'Queer Elvis Open Mic night'. Memories of ElvisCon flood back, how unwelcome she was made to feel, how even being a woman, let alone gay, meant that she was rejected.

'I don't know,' she said. 'My relationship with him is something else that's a bit...'

'Complicated? I hear you. But sometimes you gotta sing it out. Just think about it, honey,' he nods. 'You never know, it might be what you're looking for.'

'Looking for?' she asks.

'That's why we're all here, we're all passing through, searching for something or someone. I hope you find it. And if you're still looking, come to the Open Mic, you might enjoy it more than you think.'

As the door closes behind her, the singing stops, and the applause is louder than before; perhaps this will be the singer's break after all. Ambling back up Beale Street towards her hotel, Jess hears all that music again, one Blues riff melting into another Country stomp. The bars are so full that people sit against the windows, facing out, knees pressed against the glass, eating and drinking. An overweight man pushes a disintegrating burger and bun into his mouth, grease slicked on his cheeks. His elbows anchor him to the serving counter, and he's staring out at the street. Lonely, or alone.

Jess wonders which one she is too. She walks the last few blocks back to her hotel, nods at the bellman, and then goes up to her room where she hopes a jet-lagged sleep will overtake her at last.

Chapter Twenty-seven
Honey, He'd Sing

Felled by exhaustion and the stunning fact that she is here, at last, Jess has to keep sitting on the hotel bed to convince herself not to curl up under the covers and go to sleep. Getting here felt like such a huge step that the effort of doing anything else is beyond her. She'd wanted to embrace every moment and throw herself into Memphis life, let the King infuse her, but guilt and tiredness are creating a barrier she can't knock down. Thoughts of her dad swim into her face around every corner when she's awake and when she's asleep. 'Come on, King, if you're here, make it count,' she hears him say. And yet, the day slips by, she isn't making it count yet.

All confidence gone, Jess had decided not to go to the Open Mic night, then changed her mind. Something about Don, the shadows of her father etched on his leathery face, tells her she needs to go. Another evening of bad food on Beale Street would feel like defeat. Costume-less, Jess struggles with what to wear. Aside from tech rehearsals, she's never been Elvis without her suit. In the end, she puts on black jeans and a black shirt; her silver belt buckle is her only accessory.

Well, not only. Tucked in her pocket are her Elvis rings, kept tucked in the pouch during the shoot and only taken out after a bad day, and here with her now. Before she leaves, she places the black onyx and diamond one on her pinkie. She won't be singing, she's not ready for that, but to carry a part of him with her feels important. The only other visible concession to her life as Elvis is her hair, quaffed high.

She gets in the elevator, walks past the concierge ('you have a great night, now ma'am') and is out on the street before she can change her mind again.

Standing on the pavement, she has no idea what the interior is like because the windows of the Hideaway are blacked out. Once inside, the decor is not so different from other gay venues she used to go to, back when she used to go out regularly anywhere. Her trainers peel off the sticky floors with a crackle. The black breeze-block walls are covered in posters and signed photographs from decades of events and live performances. It smells of bleach and stale beer and it's almost completely empty.

She panics. Has she got the wrong night? The wrong place? She stands at the bar, unsure what to do next. She was sure the flyer said 8pm. Digging it out of her pocket again, she hears a voice boom out from the back of the space.

'Honey! You made it!' Don glides towards her, fully quiffed black hair glistening with pomade, his white jumpsuit a stark contrast to the jeans and shirt he was wearing a few days ago. His voice softens and he reaches out to kiss her hand. 'I'm proud of you. Steppin' out ain't easy. Come with, I've got some people for you to meet.'

Don takes her hand with that familiar soft grip that makes her want to cry. 'She came!' Don calls out. 'The British girl I was telling you about. I knew she would.'

The whiff of camp that Jess only detected after he revealed that he was gay feels more pronounced now. His comfort in this queer space, the power of his costume, have removed any of the harder edges in the Thirsty Moose. Don fills his jumpsuit perfectly, immaculately tailored to suit his shape. From behind, he could be Elvis in his later years. From the deep slit in his shirt, she sees that the hair on his chest has been dyed black to match his hair and a thick gold chain nestles in the thick fuzz.

'Sit, honey, sit,' Don instructs. 'Drink?'

'I thought there might be more people here,' Jess confesses. 'Did I get the wrong night?'

'I told you to reprint the flyers.' Don chides one of the other people at the table and then turns back to Jess. 'It actually starts at 9:30pm. Don't worry, there'll be quite the crowd. You'll see.'

'Don says you're from London?' one of the other men asks. He's wearing a version of the fawn uniform that Elvis wore in the film, *GI Blues*, with identical badges and insignias, his black tie tucked in between the shirt buttons, a woven black belt around his thin hips. He's a youthful Elvis – the pronounced cheekbones, smooth skin, the same shadow of nerves flickering in his eyes. The only difference is that there is no quiff, just closely shaven, bleach blonde hair. 'I've been to London.'

'How was the weather?' she says, hating herself for it the minute she asks.

'Chilly, and what is the word that you use? It was all a bit snooty.'

'That sounds about right,' Jess laughs. 'We lack a certain something in the charm department.'

'You Brits! Stiff upper lip and all that.'

'I'm Aaron, by the way.' He holds out his hand.

Another man stands and leans over to Jess. 'Not his real name, obviously. I'm Lips. Which is obviously not my real name either.'

Lips is the Elvis of the '68 Comeback special. His leather trousers and jacket fit snugly around his hips and chest, the collar high and stiff. The only obstacle to a perfect match is that he's Chinese and achieving the perfect quiff has been hampered by the fineness of his hair.

'And this is Bobby.' Lips turns to a silver-haired third man at the table who, looking like he's in his seventies, is easily the oldest of the bunch. The most 'like Elvis' in his broad shouldered, slight-hipped frame, a haunting vision of how Elvis might have looked if he hadn't passed away or experienced the weight-gain. He's wearing a silk paisley shirt undone a few buttons deep, tight dark trousers and shiny black boots. Elvis at leisure.

'Enchanté,' Bobby says. 'And I'm another Queen who loves her King.'

'Bobby's the host.' Lips leans in with a mock-whisper. 'He's the one you've got to be nice to.'

'You should try it sometime,' Bobby deadpans.

Don, back from the bar, hands drinks around and gestures Jess to sit. Even this feels like a symbol of acceptance, a coming together of differences. Here they all are, in Memphis, queer and confident. Each in their own way, Elvis.

'Don said you're an ETA too?' says Lips. 'That's amazing. I didn't think the Brits would be so accepting of you, a lady Elvis, if you don't mind me saying so. They're not that hot on us gay boys having a go, so we tend to stick to ourselves. Honestly, I was about as welcome as a shit sandwich, 'scuse my French. I was more of a performer, to be honest, did my own show. The ETA world was a new one to me and a bad experience at a competition really threw me. Thought I'd have the confidence to ride it out but turns out I didn't.'

'Girl, we've all got a whole lotta life going on,' says Aaron.

'Amen to that.' Lips raises his glass.

'Tonight, let it go. Relax. You're with us now. A friend of Don's is a friend of ours.'

As Don promised, while they've been talking the bar has filled up. The volume has increased, so they have to talk louder to be heard. Jess is relieved to see that she's not the only one who is not dressed as Elvis. The room is peppered with a few drag queens, some with Priscilla's beehive and others dressed to kill. Others aren't in costume but are wearing shirts with pictures of Elvis's face on them, jeans, and cowboy boots. So far, though, she is still the only woman.

'Ladies...' Bobby gingerly levers himself up from his chair and heads to the small stage. 'I reckon it's time to get this Presley party started.'

'Is he alright?' Jess asks Aaron.

'He's preserving his energy for the moments that count.'

'Come on, Bobby!' Lips hollers. 'Let rip!'

Sure enough, as soon as Bobby gets on stage, he transforms. Jess remembers how this feels, this ability to embody another, and feels a flicker of sorrow for what she's given up. The gels from the rig above lend colourful shimmers through the silk of his shirt. His fingers, heavy with diamond and gold rings, shoot shards of light into the audience. Clusters of people still loitering by the bar push forward to fill out the tables down at the front.

Despite the number of other ETAs and fans in the room, each with their own crowd, unlike ElvisCon there is no sense of rivalry. In fact, the cheering, whooping, and hollering are the opposite. Everything about this evening already feels like something damaged in her is being mended. Her shoulders feel lighter, she can feel the same spirit of transformation that she hasn't experienced in a long time. It feels good, and finally she can sense why she has come, not to the bar, but to Memphis.

Standing close to the microphone, Bobby calls out, 'Y'all ready to take care of a little bit of business?' The audience shouts out in return. He waits for the sound to subside and then yells out again, 'I said, are y'all ready to take care of business?'

The sound that comes back at him is even louder. It's a line she's heard more than once already since she's been here and it's the line that she and her dad used to each other on their calls. Hearing it now, she's reminded of him, and she touches the heavy rings. Whatever answers this trip brings, or whether it just creates further questions, the love for her dad is the surest thing she knows.

Jess instantly recognises the opening bars of 'Viva Las Vegas', the song she'd dreaded hearing again after ElvisCon, but it is perfect here.

The fast beat of the bongo drums kick-off and Bobby shimmers his way forwards and backwards, clicking his fingers, shrugging his shoulders, tapping his thighs, his head swivelling to connect with as many of the audience as he can. Each time he approaches the chorus, he motions to them and they shout it back at him, in perfect time. Jess is so captivated that she doesn't notice four of the glitziest drag queens join him on stage. He shimmies over to them, one by one, dances with them, and then towards the end of the song, joins them in a conga line across the stage. As the song ends, the audience continues to stomp and holler. The man who practically limped to the stage has shucked off the pain and become a true King.

The whole performance has lasted only two and a half minutes, but Jess feels that connection, that desire, that awe for Bobby that an audience must have felt for Elvis, and she too is up on her feet, shouting. He grabs a bottle of water that's passed to him from the front of the stage and then tips a little down his silk shirt.

'Whoa,' he says, shaking his chest like a dog. 'Hot, ain't it, ladies?' And then, in response to the wolf whistles, 'You like that, huh?'

Don catches Jess's eye.

'Not quite what you expected?' he laughs.

'Honestly. This is incredible. I'm stunned. We would never have this happening in the UK. Never. Not like this.'

'Hell, you ain't seen nothing yet. We'll have you up there by the end of the night.'

'No way,' she mouths back at him, but it's too late. He's already back watching Bobby pace the stage, applauding.

'Y'all not here to listen to me though, are you, folks?' Bobby calls out. 'We've got a night of rocking and rolling, jiving, and swinging (not that sort of swinging, you naughty gals), and we've got some amazing performances lined up for you. If you're here for it, we're here for it. Let's give it up for our first performer. Aaron, get up here, honey. It's our first act of the night, and welcome to Memphis's only, hell, maybe the world's only Queer Elvis Open Mic night.'

Don, Lips, and Jess blow kisses at Aaron as he grabs his peaked army cap and guitar and jogs over to the stage. She'd expected a pulsing, energetic performance, so she's caught off guard when he simply stands still and taps his guitar in time with a lilting backing track. It's not the boom of 'Blue Suede Shoes', but a less well-known track from *GI Blues*, 'Pocket Full of Rainbows'. Like Bobby, he's note-perfect, managing to capture all of Elvis's mannerisms with the slightest twitch and shake. At the end, as he's singing the final lines, he puts his hands in his pockets and pulls out handfuls of multi-coloured confetti, tossing it gently onto the audience below.

His transformation into Elvis is breath-taking – this slim-hipped man, androgynous and beautiful, tender and unbroken by whatever future is ahead of him. Jess's eyes water, and she just has time to shake out her tears before he too is back at the table.

'Oh my god.' She stands back, claps harder. 'You were incredible.'

'Thanks, hun,' he giggles. 'You've got to love a little rainbow, right?'

A few more Elvises take the stage, each one amazing, brilliant but with a nod to transgression in their own way. It's exhausting, and Jess's face aches from smiling so much. Bobby gets back on stage a final time and doesn't reprise the entire number but whoops the audience into a few more shouts of 'Viva Las Vegas' before he announces a short break.

Aaron, his elbows on the table, cups his chin in his open palms.

'So, honey, tell me, what's your story? Tell me everything. Where did it all start for you?' His eyelashes bat coquettishly.

Jess takes a moment to answer, unsure how much honesty Aaron really wants to hear.

'I guess it all started with my dad.'

'A Daddy story!' he interrupts. 'Tell me about it! As soon as I knew I wasn't going to be batting for the little league team, I was out, out, out. Until I left and then I was...' He punctuates with a twist of his hips. 'OUT, OUT, OUT. Never looked back.'

'Mine's a bit different, actually,' Jess explains. 'He's actually fine, was fine, with me being, you know...'

'A lady lover?' says Lips, who's been inching closer. 'You better believe it, Mrs!' He snaps his fingers at her.

'I wish! No, both my parents really were pretty decent about it all. I'm married, we've got a daughter. Claudie, she's incredible.'

'And yet here you are,' Aaron chimes back in, 'so perhaps not as happy families as all that.'

'I don't know, honestly.' Jess tries to explain, surprised how quickly they've detected the wrinkles. 'I love them all. Then my dad died, and

I wasn't expecting it. I used to perform as Elvis because of him, but I feel like I've lost him. I think that's why I'm here. I haven't behaved well, I've been a shit to be honest. I've come to get my head together, figure stuff out. Say goodbye. Just got to figure out what I'm really here to say goodbye to.'

'Oh sweetie, it sounds like a mess,' Don says and covers her hand with his own. 'You've got it bad. You wanna know what I always say?' He pauses, sits back, and takes a swig of his drink. 'Love will always find a way.'

'Maybe,' Jess replies. 'I don't know if I know what that means anymore.'

'Honey, you know what Elvis would do if he needed to figure something out?'

'What?'

'Honey, he'd sing.'

'How bad can it be?' she thinks as she climbs onto the stage. Her tee-shirt, jeans, and trainers are a far cry from the costumes of all her predecessors, or the one she used to wear. The nerves kick in. Jess hasn't performed, not like this, for months. The last time she was in full costume, in Birmingham, was a disaster. She'd failed to connect and then worse, she'd been rejected. And that rejection had precipitated one of the stupidest things she'd ever done. Created the mess she's in now.

Her nerves get even worse when the crowd, gone wild for other performers, goes silent as she's given the microphone, and she walks to the centre of the stage. But it's not hostile, they're waiting. In the few seconds of silence, before the track starts playing, she hears a wolf-whistle from deep in the bar. One of her four new friends.

Flicking the microphone cable behind her, she's grateful to have about twenty seconds to steady her breath before she needs to start singing. She turns left and right, as if checking something behind her, and then stands to face the audience. Her way.

As soon as she starts singing, she knows it's still there. He's still there. This performance doesn't require her showier moves. The tiniest gestures are all she needs to ensure that all attention is on her face, the angle of her cheekbones, the words that she can sing with a slight, sad smile, the glances at the ceiling. She sings about regrets, plans unfulfilled, plans still yet to make. About love, about beginning and endings.

She ends 'My Way' side-on to the audience. She's faced it all. The connection is complete. She doesn't need to look at them to know they've truly seen her. And him. They don't know her story, but they know what she's lost, are perhaps guessing what she's looking for. She hangs her head, grief and loss and hopes heavy on her shoulders, once more wishing she could right the wrongs, apologise for things she's said and done and the things she hasn't done or said yet. She won't sing like this, like Him, again.

Chapter Twenty-eight
Graceland

Jess is disillusioned by her Graceland experience the minute she's picked up by the shuttle bus that collects her from the hotel lobby.

Only once they're all onboard does her tour guide, Cherry, stand at the front with her clipboard in hand and headset microphone, and smile. Then it's full beam and straight into a deft introduction to the tour and what they should expect of the next few hours. She calls out to the rows of tourists to sing out the answers to her questions, recite lines from his most famous songs. Jess hunkers down in her seat, staring at the buildings that Cherry is pointing out along the way. The jollity that pervades this bus is not one that she feels in her heart.

'There's the Memphis Music Hall of Fame,' Cherry cries. 'Tickets also available from us and a special discount for you folks. See that corner there? Well, I gotta tell you, that's the best landmark we have. It's where I was proposed to by my own school sweetheart.' The more enthusiastic people on the bus coo. 'Thank the Lord I said no as he's doing time for armed robbery!'

Everyone laughs, even though they know she tells the same joke several times a day. They pause at a hotel, a glorious 1920s edifice of pale stone.

'And that, folks, is The Peabody Hotel. Heard the story of the ducks? That's right, folks, twice a day, those ducks walk through like they own the place. And given the price of a night there, they probably do!'

Cherry tells them to sit back and enjoy the view during the fifteen minutes it will take them to get to Graceland. Jess knows she should sit up, smile, show her appreciation, but can't summon up the charm. The seat next to her feels empty. Her dad should be here, she thinks. He'd join in the game, he'd ask questions, holding back the fact that he also knew the answers. Eventually, they pull into a parking lot. It's on the other side to the white mansion she can see in the distance, those famous wrought iron gates.

The pneumatic doors whoosh open, and Cherry stands at the bottom, not asking for, but still expecting the crumpled dollar bills that are pushed into her hand by the passengers as they disembark. Jess hasn't brought enough small notes for tips, so she has to hand over a twenty-dollar bill.

'Why, thank you, ma'am. I gotta say it, you kinda look like him, you know.'

'I'll take that as a compliment,' Jess smiles.

A Graceland branded shuttle glides to a stop, and they all pile on. There's no docent this time, but as soon as they take off, the whole three-minute drive across the road and through the gates of Graceland, a pre-recorded message shares a few well-known facts about the Presley family and lays out a few of the ground rules for their visit. There will be no freedom for solo exploring.

The bus pulls up a little way down the sloping driveway that leads up to the house. Instantly, everyone starts taking photos – of everything. Jess walks ahead, trying to put some distance between herself and these others; this is an experience she wants to have with as much solitude as possible.

Graceland is not the palatial mansion that she's imagined. Docents guide visitors along the prescribed route, admonishing anyone caught recording, reminding them not to use flash, keeping them moving at the carefully orchestrated pace. No time to linger at the doorway to the ground floor living room, the pristine white suite, the photos of Elvis's parents, Gladys and Vernon, on the small table, or to peer beyond the peacocks in the stained-glass windows over the gleaming white grand piano beyond. No time to tilt over the ropes to catch glimpses of the polished silver ornaments in the solid wood cabinets in the dining room, or time to stop as they pass through the kitchen and to imagine the bevy of maids preparing late-night snacks for Elvis and his friends. The three TVs flicker with period imagery in the bright yellow snug, but there is no time to imagine him kicking back in here, maybe on his guitar, maybe playing with Lisa Marie, or canoodling with Priscilla before their marriage went South.

Down the mirror-clad staircase, and they're in the Jungle Room. The thick green carpet, the enormous leather chairs with ornately carved arms, the monkey ornaments, and the brick wall beyond. But there is no time to pause and think of Elvis down here, recording his final album with RCA, summoning the musicians at any hour of the night or day, the light kept out.

Before she knows it, they are pushed out into the daylight. They can walk across the pathway to see Vernon's office, the pool, the fields that would have held Lisa Marie's ponies. Or they can exit through the trophy gallery of childhood treasures, platinum albums, costumes. Funnelled through, offered a headset that she refuses, Jess is bewildered. If the ghost of Elvis is here and has a message for her, she has not found it yet. When she'd told Don she was heading to Graceland, he'd tempered her expectations of magic or moments. He was right.

She skips the final part of the tour and ends up in the final stop before the museum, the Meditation Garden. Like everywhere else at Graceland, it's manicured, pristine, guarded. Mercifully quieter here, a docent stands by to stop anyone getting carried away and climbing over the short fences to the graves of Elvis and his family. For the first time since she's got here, Jess feels alone, but she knows she won't be for long.

The reality of where she is hits her all of a sudden. There is so much love and heartbreak here. Imperfect, impossible loves. Gladys and Vernon, Elvis and Priscilla. The love stories we think we know, but each ended up broken, messy. She knows she is one of hundreds of thousands who stand here each year, but her own pain and sense of loss are hers alone. Grief and confusion wind her. She takes a few steps back to rest against the curved wall encasing the space. Tears run down her cheeks. The docent comes up beside her and hands her a tissue.

'We never get over the loss,' he says. 'It's often here when it happens.'

Jess sniffs, nods thanks for the tissues, wipes her eyes.

'Happens?' she asks.

'We find him. He's been here all along, maybe he never left. You take care of yourself, now, ma'am. And have a safe journey home.'

Soon, she thinks. As soon as she figures out what home means.

CHLOË FOWLER

Chapter Twenty-nine
The Road to Tupelo

Don toots his horn, winds his window down, and rotates his wrist in a regal wave. Whatever Jess was expecting when he suggested this pilgrimage, as he called it, it was not this. He's rocked up in a vintage pink Cadillac, all fins and gleaming curves. 1960s pop blares out. It's not the car that makes her laugh, pressing her hands to her mouth. Don, Aaron, Lips and Bobby are resplendent in full King. Unlike the other night when they'd each been a different version of him, today they're in matching white jumpsuits, coloured rhinestones set against gleaming satin. Their shoulders and lapels wink in the sun, and the hands they wiggle at her are laden with diamante rings. Lips, Bobby and Don have swept their natural hair up in a quiff. Aaron is wearing a perfectly set black wig.

'Oh my god,' she cries, 'you all look amazing. And I'm such a scruff bag. Again! I'm going to totally ruin the effect. I'm so grateful for today. I can't tell you.'

'Hush now.' Don waves again, engine idling. 'Your carriage is here, it's time to start this journey. Step aboard, ma'am.'

A small crowd gathers on the sidewalk, holding up their phones to capture the spectacle. A Chinese couple asks if they can have their photo taken with Lips, and they huddle together, their hands over their mouths in delight. Jess already feels lighter with these men, accepted, ready.

'Come on,' Bobby says from the passenger seat next to Don, his age and status conferring him a right to travel in comfort, 'before we get mobbed.'

Aaron shuffles up and pats the seat next to him. Jess dips down and gets in, a wave of leather and polish in her nostrils. Lips extracts himself from the tourists and squeezes beside her on the far right.

'Been a while since I've been in between two such beautiful boys,' Jess laughs, wiggling forward so that Lips can do up her seatbelt for her.

'Been a while since I've touched such a pretty woman's rear end,' he says, clicking the clasp into place.

'Are we ready?' Don calls back.

'Ready,' they call back in unison.

'Then let this pilgrimage commence.'

As they drive, phones swivel to capture the final purr as they disappear.

'This is literally the most amazing car I've ever been in,' Jess says. 'Is it the same as Elvis's?'

'Younger sister, maybe. That was a Fleetwood. This is a Deville. But we're not complaining,' Don explains. 'I pulled in a favour.'

The silhouette of the pink 1960s Cadillac is distorted by windows as they glide past; people stare and point. Jess feels the vibration of the engine under the springs of the cream leather seat beneath her. Aaron, to her right, is so tall that his quiff is squashed by the roof.

'Mind you don't get any hair muck on the leather,' Don warns.

'Maybe take your wig off,' suggests Bobby. 'We're on the road for a while, no one will see.'

'No chance,' Aaron quips, 'a lady never takes her wig off in public.'

Their early banter wears off a touch as Don signals for silence to negotiate the complex lane changes to the highway out of the city. The car sits low to the tarmac, more boat than car, and the antique mirrors are out of step with the higher vehicles surrounding them. Don cranes his neck, sticking his bejewelled arm out to ensure his antique indicator lights are spotted.

Bobby, the group's elder, is in charge of the radio, slightly aloof as though surrounded by squabbling children. His skin is pale and taut, a masterclass in SPF and Botox. He's neither as old as Elvis would be if he'd lived or as young as Elvis was when he died but is stuck somewhere else. Timeless, regal. But having seen him on stage, Jess knows that he stiffens with electricity, only slackening when he's in repose.

Aaron, the youngest, is treated as the baby of the group. Impish, aware of his charm and at times camp and bitchy. When he's not on show he's quieter, reflective, and perhaps more than all of them, Jess feels a connection. Lips is funny, makes jokes about the being the only Chinese Elvis, and wears his status as the 'different one' as a badge of honour. He makes comments that none of the others would dare to, prone to exaggeration.

'We'll take the 55,' Don explains, and the others groan.

'I know, it's ugly, but we've got to pass Graceland, right, if we're doing this properly.'

Jess sits up straighter, but Aaron pats her wrist.

'You won't see it from the highway, hun,' he says. 'But you'll know it's there.'

They pass block after block of suburban Memphis. The grass verges give way to low, flat houses, so different from the neon wealth of downtown. Bikes lie prone, discarded on patches of scrubby yard, and small tumbledown sheds and wire fencing back onto the highway. There are references to Elvis, BB King and other Rock and Roll or Blues greats emblazoned on every passing restaurant, strip mall, and street name, but out here there is none of the neon glamour of downtown. Wires stretch across the highway; suspended road signs and lights dangle in the breeze. They pass Dixie Queens, BBQ joints, auto shops. Nail bars, dollar stores, pharmacies – each one charmless, and not intended for tourists.

'Don't know why you chose the 55 anyway,' Bobby grumbles from the front seat. 'It's really so ugly.'

'It's quicker,' explains Don. 'And once we're on the 22, you can quit your carping.'

Jess has not asked how long the journey will be. Craning her neck to see if Don has attached a sat nav to the dashboard, relying on at least one modern gizmo in this beautiful old car. But he is clearly driving from memory, so she sits backs again as the boys bicker lightly between themselves.

'Is this a trip you make every year?' Jess eventually asks.

'Not always,' Don says. 'But we know when someone needs a little remindin'. A little truth-seeking if you know what I mean.'

Thirty minutes or so later, the grey, over-baked suburban roads give way to wide-open spaces and forests stretching either side.

'Where are we now?' Jess asks.

'Holly Springs National Forest,' explains Bobby.

It's beautiful, and the sight of nature reminds her of an America that she didn't expect to see on this trip. They pass a sign to the exit ramp to Tupelo. Like Memphis, the city's outskirts morph from rundown neighbourhoods to more gentrified areas, signs to gated communities and city attractions. After following several signs to Elvis's birthplace, they pull into a parking lot. Signs point to the museum, there's another vintage car parked under a gazebo, and a tiny, unassuming building – a shack really – is tucked under some trees on the right. It's early; theirs is the only car in the lot.

Don gets out and opens the rear door, so Aaron, Lips, and Jess can climb out. Bobby stretches, shakes his legs.

'You go on over, honey,' says Don. 'We'll give you a moment alone.'

Once she's paid for her entry ticket, Jess walks down the red paving, passing manicured lawns and tubs full of flowers. Just a few minutes away from the urban sprawl, but all she hears are birds, and the faint sound of Elvis coming from speakers embedded in the bushes. She pauses at the copper sign outside the plot. 1935 he was born, right here.

The suspended green bench on the porch swings as she walks towards it, though there's no breeze or person around to have disturbed it. Climbing up the two whitewashed wooden steps, she stands in front of the open door. This tiny building, the birthplace of the King.

The silence inside is eery, just the faint whirr of the highway, and even the birds have melted away to nothing. A log-burning stove sits underneath a brick chimney, a green-checked tablecloth on a table is set for three people, a highchair set to one side. She pictures a tiny, red-cheeked baby, kicking his chubby heels against the footrest, smiling, unaware of the impact of the life ahead of him. The family's meagre possessions are stowed in a small corner cupboard, a few pots, and pans, nothing that doesn't serve a purpose.

A door leads through to the bedroom on the left-hand side. A small bed, impossibly sized for two grown adults, a mirrored dresser, two comfortable chairs. She imagines Elvis's mother, Gladys, sitting up late at night, nursing a restless infant, mourning the loss of his stillborn twin, unaware of the legend that lives. His father, Vernon, in one of his rare visits home, fast asleep. The busy floral wallpaper presses in. A vase of red roses is silhouetted against a netted window. There is a faint musty smell, polish, a chemical undertone of whatever they've used to preserve this tiny space.

The collision of ghosts, memories and premonitions are suddenly too much, and Jess walks quickly out and sits down on the bench outside, worrying for a moment if the porch ceiling will take her weight. Her feet barely reach the floor, but she balances her toes on the wooden floorboards and pushes off gently.

As Jess swings, the silence makes way for more imaginary sounds.

A baby crying, laughter, the tentative picking out of tunes on a guitar, the sounds of iron pots on the stove. She thinks about what it must have taken for Elvis's parents to pack up their lives in Tupelo and move to an uncertain future in Memphis. A decision that changed everything, including the future of music. She thinks about Elvis, Priscilla, and their little girl, Lisa Marie. Is Elvis, the King, eternally disappointing for abandoning his wife and daughter? Or was there courage in his act?

It was the part of his story that her own father refused to talk about. He always wanted there to be a happier ending. It would never have occurred to him that his own daughter might derail her own happy life for something different. His disappointment would have crushed her.

Jess tries to picture their new baby. She hasn't allowed herself to do this before; it has felt premature and she knows it still is. She hasn't wanted to imagine to life a person when she isn't yet sure she wants them to exist.

Now she sees a son. Asleep in a cradle, a fist pressed up against his plump cheek. Perfect. But does she want him? Can she give him what he needs? Is there enough love, enough will, to get her that far? And although Jess tries to train her mind on her family, the other woman constantly resurfaces into her mind. The woman who excites her, believes in her and who she finds herself drawn back to, time and again.

Footsteps. Jess looks up, tears on her cheeks, imagining for a moment that it will be her own father coming up the path to meet her. He would be walking slowly, a little stooped, careful of his knees. He'd look up at her, smile.

'You coming home, love,' he'd say. 'It's time.'

She takes her phone out of her pocket and taps out a message.

Can we talk? I need to hear your voice. xx

The swing rocks beneath her as she stands up too quickly, relief propelling her upwards.

Of course, it is not her dad's footsteps walking towards her. It is Bobby, Aaron, Lips, and Don. Four Elvises, in perfect formation, coming towards her. They stand at the bottom of the stairs, and Don hands her a linen handkerchief. She notices Elvis's embroidered initials, EAP, picked out in blue on the cotton. She holds it back out and smiles at him.

'It's the little things,' he says.

'Thank you,' she smiles, 'for bringing me here.'

'Did you find him?'

'I think I did. I think so.'

'We thought you would,' Aaron says. 'Most people think he's at Graceland, but he's not. Or maybe only part of him is.'

'You take your time,' Bobby says. 'We're ready when you are. We have one more stop to make.'

'I'm coming,' she says. 'I won't be long.'

The four men stroll away, their capes swinging behind them. She stands up and walks into Elvis's first home one more time, this tiny, coveted and then abandoned space. The Tupelo home the Presleys left to ensure that Elvis had a future, one they would fight for, both together, but also apart.

Chapter Thirty
The Lake

Jess's thoughts crowd in on her during the drive back to Memphis and she can already feel impatience coursing through her blood. She feels a hunger and a sureness within her that she's been pressing down but is impossible to ignore any longer. The slow purr of the Cadillac makes her feel faintly queasy, hemmed in by the hot thighs of Aaron and Lips either side of her. She's so grateful to these men for showing her the way, but now all she wants is to be alone so she can make that call. But as Memphis grows closer, they suddenly turn off. A sharp left at signs that announce they are entering the Holly Springs National Park. Assuming they are making a pitstop for the loo, her heart sinks when they crawl through the roads until they reach a wooded area.

'Ready?' Aaron turns to her.

Jess feigns an enthusiasm she doesn't feel.

Don gets out of the car first and opens the doors so the others can spill out and shake stiffness from their legs. He walks to the trunk and gets out a small brown suitcase. The leather looks old, the clasps are rusty. Aaron and Lips are already setting off towards the trees.

'Not going to lock it?' Jess asks, nodding at the car as Don ushers for her to follow him.

'Round here?' he says. 'We'll be the only people for miles. Trust me.'

Bobby splits off between some trees. There are no obvious markers to suggest this is where they should turn, but it's clear he knows the way. Despite wearing full rhinestone jumpsuits, capes flowing, these four men confidently pick their way over the roots, clumps, and branches that litter the trace of a path. Jess is embarrassed that she's so quickly breathless, not wearing shoes designed for cross-country terrain.

Trudging up a steep hill, forest twigs and leaves crunch as they're crushed, the only other sounds are the occasional curse words when they lose their balance. Aaron, the fittest, has forged further ahead, and all she can see is the occasional flash of his white cape through the dense trees. It smells damp, vegetal, of pine and earth.

Jess goes to check her phone, desperate to see if she's had a reply, but it's tucked in the deep leather pocket behind Don's seat, and she doesn't want to cause a fuss, and is not confident enough to turn back on her own. She walks on automatically, focusing so hard on what's under her feet that she becomes dizzy.

Finally, she hears a distant woo-hoo coming through the trees. Don, ahead of her, turns to check she's still behind him. 'Just a bit further,' he says.

'Nobody said anything about a hike,' Jess laughs, hoping that her tone comes out a little more chipper than she actually feels.

'Oh, this ain't a hike, honey, this is a stroll.'

The trees stop, and they're on the shores of a small lake. Not much bigger than an Olympic-sized pool, the murky green water is only disturbed by an occasional ripple. There is no jetty, no buildings, just a small rocky shore that slopes down to the water, flanked on all sides by tall trees.

'Oh my god,' Jess says, 'it's so beautiful.'

'There's a larger lake up the road,' Lips explains. 'But it's not so private.'

In the few seconds it takes for Jess to wonder why privacy would be desirable, she sees Aaron carefully untying the bow to his cape, laying it on a nearby rock, and then unbuttoning his trousers. He speeds up against the chill, pulling off his pants, his socks, his undershirt. Finally, he peels off his wig. His hairless torso is so lean it's almost translucent, though muscles are defined on his chest, and his skinny calves bulge when he walks. He tip-toes gingerly to the edge, his arms straight out for balance. Without pausing, he walks in until the water is lapping at his thighs. When he turns around to beckon them in, he doesn't bother to hide himself, and Jess flinches at the sight of his naked body.

'Hurry up,' he calls out as Lips and Don start peeling off their clothes.

'Not you?' she asks Bobby, who has gone to sit on a large rock.

'My paddling days are over,' he says and waves at the water, 'but you must.'

'Come on,' Lips says to her, 'it's part of the ritual.'

'Ritual?' says Jess. 'I'll think I'll sit and wait with Bobby.'

But even as she says it, she starts to regret her decision, not because they will judge her but because this is another experience she's being gifted. Looking around to see if there's a rock or tree big enough for her to hide behind, wishing she had a towel at least so she could wear it down to the water's edge and ditch it at the last minute. She is shy in the face of their bold nudity, but off come her jeans, t-shirt, bra and finally her pants, her feet pale and slim against the rocks.

'Here, I'll steady you,' Don says and holds out his hand. Initially, their nakedness puts her off, unsure where to look. Now, with her own skin being brushed by the autumn breeze, she realises its power. Her nipples harden in the cold, and she fights the urge to cover them with her free arm.

The water is freezing. Her muscles go into shock, and her lungs constrict, she breathes deeply to stem the panic and walks one step and then a few more. Don and Lips swim serenely into the centre of the water to join Aaron, who's creating small waves as he moves his arms back and forth to keep his head above the water. As she swims towards them, soft weeds stroke against the goosebumps on her shins.

Without pre-meditating, she dives under, flinching with the cold slap of water on her cheeks and forehead. Risking opening her eyes, her pale arms paddle ahead, legs kicking for balance. She has taken in enough air to push herself forward a little way but then comes up again to breathe.

She drifts towards the others, shaking her head so her tears merge with the lake. The three men lie on their backs, wafting their arms beneath them to keep afloat, toes peeping above the waterline, pubic hair clumping in their navels. It is not shocking. Tilting her own head back, she feels water sloshing in her ears, deafening and then rushing out again so she can hear the waves, her own breath.

The sky is bright white and instead of allowing herself to blink, she stares straight up, forcing herself to feel the ache of cloud blindness. This is pain she deserves, even craves. The realisation that she's become so one-tracked and side-tracked by being Elvis, then Em. How little she's been herself, the shame of being another cliché of fame. She said yes to a new baby because Sarah wanted her to, and she's felt guilty ever since. Guilty that the decision was made in a moment of shame, guilty that she still doesn't know if she has enough love, or desire, to parent a newborn again. She loves Claudie to the ends of the earth and is so proud of the little person that she's becoming, but can she still parent her if she's not in her life every day?

And then there's Tiff. A woman who she's only known for a short time but feels so close to. A woman who she wants to know so much more about, to be under her skin in the same way that Tiff is under hers. Fuck, she thinks. Fuck. She punches the water beneath her.

So desperate to please others, to *be* others, so incapable of being the woman she wants to be. The lake can't wash away her fear, but Jess knows she is close to knowing what she has to do.

Hands reach under her shoulders, tilt her upright. It's Don.

'Best get out, honey. You don't want your bones to freeze.'

In silence, Jess swims with the others towards the shoreline, and then picks her careful way up to the rocks, wincing as pebbles pierce the puckered soles of her feet. Don opens the suitcase and brings out a bottle of tequila and some glasses, a little Tupperware tub of lemons. He pours them each a drink, and they sit dripping, shivering, waiting for the air to dry their wet bodies.

Don hands her a tumbler.

'Medicinal purposes,' he says.

Once they each have a glass, they take turns to say a few words, only tilting the liquid down their throats once they've spoken.

Lips goes first.

'For my voice, for my family, for my past, thank you, buddy.'

Then Aaron.

'For giving me the courage to carry on. For giving my family the strength to accept me for who I am.'

Bobby: 'For David. I miss you.'

From Don: 'For the wisdom we all need to make the right decisions when the time comes.'

Finally, Don nods at Jess.

'For my Dad because I never got to say thank you. And to my family, I'm sorry.'

The tequila burns her throat as it slips down.

'Back on the road?' Don asks, and they all nod and slowly get dressed. Jess's jeans stick to her calves, she tugs her socks over her wet feet. The four men head off but Jess trails behind. She fishes in her pocket and takes out the small pouch where she keeps her rings. Selecting one carefully, she bends down and scrabbles in the earth, dislodging leaves and pebbles. She places one in the small well, and crouches down.

'Goodbye Dad,' she says softly, aloud. 'Goodbye Elvis. Thank you both, so much.'

Back in the car, Jess drinks in the landscape one last time. Even now, her resolve is faltering. She's read about affairs, they're the stuff of countless TV programmes, films and songs. She knows the act of truth-telling is often pictured as a selfish desire for absolution from one, a passing on of hurt to another. She also knows that telling the truth is the only option she has.

An AT&T billboard reminds her to check her phone; she has no idea of the time. She fishes deep into the leather seatback pocket, careful not to wake Aaron, who instinctively moves his leg aside as she reaches across him. She presses the on button and a few seconds later, a string of notifications pop up on the screen. Ten missed calls, text messages, WhatsApps and an email. All from Sarah. All sent nearly an hour ago when Jess was lying, face-up, naked in a stupid fucking lake in the middle of fucking nowhere. In a country her wife does not know she is even in. The possibilities of an accident, something that's happened to Claudie, crush in on her as she panics. Not now, she thinks, not now.

She leans forward, desperate for Don to stop, and a new notification pops up.

'Don. Don.' She leans forward and taps him on the shoulder. 'Please hurry. Please. It's my wife, she's been trying to get hold of me urgently. I need to call her back.'

'Don't worry, honey, we'll be back soon.'

'You don't understand, Don. It's Sarah. Something's happened.'

'Just hold tight. We'll get you there.'

Don puts his foot on the gas. The commotion causes the others to wake up, but they remain silent in the face of potential bad news. Jess knows they have at least an hour to go. Her back is stiff with tension, the car is suddenly unbearably small and she's desperate to get out.

'Maybe this will distract us,' Don says as he flicks on the radio. But one of Roy Orbison's songs comes on, 'It's Over'. It takes them all a while to spot the danger in the words ahead, and as his beautiful voice starts singing that *your baby won't be near you anymore*, Don reaches forward and flicks the radio off again.

'Be my eyes, boys. Jess, honey, you hang on in there.'

The roads they travelled earlier were full of possibility, a trip to come. Now, each landmark is loaded with fear, one mile and then another, closer to catastrophe. In the face of what she's about to hear,

Jess wonders how she will ever be able to tell Sarah the truth. Perhaps it is irrelevant now. When the car finally pulls up at her hotel, the four men pile out as quickly as they can and all Jess has time to do is throw a thank you over her shoulder as she charges through the revolving doors, passing tourists lingering in reception and then travels up, up, up in the lift.

Back in her hotel room, the line rings interminably, and her terrified thoughts crowd in. She knows Sarah and Claudie are at Center Parcs with Sarah's family. Has something happened to Claudie? What if Sarah's body is reacting badly to the hormones, or something has shown up in a blood test and she's been rushed to hospital? She might not be allowed her phone, so how will she know if she's okay? If Sarah can't answer the phone, who will? Will it be Sarah's parents, her brother, that tell her the news? Can she get home in time? In time for what?

A click. The voice that answers is groggy, but it is at least her wife's. Jess's relief is so strong she has to sit on the bed to steady herself, but she knows it doesn't mean anything. Claudie's life could still be in danger.

'Sarah. Thank God.' There is a long silence on the other end of the line. 'Sar? Are you alright? Is it Claudie?'

'Where the fuck are you, Jess?'

Sarah's voice is clearer now. The grogginess Jess heard was because she'd been asleep. Forced to abruptly U-turn her emotions to self-defence rather than panic, she's not prepared with an answer quickly enough. She's clearly taking so long to wheel through the possibilities that her wife has to speak again. Cold.

'Where the fuck are you?'

Blind-sided, Jess stalls.

'What is it? Please, just tell me.'

'We're fine.' The volume of Sarah's voice rises to a hoarse whisper. 'One more time...'

'Sarah, look, I'm so sorry. I'm not where I said I was. I'm not at home.'

'Well, that's pretty fucking obvious.'

'What do you mean?' It's too late, Jess panics, Sarah knows. But how much?

'Guess who got a call from the neighbours? They kindly rang to tell me that a massive parcel of something marked perishable turned up at the house. Wondered if I wanted them to open it, say who it was from, put it in the fridge. It was from your director, Jak. The card reads, and I quote, '*Hope you're settling in back at home with the fam. Thanks for everything.*' So, I'm thinking to myself, Jess, why does the director of the show that you're supposed to be still shooting, because they needed you for an extra few days, think you're at home already? Which means where, exactly, the fuck are you?'

'I was going to tell you, I was. I'm in Memphis.'

Seconds of silence tick by. Jess tries to picture her wife, sitting up in bed, trying not to wake Claudie so early, her face illuminated by the screen, trying to compute how far away from each other they really are.

'I had to come here. I couldn't come home. There are too many reasons to explain now. But I'm so sorry.'

'You're in Memphis? As in America? Without us? What the fuck?' Sarah hisses. 'Are you with someone?'

All Jess's resolve to tell Sarah the truth evaporates. She can't do this, she can't break something that's already so fragile, not like this.

'I'm here alone,' she says. This, at least, is not a lie. 'Who would I be with?'

If Sarah guesses the truth, she will say Tiff's name, and it will all be over. Sarah pauses.

'How should I know?'

Jess feels relief first, then wheels through guilt, regret and shame. She lands on self-righteous anger that her loyalty is being questioned, despite knowing how far across the line she has stepped in the last few months.

'I swear, I'm here alone. I just needed to be here. It's complicated.'

'*Complicated*? So complicated you can't tell your own wife? What the hell, Jess? You just keep lying to me.'

'I know, I know and I'm so sorry. But is this really all my fault?' Jess's volume rises.

'I don't know whose fault it is! We can't have this conversation now, can we? Not while you're in Memphis, and I'm stuck in Center Parcs with my entire family. Who, by the way, are already pretty furious with you for doing the shoot in the first place.'

'They said they were proud,' Jess says.

'Of course, they did. They're nice people, my family. We support each other, even if it's not totally convenient. It's what we do.'

'What are you trying to say?'

'I'm so tired, Jess. I'm tired of feeling like shit and being totally alone. I'm tired of being the only parent for Claudie, for months now. I'm tired of not knowing what our future is. I'm tired of fighting. Of being so disappointed.'

'I'm tired too.'

'Jess, this isn't just about you, you know. I know you think that all this is because of how you're feeling and the decisions you've made. But time apart has made me realise that where we're at is bigger than that. I've been thinking too.'

Jess is stunned into silence. Sarah is so quiet that Jess has to ask if she's still there and when she does speak, it's with a question. The one that Jess couldn't answer before, because the answer would have been a lie.

Sarah's voice is now a sad, low whisper, coming at her from thousands of miles away.

'I have to ask you some questions I never wanted to ask. But I can't handle not knowing anymore.'

Jess grips the bedsheets in her hand, knuckles taut. Barely breathing but needing to stand up, Jess moves to the bedroom window. It's sealed shut, preventing any urge to jump. Down to the scrubby car lots, the rooftops littered with aircon generator boxes, the alleys where the bins gather. She wants to be anywhere, anywhere but here. A voice so quiet she can barely hear it.

'How close are we to losing each other? Do you even want another baby? Do you want to be part of our… my family? Because if you don't, then I need to know, and I need to know now.'

'Oh Sarah, I'm so sorry.'

'Shit.' Sarah's voice shifts from quiet fear to anger. 'This isn't the way this is supposed to go.'

'What do you mean by 'this'?'

'This conversation. This marriage. Us.'

Jess pauses, but she knows the right answer, she's surer than she's ever been.

'You've done so much for me, Sarah. And I've tried so hard.'

'But that's not the point, is it?' Sarah whispers. 'It shouldn't have to feel like such hard work for you. That isn't good enough. And I don't need you to be grateful either.'

'I don't know how to talk to you about how I'm feeling. I thought I'd lost so much when dad died. Elvis too. Everything just feels empty, and I've just felt so lonely. I don't know if we're the same people that we were. Or at least I think *I've* changed, or am changing. I don't know. Everything just feels different. And I feel like you sense it too. I used to think it was just me, but I'm not so sure.'

As she's speaking, Jess presses her forehead against the cool glass of the windowpane. Presses so hard that her head hurts. High in the air, just able to look out, across, up, and down, as if there is nothing tethering her to the ground. To reality. Sarah's voice interrupts.

'What does all that actually mean, though? What are you saying? Are you asking me something? Or telling me?'

'I wish we weren't having this conversation in two different places.' Jess's legs shake and she feels sick. She moves away from the window and sits down on the end of the bed. It's a little too high off the ground, it's uncomfortable, but so is everything else about this terrible moment. 'I think I need more. I don't mean a house, or a new life in Brighton.'

'Or a baby?'

'Maybe even that. I just can't see a way that we can both get what we want right now, and I feel like I've spent a lot of our marriage doing what *you* want. I need to perform. I don't know if I'm saying it right, but I need to figure out how I can be someone else, not Elvis, but also be myself. I want to be taken seriously as a performer. I miss it, and I've realised that I'm good at it. Like, really good at it. And it's been so long since I've felt that I had a voice, a talent, something to be great at. Does that make any sense?'

'Oh, Jess.' Sarah is crying now. 'Is that really true? How long have you been feeling like this? Have I been so difficult to talk to that you couldn't have said this earlier?' Her voice gets louder, panic and anger rising in her. 'Do you really see me as the person who's stopped you being who you want to be? I thought I'd supported you in everything, everything you've wanted to do. I've never mentioned the money! I've been there. I've made it happen. I've even pushed you...'

'I am grateful,' Jess says quietly. 'I'm just telling you how I feel. Felt.

I know I'm to blame. It's my fault, I never asked for anything different. I didn't know there was something else that I wanted. I don't even know what I want, I just know that I don't think it's the same as what we've got now.'

'Are you telling me that you've met someone else? Is that what this is?'

Jess clenches her eyes shut and pauses, weighing up whether to lie to spare Sarah the truth, at least for now, or compound her misery.

'It's not about someone else. It's about me. Just me.'

Sarah's voice rises, her earlier patience and sadness running low.

'But it's not just you, is it Jess? What about Claudie? Me? The new baby that from what you're saying now we aren't ever going to have, that maybe you never even wanted.'

The room has grown dark. It's not just the time zones that separate them. Sarah, sitting amongst the tasteful décor of a holiday chalet, children's toys scattered around her. Jess in Memphis, in an anonymous tourist hotel. Both of them so far from home, and from each other.

Despite this conversation, the conviction she had in Tupelo – the lake, her new friends – is still there.

'There's so much more I want to say. Please, Sarah, just give me the chance to explain. I'm coming home. Please, let's just talk. I need to know what *you* want.'

Sarah's anger fades again and her voice is quiet.

'I don't know what I want. I thought I did, but I'm not sure. We'll talk. When you're back. You're right, this isn't just about you. Maybe what I want is changing too. If you can't be on the journey with me, or I'm stopping you from getting what you really want, then I'm strong enough to go it alone. I really am.'

While Jess is trying to figure out if this is a threat or a fact, she hears a shout down the line. Someone opens a door, calls out to Sarah and she says she has to go. She hears a shout and then Claudie crying.

'What's happened? Is she okay? Sarah?'

'I've got to go. Our daughter needs me. And right now, only one of us can make it better. The one of us that's actually here.'

'Please,' Jess swallows. 'Please just call me back.'

It's too late, Sarah has hung up.

Chapter Thirty-one
A New King

Bagless, with too many hours to kill, Jess puts off heading into the Departure Lounge. Numb, not sure if she's hungry, thirsty, wide-awake, or exhausted, she sits on a bench and watches queues fill and empty, fill and empty again. She checks her phone endlessly, pressing it on, hoping and then pressing it on again the minute it goes dark. Just one message, she thinks. Just one word. And I'll be there.

Looking up at the departure board she sees the flights tick by as gates are announced, to Berlin, New York, LA, London. The city that is her home but where everything has changed. The grief for her father and Elvis may have receded, but losing Sarah is something she's not able to comprehend yet.

But she knows now that her marriage has ended.

She can't yet process the guilt, the anger and the sadness as the dismantling of their life together begins. The potential impact on Claudie is terrifying, but she knows that she and Sarah will do their best to spare her the worst. Marriages end, homes break, parents cope, children adapt. The unimaginable consequences of a momentous decision are also the only ways to find their truths.

They have arrived at a moment when they both have a choice, and while there is pain in all directions, Jess knows that there is only one that comes with hope. And love.

Tiff. The woman she prays will accept her heart, and return it. With her, she might be the person she wants to be. Perhaps she can do the same for Tiff in return.

Her gate is announced, and suddenly she's late. She stands up, rushes to the escalator and grips on to the rubber rail as it ferries her up to Security. Sensing a commotion, she turns. Four men hurry towards her and then follow her up. Don first, then Aaron, Lips and finally, slower than the rest, Bobby. White jumpsuits, leather boots, wide belts, gemstones glistening.

'You came!' Her emotions catch up as she waits at the top. 'I almost missed you.'

'Girl, gonna leave without saying goodbye?' says Aaron, hand on his hip in a mock pout.

'Don called,' Lips explains. 'He got your message in time.'

'Sweetie,' Bobby says, 'you look pretty beat.'

'I'm sorry, I have to leave. It's sudden, I know.'

Don peers into her face.

'Taking care of business?'

'I might be too late. But I have to try, at least.'

He pulls her into a hug.

'Remember Elvis, embrace the mess. It's life honey, it's just life.'

'I will, I promise.'

She quickly puts her arms around Lips, Aaron and then Bobby, picks up her carry-on bag and runs. Forced to pause through Security, she pats her pockets one last time to check they're empty. They're not, there's a ring in there. It's not like the one she buried back in the forest, but it means the same. The lightning bolt, the stones, the heavy gold. Slipped into her pocket by Don as they parted.

She will never forget these men, their kindness, intuition, how at peace they are with themselves. Jess knows who she is, and who she is meant to be.

She may never see them again, but they will always be with her. The tall one, the elfin one, the funny one, the wise one, her father, and Elvis himself. Shoulder to shoulder. Each of them, forever Elvis.

Once through security, Jess sprints through the departure lounge towards her gate. Breathless, sweating, bag knocking into others as she passes. One of the last to board, there are tears running down her face as she fastens her buckle, ignoring the concerned faces of people sitting around her. The flight attendant reminds them to turn off their phones.

In her hand, it suddenly rings. She ignores the tutting around her.

'Hey.'

The voice on the other end is tentative.

'Hey back,' Jess smiles, despite herself. The agony of the last few days and hours suddenly evaporates. 'I didn't know if you'd be able to talk.'

'I wanted to. It's all I've wanted since last week. To hear your voice. How are you?'

'I'm good,' says Jess. And now, hearing Tiff's voice, she is. Despite the agony and exhaustion of the last few days, she feels a smile on her voice. 'It's good to hear your voice too.'

'Yeah?' Tiff asks.

Dings sound to remind passengers to fold up their tables, put their bags under seats, turn off devices. Stewards wander up and down the aisles, craning their necks to check on seatbelts, touching overhead lockers to check they're shut. One stands near Jess's seat to do the pre-flight demo, shooting her angry looks that she should turn off her phone.

'I'm on the plane, we're about to leave.' Jess whispers. 'They're telling me to turn off the phone. But I just had to speak to you.'

'The plane home?'

'London. But not home.' Jess says.

The plane, the air stewards, the passengers melt away and Jess feels the familiar warmth of the spotlight on her neck, warming her bones, making her whole. Transforming her not into someone else, but into being finally herself. If she was alone, she would punch the air. Instead, she grins and squeezes her eyes shut so she can revel in this feeling for a moment longer.

'Actually, I wondered if you might be able to meet me at the airport.'

'Really?'

'Really. Tiff, thank you, for everything.'

'I've got you, Jess. I always have. I'll be there.'

'Night,' Jess says. 'I'm on my way.'

'Night,' Tiff replies. 'I'm ready.'

The engines thrust as the plane makes the final turn before the runway. A flight attendant still hovers, but Jess clings tightly to the phone pressed against her ear, sweaty in her palms. As the air steward approaches once more, leaning over to tell Jess one last time that she really must turn off her phone, she hears laughter down the line.

Reaching across the ocean, she meets it halfway and they laugh together. And it is everything. Jess's head falls back against the headrest as Memphis falls away beneath the wings. There is nothing about what's next that will be easy, but the King is ready. Ready to face the music.

Acknowledgements

Thank you to my course mates and tutors from Arvon, Faber Academy, and the editorial team (especially Lily Lindon) at The Novelry. Thank you to my editor Jeremy Sugden, and illustrator Ileana Hunter who brought *King* to life for readers.

Thank you to Carla, my first reader, my fiercest critic and above all, my friend.

Thank you to all my friends and family who shared their wisdom and encouragement, especially those who share my love of Elvis.

Song references

'I Just Can't Help Believin' – Barry Mann and Cynthia Well, recorded by Elvis Presley in 1970.

'Also Sprach Zarasthustra' – Richard Strauss, 1896.

'See See Rider' – first recorded by Gertrude "Ma" Rainey in 1924, recorded by Elvis Presley in 1970.

'Heartbreak Hotel' – Mae Boren Axton & Tommy Duren in 1955, recorded by Elvis Presley in 1955.

'Surrender' – Doc Pomus, recorded by Elvis Presley in 1961.

'Are you Lonesome Tonight?' – Roy Turk & Lou Handman in 1926, recorded by Elvis Presley in 1960.

'Let Yourself Go' – Joe Byers, recorded by Elvis Presley in 1967.

'Separate Ways' – Red West & Richard Mainegra, 1972, recorded by Elvis Presley in 1972.

'The Wonder of You' – Baker Knight, 1958, recorded by Elvis Presley in 1970.

'Always on My Mind' – Wayne Carson, Johnny Christopher & Mark James, 1972, recorded by Elvis Presley in 1972.

'Just Pretend' – Guy Fletcher & Doug Flett, recorded by Elvis Presley in 1970.

'Don't Cry Daddy' – Mac Davis, recorded by Elvis Presley in 1969.

'A Little Less Conversation' – Mac Davis & Billy Strange, recorded by Elvis Presley in 1968.

'Hound Dog' – Jerry Lieber & Mike Stoller, recorded by Elvis Presley in 1956.

'Blue Suede Shoes' – Carl Perkins, 1955, recorded by Elvis in 1956.

'Viva Las Vegas' – Doc Pomus & Mort Shuman, recorded by Elvis in 1964.

'Fever' – Eddie Cooley & Otis Blackwell, recorded by Elvis Presley in 1960.

'Jolene' – Dolly Parton, 1973.

'Heart's Content' – Brandi Carlile, Tim Hanseroth & Phil Hanseroth, 2012.

'Landslide' – Stevie Nicks, 2002.

'Turpentine' – Brandi Carlile, Tim Hanseroth & Phil Hanseroth, 2007.

'The Story' – Brandi Carlile, Tim Hanseroth & Phil Hanseroth, 2007.

'Late Morning Lullaby' – Brandi Carlile, Tim Hanseroth & Phil Hanseroth, 2007.

'Pocketful of Rainbows' – Fred Wise & Ben Weisman, recorded by Elvis Presley in 1960.

'It's Over' – Roy Orbison & Bill Dees, recorded in 1964.

About the author

Chloë Fowler lives in East London. She has no dogs, cats or children. She does have a penchant for anything related to cowboys and Westerns. And a genuine passion for Elvis. She was Longlisted for the inaugural Women's Discoveries Prize in 2021. King is her first novel.